THE ANNOTATED
PHANTOM TOLLBOOTH

THE ANNOTATED PHANTOM TOLLBOOTH

NORTON JUSTER

Illustrations by JULES FEIFFER

INTRODUCTION AND NOTES BY LEONARD S. MARCUS

Alfred A. Knopf New York

THIS IS A BORZOI BOOK PUBLISHED BY ALFRED A. KNOPF

Text copyright © 1961, copyright renewed 1989 by Norton Juster
Illustrations copyright © 1961, copyright renewed 1989 by Jules Feiffer
Introduction and notes copyright © 2011 by Leonard S. Marcus

For picture credits, please see page 273.

Visit us on the Web! www.randomhouse.com/kids

Educators and librarians, for a variety of teaching tools, visit us at
www.randomhouse.com/teachers

Library of Congress Cataloging-in-Publication Data
Juster, Norton.
The annotated Phantom tollbooth / by Norton Juster ; illustrations by Jules Feiffer ;
introduction and notes by Leonard Marcus. — 1st ed.
p. cm.
ISBN 978-0-375-85715-7 (trade) — ISBN 978-0-375-95715-4 (lib. bdg.)
1. Juster, Norton. Phantom tollbooth. I. Feiffer, Jules. II. Marcus, Leonard S. III. Title.
PS3560.U8P47 2011
813'.54—dc22
2011013174

MANUFACTURED IN CHINA
October 2011
10 9 8 7 6 5 4 3 2 1

First Annotated Edition

For a Milo named
Jacob, with love
—L.S.M.

CONTENTS

Marco Polo describes a bridge, stone by stone.

"But which is the stone that supports the bridge?" Kublai Khan asks.

"The bridge is not supported by one stone or another," Marco answers, "but by the line of the arch that they form."

Kublai Khan remains silent, reflecting. Then he adds: "Why do you speak to me of the stones? It is only the arch that matters to me."

Polo answers: "Without the stones there is no arch."

—from *Invisible Cities*, by Italo Calvino

Outside of a dog, a book is man's best friend.
Inside of a dog, it's too dark to read.
—Groucho Marx

INTRODUCTION

In the spring of 1960, a thirty-one-year-old New York architect named Norton Juster won a Ford Foundation grant to write a children's book about urban planning and design. Young people were not an obvious audience for a book on this theme. But as Juster had noted in his intriguing grant proposal, the future of America's cities was far from assured, and it would soon be up to the current generation of baby boomers, many of whom called the suburbs home, to decide the fate of these aging urban centers. A book aimed at inspiring young readers to give cities a closer look might make the greatest difference of all. Juster promised to reveal the "visual delights and pleasures of living in cities—the beauty and ugliness that we create and that have been created—and the way in which every human activity finds expression in forms that reflect the life and values of its participants." But most important, his goal would be "to stimulate and heighten perception—to help children notice and appreciate the visual world around them—to help excite them and sharpen their interest in an environment that they will eventually reshape."

A letter dated June 13, 1960, from Joseph M. McDaniel, Jr., secretary of the Ford Foundation, to Norton Juster, informing Juster that he had been awarded a grant under the foundation's newly established "Fellowship Program for Studies in the Creative Arts" (microfilm roll 912, Ford Foundation Archives).

If Juster had dreamed up an imaginative plan for helping to save the American city, he had also hit upon an elegant scheme for jump-starting his own career in architecture, which had begun to stall out at the small

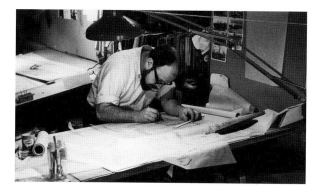
Architect Norton Juster at the drafting table, 1960s.

Manhattan firm where he was currently employed. The grant not only put a prestigious feather in his cap but it also bankrolled him for an extended break from the daily grind at the drafting table. (On receiving word of the fellowship, he rolled the dice once again and, rather than request a leave of absence from the firm of Raymond & Rado, simply resigned his job.) Juster relished his new-found leisure to mull over ideas about urban design and human perception that had intrigued him for years. No sooner, however, had he settled in to the laborious task of writing his proposed masterpiece than the tall stacks of note cards on which he had amassed his research assumed an ominous appearance. Suddenly, and quite alarmingly, it was as though he were back in grade school again, and about to be buried alive under a mountain of facts.

Deciding he needed a break from his break, Juster headed to Fire Island, a vacation spot located off the South Shore of Long Island, to walk the beaches and visit with friends. As a further distraction, he took notes for what he thought might become a short story based on an amusing incident in a Brooklyn restaurant a few days earlier. A boy of about ten had sat down next to him and launched into a freewheeling conversation about math. "What is the biggest number there is?" the boy had gamely demanded. "I already knew," Juster later recalled, "that when a kid asks you a question, you answer with another question. . . . So I said, 'Tell me what *you* think the biggest number is.' His reply was something like, 'A billion skillion katrillion.' Then I said, 'Well, add one to it.' Then we started talking back and forth, and we were very quickly talking about infinity" (*Funny Business,* compiled and edited by Leonard S. Marcus; Somerville, MA: Candlewick Press, 2009, pp. 129–130).

Juster returned to Brooklyn refreshed and with a renewed sense of purpose—to put the Ford Foundation fellowship out of his mind for a while and finish his story about a boy who asked too many questions. Juster's restaurant encounter had unleashed a torrent of childhood memories. It was all he could do to write them down fast enough.

The man behind Milo was born in Brooklyn, New York, on June 2, 1929—just months before the onset of the Great Depression. "There are still a number of people," he would later claim, "who attribute that catastrophic event directly to [my] birth" ("A Note from the Author" by Norton Juster, *The Phantom Tollbooth* Essential Modern Classics edition; London: HarperCollins, 2008). His father, Samuel Juster, was a Romanian-born Jew who immigrated as a boy to the United States accompanied

Samuel Juster, the author's father, c. 1947.

by his widowed mother. The latter died when he was eighteen, leaving Samuel to fend for himself. As a teenager with only one year of high school behind him, he set his sights on a career in architecture and pounded the pavement in search of an apprenticeship, only to be told that in America architecture was a "gentleman's profession," which in his case meant that it was closed to Jews. Juster refused, however, to abandon his dream, finally earning his license via a correspondence course. In partnership with Anthony J. DePace, a former associate of famed New York architect Cass Gilbert, he formed a small firm that built up a thriving business in church and school design. Later, the hardwood and marble samples that were the stock-in-trade of an architect with a practice like his would do double duty as his son Norton's toy blocks.

Juster's mother, Minnie Silberman, came from equally humble beginnings: a hardscrabble Polish-Jewish family who survived on piecework—cigar-making and the like—done at the kitchen table of a crowded Brooklyn apartment. As a girl, Minnie proved her worth as a go-getter and craftsperson. Years later she would do so again as the manager both of her husband's architectural office and the Juster household—a family of four after the birth of the couple's two sons, Howard and, four and a half years later, Norton. It was Minnie who oversaw the children's homework, typed their school reports, and sewed their costumes, and who maintained herself in a constant state of red alert in her children's defense. The Justers, who occupied half of a trim two-family brick

Minnie Juster, mother of Norton Juster, c. 1955.

house in the upwardly mobile Flatbush section of Brooklyn, had done a fine job of lifting themselves above their tenement beginnings. But they had done so in a social environment unstable enough (when not outright hostile) for their hard-won respectability to feel perpetually up for grabs. It was of no small concern to Minnie that her sons should have on smart clothes whenever they ventured outdoors, lest a tongue-wagging neighbor chance to spy them shabbily dressed and jump to conclusions that might tarnish the family reputation for a thousand years.

Samuel, a quiet, precise man, had a soft spot for puns

Norton Juster, about age nine, dressed for school.

and, without warning, would step out of character now and then to regale his appreciative younger son with a manic hail of Marx Brothers patter: "Aha! I see you're coming early. You used to be behind before, but now you're first at last." "I'd look at him," Juster later recalled, "and not know what the hell he was saying." But the intent was clear: "Pure delight . . . that marvelous sense of things being out of context" (*Funny Business*, p. 124). Samuel Juster adored Groucho Marx, not least for the wild-eyed comedian's mordant contempt for the social snobbery that in America, as Samuel knew all too well, so often masked deep-seated religious prejudice.

Throughout their school years, the two boys shared a bedroom. For Norton, the gap in their ages meant that Howard was "just big enough to knock the crap out of me and that I couldn't get even or even dream of getting even" (*Funny Business*, p. 120). Handsome, athletic, and smart as a whip, Howard was a golden boy, whose triumphal march through the streets of Flatbush and Brooklyn's public schools would have been a hard act to follow for any younger sibling. For the first several years, Norton seems not to have tried but instead to have beaten a tactical retreat into the shadows of Howard's magnificence, where he found ample cover to pursue his own more idiosyncratic ways undisturbed. Easily bored and just as easily distracted, Norton devised elaborate solitary routines that more than occasionally mystified his parents. When he spoke up at home, it was usually to ask a quirky question.

The Justers go swimming in upstate New York. Howard Juster (far left) stands head and shoulders above his younger brother.

Home for this elusive child was a more frightening place than his parents could have imagined: a world, as he later described it, in which "there were no inanimate objects—shoes, chairs, silverware, vegetables, dishes, toothpaste tubes—everything had a life and a personality of its own and each 'thing' had to be dealt with in its own special way. Some were friendly and understanding like the dining room table, others quite stern or antagonistic like all the marbles that were blue. There were enemies and alliances, touching loyalties and base betrayals and, of course, a few 'things' who were simply not trustworthy and given the slightest opportunity would surely do harm. It was a vastly complex world—crammed with subtle and intricate relationships" (unpublished speech titled "How to Write a Children's Book—and Why," presented at the Conference on

Techniques in Children's Literature, Long Island University, February 15, 1967, p. 1).

All small children pass through a stage of animistic thinking marked by the conviction, as Jean Piaget long ago reported, that everything is alive and endowed with feeling, intentionality, and will. Piaget observed that children aged two to six typically hold this view before relinquishing it in favor of a more mature, reality-based understanding of the difference between "inanimate" and "alive." In some children, however, the tendency to invest inanimate objects with lifelike powers is not so quickly outgrown or unlearned, and Juster (together, one imagines, with the vast majority of future fiction writers) belonged to this latter group. It later seemed to him that his predisposition to see characters—and, in particular, demons—everywhere "made my so-called

A very young Norton Juster strutting his stuff at a Brooklyn playground.

'real life' very much easier. . . . Coping with conventional living things like teachers, and people, became a much less difficult problem, and facing angry parents was often far less harrowing than knowing that a treacherous hat rack was waiting for you just inside the front door" ("How to Write a Children's Book," p. 1).

Another indicator of an unconventional mind revealed itself in the young child's early struggles with math. For a time, Juster was unable to think clearly about numbers or grasp the most basic rules for manipulating them. Nothing his teachers said or did seemed to help. When he finally did gain ground on the problem, it was by means of a strategy that students of the neurological phenomenon known as synesthesia would today be quick to recognize: Juster—doubtless driven by sheer frustration—had discovered that it felt right to associate each of the numbers from zero to nine with a different color. By applying this private color-coding system as he wrote out a math problem with colored pencils, he made addition and subtraction into manageable operations. The struggle that preceded this breakthrough had been a painful one, and the experience served to underscore for him the truth that childhood was a dismal, largely unrewarding line of work; he longed for the simple, carefree life of an adult ("How to Write a Children's Book—and Why," p. 1).

Still, Juster found much to amuse and absorb him at home. For reading, there were the Oz books, treasured copies of which had come to him as holiday gifts, and his parents' shelf of Yiddish literature in translation, which he *pretended* to read, the ornate prose almost a foreign

The front cover of the first edition of one of Norton Juster's favorite childhood books, L. Frank Baum's *The Wonderful Wizard of Oz* (1900).

language in itself. Reading in this abstracted manner fueled the game of repeating a random word or phrase until it split off from the realm of meaning to reconstitute itself as a mantra-like hum: a magic sound or string of sounds that no longer belonged to English or Yiddish, or any language, but only to him. One of the special appeals for him then of Kenneth Grahame's *The Wind in the Willows* was that fantasy's "dazzling display of words, [even though] many of them," as Juster learned years later, were considered by educators to be "far over the heads of kids." When Juster himself turned his hand to writing for children, he did so with the lesson he had gleaned from his first experience of Grahame's book firmly in mind: the vocabulary level of a children's book "[did not] matter much. . . . All that matters is that the book has a unifying rhythm to it, a rhythm to keep you going past the words you don't understand" (*New York Herald Tribune*, November 22, 1961, p. 23).

The most fascinating and frustrating of the books he read at home were the twenty stout volumes of *The Book of Knowledge*. He read them from cover to cover in an excited, trance-like state from which he invariably emerged, however, with an equally strong sense of futility. Immersing himself in the encyclopedia made him keenly aware that the very books that put him in command of "the greatest treasury of disembodied facts" also left him clueless as to their real-world significance (*Funny Business*, p. 122). A dim suspicion darkened to certainty: fact learning and true knowledge had surprisingly little to do with one another. The longer he thought about this, the more it seemed that facts raised more questions than they answered. Just as Milo would do, he began to question the point of learning. As his hunger for understanding increased, Juster grew more talkative. He began to ask more questions in class—cascades of probing, often vexingly unanswerable questions. Having already laid the groundwork at home, he now cheerfully embarked on his first great mission in life as the "thorn in the side of my teachers" (unrecorded conversation with author, 2009).

After school, Juster might tune in to his favorite radio serials—*Jack Armstrong, the All-American Boy* and *Don Winslow of the Navy*—or escape to the basement, where, in a Depression-era gesture of generosity toward the less fortunate, his father had given an itinerant handyman the run of his workbench and tools. A master

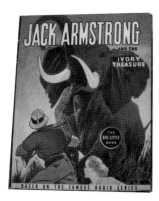

Nineteen-thirties children who did not get their fill of Jack Armstrong, the all-American boy, by tuning in to the popular radio adventure series of that name could purchase these action-packed volumes for a dime each. Escapist literature pure and simple, *Jack Armstrong and the Ivory Treasure* (Whitman, 1937) and *Jack Armstrong and the Mystery of the Iron Key* (Whitman, 1939) were printed on pulp paper in a pocket-sized novelty format that made them easy to hide from disapproving parents.

carpenter who had fallen on hard times, this kindly, taciturn old man, Mr. Brickman, would pause over his work to explain a woodworking technique or let his wide-eyed onlooker feel the weight of a tool in his own small hands. The lessons learned during these interludes were as much about philosophy as craft. From then onward, Juster took it for granted that no job done well was apt to come easily (*Funny Business*, p. 134) and that care and craftsmanship were their own rewards.

In time these basement retreats and solitary activities became less important to him. At sleepaway camp at age ten or eleven, he even took up acting. Cast in the starring role in *My Client Curley*, a screwball comedy about a boy showman and his dancing caterpillar, he found that he loved the sound of thunderous applause.

Gradually, the pleasures of food also revealed themselves to the formerly impossibly picky eater. By the time he entered Brooklyn's James Madison High School, Juster was no longer the shy, skinny, querulous eccentric who had baffled his parents but a gregarious social being with a sonorous baritone voice, an elfish glint in his eye, and a love of adventure. He joined the track team, threw himself—sometimes literally—into the fray of any football scrimmage that would have him, and scored the honor of directing the senior play. With a firm grip on once-nettlesome subjects like math, he earned high grades—and a place at the University of Pennsylvania's school of fine arts as a member of the class of 1952. Howard had followed Samuel Juster into a career in architecture, and now Norton was about to do so, too. By his account, it had never occurred to him to consider any other future for himself. But he had also decided to make his own mark.

With a client list headed by the Archdioceses of New York, Bridgeport, and Hartford, DePace & Juster was known for its impeccably designed—but wholly conventional—work, a far cry from the headline-grabbing pyrotechnics of architectural innovators like Frank Lloyd Wright and Le Corbusier. With the arrogance of youth, Juster's younger son set off for college with dreams of showing up his father and grabbing modern architecture's brass ring. Penn was a fine place to entertain such overarching ambitions. During Juster's four years there, the charismatic visionary Louis Kahn came to lecture and Frank Lloyd Wright, furled cape and all, did a memorable turn as he collected a prestigious award. But for Juster, the high point of his undergraduate education was the chance to study with Lewis Mumford, America's leading authority on urban history and design and the architecture critic at the *New Yorker*. An inspirational teacher, Mumford championed enlightened urban planning and took it as an article of faith that architects had an important role to play in the work of civilization. It impressed Juster that this widely read and worldly professor, whom Malcolm Cowley called "the last of the great humanists," was a down-to-earth and largely self-educated man. An elegant writer, Mumford, in conversation, joked freely about sex and was at his best during long campus walks when, as a kind of party trick, he would show off his extraordinary powers of observation. Student and teacher became lifelong friends. At graduation, Juster collected a quiver of academic prizes along with his Bachelor of Architecture degree. With Mumford's blessing, he sailed for England on a Fulbright Scholarship for a year of advanced study in the department of civic design at the University of Liverpool's School of Architecture.

Economically devastated after years of wartime aerial bombardment and still suffering from shortages of many basic commodities, England during the early 1950s was a grim, gray place. But for Britain's architects and urban planners, the war's end had brought with it unprecedented opportunities, the chance in a nation freighted with centuries-old traditions to reimagine its cities and towns, in some instances literally from the ground up. To a first-time visitor from America, especially one who had grown up daydreaming his way through the novels of Arthur Ransome and E. Nesbit, plenty of the old storybook England remained to be seen and savored—especially if, like Juster, one happened to have a motorbike at one's disposal and the urge to explore London and points beyond. Damp, wind-whipped overnight ferry crossings to Ireland in the company of a tight band of drinking friends were also on order. During one such excursion, Juster met an up-and-coming young Irish actor named Milo O'Shea. The two never crossed paths again, but the name Milo lodged in his memory. At the 1952 departmental Christmas dinner, "a freshman, Mr. N. Juster," was accorded the honor of giving the student response to the faculty toast to the

Norton Juster on his sporty motorbike, England, 1952.

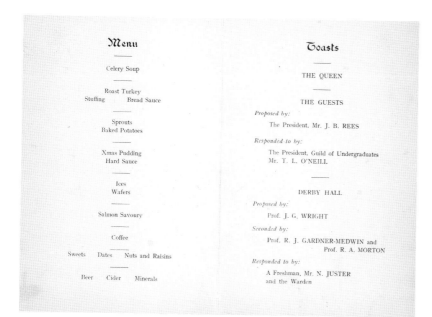

Menu

Celery Soup

Roast Turkey
Stuffing   Bread Sauce

Sprouts
Baked Potatoes

Xmas Pudding
Hard Sauce

Ices
Wafers

Salmon Savoury

Coffee

Sweets   Dates   Nuts and Raisins

Beer   Cider   Minerals

Toasts

THE QUEEN

THE GUESTS

Proposed by:
The President, Mr. J. B. REES

Responded to by:
The President, Guild of Undergraduates
Mr. T. L. O'NEILL

DERBY HALL

Proposed by:
Prof. J. G. WRIGHT

Seconded by:
Prof. R. J. GARDNER-MEDWIN and
Prof. R. A. MORTON

Responded to by:
A Freshman, Mr. N. JUSTER
and the Warden

The commemorative program and menu for the 1952 Christmas dinner that Norton Juster attended as a Fulbright Scholar, at the University of Liverpool.

future of dear old Derby Hall (program and menu for the University of Liverpool Hall of Residence for Men Christmas Dinner, December 11, 1952). The world was opening up to him.

As Juster's British interlude drew to a close, the prospect of military service back home loomed. The Korean War was winding down, but the military draft remained in force, and Juster knew that he could either wait to be called up for a two-year tour of duty or enlist in the reserves for three years and have more control over his destiny. He chose the latter option and in 1954 elected to enter the Civil Engineer Corps of the United States Naval Reserve, where he rose to the rank of Lieutenant Junior Grade.

A plum posting in sun-splashed Morocco started his tour of duty off well, but the navy's next plan for him more than made up for it. Juster later recalled Argentia, Newfoundland, as a "dreadful place where the Labrador

Navy reservist Norton Juster looking sharp at Officer Candidate School, Newport, Rhode Island, 1954.

Current and the Gulf Stream meet, generating fantastic amounts of fog and misery" (*Funny Business*, p. 128). Quartered on a barracks ship where boredom was the main enemy, Juster took up four-wall handball and, on a whim, began to write and illustrate a story for children. After each painting session, he would hang his watercolors to dry in the ship's corridor, and it was not long before the commanding officer called him in to tell him that navy men did not paint pictures or write children's

An ink and watercolor illustration by Norton Juster for "The Passing of Irving," the unpublished picture-book fable he created to distract himself while serving as a navy reservist in frigid Newfoundland.

stories, and that Juster was to stop doing so immediately, before he inflicted further damage on the ship's morale. Somehow Juster still managed to complete "The Passing of Irving," a satirical fairy tale about a mythological beast who, in a case of identity confusion, believed himself to be real. Whatever the inspiration—the barren northern landscape, the bone-chilling cold, or the surreality of military routine—Juster had reconnected with the storytelling voice that had enthralled him as a child. It would not be the last time he did so when in need of solace, distraction, or out-and-out escape.

Juster's final posting, at New York's Brooklyn Navy Yard, was another soft assignment. It came with a modest housing allowance, which he used to rent a garden apartment in nearby Brooklyn Heights. All brass and nervous energy as he ran out the clock on a meaningless desk job, Juster summoned his acting skills to recast his life as a kind of Marx Brothers routine and make the most of his arrival in the big city. First, he dreamed up a nonexistent military publication—the *Naval News Service*—as a pretext for requesting interviews with the attractive women he saw pictured each morning in the *New York Times*'s theater pages. Few people, he had discovered, ever turned down a serviceman with a reasonable-sounding request. The ruse worked so well as a scheme for getting dates that he soon had one of his neighbors begging to tag along as his assistant. Inspired by a statue in Washington Square Park, Juster called his next venture the Garibaldi Society. It existed, to the extent that it did exist, for the sole purpose of rejecting the overtures of anyone foolish enough to apply for membership. Juster went to the trouble of designing an impressive Society logo and preparing both an elaborate application form and a heart-stabbing rejection letter. If the navy was going to browbeat him into engaging in hour upon hour of mindless paperwork, Juster at least was not going to be outdone by it.

Military life and these extracurricular pranks somehow still left him with an inordinate amount of nap time, or so it seemed to the neighbor he met one morning as they were both taking out the trash. Jules Feiffer lived alone in a furnished, one-bedroom apartment two floors above Juster's slightly less scruffy garden digs. Standing side by side, the two men, who were just a few months apart in age, looked nothing like brothers but might easily have been mistaken for a comedy team—a Jewish Laurel and Hardy or Abbott and Costello—with Juster in the role of the short, pugnacious wiseacre and Feiffer as the tall, shy, rail-thin straight man with the perpetually bemused expression. "Nortie," as Feiffer took to calling his fun-loving friend, was hardly the archetype of the military man, making the sight of him all the more amusing to the cartoonist when Juster paraded about the neighborhood in his crisp navy uniform.

Both Feiffer, who had last lived in a series of cheap Lower Manhattan apartments, and Juster, who had grown up in a far less stylish part of the borough, felt lucky to have landed in Brooklyn Heights. Manhattanites might regard the Heights as worlds away from their skyscraper city—but in reality it was a quick subway or cab ride from Midtown and a place with a rich history of its own. Just up the hill from the Brooklyn Bridge and the pier where Walt Whitman had boarded the ferry for Manhattan every morning, the Heights was a honeycomb of narrow, tree-lined streets, historic churches, and brownstone, brick, and clapboard houses, many of them dating from the age of Abraham Lincoln. By the 1950s, the once grand, now largely tumbledown enclave had become a magnet for artists, writers, and intellectuals, with a roster of recent or present-day residents that included William Zorach, Truman Capote, Arthur Miller, Alan Arkin, Norman Mailer, W. H. Auden, and W. E. B. Du Bois. "We have so many people . . . who work in cultured fields," deadpanned Ira Jan Wallach, author of *Hopalong-Freud,* to a reporter for the *New York World-Telegram and Sun,* "that even the most casual conversations are in hi-fi" (Bernard Krisher, "Heavy Artistic Content," January 23, 1957). As that article intimated, Brooklyn Heights was fast becoming the city's second Greenwich Village, a lower-key version of the legendary artists' quarter, but with none of the latter's clamorous tourist traffic or ersatz bohemianism.

As the birthplace of Abstract Expressionism during the immediate postwar years, New York had leapfrogged past Paris to stake its claim as the undisputed art capital of the world. Greenwich Village, long New York's Left Bank, reaffirmed its role as the city's artistic epicenter, the preferred gathering (and drinking) place of the new abstractionists. Led by Jackson Pollock and championed by a cadre of critics with the aloof, cocksure manner of high priests, they became overnight celebrities, their photographs splashed across the pages of *Life.* But for the stalwart figurative painters of the 1940s and 1950s who chose to resist the tide, the Village now became alien territory. Seeking safety in numbers, several of these artists took refuge in Brooklyn Heights.

One of the central figures of this group of exiles was a young portrait painter named David Levine.* Levine never forgot the scorn heaped on artists like himself by the most imperious of all the city's art critics, Clement Greenberg, for what the latter deemed their slavish

* Levine was soon to win renown as the *New York Review of Books's* resident political caricaturist.

dependence on external subject matter and the favor of clients. Painting with a broad brush of his own, Greenberg dismissed all representational art as "illustrative." A comic-strip illustrator like Jules Feiffer did not even figure in the pecking order.

Feiffer had found his way to the Heights thanks to an artist friend, Harvey Dinnerstein. As he got to know Levine and the other neighborhood painters—Burton Silverman, Aaron Shikler, and others—Feiffer, a habitual loner, discovered that he enjoyed their company, the first group of artists he had ever called friends. They shared his leftist politics and eagerness to debate big ideas. Like them, Feiffer too was glad to have put himself at a healthy remove from the fiercely competitive Village art maelstrom.

He settled in to his new life across the East River with his work cut out for him. Feiffer had recently launched a weekly satirical comic strip in—the irony was not lost on him—the *Village Voice*. Within weeks of its debut on October 24, 1956, *Sick, Sick, Sick* (soon to be renamed *Feiffer*) had become required reading for New York hipsters and the entire publishing industry. As he wrestled with the blank slate that the *Voice*'s laissez-faire editors had given him, Feiffer drew each of the first few strips in a different graphic style. Although far from satisfied with his efforts—was he *ever* satisfied?—he "wasted no time," as historian and publisher Gary Groth would observe, "confronting the social and psychological, the private and public issues that defined his generation, described by Auden as the postwar generation living in the Age of

Jules Feiffer reviewing proof sheets of his first book, *Sick, Sick, Sick* (1958).

Anxiety" (Jules Feiffer, *Explainers: The Complete* Village Voice *Strips (1956–66)*; introduction by Gary Groth; Seattle: Fantagraphics Books, 2008, p. vi). The *Voice* paid him nothing for his services, but Feiffer had made the shrewd calculation that to have so visible a showcase for his work was bound to yield tangible benefits sooner or later. Fame and national syndication would follow in fact in short order. In the meantime, he could take justifiable pride in having achieved a position of consequence: a public perch from which to take the measure of American social codes and sexual mores, disentangle governmental doublespeak, and decipher the mixed messages of everyone from self-loathing advertising men to outwardly liberated but secretly terrified with-it couples out on a date.

Up until then, Feiffer had been all too accustomed to things not going well. When the *Voice* chance arose, he had been drifting on and off unemployment while scrambling to establish a toehold as a cartoonist. His earlier life had been a mishmash of thwarted dreams and only occasional glimmers of something better. Born in the Bronx into a poor and seemingly luckless Jewish family, Feiffer fell in love as a boy with the garish galaxy of comic-book superheroes whose adventures he and his schoolmates devoured weekly. With a father who had trouble keeping a job, he decided at an early age that there could be no better life for himself than that of an artist who got paid to bring heart-stopping comics magic into the world. At five, he won a gold medal in an art contest and was soon drawing comics of his own, assigning a cover price of eight or nine cents to his surprisingly accomplished efforts—a penny or two less than what the professionals charged. School was another matter: he was a mediocre student. After being rejected by the art programs of New York University and Pratt Institute, Feiffer overcame his chronic shyness long enough to talk his way into an assistant's job in the studio of comics master Will Eisner, creator of *The Spirit*. A generous mentor, Eisner entrusted him with writing entire episodes of the series and eventually gave him a one-page strip of his own, called "Clifford," on the last page of the weekly *Spirit* section. The apprenticeship lasted three years. Then restless, painfully self-critical, and aware that he would soon be drafted into the army, Feiffer, still in his teens, took off with a friend on a month-long cross-country road trip.

Months later, as an army private stationed in New Jersey, Feiffer found time to draw, and produced a comics-style send-up of military life, in book form.* In *Munro*, he chronicled the misadventures of a four-year-old boy whom the army, in a classic case of bureaucratic boneheadedness, mistakenly drafted into its ranks and then refused to discharge. He hoped the clever little book would be his ticket to success as an illustrator. But following his own return to civilian life, when Feiffer made the rounds of publishers, he found no takers, in part because the forty-five-page-long comic straddled the line between traditional categories: it looked like a children's book but read as satire for cynical grown-ups.

Jules Feiffer at age nine.

* Feiffer served in the Army Signal Corps from 1951 to 1953.

"SEE THAT MAN!" said the sergeant suddenly pointing at Munro. All the new men looked.
"THAT'S A **SOLDIER**!" said the sergeant proudly. "THAT'S WHAT WE'RE GOING TO TRAIN **YOU** TO BE!"

A page from *Munro*, the "children's book for adults," which Jules Feiffer produced while serving as a U.S. Army private stationed in New Jersey.

Feiffer, who by then knew the comics tradition cold, was well aware of the originality of his book but not, at first, of the predictable reluctance of publishers to stick their neck out for an unknown talent. Moving into the "known" column now became an all-consuming obsession. Two of Feiffer's heroes—William Steig and Saul Steinberg—drew for the *New Yorker*, but Feiffer was convinced he lacked the polish as a draftsman to approach that magazine, which he simultaneously loathed for its insouciant air of moneyed self-importance and revered for the kick-ass brilliance of its art. As he cast about for his big break, he tested the waters of the juvenile book market by presenting his portfolio to Harper & Brothers' Ursula Nordstrom. As they chatted, the legendary editor brought out examples of the work of a rising star on her list, Maurice Sendak. One look at *A Hole Is to Dig*—whose author, Ruth Krauss, was married to another Feiffer hero, cartoonist Crockett Johnson—

was enough to persuade him that that field's top spot was already taken. He would need to seek his glory elsewhere.

With that history of rejection as prologue, the *Village Voice* opportunity came about more casually than Feiffer would have dreamed possible. He simply dropped by the weekly's offices without an appointment one day and introduced himself to the editors, who passed around his portfolio, laughing appreciatively at the humorous bits in *Munro* and at his samples for a new cartoon strip about conformist behavior called *Sick, Sick, Sick*. After a brief discussion amongst themselves, the editors told him—just like that—that they would be happy to publish anything he wished to do for their newspaper. Feiffer had been in and out the door in half an hour. When he stepped back out onto the street on

© Jules Feiffer

The first installment of *Sick, Sick, Sick*, the satirical *Village Voice* strip that was soon renamed *Feiffer*.

his long, spindly legs, he felt at once exhilarated, dazed, and doomed: which is to say, like a living, breathing *Feiffer* character—a dumbstruck Bernard in the making.

Just then, things were looking up for Norton Juster as well. Six months after he and the cartoonist first met, Juster's military discharge papers came through and he traded his navy uniform for a jacket and tie and a job at a Manhattan architectural firm. With energy to burn, he also accepted a part-time teaching job at Brooklyn's Pratt Institute and began contributing occasional pieces on architecture to the *New York Herald Tribune* and the *Village Voice*. Meanwhile, as the success of Feiffer's *Village Voice* strip grew, the larger career goals it had been meant to serve were being realized. In 1958, his first book, *Sick, Sick, Sick: A Guide to Non-Confident Living*— a compilation of the early *Voice* strips—became a best-seller. The following year, *Feiffer* went into national syndication.

When the two men's leases expired, they and a third friend pooled their resources and rented a duplex apartment in a blue-shuttered row house at nearby 153 State Street. In return for agreeing to do most of the cooking, Juster took over the entire fourth floor, where the kitchen was located; Feiffer shared the third floor with an Englishman named Max Eckstein, who taught comparative education at Queens College.

With Juster firmly in control of the food supply, the situation was ripe for mischief. He had observed that his cartoonist friend, always a creature of habit, came

153 State Street, Brooklyn, New York. Norton Juster wrote— and rewrote—*The Phantom Tollbooth* in his apartment in the uppermost reaches of this quintessentially charming Brooklyn Heights row house while, one floor below, Jules Feiffer turned out scores of sketches.

upstairs every morning to put two eggs up to boil, then returned to his rooms and reappeared just in time to claim his breakfast. One morning as this daily ritual was being played out, the architect lay in wait. With seconds to go before Feiffer's return, Juster rushed to the stove and substituted a raw egg for one of the two tumbling deliriously in the water. When the easily flustered artist sat down to breakfast that morning, he found himself confronted with an unnerving mystery: how one of his eggs could have cooked perfectly while the other one, put up to boil at the same time, had remained practically raw.

Juster had long since come to know Feiffer's artist friends, several of whom (along with Norman Mailer) rented studio space in an old loft building on the edge of Brooklyn Heights. He would stop by to chat with the

Ovington Studios gang, one of whom stood out from the others both for being a much older man and for being a much better elevator mechanic than he was a painter. While Juster viewed Emil Goldfus as a kindly, avuncular presence, Feiffer saw him as "something of a burnt-out case," a nowhere man who ingratiated himself by being the one good listener in a crowded field of "cocky . . . self-absorbed" talkers (Jules Feiffer, *Backing into Forward*, p. 225). Then one evening as the cartoonist was on his way home from Manhattan, a newspaper headline stopped him in his tracks: RED POSING AS B'KLYN ARTIST INDICTED AS TOP SOVIET SPY. There, framing Emil Goldfus's police mug shots on the front page of the *New York Journal American,* was the stupefying news that the mild-mannered sad sack with whom Feiffer shot the breeze from time to time was in fact Colonel Rudolf Abel, a top Soviet spy. The FBI had been shadowing Abel for years, including, presumably, his comings and goings at the Ovington Studios. When Feiffer reached State Street, he found Juster stretched out faceup on the couch in his favorite napping position and dropped the paper on his chest, bringing him to. Juster's eyes popped at the incredible revelation, but Feiffer was more shaken than Juster by the incident. As he later recalled: "I, in particular, was confident of my powers of analysis and my ability to understand people. That was one of my strong points: reading between the lines, understanding the subtext. It's what I did in my cartoons.

"But now I began to doubt everything. If Emil was not Emil, if Emil was a Russian whose name was Abel. And he was a spy. And I never suspected. What else out there did I have all wrong?" (*Backing into Forward,* p. 228).

Evenings at home, Juster was a restless, percussive pacer. Night after night, Feiffer would hear his agitated footfalls overhead and wonder peevishly what the commotion was all about. Finally, one evening he decided to investigate. Feiffer knew about his friend's Ford Foundation fellowship and supposed that he must be hard at work on his proposed book. So it came as a big surprise to learn that Juster was instead writing a work of fantasy fiction—roughly speaking, an outrageous cross between *The Wonderful Wizard of Oz* and *On the Road* salted with Marx Brothers high jinks and wordplay. With his secret thus exposed, Juster shed all reluctance to talk about it and handed Feiffer a sheaf of pages containing everything—disconnected episodes and dialogue fragments—he had written so far. Feiffer liked what he read and said so. Thus encouraged, Juster made sure from then onward to show Feiffer *all* his latest pages. Without further prompting, Feiffer in turn began sketching. It was never formally decided that he would illustrate *The Phantom Tollbooth.* That hadn't been necessary. "Nortie did the cooking," Feiffer later explained, "and if I wanted to eat I knew I would have to illustrate it" (interview with author, April 24, 2009).

It was at about this time that Feiffer met Judy Sheftel, the charismatic young editor who in 1961 would become his first wife. Sheftel worked at American Heritage

Judy Sheftel Feiffer, no date. Photograph © Mary Ellen Mark. (Reproduced by permission of the photographer.)

and was a gregarious "connector" who knew everyone in publishing and loved to put people and deals together. (It was she who later persuaded Maya Angelou to write about her traumatic formative years in *I Know Why the Caged Bird Sings* and coaxed Joan Crawford's daughter into publishing the quintessential Hollywood tell-all, *Mommie Dearest*.) Sheftel was out walking on Columbus Avenue one day when she spied a publishing friend coming toward her. Jason Epstein was one of Random House's top editors and among the book world's most influential figures. Throwing her arms wide in greeting, she deftly segued into pitch mode to sing the praises of a project then very much on her mind: "There's a wonderful children's book," Sheftel declared, "and you *have* to publish

it!" (Jason Epstein, interview with author, December 16, 2008). Epstein promised to read the manuscript that his friend's famous cartoonist boyfriend planned to illustrate, and continued on his way.

Theirs had been a most fortunate encounter. American children's book editors of the time took little interest in fantasy fiction—apart from the best of what reached their desks with an unassailable British pedigree: Mary Norton's Borrowers series and Lucy M. Boston's tales of Green Knowe. Realism was what sold—and won awards. Year after year, the Newbery Medal went to a work of historical fiction or a realistic novel set in foreign lands. A text like Juster's had a second strike against it as well. It ran circles around the postwar-era education world's pinched efforts to minimize young-reader frustration by means of a restricted vocabulary.

But Jason Epstein was in a position to sail above most such parochial concerns. He prided himself on his maverick approach to publishing and, in particular, on his proven talent for spotting golden opportunities that defied the common wisdom. What was more, unlike many of his editorial peers, who dismissed publishing's "juvenile" sector as a quaint (albeit often surprisingly profitable) backwater operation, Epstein genuinely cared about books for young readers. Not long before, he had started a small company of his own dedicated to reissuing children's classics at affordable prices. As Sheftel launched into her spiel, she was well aware of the fact that Epstein & Carroll, as the venture was called, did not acquire original manuscripts. But as Sheftel also knew,

Jason Epstein in his office at Random House, 1960s.

Epstein was never one to foreclose his options.

In the days when Norton Juster was finishing his coursework at Penn and Jules Feiffer was bracing for his slog in army drabs, Jason Epstein was already kicking up dust in New York as a hard-driving Doubleday publishing trainee. Within a year's time, Epstein had single-handedly laid the groundwork for Anchor Books, Doubleday's history-making quality paperback line. Anchor tapped into a vastly lucrative market by addressing the reading needs of millions of budget-minded postwar American college students and graduates. Its spectacular success made Epstein the publishing industry's wunderkind.

In 1958, when Doubleday declined to publish a controversial novel the young editor felt strongly about acquiring—the book in question was Nabokov's *Lolita*—Epstein packed up his blue pencils and moved to Random House, where Bennett Cerf had offered him a job on special terms: Epstein would be free to launch any publishing venture of his own devising so long as it was noncompetitive; if Cerf liked the idea, he would lend his company's support. Before long, Epstein and his former Doubleday colleague Clelia Carroll had mapped out plans for a "children's counterpart to Anchor Books" to be called the Looking Glass Library. Random House agreed to manufacture and distribute the line and provided office space in the attic of the old Villard Mansion, where the larger house was headquartered, on Madison Avenue across from St. Patrick's Cathedral.

While Epstein labored belowdecks in the Random editorial offices, Carroll, up in the eaves, attended to Looking Glass business, aided by a secretary and another Doubleday émigré, Edward Gorey, who had signed on as art director. Just down the hall from them was the skeleton crew of a second 1958 start-up—Beginner Books—headed by Ted Geisel, aka Dr. Seuss, and his business partner, Phyllis Cerf (Bennett Cerf's wife). Beginner Books aimed to build on the phenomenal success of Geisel's own *The Cat in the Hat*, published a year earlier, by generating an entire line of fun-to-read primers by Geisel and a hand-picked stable of other writers and illustrators. The inaugural title, Geisel's own *The Cat in the Hat Comes Back*, promised to start things off with a bang.

Children who outgrew Beginner Books would be ready to move on to the riches of the Looking Glass Library, which launched in the fall of 1959 with nine old favorites on its list, including E. Nesbit's *Five Children and It*, Sir Arthur Conan Doyle's *The Lost World*, and, as a kind of dessert, a book of vintage ghost stories compiled by Edward Gorey—*The Haunted Looking Glass.*

The compiler of this 1961 Looking Glass Library treasury, Hart Day Leavitt, was a popular English teacher at Phillips Academy, Andover, where his students included George H. W. Bush and Jack Lemmon.

Epstein undertook this new project certain that his Doubleday experience would stand him in good stead. In practice, however, the Anchor model could carry him only so far. For practical as well as what might be considered philosophical reasons, schools and public libraries during the 1950s and 1960s—the primary American market for juvenile books—refused to purchase paperbacks. It was not just that paperbound books lacked the durability of hardcovers. Paperbacks also had unsavory down-market connotations—shades of dime novels and pulp fiction!—that were not easily set aside by tradition-bound institutions. It simply did not work to think of Looking Glass in terms of a paperback line.

As an alternative, Epstein & Carroll chose the more elegant yet still relatively low-cost format known in the industry as paper-over-board, for which sturdy cardboard front and back covers are overlaid with paper rather than cloth. To burnish their credibility with children's literature's gatekeepers, the partners enlisted the aid of an illustrious advisory board of writer friends including W. H. Auden, Edmund Wilson, and Phyllis McGinley.*

All this was in progress while Epstein was also busy directing Random House's high-stakes Vintage paperback line, the company's answer to Anchor. Amid a blizzard of competing demands on his time, Epstein took his eye off the Looking Glass list long enough for an inferior grade of paper to have been ordered for the first ten books and for some volumes to have gone to press

* Norman Podhoretz also served on the board for a time but found the work too hazardous after contracting chicken pox during a library research excursion. Of the three remaining board members, Phyllis McGinley, as an author for children, had the most immediately pertinent credentials. But according to Epstein, Edmund Wilson cared deeply about children's literature and treasured his childhood copies of *St. Nicholas* magazine; and Auden *was* a child. In a *New York Times Book Review* essay titled "Today's 'Wonder-World' Needs Alice," Auden would make the case for children's books as a legitimate literary genre. "There are some good books which are only for adults because their comprehension presupposes adult experiences," argued Auden in a piece marking the centenary of Lewis Carroll's *Alice's Adventures Underground*, "but there are no good books which are only for children" (Robert Phillips, ed., *Aspects of Alice: Lewis Carroll's Dreamchild as Seen Through the Critics' Looking-Glasses*; New York: Vintage, 1977, p. 11).

with overcrowded page layouts. When the crucial first reviews were mixed and initial sales fell short of expectations, Epstein was not surprised. By their third season (fall 1960), Epstein & Carroll was clearly on the defensive, having trimmed the list to eight new titles and raised the uniform retail price from $1.50 to $1.95—the latter development especially worrying for a venture built on the promise of a bargain. It was just about then that Sheftel and Epstein chanced to meet on a crowded city street, and that Epstein—whether out of friendship, curiosity, or the need to jolt his struggling firm back to life—promised to read a manuscript unlike any that he and his partner, until that moment, had had any notion of publishing.

The manuscript that Sheftel had touted so effusively was itself something of a phantom, the author having thus far produced a polished draft of only the first seven chapters of an as-yet-unplotted novel of indeterminate length. Sheftel, unfazed, informed Feiffer and Juster of the great stroke of luck that had befallen them thanks to her quick thinking, and offered personally to deliver the manuscript to Random House. Juster, she said, should first prepare an outline of the rest of his story—providing just enough detail to give Epstein confidence that the author knew what he was doing. Juster in fact had only the vaguest idea about where his story was headed, but he scribbled three pages of what *sounded* like a synopsis, had his mother type a fair copy, and authorized Sheftel to proceed. About three weeks later, he received a telephone request for a

Page one of the *Phantom Tollbooth* synopsis that Norton Juster hastily prepared for submission to Jason Epstein.

meeting with Epstein. Much to his astonishment, Epstein & Carroll had decided to publish his book.

Juster was quick to see a dark side to the good news. Suddenly his amusing pastime had become "BUSINESS," as he would later recall. "I didn't own it—IT OWNED ME" ("The Current Speech—Always Changing," unpublished lecture notes by Norton Juster, n.d., note 23, collection of N.J.). Milo has a similar response when, as he wheels his toy car out onto the open road at the start of chapter two, he sighs, "This game is much more serious than I thought" (p. 16).

The opening lines of the typescript Juster submitted to Jason Epstein read:

Milo didn't know what to do with himself—Not just sometimes, but always.

When he was in school he longed to be out and when he was out he longed to be in. On the way he thought about coming home and coming home he thought about going. Wherever he was he longed to be somewhere else and when he got there he wondered why he'd bothered.

Nothing interested him—especially the things that should.

"It seems to me that almost everything is a waste of time," he said one day as he walked dejectedly home from school (Lilly Library, box 3, folder 23).

Apart from the all-important first sentence, which would undergo fine-tuning at every stage, Juster's text—the little there was of it—was in near final form. Details remained to be filled in: except for "Faintly Macabre's Story," the chapters of the sample manuscript lacked titles. The punctuation and paragraphing were a bit wobbly, and an occasional word or exchange of dialogue cried out for reconsideration. All in all, however, Juster had crafted an impressive, not to say hilarious, beginning. What was more, he had written the synopsis Sheftel had asked for with equal conviction, taking the

assignment as an occasion to brainstorm potential plot twists and yet-to-be-encountered characters. The latter included Rhyme and Reason, the pair of allegorical princesses whose off-stage abduction and climactic rescue would ultimately give direction to Milo's wanderings and shape to the narrative.

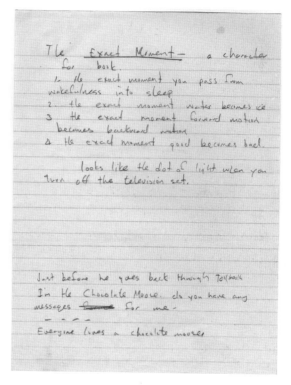

The author's notes for two characters he ultimately chose not to include in *The Phantom Tollbooth*.

Juster's working method, apart from his pacing, was to write in longhand with a number-2 pencil on a wide-ruled tablet, the kind of composition paper well known to schoolchildren. He enjoyed the element of manual labor involved in writing this way, as tedious as it also was. As he wrote, he listened intently to the sound and rhythm of his words. He would revise and recopy a passage again and again, until the language and rhythm fell precisely into place. At three or more stages, Minnie Juster retyped the manuscript for her son, the better for him to attack the material with a fresh eye and, where further rewrites were needed, with a red pencil.

Scraps of paper became repositories of notes for a section in progress. On a page headed "SIGHT," for instance, Juster scribbled six thematically related ideas, starting with:

> 1. Color organ—played by Chroma the Great. An enormous machine with rows of notes and pedals below and many pipes of all sizes above. The pedals are used perhaps to hold colors, provide breezes and highlights.
> 2. The city of sight could be invisible.
> 3. The Didja—Didja ever notice how many cracks were in the sidewalk? Tells of the many things that people fail to notice: sunsets, trees, flowers, wet streets (Lilly Library, box 5, folder 42).

And then there were the lists—of synonyms, characters' names, idiomatic expressions, and comic "business" ("No noise is good noise"; "When a baby wants food he cries. When a river wants water it creaks") and of matters requiring further thought ("How do sounds look?").

How, indeed. Memo to self: "Quite often the road to Rhyme and Reason is through the right mistakes." Idea for dialogue: "'It's amazing how many things which make no sense at all are quite logical,' says Milo." "The *Exact Moment*—a character for book. 1. The exact moment you pass from wakefulness into sleep; 2. The exact moment water becomes ice; 3. The exact moment forward motion becomes backward motion; 4. The exact moment good becomes bad. Looks like the dot of light when you turn off the television set" (Lilly Library, box 5, folder 34). Many of these notes ended up on the cutting-room floor, but all grew from the same relentless drive to generate comic sparks from the flinty imprecision of everyday thought and perception and the inherently slippery nature of words.

In the opening scene of the earliest extant draft of *The Phantom Tollbooth*, a doorman takes delivery of a mysterious package that becomes the object of excited speculation by not only the story's hero—a ten-year-old here named Tony—but also by his parents:

> Nobody knew where it had come from. It certainly hadn't been ordered. It was no one's birthday and Christmas was still two months away—yet it was unmistakably there in the hallway, a large box with most extraordinary designs all over it, no name or address or

label or number or even a "fragile" or "this end up" sticker on it.

"Well, I suppose we ought to have a look at what's inside"—Mr. Flanders was a most practical man and this seemed like the logical thing to do—although even he was a bit uneasy about opening a package which had been delivered when no one was home and as the doorman said by a small wild eyed little man who kept repeating breathlessly

Page two of the earliest known version of the story's opening scene (Lilly Library, box 5, folder 37).

"here it is, here it is," as he carried it into the lobby, and then before any questions could be asked or answered disappeared down the street with only a parting, "It's for Flanders, you know."

Cautious Mrs. Flanders counsels leaving the package unopened as its delivery to the family must surely have been a mistake, but she is outvoted by her husband and son. Then comes a rather elaborate description of the packing materials, followed by the discovery of an "announcement" reading: "One Genuine Highway Toll Booth . . . easily assembled at home . . . and for use of those who have someplace to go—Instruction book and traffic regulations inside" (Lilly Library, box 5, folder 37).

As Juster searched for a credible device for drawing readers into the magical realm of the child's adventure, he struggled with the rationalist's urge to account for the mechanism behind the make-believe—the how and the why of the tollbooth's mysterious appearance. Juster's breakthrough came with the realization that the reader's own wish to escape from the boredom of daily routine would itself go a long way toward propelling the fantasy. As J. R. R. Tolkien had observed in the essay "On Fairy-Stories" (1947): "Fairy-tales were plainly not primarily concerned with possibility, but with desirability" (J. R. R. Tolkien, *The Tolkien Reader*; New York, Ballantine, 1966, p. 63).

Few of the details laid out in Juster's sketchy first draft proved to have much traction. The mystery package came with a map, but a map that indicated "Numeropolis" as a possible destination—not the more toe-tappingly staccato "Digitopolis" of later drafts. "Tony" of course became "Milo," and the boy's parents and doorman dropped from view, never to be seen or heard from again (Lilly Library "Rejects," box 5, folder 37). Juster would continue to fiddle with his hero's age, in various subsequent drafts specifying it as eight or nine before concluding at a late stage that it was not only unnecessary to be that precise but probably more prudent not to do so, lest some readers decide they were too old to care about Milo's adventures.

In addition to the sample chapters submitted by Juster to Epstein, two subsequent, more or less complete typescripts of the book have survived, including the so-called "Final Typed Draft," from which Epstein & Carroll prepared the first set of galleys. The opening sentence of chapter one of the latter draft reads: "There once was a little boy named Milo who didn't know what to do with himself—not just sometimes, but always." On reading the galleys, Juster struck the word "little" with a single stroke of his pencil.

It was also at this late stage that Epstein or Juster—neither could recall later whose idea it was—decided to do a major reshuffling of the middle chapters of the book. Entire scenes from chapters nine to thirteen—i.e., those framing the central Chroma episode—were exchanged for each other. In the published book, Milo meets Alec Bings immediately after leaving Digitopolis. He then encounters Chroma, followed by Dr. Dischord.

But in the manuscript, upon departing Digitopolis, Milo and company come first to the doctor, then proceed to the Silent Valley and from there on to Alec, Chroma, and the Island of Conclusions. It is from Alec Bings, it might be said, that Milo learns a fortifying lesson about the importance of believing in one's own point of view, while the Chroma episode balances that message with a reminder of the harm that can easily come of naively assuming one has *all* the answers. Both these lessons stand Milo in good stead as he ventures deeper into the Lands Beyond, so it would seem there was good reason to reorganize the material, however late in the game Juster (or his editor) thought to do so.

As Juster finalized the text, Jules Feiffer was in a state of high panic, having all but convinced himself that he was not up to the task of illustrating *The Phantom Tollbooth*. It was not just that he had never illustrated a children's book before. Notwithstanding the resounding success of his *Voice* strip, he remained far more confident in his writing ability than in his drawing. Key elements of the text seemed certain to shine a harsh light on his technical limitations—his inability to draw dogs, for instance. Feiffer would later describe his interpretation of Tock as a "kind of cartoon man on all fours" (interview with author, April 24, 2009). Believing himself no better at drawing horses, he tried in vain to talk Juster into having the armies of Wisdom ride into battle on the backs of cats. Still more troubling to him, Juster's text, having sounded the exuberant note of full-dress British comic fantasy, clearly called for illustrations in the same vein as those created with such finesse by Sir John Tenniel for Lewis Carroll's Alice books (and of the same high caliber, Feiffer admonished himself). The contemporary precedent of Edward Ardizzone, another English line artist of dazzling virtuosity, also leapt intimidatingly to mind. Nor was that all. Feiffer's work up until then had largely been adversarial in stance—a sharp jab at this or that perpetrator of moral hypocrisy, government malfeasance, or human folly. Feiffer now questioned his suitability as the illustrator of a children's book that, however raucous and satire-laced, was ultimately a story with a good-natured view of life.

Short of cash and sure that he would have to discard a great many false starts along the way, Feiffer opted to draw the illustrations on inexpensive tracing paper rather than on a more costly (and durable) paper like Fabriano. Years later, when the originals began to crumble, he greatly regretted the choice. At the time, however, using cheap paper had a much-needed liberating effect, freeing him to draw with abandon. Even so, on completing the work, Feiffer made a characteristically downbeat assessment. Far from judging that he had done a first-rate job, he told himself, "Well, I got away with it." One of the few illustrations he counted a complete success was the teeming double-page spread of the assembled cast of demons.

For all the angst the project induced in him, Feiffer still managed to have some fun with it. Once under way, both he and Juster approached their collaboration as an extension of their easygoing camaraderie, another chance for the two friends to tease and top one another: Feiffer by caricaturing Juster and contriving clever ways to avoid illustrating subjects he preferred not to draw, Juster by inventing characters and scenes the cartoonist would be hard-pressed to illustrate (for example, the Triple Demons of Compromise, "one short and fat, one tall and thin, and the third exactly like the other two"). For Feiffer, the experience also yielded a surprising, and ultimately career-changing, discovery: the realization that as a children's book illustrator he could be "more playful, even silly" on paper, and that he "loved engaging that side of myself" (interview with author, April 24, 2009).

During the six months that he worked on the manuscript, Juster met with Epstein from time to time, the latter always enthusiastic if also a bit preoccupied, and in any case not given to small talk. If Juster arrived early for an appointment, he knew better than to head straight to Epstein's office but rather would look in on Bennett Cerf, the pun-loving president of the firm, who might have his color television tuned to a baseball game, and who was always good for a rapid-fire exchange of puns. The one section of the book that Epstein and Juster disagreed about was the Chroma episode, in which Milo discovers a mysterious orchestra whose music-making is responsible for bringing color into the world. Epstein thought this mystical scene was out of character with the playful mood of the rest of the book. He urged Juster to remove it. When the author refused, Epstein deferred to his judgment but with a disclaimer that sounded ominously to the first-time author like a forecast of certain catastrophe. "Well, it's your book," Epstein said, "do what you want."

Unseen hands worked on the book at critical stages. When the copy editor responsible for reviewing the finer points of the text returned Juster's typescript to him with a list of queries and suggested revisions, the author was appalled to see that the editor had completely missed the comedic point of scenes like the ones in which King Azaz's advisors let loose with a barrage of synonyms. ("'Of course.' 'Certainly.' 'Precisely.' 'Exactly.' 'Yes,' they replied in order.") Didn't the author feel he could do without quite so much redundancy in the dialogue? The copy editor had proceeded to strike some of these instances of repetitiveness. Fortunately, Juster was given the time and the opportunity to repair the damage. Closer to publication, he was shown a set of page layouts prepared by Edward Gorey. The placement of the illustrations in relation to the text struck Juster as needlessly complex and fussy, to the point of being confusing. As an architect, he thought nothing of tearing apart a colleague's work (or of having the same done to his own) for the sake of advancing a problem toward its optimum solution, so he felt no reluctance now about redesigning the book from start to finish; Juster's design for *The Phantom Tollbooth* is the one that readers would come to know.

Epstein & Carroll published *The Phantom Tollbooth* in September of 1961, in the same year that saw the release of Roald Dahl's *James and the Giant Peach* (Knopf); Edwin Tunis's historical novel *Frontier Living* (World Publishing Company); and *The Bronze Bow* (Houghton Mifflin), the story, set in biblical times, that would win Elizabeth George Speare her second Newbery Medal in three years.

Like all first-time authors, Juster was keen to see his book on store shelves and, when this did not happen immediately, was convinced that it must have been distributed "in the dead of night, in plain unmarked cartons that were immediately put in bookstore basements, never to be seen again" ("The Current Speech—Always Changing," unpublished lecture notes by Norton Juster, n.d., note 36, collection of N.J.). Leaving nothing to chance, Minnie Juster swung into high gear, haunting New York City's bookstores, where, brimming with fierce maternal protectiveness and pride, she "terrorized" booksellers on her son's behalf (*Funny Business*, p. 125).

Then, one by one, the spectacular reviews rolled in. In a rhapsodic full-page essay, Emily Maxwell, writing in the *New Yorker*, stated plainly that she loved the book. Maxwell, the magazine's children's book reviewer since 1957 and the wife of its fiction editor, called *The Phantom Tollbooth* an "odd, very fine book" as she noted with amazement: "[This] is my first experience of opening a book with no special anticipation and gradually becoming aware that I am holding in my hands a newborn classic, still sticky from its chrysalis." After giving an elaborate plot summary, Maxwell concluded: "As *Pilgrim's Progress* is concerned with the awakening of the sluggardly spirit, *The Phantom Tollbooth* is concerned with the awakening of the lazy mind. One is also reminded of *Alice in Wonderland*—not to mention the fantasies of James Thurber . . . but the book remains triumphantly itself, lucid, humorous, full of warmth and real invention." She closed with an appreciative nod to the first-time author responsible for the magic: "Mr. Juster is thirty-two years old and is a practicing architect. According to the jacket, he is preparing a book on urban aesthetics, on a grant from the Ford Foundation. I have great hopes for any city he has a say about."

By then, the *New York Herald Tribune* and the *New York Times* had weighed in with equally laudatory notices. In the prologue to an interview with Juster in the *Tribune*, John Crosby wrote: "In a world which sometimes seems to have gone mad, it is refreshing to pause and consider for a moment a book for children which contains a character called 'Faintly Macabre, the not so wicked Which.' The name of the book is *The Phantom Tollbooth* and it was written by a bearded elf named Norton Juster and illustrated by Jules Feiffer, who is the cleverest of the younger neurotics." Crosby went on to place the book in the exalted company of *Alice's Adventures in Wonderland* and *Gulliver's Travels*. In addition to making what was fast becoming the obligatory comparison with the Alice books, the *Times*'s reviewer, Ann McGovern, cited *The Wonderful Wizard of Oz*. Critics, it seemed, had begun vying with each other to name the classic that Juster's remarkable book most nearly resembled. McGovern noted as well that while "most books

An advertisement published in the *New York Times Book Review*, December 3, 1961.

advertised for 'readers of all ages' fail to keep their promise," Juster's "wonderful fantasy" did indeed have "something wonderful for anyone old enough to relish the allegorical wisdom."

The *Village Voice* chimed in that December with an appreciative review by Jane Jacobs, the urban-design critic and neighborhood activist whose monumental *The Death and Life of Great American Cities* had recently appeared. Jacobs, who was a friend of Juster's, made one of the more astute comments about the book when she remarked that *The Phantom Tollbooth* derived its special flavor from a fusion of the "most outrageous fantasy" with an "urgent and vivid sense of reality." As for the illustrator, Jacobs wrote: "Jules Feiffer [is] a man who can draw an idea."

In another reflection of the children's book world's low regard for fantasy, the only dissenting opinions came from two journals read primarily by librarians and educators. The *Bulletin of the Center for Children's Books* dismissed *The Phantom Tollbooth* as an "intensive and extensive fantasy, heavily burdened with contrivance and whimsy" (March 1962, vol. xv, no. 7, p. 112). The venerable *Horn Book Magazine*, where omissions were never accidents, simply ignored it.

The following fall, Collins published the English edition. Astoundingly, as the book ran the gauntlet of British critics, it received a second round of toasts and accolades. Much to their credit, England's reviewers, instead of waxing proprietary, took it in stride that an American author might be capable of diving fearlessly into the great stream of English fantasy writing and produce a masterpiece worthy of the likes of Carroll and Grahame. As the *Guardian*'s Andrew Leslie observed: "To those grown-ups who, either cheerfully or stoically, perform the bedtime duty of reading to the children—and occasionally wish it wouldn't go on quite so long—I recommend outright purchase of Norton Juster's *The Phantom Tollbooth*. . . . The story is always charmingly inventive—Jules Feiffer's drawings splendidly catch the spirit of it all—and in some families I think it could become a well-thumbed classic" (November 16, 1962).

In 1963, Juster followed up on his triumphant authorial debut with *The Dot and the Line: A Romance in Lower Mathematics*, a hipster fable about a modern love triangle. The author had upped the ante by creating his own illustrations. In a witty brew of drawing and collage, he combined straight lines, squiggles, and circles with a grab bag of images pilfered from the history of art. Jason Epstein once again published Juster but this time under the Random House imprint, Epstein and Clelia Carroll having by then dissolved their partnership. *The Dot and the Line* was a novelty book, whose primary audience—"readers of all ages from middle to dark," as the author archly stated in the flap copy he prepared for it—was a perfect match for the readership of *Feiffer*. For *Phantom Tollbooth* fans clamoring for a sequel on the order of Lewis Carroll's *Through the Looking-Glass*, the new book may have come as something of a disappointment. Juster, however, was not one to repeat himself, and *The Dot and the Line* settled in to respectable sales as a perennial gift book, especially around Valentine's Day. Then in 1965, he surprised his fans again by publishing *Alberic the Wise*, a collection of three lyrical quest tales with a medieval flavor, each an exploration of one of life's big questions: the meaning of wisdom, happiness, and truth.

During these years, Juster devoted much of his time to his architectural practice, which was growing steadily, if not quite in the glamorous direction he had imagined for himself during his student days. Rather like his father, he had become a partner in a small firm with an eclectic practice that included the design of private homes and of school and museum structures. He continued to teach part-time as well—first at Pratt Institute and later, after he and his wife moved to Massachusetts, at Hampshire College.* When asked which of his three part-time occupations he preferred, Juster would always give a Milo-like response: "The most appealing of the three are the two I am *not* doing at the time" ("The Current Speech—Always Changing," unpublished lecture notes by Norton Juster, n.d., note 43, collection of N.J.).

Every now and then, Juster published another new book. He did so to the delight of some fans as well as to the befuddlement of those who still had not learned to look beyond their expectations about the author. Among these later works were his wordplay collections, the first of which, *Stark Naked: A Paranomastic Odyssey* (1969), was not intended for children, while the other books were: *Otter Nonsense* (1982) and *As: A Surfeit of Similes* (1989). *So Sweet to Labor* (1979, later retitled *A Woman's Place: Yesterday's Women in Rural America*) was a bigger surprise than most: a scholarly work of regional history in which Juster, having moved from New York City to an old western Massachusetts farm, resumed his reflections on the balanced and considered life, but this time in reaction to the social practices and belief systems of nineteenth-century rural America rather than those of the modern city. Then, as a grandparent and a man in his seventies, he turned to writing picture books, the first of which, *The Hello, Goodbye Window* (2005), won the Caldecott Medal for its illustrator, Chris Raschka. He never completed his Ford Foundation fellowship project, but nor did he rule out the possibility of doing so either. "Maybe someday I'll get back to it," he said once, "when I'm trying to avoid doing something else" (Norton Juster, "A Note from the Author," in *The Phantom Tollbooth*, Essential Modern Classics edition, London: HarperCollins Essential Modern Classics, 2008).

Norton and Jeanne Juster, c. 1970.

* In 1970, Juster joined the faculty of Hampshire, a newly created small liberal arts college located in the wooded outskirts of Amherst, Massachusetts. In the countercultural spirit of the times, Hampshire set out to offer a largely unstructured, alternative educational experience to highly motivated, self-directed students. It was a place for teenage Milos to take to the open road, with just an occasional bit of judicious guidance from their elders, and, not surprisingly, Juster felt right at home there.

Jules Feiffer, at a Manhattan bus stop displaying the poster for his New-York Historical Society retrospective exhibition, 2003.

The Phantom Tollbooth's stunning initial success had surprisingly little impact, in the short term, on Jules Feiffer's professional life. It did not, as one might have expected, prompt a great flurry of telephone calls from publishers eager for his services, and the silence only fed his lingering doubts about the drawings. Not that Feiffer was suffering in obscurity. By 1961, syndication of his *Voice* strip was up to forty newspapers nationwide. Earlier that year, he had won both a George Polk Award in journalistic excellence for *Feiffer* and an Academy Award as the writer of the Best Animated Short Film for *Munro*, a film based on the book that for years no publisher had wanted. During the 1960s, to the delight of his growing legion of fans, a new Feiffer book (whether a *Voice* compilation or something original) be-

came an almost annual event. Starting with *Little Murders* (1967), he branched out further by writing for the stage, and he added to his film credits as the screenwriter of *Carnal Knowledge* (1971) and *Popeye* (1980). Amid this torrent of creativity, Feiffer might well have left *The Phantom Tollbooth* far behind. Instead, in "Excalibur and Rose" (1963), he attempted a literary fairy tale of his own in the earlier work's grand comic manner.* Looking back at the experiment, he found (for once) that the text was the weak link and that in the accompanying drawings he had finally achieved the technical mastery and ripeness of vision that he had longed for, and only partially attained, in *The Phantom Tollbooth*.

Feiffer soured on playwriting when *Elliot Loves*, a drama directed by Mike Nichols, opened off-Broadway with a first-rate cast in June 1990—and closed only weeks later thanks to a brutal review by *New York Times* critic Frank Rich. The experience devastated him and prompted him to rethink his involvement in a creative realm where one's best efforts could be crushed so summarily. It was then that Feiffer recalled the intense enjoyment that—his persistent misgivings at the time notwithstanding—he had felt as *The Phantom Tollbooth*'s illustrator.

Serendipitously, an artist friend, Edward Sorel, had recently asked him to write a story for children for Sorel to illustrate—then, without telling Feiffer, changed his mind and wrote the book himself. Feiffer, furious, plotted his revenge—rather quixotically—by plunging headlong into the children's book world himself, with

* Feiffer created "Excalibur and Rose" for *Feiffer's Album* (New York: Random House, 1963).

the intention of writing circles around Sorel. In a burst of creativity, he produced *The Man in the Ceiling* (1993), an illustrated novel about a boy with dreams of being a cartoonist, and then quickly followed it with two more novels and the first of many picture books. Feiffer, at sixty-four, had embarked on a major new career path that, following the cancellation of his *Voice* strip in 1998 after a forty-two-year run, came to mean more and more to him. Among the collaborators he now worked with were his own eldest daughter, the writer Kate Feiffer; Florence Parry Heide; Lois Lowry; and, in 2010, for a picture book called *The Odious Ogre*, Norton Juster—the old friends' first creative reunion in nearly fifty years. Most collaborators would have thought this rather a long gap between projects, but Feiffer and Juster had always prided themselves on doing things in their own good time. Perhaps Juster, an arch-procrastinator from way back, had finally run out of excuses *not* to write another book for his friend to illustrate. Or perhaps, like Milo home from the Lands Beyond, they each had had so much else to do.

The Phantom Tollbooth is one of those rare books that readers cite time and again as having changed their lives. Writing in *The Harvard Guide to Influential Books*, Martha Minow, a Harvard law professor and former clerk to U.S. Supreme Court justice Thurgood Marshall, praised it for "remind[ing] us that we might well be able to do things that people say could never be done" (*The Harvard Guide to Influential Books*, edited by C. Maury

Norton Juster, posing as a gargoyle, 1992.

Devine, et al.; New York: Harper & Row, 1986, pp. 175–76). Novelist Cathleen Schine spoke for many when she recalled: "When I first read *The Phantom Tollbooth* (it was actually read to my fourth-grade class by our homeroom teacher), it was as if someone had turned on the lights. The concepts of irony, of double entendre, of words as play, of the pleasure and inevitability of intellectual absurdity were suddenly accessible to me. They made sense to me in an extremely personal way. It was a new way of seeing the world, but a way that I recognized, as if I'd been waiting for it" (*Barnard*, Winter 1994, p. 26).

As a child, novelist Michael Chabon was so excited by *The Phantom Tollbooth* that he reread it eleven or twelve times and then, inspired by the example of the American frontiersman (and early Boy Scout leader) Dan Beard, pricked his finger and signed his name in blood on the flyleaf (*New York Post*, August 26, 2001). The family of British fantasy writer Diana Wynne Jones, the author of *Howl's Moving Castle* and *Castle in the Air*, reread their copy so often that it fell apart and somehow "got covered with strange stains that nobody would admit to making." Years afterward, she was amused to realize: "It didn't occur to us that it might be about something. It struck us as a little like *The Wizard of Oz*, only better.

"You can read it that way and enjoy it thoroughly, but," Jones continued, "it is about something. When you see that it is, it adds a whole extra dimension to the story. It is about getting educated. It is about everyone's complete puzzlement over all the weird and useless things they make you learn at school" ("Why You'll Love This Book," by Diana Wynne Jones. Foreword to *The Phantom Tollbooth* Essential Modern Classics edition; London: HarperCollins, 2008).

Then there was the ardent fan who, identifying himself only as "Milo" in a letter to *Rolling Stone* published at the height of the counterculture, admonished fellow readers: "If you want to get freaked out of your undernourished head, pick up *The Phantom Tollbooth*, by Norton Juster. They tell you it's a kids' book, but take my word for it, no one who reads it is ever the same. No hype" (October 29, 1970).

In *The Child That Books Built*, English journalist Francis Spufford reflects on the unique summons by which each of the books he most prized as an avid child reader of the 1960s lured him into its imaginative orbit: "Be a Roman soldier, said a book by Rosemary Sutcliffe. Be an urchin in Georgian London, said a Leon Garfield. Be Milo, 'who was bored, not just some of the time but all of the time,' and drives past the purple tollbooth to the Lands Beyond. Be where magic works" (New York: Metropolitan Books, 2002, p. 80).

In its first half century, more than three million copies of *The Phantom Tollbooth* had been sold in the U.S. alone. And in a turn of events that boredom-prone Milo might have appreciated, Juster's book by then had found its way into middle-grade classrooms throughout the country, amusing untold numbers of schoolchildren even as it challenged them to question authority and think for themselves. Foreign-language translations included editions in Catalan, Chinese, Croatian, Dutch, French, German, Greek, Hebrew, Italian, Japanese, Korean, Lithuanian, Polish, Portuguese, Russian, Spanish, Swedish, Thai, and Turkish. The first major adaptation, a feature-length live-action/animated film directed by Chuck Jones (1970), failed to catch on and had only a very limited and short-lived theatrical release. But a family opera commissioned in 1995 by OperaDelaware, with music by Arnold Black and lyrics by Juster and Sheldon Harnick, was well received and led to the "musical" version by the same collaborators, which debuted to rave reviews at the John F. Kennedy

Center for the Performing Arts in Washington, D.C., in 2008, and then embarked on a national tour.

After "Max," the name of *Where the Wild Things Are*'s doughty young hero, "Milo," it would seem, is the name most commonly given to an American child out of affection for a children's book. Madeleine L'Engle's *A Wrinkle in Time* (1962) and Louise Fitzhugh's *Harriet the Spy* (1964) are two of the handful of children's literature classics that, in surveys of books remembered from childhood, are almost always singled out as transformative experiences. *The Phantom Tollbooth* is another such book.

It is no small feat for an author who has transported readers to a magical place like the Lands Beyond to bring them back to reality again. Handling it awkwardly, an author may stir up feelings of betrayal or letdown. Juster met this final challenge with one last, grand flourish. Like Candide returning from his far-flung travels to discover a world of possibility in his own garden, Milo arrives home to survey his room with newly appraising eyes. "There were books," he now saw, "that could take you anywhere, and things to invent, and make, and build, and break, and all the puzzlement and excitement of everything he didn't know." "Reading becomes the new portal for adventures," writes literary historian Maria Tatar of Milo's epiphany (Maria Tatar, *Enchanted Hunters: The Power of Stories in Childhood*; New York: W. W. Norton, 2009, p. 153). Or, rather, it becomes one portal among many to the infinity of worlds that a child like Milo—which is to say, *any* child—might imagine "and then someday make real."

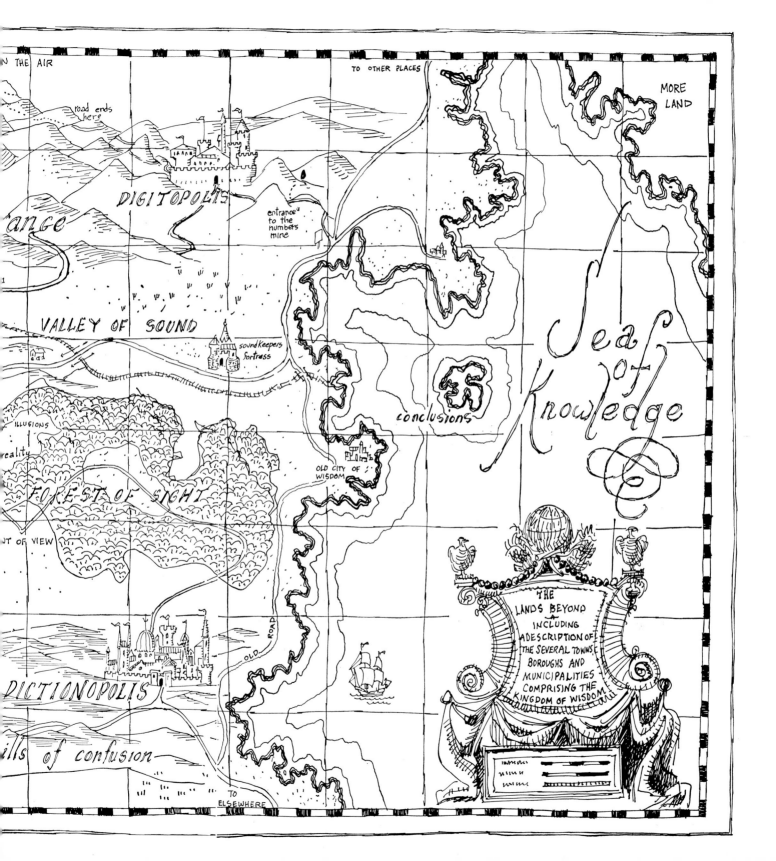

Annotator's Note

Please note that the main text begins on page 9, following the pagination of the original book. This reflects the style of numbering books from the very first page, including front matter, that was customary at the time of publication.

1. Milo

There was once a boy named Milo who didn't know what to do with himself—not just sometimes, but always.

When he was in school he longed to be out, and when he was out he longed to be in. On the way he thought about coming home, and coming home he thought about going. Wherever he was he wished he were somewhere else, and when he got there he wondered why he'd bothered. Nothing really interested him—least of all the things that should have.

"It seems to me that almost everything is a waste of time," he remarked one day as he walked dejectedly home from school. "I can't see the point in learning to solve useless problems, or subtracting turnips from turnips, or knowing where Ethiopia is or how to spell February." And, since no one bothered to explain otherwise, he regarded the process of seeking knowledge as the greatest waste of time of all.

1. Milo

In 1952–53, as a Fulbright Scholar in city planning at the University of Liverpool's School of Architecture, Juster occasionally took the night ferry to Dublin for weekend holidays with his actor friends. During one such excursion, he met character actor Milo O'Shea, who was just becoming known on the Irish stage, and remembered his name. A decade later, O'Shea catapulted to world fame with his screen roles in *Ulysses,* Franco Zeffirelli's *Romeo and Juliet,* and *Barbarella,* among other major films.

Serendipitously, 1961 also saw the advent of a second fictional Milo. Lieutenant Milo Minderbinder, the U.S. Army Air Forces mess officer who figures prominently in Joseph Heller's antiwar satire *Catch-22,* is an amoral schemer and entrepreneur who, as the driving force behind M & M Enterprises, finds innumerable ways to game the U.S. military's lumbering bureaucracy for fun and profit. As a master of circular logic and organized chaos, Heller's Milo might easily be imagined as making an appearance along the road to Juster's Rhyme and Reason.

2. When he was in school he longed to be out, and when he was out he longed to be in.

Milo's complaint runs deeper than the schoolchild's usual professions of boredom. Max Weber was among the pioneering sociologists to analyze the modern industrial city as a breeding ground for disaffected feeling and alienation. As a student of urban planning, Juster too was interested in the psychological impact, both for good and for ill, of city living. Juster's friend Jane Jacobs published her landmark book on this theme, *The Death and Life of Great American Cities,* in 1961, the year in which *The Phantom Tollbooth* also appeared. Coincidentally, the same Random House editor, Jason Epstein, shepherded both books into print.

Juster was hardly the first writer to deal in comic

terms with the malaise of alienation. As a child, he was treated at the movies to one of its classic formulations upon hearing Groucho Marx, as Captain Geoffrey (or Jeffrey) T. Spaulding in *Animal Crackers* (1930), croon the woolly mock lament "Hello, I Must Be Going."

As he and his unhappy thoughts hurried along (for while he was never anxious to be where he was going, he liked to get there as quickly as possible) it seemed a great wonder that the world, which was so large, could sometimes feel so small and empty.

"And worst of all," he continued sadly, "there's nothing for me to do, nowhere I'd care to go, and hardly anything worth seeing." He punctuated this last thought with such a deep sigh that a house sparrow singing nearby stopped and rushed home to be with his family.

Without stopping or looking up, Milo dashed past the buildings and busy shops that lined the street and in a few minutes reached home—dashed through the lobby—hopped onto the elevator—two, three, four, five, six, seven, eight, and off again—opened the apartment door—rushed into his room—flopped dejectedly into a chair, and grumbled softly, "Another long afternoon."

He looked glumly at all the things he owned. The books that were too much trouble to read, the tools he'd never learned to use, the small electric automobile he hadn't driven in months—or was it years?—and the hundreds of other games and toys, and bats and balls, and bits and pieces scattered around him. And then, to one side of the room, just next to the phonograph, he noticed something he had certainly never seen before.

Who could possibly have left such an enormous package and such a strange one? For, while it was not quite square, it was definitely not round, and for its size it was larger than almost any other big package of smaller dimension that he'd ever seen.

Page 11

3. and in a few minutes reached home

Home for the Justers was a two-family semidetached house in the Flatbush section of Brooklyn, New York. Juster made Milo an apartment dweller on the assumption that more young readers would be familiar with that type of setting.

4. "Another long afternoon."

For young Juster, tuning in to radio serials like *Jack Armstrong, the All-American Boy*, which aired each weekday afternoon in fifteen-minute-long installments, provided a welcome alternative to homework and chores during the long hours before supper.

5. the small electric automobile he hadn't driven in months

The luckiest real-life Milos among the book's first readers could have had a battery-powered car of their own. The 42-inch-long Stutz Bearcat Ride-On Roadster, for example, a scaled-down replica of the 1914 original, was first marketed in 1961 by Louis Marx and Company. As a boy, Juster was the proud owner of a more modest pedal car that, at age six, he used as a getaway vehicle on the one occasion when he ran away from home. The first grader had packed his father's necktie collection to be bartered for food and drink on the open road. His uncle Bill caught up with him a few blocks away. Cars remained a symbol of freedom and escape for him, as they did for so many Americans.

An irresistible Marx "Ride-On" car, c. 1960.

Page 12

6. "ONE GENUINE TURNPIKE TOLLBOOTH"

Turnpike is an old-fashioned term for a type of road whose use requires the payment of a fee or toll. *Pike* is the old name for the moveable barrier used to bar the traveler's progress prior to payment. This arrangement for financing road construction and maintenance, and for replenishing government coffers, dates back thousands of years, with one toll road known to have been in operation in the Neo-Assyrian Empire as early as the seventh century BC. Perhaps the dimwitted troll in the Norwegian trickster tale "Three Billy Goats Gruff" was intended as a caricature of an overzealous toll collector, attempting in vain as he does to set the price of crossing his bridge at the forfeiture of a traveler's life.

In the United States during the years following World War II, millions of veterans and their families moved to the suburbs, where car ownership was a necessity. President Dwight D. Eisenhower accelerated the trend when he signed into law the Federal-Aid Highway Act of 1956, which provided for the creation of a vastly expanded interstate network of roads. Justified in part as an essential element of the nation's defense apparatus, the monumental public-works project proved a major boon to the American auto industry. As cars proliferated, the automobile's importance as a status symbol for millions of middle-class Americans in the fifties and sixties grew as well. Young Milo's real-life counterparts of that era would have known all the latest American-made cars by make, model, and fin type, and tollbooths would have been familiar landmarks.

7. "EASILY ASSEMBLED AT HOME"

Juster recalled: "When I was a child, almost all presents, it seemed, came in pieces and had to be put together. Some I loved, like erector sets and model airplanes. In fact, I think I learned to read well, and

Attached to one side was a bright-blue envelope which said simply: "FOR MILO, WHO HAS PLENTY OF TIME."

Of course, if you've ever gotten a surprise package, you can imagine how puzzled and excited Milo was; and if you've never gotten one, pay close attention, because someday you might.

"I don't think it's my birthday," he puzzled, "and Christmas must be months away, and I haven't been outstandingly good, or even good at all." (He had to admit this even to himself.) "Most probably I won't like it anyway, but since I don't know where it came from, I can't possibly send it back." He thought about it for quite a while and then opened the envelope, but just to be polite.

"ONE GENUINE TURNPIKE TOLLBOOTH," it stated—and then it went on:

"EASILY ASSEMBLED AT HOME, AND FOR USE BY THOSE WHO HAVE NEVER TRAVELED IN LANDS BEYOND."

"Beyond what?" thought Milo as he continued to read.

"THIS PACKAGE CONTAINS THE FOLLOWING ITEMS:

"One (1) genuine turnpike tollbooth to be erected according to directions.

"Three (3) precautionary signs to be used in a precautionary fashion.

"Assorted coins for use in paying tolls.

"One (1) map, up to date and carefully drawn by mas-

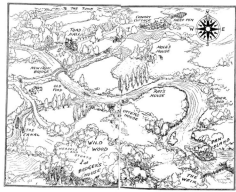

carefully, by poring over the directions for putting together model airplanes. . . . To me any real present required participation and patience" (N.J. Notes I, p. 4).

8. "Three (3) precautionary signs"

Here Juster gives a modest demonstration of circular logic, in a statement that sounds like a useful instruction but which in fact conveys no useful information whatsoever.

Pages 12–13

9. "One (1) map, up to date and carefully drawn by master cartographers"

Among Juster's first ideas about the book was that it should have endpaper maps like those he recalled poring over as a child in Arthur Ransome's Swallows and Amazons series and Kenneth Grahame's *The Wind in the Willows*, illustrated by Ernest Shepard. When Jules Feiffer reacted coolly to the suggestion, the author took it upon himself to sketch a map of the Lands Beyond and left it to his collaborator to retrace and finish the work in his own signature pen line.

Endpaper map by Ernest Shepard for Kenneth Grahame's *The Wind in the Willows* (1908).

ter cartographers, depicting natural and man-made features.

"One (1) book of rules and traffic regulations, which may not be bent or broken."

And in smaller letters at the bottom it concluded:

"RESULTS ARE NOT GUARANTEED, BUT IF NOT PERFECTLY SATISFIED, YOUR WASTED TIME WILL BE REFUNDED."

Following the instructions, which told him to cut here, lift there, and fold back all around, he soon had the toll-

Page 14

10. and even the names sounded most peculiar.

Place names such as Mountains of Ignorance and Foothills of Confusion herald a tale at once allegorical and comedic. In her rave review of *The Phantom Tollbooth* in the *New Yorker*, Emily Maxwell wrote, "As *Pilgrim's Progress* is concerned with the awakening of the sluggardly spirit, *The Phantom Tollbooth* is concerned with the awakening of the lazy mind" (November 18, 1961). Writing in the *New York Herald Tribune*, critic John Crosby hailed the book as an "amalgam between *Gulliver's Travels* and *Alice in Wonderland*" (September 22, 1961).

booth unpacked and set up on its stand. He fitted the windows in place and attached the roof, which extended out on both sides, and fastened on the coin box. It was very much like the tollbooths he'd seen many times on family trips, except of course it was much smaller and purple.

"What a strange present," he thought to himself. "The least they could have done was to send a highway with it, for it's terribly impractical without one." But since, at the time, there was nothing else he wanted to play with, he set up the three signs,

SLOW DOWN APPROACHING TOLLBOOTH

PLEASE HAVE YOUR FARE READY

HAVE YOUR DESTINATION IN MIND

and slowly unfolded the map.

As the announcement stated, it was a beautiful map, in many colors, showing principal roads, rivers and seas, towns and cities, mountains and valleys, intersections and detours, and sites of outstanding interest both beautiful and historic.

The only trouble was that Milo had never heard of any of the places it indicated, and even the names sounded most peculiar.

"I don't think there really is such a country," he concluded after studying it carefully. "Well, it doesn't matter anyway." And he closed his eyes and poked a finger at the map.

"Dictionopolis," read Milo slowly when he saw what

his finger had chosen. "Oh, well, I might as well go there as anywhere."

He walked across the room and dusted the car off carefully. Then, taking the map and rule book with him, he hopped in and, for lack of anything better to do, drove slowly up to the tollbooth. As he deposited his coin and rolled past he remarked wistfully, "I do hope this is an interesting game, otherwise the afternoon will be so terribly dull." 11

Page 15

11. "an interesting game"

Although "interesting" is among the English language's most overused descriptives, Milo employs it here with striking precision. Derived from the Latin, "interest" literally means "between beings." Milo's first challenge is indeed to get outside of himself and make meaningful contact with the larger world.

1. Suddenly he found himself speeding along an unfamiliar country highway

Juster brings about Milo's swift, matter-of-fact passage from mundane reality to the surprise-laden Lands Beyond in one of modern fantasy literature's deftest sleights of hand. For Milo, taking a toy to heart is all that's required to cross over into the world of the imagination. About his choice of a tollbooth as Milo's magic portal, the author observed: "I wanted something that most children would be familiar with. In our automobile-dominated society, the tollbooths on major highways seemed to fit the bill" (N.J. Notes I, p. 4).

Every work of fantasy involving an alternate world needs some such narrative gateway or pivot, a device for transporting the hero while maintaining the modern (i.e., inherently skeptical) reader's willing suspension of disbelief. Juster's literary forebears attempted this feat in a variety of ways. According to Martin Gardner (*The Annotated Alice*, p. 27), Alice's fall down the rabbit hole gained in credibility with the author's contemporary readers because it alluded to a scientific debate that was then the subject of "considerable popular speculation": the question of "what would happen if one fell through a hole that went straight through the center of the earth." In *The Wonderful Wizard of Oz*, L. Frank Baum relies on the forces of nature to lift Dorothy out of prosaic Kansas and set her down on the road to the Emerald City. E. Nesbit trades on the modern reader's fascination with ancient civilizations as well as their lingering sympathy for the supernatural when in *The Story of the Amulet* she places one half of a curious amulet in her child characters' hands and empowers it to transform the children into time travelers. C. S. Lewis uses an unremarkable-looking wardrobe to transport his child characters to Narnia, albeit a wardrobe crafted (as it turns out) from the wood of an otherworldly tree planted by the magician's nephew.

2. Beyond Expectations

1 Suddenly he found himself speeding along an unfamiliar country highway, and as he looked back over his shoulder neither the tollbooth nor his room nor even the house was anywhere in sight. What had started as make-believe was now very real.

"What a strange thing to have happen," he thought (just as you must be thinking right now). "This game is much more serious than I thought, for here I am riding on a road I've never seen, going to a place I've never heard of, and all because of a tollbooth which came from nowhere. I'm certainly glad that it's a nice day for a trip," he concluded hopefully, for, at the moment, this was the one thing he definitely knew.

2 The sun sparkled, the sky was clear, and all the colors he saw seemed to be richer and brighter than he could ever remember. The flowers shone as if they'd been

16

cleaned and polished, and the tall trees that lined the road shimmered in silvery green.

"WELCOME TO EXPECTATIONS," said a carefully lettered sign on a small house at the side of the road.

"INFORMATION, PREDICTIONS, AND ADVICE CHEERFULLY OFFERED. PARK HERE AND BLOW HORN."

With the first sound from the horn a little man in a long coat came rushing from the house, speaking as fast as he could and repeating everything several times:

2. all the colors he saw seemed to be richer and brighter

As a city child who rarely had the chance to venture far from his neighborhood, Juster grew up knowing more about the maps of faraway places that fascinated him than he did about the places themselves. The Justers' occasional family car trips into the countryside seemed magical to him, if also disappointing in one respect. With his beloved maps as his primary frame of reference, Juster recalled: "I always expected places to change color as you crossed borders or state lines—from pink to pale blue to light yellow" (N.J. Notes I, p. 5).

Page 17
3. "WELCOME TO EXPECTATIONS"

In countless Jewish American households like the Justers', where memories of immigrant struggle remained raw, high parental expectations set the tone of family life. Youngsters were under constant pressure to do well at school, and reminded of the many sacrifices their parents made for them. Juster recalled a typical joke of the time: A schoolchild proudly announces at the dinner table, "I got 97 on the math test." The parents reply, "Who got the other 3 percent?" Not all children suffered equally under the burden of these demands, however, and Juster himself was fortunate that his parents chose to place their highest hopes not in him—the family daydreamer—but rather in his elder brother, Howard. Yet even as a child he sensed, as he listened to the conversations of the adults around him, the "great tragedy" of living a life governed entirely by expectations (N.J. Notes I, p. 8). In the decades that followed, many of Juster's literary contemporaries—Richard Yates in *Revolutionary Road*, Allen Ginsberg in *Howl*, and sociologist William H. Whyte in *The Organization Man*, among others—would critique post–World War II American society from this same perspective.

4. Illustration

The drawing of the Whether Man as a "short, plump, balding semi-lunatic in a toga" is Feiffer's teasing portrait of his collaborator. In his afterword to the British paperback edition, Juster declared this depiction of himself "quite unfair, since everyone knows I never wear a toga."

5. "Is this the right road for Dictionopolis?"

Milo's exchange with the Whether Man recalls Alice's conversation, in Wonderland, with the Cheshire Cat:

> "Would you tell me, please, which way I
> ought to go from here?"
> "That depends a good deal on where you
> want to get to," said the Cat.
> "I don't much care where—" said Alice.
> "Then it doesn't matter which way you
> go," said the Cat.
> "—so long as I get *somewhere*," Alice added
> in explanation.
> "Oh, you're sure to do that," said the Cat,
> "if you only walk long enough."

As Martin Gardner points out in *The Annotated Alice*, another "echo" of this oft-quoted passage appears in Jack Kerouac's "forgettable"(!) novel of 1957, *On the Road*:

4

5

"My, my, my, my, my, welcome, welcome, welcome, welcome to the land of Expectations, to the land of Expectations, to the land of Expectations. We don't get many travelers these days; we certainly don't get many travelers these days. Now what can I do for you? I'm the Whether Man."

"Is this the right road for Dictionopolis?" asked Milo, a little bowled over by the effusive greeting.

"Well now, well now, well now," he began again, "I don't know of any wrong road to Dictionopolis, so if this road goes to Dictionopolis at all it must be the right road, and if it doesn't it must be the right road to somewhere else, because there are no wrong roads to anywhere. Do you think it will rain?"

"I thought you were the Weather Man," said Milo, very confused.

"Oh no," said the little man, "I'm the Whether Man, not the Weather Man, for after all it's more important to know whether there will be weather than what the weather will be." And with that he released a dozen balloons that sailed off into the sky. "Must see which way the wind is blowing," he said, chuckling over his little joke and watching them disappear in all directions.

"What kind of a place is Expectations?" inquired Milo, unable to see the humor and feeling very doubtful of the little man's sanity.

"Good question, good question," he exclaimed. "Expectations is the place you must always go to before you get to where you're going. Of course, some people never go beyond Expectations, but my job is to hurry them along whether they like it or not. Now what else can I do for you?" And before Milo could reply he rushed into the house and reappeared a moment later with a new coat and an umbrella.

"I think I can find my own way," said Milo, not at all sure that he could. But, since he didn't understand the little man at all, he decided that he might as well move on—at least until he met someone whose sentences didn't always sound as if they would make as much sense backwards as forwards.

"Splendid, splendid, splendid," exclaimed the Whether Man. "Whether or not you find your own way,

"We gotta go and never stop going till we
   get there."
"Where we going, man?"
"I don't know but we gotta go."
  Unlike Alice, however, and for that matter Kerouac's burnt-out drifters, Milo has a destination squarely in mind.

Page 19

6. But, since he didn't understand the little man at all
  This passage likewise echoes *Alice's Adventures in Wonderland*, the moment in chapter one when, as Alice tumbles down the rabbit hole, she drowsily mutters to herself, "'Do cats eat bats? Do cats eat bats?' and sometimes, 'Do bats eat cats?' for, you see, as she couldn't answer either question, it didn't much matter which way she put it." In contrast to Carroll's heroine, Milo keeps his head and remains wide awake as he ventures deeper into unfamiliar territory.

6

7. "Expect everything, I always say, and the
unexpected never happens."

Juster recalled this intriguing maxim, spoken by the
Whether Man, as a favorite of Jules Feiffer's mother.

you're bound to find some way. If you happen to find my way, please return it, as it was lost years ago. I imagine by now it's quite rusty. You did say it was going to rain, didn't you?" And with that he opened the umbrella and looked up nervously.

"I'm glad you made your own decision. I do so hate to make up my mind about anything, whether it's good or bad, up or down, in or out, rain or shine. Expect everything, I always say, and the unexpected never happens. Now please drive carefully; good-by, good-by, good-by, good…" His last good-by was drowned out by an enormous clap of thunder, and as Milo drove down the road in the bright sunshine he could see the Whether Man standing in the middle of a fierce cloudburst that seemed to be raining only on him.

The road dipped now into a broad green valley and stretched toward the horizon. The little car bounced along with very little effort, and Milo had hardly to touch the accelerator to go as fast as he wanted. He was glad to be on his way again.

"It's all very well to spend time in Expectations," he thought, "but talking to that strange man all day would certainly get me nowhere. He's the most peculiar person I've ever met," continued Milo—unaware of how many peculiar people he would shortly encounter.

As he drove along the peaceful highway he soon fell to daydreaming and paid less and less attention to where he was going. In a short time he wasn't paying any attention at all, and that is why, at a fork in the road, when a sign pointed to the left, Milo went to the right,

Page 21

8. Illustration

Had Jack Kerouac written *On the Road* (1957) as preteen fiction, Feiffer's drawing might have made the perfect cover illustration. Both Juster and Feiffer made cross-country road trips of their own as young men. Ever game for adventure, Juster hitchhiked solo during the summer following his junior year at the University of Pennsylvania, stopping to ride down the Grand Canyon by mule and scoring a date with a Hollywood starlet. The more timorous Feiffer, knowing his military draft number would soon be called, quit his job at Will Eisner's studio to pursue a sometime girlfriend who had hitchhiked to Berkeley and dared him to do the same. With characteristic ambivalence, Feiffer and a friend who facetiously dubbed the young cartoonist "Captain Caution" (*Backing into Forward*, p. 102) traveled as far as Chicago by bus and hitchhiked the rest of the way.

Norton Juster (right) at the Grand Canyon with one of the friends he made while traveling west.

Page 22

9.

' It looks as though I'm getting nowhere' yawned Milo

Study by Jules Feiffer of Milo in the Doldrums
(collection of the artist).

10. "You're . . . in . . . the . . . Dol . . . drums"

The expression "in the doldrums" well describes
Milo's distracted state at the time we first meet him in
his room at home. Properly speaking, he is in the
doldrums long before he drives up to the place of that
name. As British fantasy writer Diana Wynne Jones has
observed: "Milo starts in the Doldrums—where most of
us are after a few years of school—and nearly gets stuck
there—as we all do" (from the introductory note by
D.W.J. to the HarperCollins UK Essential Modern
Classics paperback edition, 2008).

The editors of the *Oxford English Dictionary* speculate
that "in the doldrums" acquired its special meaning for
seafarers—as a term for the misfortune of getting stuck
in a place of becalmed and stymieing winds—through a

along a route which looked suspiciously like the wrong
way.

Things began to change as soon as he left the main
highway. The sky became quite gray and, along with it,
the whole countryside seemed to lose its color and
assume the same monotonous tone. Everything was
quiet, and even the air hung heavily. The birds sang only
gray songs and the road wound back and forth in an endless series of climbing curves.

Mile after

mile after

mile after

mile he drove, and now, gradually, the car went slower
and slower, until it was hardly moving at all.

"It looks as though I'm getting nowhere," yawned
Milo, becoming very drowsy and dull. "I hope I haven't
taken a wrong turn."

Mile after

mile after

mile after

mile, and everything became grayer and more monotonous. Finally the car just stopped altogether, and, hard as
he tried, it wouldn't budge another inch.

"I wonder where I am," said Milo in a very worried
tone.

10 "You're . . . in . . . the . . . Dol . . . drums,"
wailed a voice that sounded far away.

He looked around quickly to see who had spoken.
No one was there, and it was as quiet and still as one
could imagine.

"Yes . . . the . . . Dol . . . drums," yawned another voice, but still he saw no one.

"WHAT ARE THE DOLDRUMS?" he cried loudly, and tried very hard to see who would answer this time.

"The Doldrums, my young friend, are where nothing ever happens and nothing ever changes."

This time the voice came from so close that Milo jumped with surprise, for, sitting on his right shoulder, so

misreading of a traveler's letter, in which a reference to a "state [of mind]" was "[mis]taken for a locality." In any case, by the mid-nineteenth century "The Doldrums" had taken its place on navigational maps as the accepted name for a shifting equatorial region of the ocean where warm temperatures generate low air pressure systems that result in windless days.

Page 24

11. "We are the Lethargarians, at your service."

The Lethargarians call to mind the race of wee people first encountered by the narrator of Jonathan Swift's pungent satiric allegory on human nature, *Gulliver's Travels* (1726). But whereas Swift's Lilliputians epitomize all manner of human spitefulness and petty behavior—the spiritual smallness of people in general—Juster's impish crew more nearly resemble comic bumblers of the Keystone Kops variety. The author does not get bogged down in feelings of contempt for the airheads, nor do we: we're simply glad to see the bright lad don his thinking cap and move on.

Juster commented about this section: "The doldrums is where I spent a large part of my childhood. . . . When I realized how important a place this was for Milo, I had to visualize what it would be like and who might live there—hence, the Lethargarians. It was great fun to write this section, especially the daily schedule they had. It reminded me so much of what my ideal day would have been like when I was ten" (N.J. Notes I, p. 11).

lightly that he hardly noticed, was a small creature exactly the color of his shirt.

"Allow me to introduce all of us," the creature went on. "We are the Lethargarians, at your service."

Milo looked around and, for the first time, noticed dozens of them—sitting on the car, standing in the road, and lying all over the trees and bushes. They were very difficult to see, because whatever they happened to be sitting on or near was exactly the color they happened to be. Each one looked very much like the other (except for the color, of course) and some looked even more like each other than they did like themselves.

"I'm very pleased to meet you," said Milo, not sure whether or not he was pleased at all. "I think I'm lost. Can you help me please?"

"Don't say 'think,'" said one sitting on his shoe, for the one on his shoulder had fallen asleep. "It's against the law." And he yawned and fell off to sleep, too.

"No one's allowed to think in the Doldrums," continued a third, beginning to doze off. And as each one spoke, he fell off to sleep and another picked up the conversation with hardly any interruption.

"Don't you have a rule book? It's local ordinance 175389-J."

Milo quickly pulled the rule book from his pocket, opened to the page, and read, "Ordinance 175389-J: It shall be unlawful, illegal, and unethical to think, think of thinking, surmise, presume, reason, meditate, or speculate while in the Doldrums. Anyone breaking this law shall be severely punished!"

12

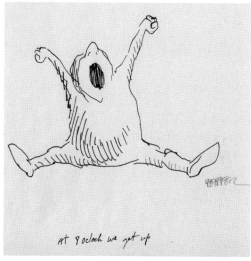

At 9 oclock we get up

Study by Jules Feiffer of a Lethargarian. A version of this elfin yawner appears in the background, right, of the finished drawing.

Page 26

13. "we have a very busy schedule"

The last memorable parody of a children's book character's "busy" day appeared in chapter four of E. B. White's *Charlotte's Web* (1952). As a defense against loneliness, Wilbur the runt pig resolves to bring structure to his life: "Breakfast at six-thirty . . . From seven to eight, Wilbur planned to have a talk with Templeton, the rat . . . From eight to nine, Wilbur planned to take a nap . . . From nine to eleven, he planned to dig a hole, or trench . . . From eleven to twelve, he planned to stand still and watch flies on the boards, watch bees in the clover, and watch swallows in the air."

14. "daydreaming"

Western culture has been of more than one mind about daydreaming. Plato wrote admiringly of Socrates's facility for losing himself in thought as he stood in the thick of Athens's bustling marketplace. Parodying Socrates for this very gift for distraction, Aristophanes, on the other hand, coined an immortal phrase when he caricatured the daydreaming philosopher as a man with his "head in the clouds." While other bold adventurers of the Age of Discovery charted distant continents, sixteenth-century French philosopher Michel de Montaigne turned to the shadowy byways of his own innermost thoughts as *terra incognita* well worth exploring. Shakespeare in *Hamlet* (c. 1600) and Cervantes in *Don Quixote* (1605 and 1615) subtly examined daydreaming as, in part, a habit of mind with the tragic—or comic—potential for inhibiting action. With less concern for nuance, John Bunyan codified the case against "sloth," the sin most often associated with a wandering mind, in *The Pilgrim's Progress* (1678). But nineteenth-century Romantics William Blake, William Wordsworth, and Samuel Taylor Coleridge rejected Bunyan and his like as they celebrated daydreaming as a portal to higher awareness. The

"That's a ridiculous law," said Milo, quite indignantly. "Everybody thinks."

"We don't," shouted the Lethargarians all at once.

"And most of the time *you* don't," said a yellow one sitting in a daffodil. "That's why you're here. You weren't thinking, and you weren't paying attention either. People who don't pay attention often get stuck in the Doldrums." And with that he toppled out of the flower and fell snoring into the grass.

Milo couldn't help laughing at the little creature's strange behavior, even though he knew it might be rude.

"Stop that at once," ordered the plaid one clinging to his stocking. "Laughing is against the law. Don't you have a rule book? It's local ordinance 574381-W."

Opening the book again, Milo found Ordinance 574381-W: "In the Doldrums, laughter is frowned upon and smiling is permitted only on alternate Thursdays. Violators shall be dealt with most harshly."

"Well, if you can't laugh or think, what can you do?" asked Milo.

"Anything as long as it's nothing, and everything as long as it isn't anything," explained another. "There's lots to do; we have a very busy schedule——

"At 8 o'clock we get up, and then we spend

"From 8 to 9 daydreaming.

"From 9 to 9:30 we take our early midmorning nap.

"From 9:30 to 10:30 we dawdle and delay.

"From 10:30 to 11:30 we take our late early morning nap.

"From 11:30 to 12:00 we bide our time and then eat lunch.

"From 1:00 to 2:00 we linger and loiter.

"From 2:00 to 2:30 we take our early afternoon nap.

"From 2:30 to 3:30 we put off for tomorrow what we could have done today.

"From 3:30 to 4:00 we take our early late afternoon nap.

"From 4:00 to 5:00 we loaf and lounge until dinner.

"From 6:00 to 7:00 we dillydally. 15

"From 7:00 to 8:00 we take our early evening nap, and then for an hour before we go to bed at 9:00 we waste time.

"As you can see, that leaves almost no time for brooding, lagging, plodding, or procrastinating, and if we stopped to think or laugh, we'd never get nothing done." 16

"You mean you'd never get anything done," corrected Milo.

"We don't want to get anything done," snapped another angrily; "we want to get nothing done, and we can do that without your help."

"You see," continued another in a more conciliatory tone, "it's really quite strenuous doing nothing all day, so once a week we take a holiday and go nowhere, which was just where we were going when you came along. Would you care to join us?"

"I might as well," thought Milo; "that's where I seem to be going anyway."

argument continued a century later when American philosopher (and proto-psychologist) William James expressed a Montaigne-like fascination with what he was the first to term the mind's "stream of consciousness" and Freud propounded a quasi-scientific rationale for associating daydreaming with the darker aspects of the human psyche. In "The Secret Life of Walter Mitty," a short story first published in the *New Yorker* in 1939 and later made into a film, humorist James Thurber did much to popularize a more forgiving view of the matter than Freud's, suggesting that everyone daydreams from time to time and with few if any adverse consequences. Recent psychological research on daydreaming, much of it built on the pioneering work of Yale psychologist Jerome L. Singer, indicates that daydreaming is not inherently harmful, and that those individuals (including children) who daydream most freely tend, on the contrary, to exhibit better concentration and a livelier manner, to show a higher tolerance for frustration, and to be less fearful, more alert, and generally happier. (See Jerome L. Singer, *Daydreaming: An Introduction to the Experimental Study of Inner Experience*, New York: Random House, 1966, and Eric Klinger, "The Power of Daydreaming," in *Psychology Today*, October 1987, pp. 36–44.)

Page 27

15. "dillydally"

The *Oxford English Dictionary* describes *dilly-dally*, semantically, as a "varied reduplication of 'dally,' with the same alternation as in zig-zag, shilly-shally, etc." Its first known appearance in print occurs in the Right Reverend Gervase Babington's dour commentary on the Five Books of Moses (1610), in which the author, then the Bishop of Worcester, writes scornfully of the unseemly lack of dispatch shown by Rebecca's family (in Genesis 24) as they prepare to send their daughter off to wed Isaac: "Such dilly dally is fitter for heathens that know not God, than for sober Christians."

(Christians? In his zeal, the good bishop seems momentarily to have strayed into New Testament territory!)

16. "procrastinating"

The word *procrastination* derives from the Latin *procrastinatus*: *pro*, for "forward"; and *crastinus*, meaning "of tomorrow." The *Oxford English Dictionary* traces its entry into the printed record to the 1540s and the historical writings of English chronicler and lawyer Edward Hall. In succeeding centuries, *procrastination* firmly established itself in the language of moral judgment as a pejorative term for the tendency to unwisely postpone or avoid action or to shirk one's responsibilities. As the English poet Edward Young would declare memorably in *The Complaint: or, Night Thoughts on Life, Death, and Immortality* (1742), "Procrastination is the thief of time." More recently, psychologists have attempted to explain chronic procrastination in terms of personality disorders such as perfectionism and low self-esteem, while neuroscientists have looked to malfunction in the prefrontal cortex, the brain's command and control center, as the root cause of procrastinatory behavior.

All of which is a bit ironic when one considers that *The Phantom Tollbooth* is itself a by-product of procrastination, Juster's avoidance of a more "serious" book project that had become too burdensome.

Page 28

17. "Everyone but the terrible watchdog"

Juster drew his inspiration for Milo's traveling companion, Tock, from a favorite character in the aforementioned radio drama of his childhood, *Jack Armstrong, the All-American Boy*. In this serial, Jack, a popular high school athlete, accompanies his best friends, Billy and Betty Fairfield, and their rich uncle, Jim Fairfield, on the latter's business trips to dangerous,

"Tell me," he yawned, for he felt ready for a nap now himself, "does everyone here do nothing?"

17

"Everyone but the terrible watchdog," said two of them, shuddering in chorus. "He's always sniffing around to see that nobody wastes time. A most unpleasant character."

"The watchdog?" said Milo quizzically.

"THE WATCHDOG," shouted another, fainting from fright, for racing down the road barking furiously and kicking up a great cloud of dust was the very dog of whom they had been speaking.

18

"RUN!"

"WAKE UP!"

"RUN!"

"HERE HE COMES!"

"THE WATCHDOG!"

Great shouts filled the air as the Lethargarians scattered in all directions and soon disappeared entirely.

"R-R-R-G-H-R-O-R-R-H-F-F," exclaimed the watchdog as he dashed up to the car, loudly puffing and panting.

Milo's eyes opened wide, for there in front of him was a large dog with a perfectly normal head, four feet, and a tail—and the body of a loudly ticking alarm clock.

"What are you doing here?" growled the watchdog.

exotic locales. Tock is Juster's cartoonish version of worldly-wise and unflappable "Uncle Jim."

Page 29

18. Illustration

Feiffer's Tock is a walking visual pun: a shaggy dog at large in the pages of a shaggy-dog story. The artist equipped Milo's guardian angel with a good head on his shoulders and an inner clock upon which the child can rely for help. Cloudlike and benevolent-looking, Tock bears a family resemblance to the dogs James Thurber loved to draw.

Commenting to publisher/critic Gary Groth on the period in his career just prior to his breakthrough success, in late 1956, as a cartoonist for the *Village Voice*, Feiffer placed Thurber on the short list of artists he particularly admired—and envied: "I had been turned down over and over again by book publishers. . . .

© Jules Feiffer   © Rosemary A. Thurber

Illustration (right) by James Thurber titled "Dogs on Islands" from *The Dog Department*, © 2001 Rosemary A. Thurber. Drawing originally illustrated the word *canary* for a book on etymology—*In a Word* by Margaret S. Ernst (Knopf, 1939). Reprinted by arrangement with Rosemary A. Thurber and the Barbara Hogenson Agency. All rights reserved.

Drawing (left) by Jules Feiffer for *Feiffer*, December 8, 1960.

I had no name, so who was going to buy this work [a book titled *Munro*] that looked like children's drawings, but was very adult material? Now, if my name were Steig, it would be marketable. If my name were Steinberg, then they could sell it. If my name were Thurber, no problem. So I had to figure out a way of becoming Steig, Steinberg or Thurber in order to get what I wanted into print. I thought of all sorts of things. I could kill somebody, and then get famous that way, and then I could get published. I could commit suicide [but] suicide was not yet established as a form of self-promotion" (from Introduction by Gary Groth, *Explainers*, by Jules Feiffer, p. vii).

Page 30

19. "Just killing time"

The first English-language reference to "killing" time dates from the early eighteenth century, a period characterized by urbanization, unprecedented social mobility, and the spirit of enterprise that culminated in the Industrial Revolution. Sir John Vanbrugh and Colley Cibber write in *The Provok'd Husband, or, a Journey to London* (1728): "What think you, if we three sat soberly to kill an hour an ombre?" For those immersed in the newly fluid, innovation-driven society, it was increasingly important to track the passage of time with precision. Eighteenth-century inventors obliged by devising a succession of ever more accurate pendulum clocks and other timepieces.

20. Illustration

Feiffer's drawing gives new meaning to the term "self-winding watch."

19 "Just killing time," replied Milo apologetically. "You see——"

"KILLING TIME!" roared the dog—so furiously that his alarm went off. "It's bad enough wasting time without killing it." And he shuddered at the thought. "Why are you in the Doldrums anyway—don't you have anywhere to go?"

"I was on my way to Dictionopolis when I got stuck here," explained Milo. "Can you help me?"

"Help you! You must help yourself," the dog replied, carefully winding himself with his left hind leg. "I suppose you know why you got stuck."

20

"I guess I just wasn't thinking," said Milo.   21

"PRECISELY," shouted the dog as his alarm went off   22
again. "Now you know what you must do."

"I'm afraid I don't," admitted Milo, feeling quite stupid.

"Well," continued the watchdog impatiently, "since you got here by not thinking, it seems reasonable to expect that, in order to get out, you must start thinking." And with that he hopped into the car.

"Do you mind if I get in? I love automobile rides."

Milo began to think as hard as he could (which was very difficult, since he wasn't used to it). He thought of birds that swim and fish that fly. He thought of yesterday's lunch and tomorrow's dinner. He thought of words that began with J and numbers that end in 3. And, as he thought, the wheels began to turn.

"We're moving, we're moving," he shouted happily.

"Keep thinking," scolded the watchdog.

The little car started to go faster and faster as Milo's brain whirled with activity, and down the road they went. In a few moments they were out of the Doldrums and back on the main highway. All the colors had returned to their original brightness, and as they raced along the road Milo continued to think of all sorts of things; of the many detours and wrong turns that were so easy to take, of how fine it was to be moving along, and, most of all, of how much could be accomplished with just a little thought. And the dog, his nose in the wind, just sat back, watchfully ticking.

Page 31

21. "I guess I just wasn't thinking," said Milo.

The author recalled: "Not thinking or paying attention was something I was constantly accused of by teachers, parents, etc. Since I daydreamed a lot it was their assumption that I wasn't thinking—not entirely illogical" (N.J. Notes I, p. 13).

22. "PRECISELY," shouted the dog. . . . And with that he hopped into the car.

Maurice Sendak singled out this scene as a favorite: "You know you're in excellent hands when, in the midst of some nutty, didactic dialogue, the author disarms you. . . . It's what Tock, the literal watchdog . . . says next that makes my heart melt, as it did on my very first reading way back when: 'Do you mind if I get in? I love automobile rides.' There is the teeming-brained Norton Juster touching just the right note at just the right moment" ("An Appreciation," by M.S. for the 35th-anniversary U.S. edition, 1996).

3. Welcome to Dictionopolis

"You must excuse my gruff conduct," the watchdog said, after they'd been driving for some time, "but you see it's traditional for watchdogs to be ferocious…"

Milo was so relieved at having escaped the Doldrums that he assured the dog that he bore him no ill will and, in fact, was very grateful for the assistance.

"Splendid," shouted the watchdog. "I'm very pleased—I'm sure we'll be great friends for the rest of the trip. You may call me Tock."

"That is a strange name for a dog who goes ticktick-tickticktick all day," said Milo. "Why didn't they call you——"

"Don't say it," gasped the dog, and Milo could see a tear well up in his eye.

"I didn't mean to hurt your feelings," said Milo, not meaning to hurt his feelings.

"That's all right," said the dog, getting hold of himself.

"It's an old story and a sad one, but I can tell it to you now. [1]

"When my brother was born, the first pup in the family, my parents were overjoyed and immediately named him Tick in expectation of the sound they were sure he'd make. On first winding him, they discovered to their horror that, instead of going tickticktickticktick, he went tocktocktocktocktocktock. They rushed to the Hall of Records to change the name, but too late. It had already been officially inscribed, and nothing could be done. When I arrived, they were determined not to make the same mistake twice and, since it seemed logical that all their children would make the same sound, they named me Tock. Of course, you know the rest—my brother is called Tick because he goes tocktocktocktocktocktocktock and I am called Tock because I go tickticktickticktickticktick and both of us are forever burdened with the wrong names. My parents were so overwrought that they gave up having any more children and devoted their lives to doing good work among the poor and hungry."

"But how did you become a watchdog?" interjected Milo, hoping to change the subject, as Tock was sobbing quite loudly now.

"That," he said, rubbing a paw in his eye, "is also traditional. My family have always been watchdogs—from father to son, almost since time began. [2]

"You see," he continued, beginning to feel better, "once there was no time at all, and people found it very inconvenient. They never knew whether they were eating

---

Page 33

1. "It's an old story"

Juster recalled: "Tock's explanation of his name was my take on the kind of detail parents were always looking for—information that might be true or logical but added very little to your essential understanding even if, at times, it made for a good story" (N.J. Notes I, p. 13).

2. "That," he said, rubbing a paw in his eye, "is also traditional. My family have always been watchdogs"

Tock's explanation of his vocational choice echoes the author's own. Juster followed both his father and his older brother into architecture. By his own account, he never seriously considered any other career.

Page 34

3. his alarm again ringing furiously.

The word *clock* derives from the Celtic *clagan* and *clocca*, both meaning "bell." It shares a common root with the French word for bell, *cloche*.

4. As they drove along, Tock continued to explain the importance of time, quoting the old philosophers and poets

One of Juster's favorite philosophers, George Santayana (1863–1952), wrote: "There is no cure for birth and death save to enjoy the interval" (*Soliloquies in England and Later Soliloquies*, 1922); and, apropos of historical time, the well-known admonition: "Those who cannot remember the past are condemned to repeat it" (*The Life of Reason*, Vol. 1: *Reason in Common Sense*).

Of his own thoughts about time, Juster commented: "Time has always fascinated me. How was it established? How and why was it broken down into seconds, minutes, hours, days, etc.? What would people do without it? How *did* people do without it before there was a way to tabulate it? What would happen if it stopped, or started to run backwards? Can you replay it or go back to it? And then there is the question of perceived time. Why sometimes it passes slowly and other times so quickly. And then there is the wasting of it or the loss of it. I guess all this underpins (and underpinned) much of my daydreaming" (N.J. Notes I, p. 14).

5. Before long they saw in the distance the towers and flags of Dictionopolis

The first of the story's dystopian cities, Dictionopolis is initially mentioned in chapter one (p. 14) as the destination Milo has chosen at random from the map that came with the tollbooth. As a city whose citizens are obsessed with words, and one where even routine communication is regularly hobbled by that very

lunch or dinner, and they were always missing trains. So time was invented to help them keep track of the day and get places when they should. When they began to count all the time that was available, what with 60 seconds in a minute and 60 minutes in an hour and 24 hours in a day and 365 days in a year, it seemed as if there was much more than could ever be used. 'If there's so much of it, it couldn't be very valuable,' was the general opinion, and it soon fell into disrepute. People wasted it and even gave it away. Then we were given the job of seeing that no one wasted time again," he said, sitting up proudly. "It's hard work but a noble calling. For you see"—and now he was standing on the seat, one foot on the windshield, shouting with his arms outstretched— "it is our most valuable possession, more precious than diamonds. It marches on, it and tide wait for no man, and——"

At that point in the speech the car hit a bump in the road and the watchdog collapsed in a heap on the front seat with his alarm again ringing furiously.

"Are you all right?" shouted Milo.

"Umphh," grunted Tock. "Sorry to get carried away, but I think you get the point."

As they drove along, Tock continued to explain the importance of time, quoting the old philosophers and poets and illustrating each point with gestures that brought him perilously close to tumbling headlong from the speeding automobile.

Before long they saw in the distance the towers and flags of Dictionopolis sparkling in the sunshine, and in a

obsession, Dictionopolis calls to mind the Tower of Babel, though in a decidedly slapstick vein. A crossroads where words are bought and sold at fever pitch also suggests 1950s Manhattan, epicenter of the American publishing, advertising, and broadcast media industries.

Page 35

6. Illustration

In his previous work as a comic-strip artist, Feiffer had shown little interest in landscape, architecture, or background details of any description. As the illustrator of a children's book, he felt compelled to modify— somewhat—his stance. Here the bold use of white space renders further elaboration of the setting unnecessary. The blank expanse at the center of the image speaks eloquently of the heightened state of not knowing in which Milo, himself no more than a tiny scribble in the lower left-hand corner, finds himself as he approaches the great walled city.

6

Page 36

7. "A-H-H-H-R-R-E-M-M," roared the gateman

According to Juster: "In my sense of things as a kid there were always gatekeepers and rituals I never understood, but [which] were important and had to be observed" (N.J. Notes I, p. 14).

8. "a happy kingdom, advantageously located"

The gateman speaks in the florid language of travel brochures. The reduction of words to tools for buying and selling, a keynote of Dictionopolis life, is well under way.

9. "WHY NOT?"

Although hardly uttered here in anything like a spirit of true inquiry, the gatekeeper's question is in essence the same one Juster poses to readers at every turn. George Bernard Shaw gave the question its most famous literary formulation in *Back to Methuselah* (1921): "You see things; and you say, 'Why?' But I dream things that never were; and I say, 'Why not?'" (Part I, Act 1).

few moments they reached the great wall and stood at the gateway to the city.

7 "A-H-H-H-R-R-E-M-M," roared the gateman, clearing his throat and snapping smartly to attention. "This is
8 Dictionopolis, a happy kingdom, advantageously located in the Foothills of Confusion and caressed by gentle breezes from the Sea of Knowledge. Today, by royal proclamation, is market day. Have you come to buy or sell?"

"I beg your pardon?" said Milo.

"Buy or sell, buy or sell," repeated the gateman impatiently. "Which is it? You must have come here for some reason."

"Well, I——" Milo began.

"Come now, if you don't have a reason, you must at least have an explanation or certainly an excuse," interrupted the gateman.

Milo shook his head.

"Very serious, very serious," the gateman said, shaking his head also. "You can't get in without a reason." He thought for a moment and then continued. "Wait a minute; maybe I have an old one you can use."

He took a battered suitcase from the gatehouse and began to rummage busily through it, mumbling to himself, "No . . . no . . . no . . . this won't do . . . no . . . h-m-m-m . . . ah, this is fine," he cried triumphantly, holding up a small medallion on a chain. He dusted it off, and engraved on one side were the words
9 "WHY NOT?"

"That's a good reason for almost anything—a bit used

Page 37

10. Illustration

During basic training at Fort Dix, New Jersey, Feiffer stumbled onto a novel way to fight boredom and win immunity from some of the more arduous demands of military routine. Marketing their talents, he and a commercial-artist friend went into business decorating the helmet liners of their superiors with customized lettering and designs. Soon every noncom and officer on base clamored for their services. The high point came during a full-dress military parade in which their "complete works" were put on display for all to see. As Feiffer recalled: "The pageantry of our artwork dominated the field, the single ray of light, pride, and celebration in a dull, forbidding winter sky. For that moment only, it made Harry and me more than two goldbricks from New York trying to con our way out of basic training. It made us proud to be in the United States Army. And why not? We were in command" (*Backing into Forward*, p. 145).

11. Illustration

A drawing by Jules Feiffer for *Munro*, the "picture book for adults" that he created during his time as a private in the U.S. Army.

© Jules Feiffer

12. "WELCOME TO THE WORD MARKET"

As a child, Juster was fascinated by the idea that there existed "an endless number of words . . . that could never all be sampled or learned," and that scattered among them were certain "especially intriguing (or delicious) words that you could learn and foist on your friends and parents." A joke recalled from that time illustrates the latter point: "A child comes home from school and says to his parents, 'I learned a new word at school today. I bet you can't surmise what it is. I'll give you three surmises'" (N.J. Notes I, p. 15).

13. "Greetings!" "Salutations!"

According to Juster, the king's synonymous ministers represent "my bafflement [as a child, at there being so] many ways . . . to say the same thing—my intrigued confusion over the richness and potential mischief embodied in the English language.

"Big words or obscure words were to my naïve intellect a sign of intelligence, worldliness—SMARTS! In my school world it was the girls who knew the words and for that reason seemed smart and intimidating. Luckily, they couldn't play ball" (N.J. Notes I, pp. 15–16).

14. Azaz the Unabridged

The 1864 edition of Webster's dictionary, published by the G. & C. Merriam Company of Springfield, Massachusetts, was the world's first lexicon to be called "Unabridged." By the time of its appearance, the dictionary's original author, Noah Webster, had been dead for twenty-one years, having lived long enough to contribute greatly to the delineation of a distinctively American version of English.

perhaps, but still quite serviceable." And with that he placed it around Milo's neck, pushed back the heavy iron gate, bowed low, and motioned them into the city.

"I wonder what the market will be like," thought Milo as they drove through the gate; but before there was time for an answer they had driven into an immense square crowded with long lines of stalls heaped with merchandise and decorated in gay-colored bunting. Overhead a large banner proclaimed:

12

"WELCOME TO THE WORD MARKET"

And, from across the square, five very tall, thin gentlemen regally dressed in silks and satins, plumed hats, and buckled shoes rushed up to the car, stopped short, mopped five brows, caught five breaths, unrolled five parchments, and began talking in turn.

13 "Greetings!"

"Salutations!"

"Welcome!"

"Good afternoon!"

"Hello!"

Milo nodded his head, and they went on, reading from their scrolls.

14 "By order of Azaz the Unabridged——"

"King of Dictionopolis——"

"Monarch of letters——"

"Emperor of phrases, sentences, and miscellaneous figures of speech——"

"We offer you the hospitality of our kingdom,"

"Country,"

"Nation,"

"State,"

"Commonwealth,"

"Realm,"

"Empire,"

"Palatinate,"

"Principality."

"Do all those words mean the same thing?" gasped Milo.

"Of course."

"Certainly."

"Precisely."

"Exactly."

"Yes," they replied in order.

Page 39

15. Illustration

Feiffer's kick line of high-stepping royal advisers suggests a Busby Berkeley routine as well as the fun-house mirror figures to be found in the Little Nemo strips of Winsor McCay—an early and powerful Feiffer influence. See, especially, the seven-week McCay sequence "Befuddle Hall" (1908), below.

15

Courtesy of John Canemaker

Page 40

16. not understanding why each one said the same thing in a slightly different way

Juster mined the thesaurus for laughs as had few writers before him. *Roget's Thesaurus*, the best-known English-language writers' aid of its kind, dates from 1852 and is the genre's foundational work. The author, Peter Mark Roget, was a British doctor and amateur lexicographer—and by all accounts an obsessive list-maker from childhood. While compilations of words can be traced back to ancient times, Roget was the first to cluster words by concept. *Thesaurus*, the word he chose for his enterprise, is of Greek and Latin origin and means "treasury" or "storehouse." Pre-Roget, the term could be used to refer to the treasure room of a temple, or, metaphorically, to a range of compendious reference works including encyclopedias and dictionaries.

17. "We're not interested in making sense"

Real-world government officials rarely display such candor.

16 "Well, then," said Milo, not understanding why each one said the same thing in a slightly different way, "wouldn't it be simpler to use just one? It would certainly make more sense."

"Nonsense."

"Ridiculous."

"Fantastic."

"Absurd."

"Bosh," they chorused again, and continued.

17 "We're not interested in making sense; it's not our job," scolded the first.

"Besides," explained the second, "one word is as good as another—so why not use them all?"

"Then you don't have to choose which one is right," advised the third.

"Besides," sighed the fourth, "if one is right, then ten are ten times as right."

"Obviously you don't know who we are," sneered the fifth. And they presented themselves one by one as:

"The Duke of Definition."

"The Minister of Meaning."

"The Earl of Essence."

"The Count of Connotation."

"The Undersecretary of Understanding."

Milo acknowledged the introduction and, as Tock growled softly, the minister explained.

"We are the king's advisers, or, in more formal terms, his cabinet."

18

Page 41

18. Illustration

Jules Feiffer had good reason to admire—and draw inspiration from—the acerbic British political caricaturist James Gillray (1756–1815). Like Feiffer, Gillray before him had fearlessly mocked the most powerful figures of his day. In the 1805 caricature "Uncorking Old Sherry," for example, he satirized Prime Minister William Pitt, depicting him as foppish, vain, and unspeakably brutish.

Page 42

19. "I didn't know that words grew on trees"

"Money doesn't grow on trees"—a popular expression during the Great Depression years—morphed, in the Juster household, into an all-purpose riposte to a persistent child's questions about the origins of things: "Where do you *think* [fill in the blank] come from? Do you think they grow on trees?" (N.J. Notes I, p. 17). Here the author turns the brittle straw of parental impatience into nonsense gold.

20. "Our job," said the count, "is to see that all the words sold are proper ones"

The closest real-world equivalent to King Azaz's cabinet is the Académie Française, the French government–sanctioned body of forty "immortals" (writers, scholars, and others) charged with resolving all questions regarding the French language and with updating the official French dictionary. The Academy was established in 1635 by Cardinal Richelieu, and has safeguarded *la belle langue* ever since, except during the tumultuous years of the French Revolution.

"Cabinet," recited the duke: "1. a small private room or closet, case with drawers, etc., for keeping valuables or displaying curiosities; 2. council room for chief ministers of state; 3. a body of official advisers to the chief executive of a nation."

"You see," continued the minister, bowing thankfully to the duke, "Dictionopolis is the place where all the words in the world come from. They're grown right here in our orchards."

"I didn't know that words grew on trees," said Milo timidly.

"Where did you think they grew?" shouted the earl irritably. A small crowd began to gather to see the little boy who didn't know that letters grew on trees.

"I didn't know they grew at all," admitted Milo even more timidly. Several people shook their heads sadly.

"Well, money doesn't grow on trees, does it?" demanded the count.

"I've heard not," said Milo.

"Then something must. Why not words?" exclaimed the undersecretary triumphantly. The crowd cheered his display of logic and continued about its business.

"To continue," continued the minister impatiently. "Once a week by royal proclamation the word market is held here in the great square and people come from everywhere to buy the words they need or trade in the words they haven't used."

"Our job," said the count, "is to see that all the words sold are proper ones, for it wouldn't do to sell someone a word that had no meaning or didn't exist at all. For instance, if you bought a word like *ghlbtsk*, where would you use it?"

"It would be difficult," thought Milo—but there were so many words that were difficult, and he knew hardly any of them.

"But we never choose which ones to use," explained the earl as they walked toward the market stalls, "for as long as they mean what they mean to mean we don't care if they make sense or nonsense." 21

"Innocence or magnificence," added the count.

"Reticence or common sense," said the undersecretary.

"That seems simple enough," said Milo, trying to be polite.

"Easy as falling off a log," cried the earl, falling off a log 22 with a loud thump.

"Must you be so clumsy?" shouted the duke.

"All I said was——" began the earl, rubbing his head.

Page 43

21. "for as long as they mean what they mean to mean we don't care if they make sense or nonsense."

Lewis Carroll's "grin without a cat" is one of many instances in the "Alice" books of the latter possibility. Logicians have devoted much thought to the nature of meaning in language. How, for instance, can certain verbal statements be both true and false, as in:

> The statement in the box is false.

For a discussion of this and other verbal paradoxes, see Robert M. Martin, *There Are Two Errors in the the Title of This Book* (p. 86).

22. Falling off a log

As a kind of warm-up exercise, Juster made list after list of idiomatic expressions that had comic potential if taken literally.

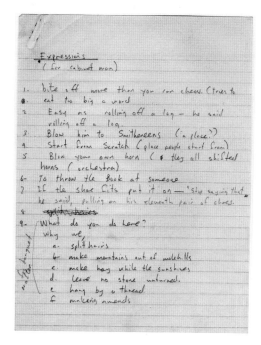

23. "Only when you use a lot to say a little"

A classic variation on this insight is seventeenth-century French philosopher Blaise Pascal's apologetic remark to a correspondent (*Provincial Letters, 1656–57*): "I have made this letter longer than usual because I lack the time to make it short." Tock's observation that words cause confusion "only when you use a lot to say a little" echoes the young Juster's own appraisal of adult conversation (N.J. Notes I, p. 44). Tock's maxim is likewise in absolute accord with one of the "reminders" for writers set down by William Strunk, Jr., and E. B. White in *The Elements of Style*: "Clarity, clarity, clarity. When you become hopelessly mired in a sentence, it is best to start fresh; do not try to fight your way through against the terrible odds of syntax. . . . When you say something, make sure you have said it. The chances of your having said it are only fair" (*Elements*, pp. 65–66).

"We heard you," said the minister angrily, "and you'll have to find an expression that's less dangerous."

The earl dusted himself off as the others snickered audibly.

"You see," cautioned the count, "you must pick your words very carefully and be sure to say just what you intend to say. And now we must leave to make preparations for the Royal Banquet."

"You'll be there, of course," said the minister.

But before Milo had a chance to say anything, they were rushing off across the square as fast as they had come.

"Enjoy yourself in the market," shouted back the undersecretary.

"Market," recited the duke: "an open space or covered building in which——"

And that was the last Milo heard as they disappeared into the crowd.

"I never knew words could be so confusing," Milo said to Tock as he bent down to scratch the dog's ear.

23 "Only when you use a lot to say a little," answered Tock.

Milo thought this was quite the wisest thing he'd heard all day. "Come," he shouted, "let's see the market. It looks very exciting."

1. "Get your fresh-picked ifs, ands, and buts."

Juster observed: "Unknown to me then but not a bad way to think about learning—as a great marketplace, with much hoopla, a lot of huckstering, and aggressive marketing. Colorful, vastly attractive, and mystifying! Intriguing but scary: all you needed was appetite, experience, judgment, and a sense of promise" (N.J. Notes I, p. 18).

4. Confusion in the Market Place

Indeed it was, for as they approached, Milo could see crowds of people pushing and shouting their way among the stalls, buying and selling, trading and bargaining. Huge wooden-wheeled carts streamed into the market square from the orchards, and long caravans bound for the four corners of the kingdom made ready to leave. Sacks and boxes were piled high waiting to be delivered to the ships that sailed the Sea of Knowledge, and off to one side a group of minstrels sang songs to the delight of those either too young or too old to engage in trade. But above all the noise and tumult of the crowd could be heard the merchants' voices loudly advertising their products.

"Get your fresh-picked ifs, ands, and buts."

"Hey-yaa, hey-yaa, hey-yaa, nice ripe wheres and whens."

"Juicy, tempting words for sale."

Page 46

2. Illustration

    Feiffer took particular pride in this drawing because, unlike the cartoon work for which he was known, it had required him to develop an elaborate mise-en-scène.

So many words and so many people! They were from every place imaginable and some places even beyond that, and they were all busy sorting, choosing, and stuffing things into cases. As soon as one was filled, another was begun. There seemed to be no end to the bustle and activity.

Milo and Tock wandered up and down the aisles looking at the wonderful assortment of words for sale. There were short ones and easy ones for everyday use, and long and very important ones for special occasions, and even some marvelously fancy ones packed in individual gift boxes for use in royal decrees and pronouncements.

"Step right up, step right up—fancy, best-quality words right here," announced one man in a booming voice. "Step right up—ah, what can I do for you, little boy? How about a nice bagful of pronouns—or maybe you'd like our special assortment of names?"

Milo had never thought much about words before, but these looked so good that he longed to have some.

"Look, Tock," he cried, "aren't they wonderful?"

"They're fine, if you have something to say," replied Tock in a tired voice, for he was much more interested in finding a bone than in shopping for new words.

"Maybe if I buy some I can learn how to use them," said Milo eagerly as he began to pick through the words in the stall. Finally he chose three which looked particularly good to him—"quagmire," "flabbergast," and "upholstery." He had no idea what they meant, but they looked very grand and elegant.

"How much are these?" he inquired, and when the

3

Page 47

3. Finally he chose three [words] which looked particularly good to him

In his review of *The Phantom Tollbooth* in the *Guardian* (November 16, 1962), English critic Andrew Leslie observed: "Words, indeed, are Mr. Juster's forte: without talking down to anyone, he recaptures that childhood awareness that words like 'quagmire,' 'flabbergast,' 'upholstery'—and let me throw in, if I may, 'linoleum,' 'haphazard,' and 'defenestration'—have a flavour and personality like some people. One can never quite understand them."

Juster's delight in "big" words stands in marked contrast to the insistence of some influential educators of the time that the vocabulary employed in children's books not exceed the young reader's presumed comprehension level. Dr. Seuss's *The Cat in the Hat* is the most famous of the era's children's books to be written from a "controlled vocabulary"—a list of 236 words deemed age-appropriate for newly independent readers.

Study by Jules Feiffer for a merchant of Dictionopolis.

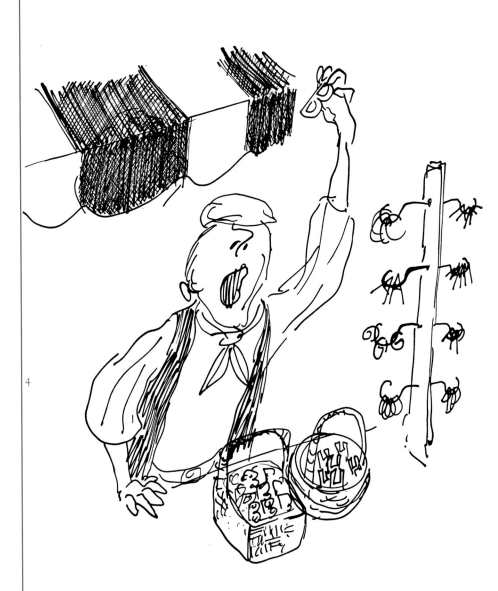

4

man whispered the answer he quickly put them back on the shelf and started to walk on.

"Why not take a few pounds of 'happys'?" advised the salesman. "They're much more practical—and very useful for Happy Birthday, Happy New Year, happy days, and happy-go-lucky."

"I'd like to very much," began Milo, "but——"

"Or perhaps you'd be interested in a package of 'goods'—always handy for good morning, good afternoon, good evening, and good-by," he suggested.

Milo did want to buy something, but the only money he had was the coin he needed to get back through the tollbooth, and Tock, of course, had nothing but the time.

"No, thank you," replied Milo. "We're just looking." And they continued on through the market.

As they turned down the last aisle of stalls, Milo noticed a wagon that seemed different from the rest. On its side was a small neatly lettered sign that said, "DO IT YOURSELF," and inside were twenty-six bins filled with all the letters of the alphabet from A to Z.

"These are for people who like to make their own words," the man in charge informed him. "You can pick any assortment you like or buy a special box complete with all letters, punctuation marks, and a book of instructions. Here, taste an A; they're very good."

Milo nibbled carefully at the letter and discovered that it was quite sweet and delicious—just the way you'd expect an A to taste.

"I knew you'd like it," laughed the letter man, popping two G's and an R into his mouth and letting the juice

Page 49

5. "DO IT YOURSELF"

The term "do it yourself" dates from post–World War II America, when millions of young families, having set up housekeeping in the suburbs, took on home-improvement projects of one kind or another as a form of weekend recreation. Prepackaged kits of tools and materials, complete with instructions, proliferated as the fashion gathered momentum, as did the publication of books and magazines inspired by the craze. Here Juster makes the witty leap to seeing dictionaries as do-it-yourself kits for writers, as in fact they are.

6. "A's are one of our most popular letters."

The *Concise Oxford Dictionary* concurs. Based on a statistical analysis of letter frequency in all main-entry words listed in the *COD*'s 11th edition (2004), the letter *E* ranks first in popularity, occurring 56.88 times more often than the least popular letter, *Q*. The letter *A* places a very respectable second at a multiple of 43.31 times that of poor *Q* (www.askoxford.com/asktheexperts/faq/aboutwords/frequency).

7. "I am the Spelling Bee"

Juster recalled: "Spelling was one of my bugaboos as a kid—a great mystery. The idea of constructing your own words intrigued me. I wish I had done more on creating your own spellings in the book. It would have been fun" (N.J. Notes I, p. 19).

6 drip down his chin. "A's are one of our most popular letters. All of them aren't that good," he confided in a low voice. "Take the Z, for instance—very dry and sawdusty. And the X? Why, it tastes like a trunkful of stale air. That's why people hardly ever use them. But most of the others are quite tasty. Try some more."

He gave Milo an I, which was icy and refreshing, and Tock a crisp, crunchy C.

"Most people are just too lazy to make their own words," he continued, "but it's much more fun."

"Is it difficult? I'm not much good at making words," admitted Milo, spitting the pits from a P.

"Perhaps I can be of some assistance—a-s-s-i-s-t-a-n-c-e," buzzed an unfamiliar voice, and when Milo looked up he saw an enormous bee, at least twice his size, sitting on top of the wagon.

7 "I am the Spelling Bee," announced the Spelling Bee. "Don't be alarmed—a-l-a-r-m-e-d."

Tock ducked under the wagon, and Milo, who was not overly fond of normal-sized bees, began to back away slowly.

"I can spell anything—a-n-y-t-h-i-n-g," he boasted, testing his wings. "Try me, try me!"

"Can you spell 'good-by'?" suggested Milo as he continued to back away.

The bee gently lifted himself into the air and circled lazily over Milo's head.

"Perhaps—p-e-r-h-a-p-s—you are under the misapprehension—m-i-s-a-p-p-r-e-h-e-n-s-i-o-n—that I am dangerous," he said, turning a smart loop to the left.

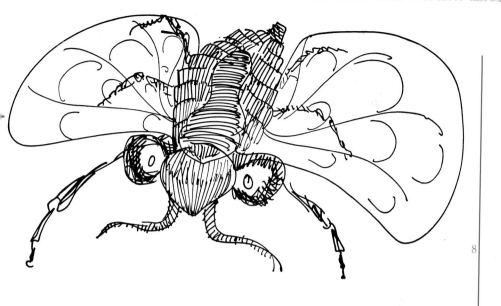

Page 51

8. Illustration

On several occasions, Juster's text compelled Feiffer to depart from his preferred subject matter—people and their endlessly self-revealing poses and expressions—in favor of animal characters.

9. "Let me assure—a-s-s-u-r-e—you that my intentions are peaceful—p-e-a-c-e-f-u-l."

The Spelling Bee's assurances recall those of Klaatu, the humanoid space alien who, in the American sci-fi film classic *The Day the Earth Stood Still* (1951), touches down in Washington, D.C., and, emerging from his flying saucer, declares his goodwill to a deeply wary crowd of onlookers.

Klaatu is immediately fired upon by one of the U.S. military personnel dispatched to the landing site. In this and subsequent scenes, Cold War Americans' pervasive fear of invasion (whether by space aliens or Communists) is explored to chilling effect.

9 "Let me assure—a-s-s-u-r-e—you that my intentions are peaceful—p-e-a-c-e-f-u-l." And with that he settled back on top of the wagon and fanned himself with one wing. "Now," he panted, "think of the most difficult word you can and I'll spell it. Hurry up, hurry up!" And he jumped up and down impatiently.

"He looks friendly enough," thought Milo, not sure just how friendly a friendly bumblebee should be, and tried to think of a very difficult word. "Spell 'vegetable,'" he suggested, for it was one that always troubled him at school.

"That is a difficult one," said the bee, winking at the letter man. "Let me see now…hmmmmmm…" He frowned and wiped his brow and paced slowly back and forth on top of the wagon. "How much time do I have?"

"Just ten seconds," cried Milo excitedly. "Count them off, Tock."

"Oh dear, oh dear, oh dear, oh dear," the bee repeated, continuing to pace nervously. Then, just as the time ran out, he spelled as fast as he could—"v-e-g-e-t-a-b-l-e."

"Correct," shouted the letter man, and everyone cheered.

"Can you spell everything?" asked Milo admiringly.

"Just about," replied the bee with a hint of pride in his voice. "You see, years ago I was just an ordinary bee minding my own business, smelling flowers all day, and occasionally picking up part-time work in people's bonnets. Then one day I realized that I'd never amount to anything without an education and, being naturally adept at spelling, I decided that——"

"BALDERDASH!" shouted a booming voice. And from around the wagon stepped a large beetlelike insect dressed in a lavish coat, striped pants, checked vest, spats, and a derby hat. "Let me repeat—BALDER-DASH!" he shouted again, swinging his cane and clicking his heels in mid-air. "Come now, don't be ill-mannered. Isn't someone going to introduce me to the little boy?" 10

"This," said the bee with complete disdain, "is the Humbug. A very dislikable fellow." 11

Page 53

10. "BALDERDASH!"

Now a synonym for nonsense, this fun word dates back to the late sixteenth century, when it referred to any frothy liquid. Later, Ben Jonson employed it to describe a weird potable concoction such as buttermilk mixed with beer. The drinker of such a brew might well be expected to jumble his words.

11. "This," said the bee with complete disdain, "is the Humbug."

Juster commented: "For the sake of balance I wanted someone who was the reverse [of Tock]—a bad influence. Someone who is a braggart, not very honest, a huckster, not too trustworthy, a self-promoter—in short, someone sure to steer Milo wrong. The kind of person who, if Milo brought him home from school, his mother would say, 'I don't want you playing with him'" (N.J. Notes I, p. 22).

Juster had no further to look for this dubious character's name than the pages of a favorite book from his own childhood, *The Wonderful Wizard of Oz,* in which the author, L. Frank Baum, refers to the fraudulent Wizard as the "great humbug."

The word *humbug* still registered as slang to the educated ear of mid-1700s England, but Charles Dickens did much to mainstream the term through the bitter outbursts of the miserly Ebenezer Scrooge ("Bah, humbug!"), in his immensely popular *A Christmas Carol* (1843). Robert Hendrickson, author of the *QPB Encyclopedia of Word and Phrase Origins,* notes that *bug* derives from *bogey,* or evil spirit. While Juster's Humbug does Milo no harm, his aid and counsel are, at best, of doubtful merit, and it is not far-fetched to regard him warily, as a distant relation of the story's many bona fide demons.

Page 54

12. "NONSENSE! Everyone loves a Humbug"

American literature would seem to bear out this brash claim, with the confidence man ranking high among the major archetypes of American fiction. In a national culture built on reverence for individualism and limitless faith in the potential for self-reinvention, con men have long trolled the darker recesses of the American dream. To trust one's own good judgment is to run the risk of being duped by one's fellows, as Melville demonstrates in *The Confidence Man* (1857) and Mark Twain does in *The Adventures of Huckleberry Finn* (1885).

Showman P. T. Barnum was merely the best-known of nineteenth-century America's real-life hucksters and sleight-of-hand men. By a delicious irony, the maxim most often attributed to Barnum—"There's a sucker born every minute"—is something he never actually said. In the psychologically inflected fiction of post-Victorian "modern" times, argues Gary H. Lindberg in *The Confidence Man in American Literature*, the scam is internalized, as when Fitzgerald's Jay Gatsby fabricates an idealized persona for himself that for a time leaves even him completely fooled.

13. "A slavish concern for the composition of words is the sign of a bankrupt intellect"

The Humbug's remark—one of *The Phantom Tollbooth*'s most quoted lines—echoes Ralph Waldo Emerson's rousing denunciation of soulless pedantry: "A foolish consistency is the hobgoblin of little minds" (from "Self-Reliance").

12 "NONSENSE! Everyone loves a Humbug," shouted the Humbug. "As I was saying to the king just the other day——"

"You've never met the king," accused the bee angrily. Then, turning to Milo, he said, "Don't believe a thing this old fraud says."

"BOSH!" replied the Humbug. "We're an old and noble family, honorable to the core—*Insecticus humbugium*, if I may use the Latin. Why, we fought in the crusades with Richard the Lion Heart, crossed the Atlantic with Columbus, blazed trails with the pioneers, and today many members of the family hold prominent government positions throughout the world. History is full of Humbugs."

"A very pretty speech—s-p-e-e-c-h," sneered the bee. "Now why don't you go away? I was just advising the lad of the importance of proper spelling."

"BAH!" said the bug, putting an arm around Milo. "As soon as you learn to spell one word, they ask you to spell another. You can never catch up—so why bother? Take my advice, my boy, and forget about it. As my great-great-great-grandfather George Washington Humbug used to say——"

"You, sir," shouted the bee very excitedly, "are an impostor—i-m-p-o-s-t-o-r—who can't even spell his own name."

13 "A slavish concern for the composition of words is the sign of a bankrupt intellect," roared the Humbug, waving his cane furiously.

Milo didn't have any idea what this meant, but it

America's first great showman, P. T. Barnum (1810–1891), once said, "Every crowd has a silver lining." Barnum's genius for publicity stunts earned him the title "Prince of Humbugs." At various times during his long and colorful career, he directed a popular New York City museum, co-owned a famous circus, and served as mayor of Bridgeport, Connecticut.

seemed to infuriate the Spelling Bee, who flew down and knocked off the Humbug's hat with his wing.

"Be careful," shouted Milo as the bug swung his cane again, catching the bee on the foot and knocking over the box of W's.

"My foot!" shouted the bee.

"My hat!" shouted the bug—and the fight was on.

The Spelling Bee buzzed dangerously in and out of range of the Humbug's wildly swinging cane as they menaced and threatened each other, and the crowd stepped back out of danger.

"There must be some other way to——" began Milo. And then he yelled, "WATCH OUT," but it was too late.

There was a tremendous crash as the Humbug in his great fury tripped into one of the stalls, knocking it into another, then another, then another, then another, until every stall in the market place had been upset and the words lay scrambled in great confusion all over the square.

The bee, who had tangled himself in some bunting, toppled to the ground, knocking Milo over on top of him, and lay there shouting, "Help! Help! There's a little boy on me." The bug sprawled untidily on a mound of squashed letters and Tock, his alarm ringing persistently, was buried under a pile of words.

---

14. "Help! Help! There's a little boy on me."

Juster recalled: "In summer, the great traumatic experience when I was a kid was having some frightening insect land on you, prepared to inflict great harm." Here the author blithely turns the tables on a situation with which most readers would have similar associations.

1. Short Shrift

In medieval times, *shrift* meant penance imposed by a priest after confession, and *short shrift* referred to the brief time allotted to a condemned man to make penance prior to his execution. Shakespeare appears to have introduced *short shrift* into English literature in *Richard III* ("Make a short Shrift, he longs to see your Head," Act III, Scene 4, line 97). According to the *Oxford English Dictionary*, the expression may not have acquired its more familiar meaning of "less than full consideration" until the late nineteenth century, as, for example, in: "Every argument . . . tells with still greater force against the present measure, and it is to be hoped that the House of Commons will give it short shrift to-night" (*The Times* of London, February 15, 1887).

Juster aptly applies the term to that modern-day arbiter of guilt and innocence, the cop on the beat. The author recalled: "When I was growing up there were two figures of authority . . . to be obeyed without question, to be respected: teachers and police officers" (N.J. Notes I, p. 24).

5. Short Shrift

"Done what you've looked," angrily shouted one of the salesmen. He meant to say "Look what you've done," but the words had gotten so hopelessly mixed up that no one could make any sense at all.

"Do going to we what are!" complained another, as everyone set about straightening things up as well as they could.

For several minutes no one spoke an understandable sentence, which added greatly to the confusion. As soon as possible, however, the stalls were righted and the words swept into one large pile for sorting.

The Spelling Bee, who was quite upset by the whole affair, had flown off in a huff, and just as Milo got to his feet the entire police force of Dictionopolis appeared—loudly blowing his whistle.

"Now we'll get to the bottom of this," he heard some-one say. "Here comes Officer Shrift."

Striding across the square was the shortest policeman Milo had ever seen. He was scarcely two feet tall and almost twice as wide, and he wore a blue uniform with white belt and gloves, a peaked cap, and a very fierce expression. He continued blowing the whistle until his face was beet red, stopping only long enough to shout, "You're guilty, you're guilty," at everyone he passed. "I've never seen anyone so guilty," he said as he reached Milo. Then, turning towards Tock, who was still ringing loudly, he said, "Turn off that dog; it's disrespectful to sound your alarm in the presence of a policeman."

He made a careful note of that in his black book and strode up and down, his hands clasped behind his back, surveying the wreckage in the market place.

"Very pretty, very pretty." He scowled. "Who's respon-sible for all this? Speak up or I'll arrest the lot of you."

There was a long silence. Since hardly anybody had actually seen what had happened, no one spoke.

"You," said the policeman, pointing an accusing finger at the Humbug, who was brushing himself off and straightening his hat, "you look suspicious to me."

The startled Humbug dropped his cane and nervously replied, "Let me assure you, sir, on my honor as a gentle-man, that I was merely an innocent bystander, minding my own business, enjoying the stimulating sights and sounds of the world of commerce, when this young lad——"

2. stopping only long enough to shout, "You're guilty, you're guilty," at everyone he passed.

Officer Shrift prejudges those around him with the imperious caprice and crazed fervor of Lewis Carroll's Queen of Hearts. But for writers and artists of Juster and Feiffer's generation, an abuser of power such as Shrift was not a purely imaginary figure. When Juster wrote this, America had recently withstood the Communist witch hunts of the McCarthy period, as a result of which the reputations and lives of countless citizens were destroyed. Feiffer, recalling his major preoccupations of the mid-1950s for historian Steven Heller, noted: "Essentially, I was affected by what was in those days called one's 'Freudian life,' and our 'Cold War life.' I felt very hemmed in politically by the blacklist, and other repressive aspects of the Eisenhower-McCarthy Cold War years; and I felt hemmed in psychologically by my life, living without women, my continual guilt about everything, and a sustaining anxiety and even rage, now and then, about it all" (interview with Steven Heller, in *The Masters Series: Jules Feiffer* exhibition catalog, School of Visual Arts, 2006).

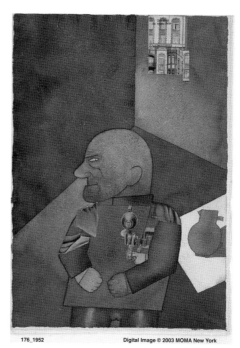

Page 61

3. Illustration

Compare Feiffer's portrait of Officer Shrift with George Grosz's *"The Convict," Monteur John Heartfield After Franz Jung's Attempt to Get Him Up on His Feet* (1920), in the collection of the Museum of Modern Art, New York.

176_1952   Digital Image © 2003 MOMA New York

© Estate of George Grosz/Licensed by VAGA, New York, NY, and the Museum of Modern Art

Born in Berlin in 1893, Grosz made his reputation as a political caricaturist and an acute satirical observer of modern life. He vigorously opposed Nazism and in 1933 immigrated to the United States, where he adopted a less combative stance for his art and, from a perch at New York's Art Students League, became one of his generation's most influential art instructors. Grosz died, an American citizen, in Berlin in 1959. Art historian

Robert Hughes has written of him: "In Grosz's Germany everything and everybody is for sale. All human transactions, except for the class solidarity of the workers, are poisoned. The world is owned by four breeds of pig: the capitalist, the officer, the priest and the hooker, whose other form is the sociable wife. He was one of the hanging judges of art."

Feiffer never met Grosz, but he greatly admired his work as a satirist.

Page 62

4. rapping his gavel three times.

The word *gavel* was in use in Britain as far back as the eighth century, when it referred not to a ceremonial mallet but rather to various forms of payment of rent or tribute. The gavels we associate with courts of law and other formal proceedings are an American invention. As a matter of tradition, the solid ivory gavel employed to maintain order in the United States Senate is shaped like an hourglass and lacks a handle.

5. "That's the shortest sentence I know."

According to Robert Hendrickson, "The longest legitimate sentence in a highly regarded literary work is a 958-word monster in Marcel Proust's *Cities of the Plain*" (*QPB Encyclopedia of Word and Phrase Origins*, p. 647).

"AHA!" interrupted Officer Shrift, making another note in his little book. "Just as I thought: boys are the cause of everything."

"Pardon me," insisted the Humbug, "but I in no way meant to imply that——"

"SILENCE!" thundered the policeman, pulling himself up to full height and glaring menacingly at the terrified bug. "And now," he continued, speaking to Milo, "where were you on the night of July 27?"

"What does that have to do with it?" asked Milo.

"It's my birthday, that's what," said the policeman as he entered "Forgot my birthday" in his little book. "Boys always forget other people's birthdays.

"You have committed the following crimes," he continued: "having a dog with an unauthorized alarm, sowing confusion, upsetting the applecart, wreaking havoc, and mincing words."

"Now see here," growled Tock angrily.

"And illegal barking," he added, frowning at the watchdog. "It's against the law to bark without using the barking meter. Are you ready to be sentenced?"

"Only a judge can sentence you," said Milo, who remembered reading that in one of his schoolbooks.

"Good point," replied the policeman, taking off his cap and putting on a long black robe. "I am also the judge. Now would you like a long or a short sentence?"

"A short one, if you please," said Milo.

4 "Good," said the judge, rapping his gavel three times. "I always have trouble remembering the long ones. How 5 about 'I am'? That's the shortest sentence I know."

Everyone agreed that it was a very fair sentence, and the judge continued: "There will also be a small additional penalty of six million years in prison. Case closed," he pronounced, rapping his gavel again. "Come with me. I'll take you to the dungeon."

"Only a jailer can put you in prison," offered Milo, quoting the same book.

"Good point," said the judge, removing his robe and taking out a large bunch of keys. "I am also the jailer." And with that he led them away.

"Keep your chin up," shouted the Humbug. "Maybe they'll take a million years off for good behavior."

The heavy prison door swung back slowly and Milo and Tock followed Officer Shrift down a long dark corridor lit by only an occasional flickering candle.

"Watch the steps," advised the policeman as they started down a steep circular staircase.

The air was dank and musty—like the smell of wet blankets—and the massive stone walls were slimy to the touch. Down and down they went until they arrived at another door even heavier and stronger-looking than the first. A cobweb brushed across Milo's face and he shuddered.

"You'll find it quite pleasant here," chuckled the policeman as he slid the bolt back and pushed the door open with a screech and a squeak. "Not much company, but ⁶ you can always chat with the witch."

"The witch?" trembled Milo.

"Yes, she's been here for a long time," he said, starting along another corridor.

6. "but you can always chat with the witch."

To the young Juster, witches were real. He believed that a witch of the more familiar, sinister variety inhabited his toy chest and came out to "wreak havoc" after the humans went to sleep. When his mother angered him sufficiently and it seemed time to haul out the big guns, he called her a witch, the worst accusation in his arsenal (N.J. Notes I, pp. 25–26).

Page 64

7. Illustration

Feiffer associated the shadow-drenched architecture and noir-ish atmospherics of this accomplished illustration with Will Eisner's drawings for *The Spirit*. Eisner's modern-day crime-fighting saga debuted on June 2, 1940, and ran for twelve years as the eight-page main feature of a nationally syndicated sixteen-page Sunday comics supplement that at its peak reached an audience of five million readers. As Feiffer, a die-hard comics fan, recalled: "*The Spirit* was unlike anything I or anyone else had ever seen before" (*Backing into Forward*, p. 45). The hard-boiled hero of the strip always donned a mask before venturing forth from his subterranean headquarters under a tombstone to stop evildoers in their tracks. In all other respects, Denny Colt (aka the Spirit) paid scant attention to his appearance and was something of a slouch—a recognizable type to anyone who, like both Eisner and Feiffer, had come of age on the mean streets of the working-class Bronx. As Feiffer observed: "[Eisner's] art crawled with Depression-era urban imagery, his drawing dark and clotted and often ungainly. Grotesque and bulky figures fighting it out in heavyweight balletic violence, the action lifelike, despite its distortions" (*Backing into Forward*, p. 48).

At sixteen and a half and having just been rejected by the two art schools to which he had applied, Feiffer screwed up his courage, and, without an appointment, knocked on Eisner's studio door and talked his way into an apprenticeship. The experience proved to be transformative, especially after Eisner, who had bluntly told the teen aspirant at their first meeting that his sample drawings "stank," discovered Feiffer's writing talent. Eisner eventually entrusted Feiffer with the writing of entire *Spirit* story sequences and, in lieu of a raise, gave him a page in the Sunday supplement on which to launch a strip of his own, called *Clifford*.

7

In a few more minutes they had gone through three other doors, across a narrow footbridge, down two more corridors and another stairway, and stood finally in front of a small cell door.

"This is it," said the policeman. "All the comforts of home."

The door opened and then shut and Milo and Tock found themselves in a high vaulted cell with two tiny windows halfway up on the wall.

"See you in six million years," said Officer Shrift, and the sound of his footsteps grew fainter and fainter until it wasn't heard at all.

"It looks serious, doesn't it, Tock?" said Milo very sadly.

"It certainly does," the dog replied, sniffing around to see what their new quarters were like.

"I don't know what we're going to do for all that time; we don't even have a checker set or a box of crayons."

"Don't worry," growled Tock, raising one paw assuringly, "something will turn up. Here, wind me, will you please? I'm beginning to run down."

"You know something, Tock?" he said as he wound up the dog. "You can get in a lot of trouble mixing up words or just not knowing how to spell them. If we ever get out of here, I'm going to make sure to learn all about them."

"A very commendable ambition, young man," said a small voice from across the cell.

Milo looked up, very surprised, and noticed for the

8. for he knew how much witches hate loud noises.

The author invented this attribute of witches for purposes of the story's plot. It has no basis in supernatural lore.

THE PHANTOM TOLLBOOTH

first time, in the half-light of the room, a pleasant-looking old lady quietly knitting and rocking.

"Hello," he said.

"How do you do?" she replied.

"You'd better be very careful," Milo advised. "I understand there's a witch somewhere in here."

"I am she," the old lady answered casually, and pulled her shawl a little closer around her shoulders.

Milo jumped back in fright and quickly grabbed Tock to make sure that his alarm didn't go off—for he knew how much witches hate loud noises.

"Don't be frightened," she laughed. "I'm not a witch— I'm a Which." 9

"Oh," said Milo, because he couldn't think of anything else to say.

"I'm Faintly Macabre, the not-so-wicked Which," she continued, "and I'm certainly not going to harm you." 10

"What's a Which?" asked Milo, releasing Tock and stepping a little closer.

"Well," said the old lady, just as a rat scurried across her foot, "I am the king's great-aunt. For years and years I was in charge of choosing which words were to be used for all occasions, which ones to say and which ones not to say, which ones to write and which ones not to write. As you can well imagine, with all the thousands to choose from, it was a most important and responsible job. I was given the title of 'Official Which,' which made me very proud and happy.

"At first I did my best to make sure that only the most proper and fitting words were used. Everything was said clearly and simply and no words were wasted. I had signs posted all over the palace and market place which said:

Brevity Is the Soul of Wit. 11

"But power corrupts, and soon I grew miserly and chose fewer and fewer words, trying to keep as many as possible for myself. I had new signs posted which said: 12

Page 67

9. "Don't be frightened," she laughed.

Juster's Which is a benevolent figure in the tradition of L. Frank Baum's Good Witch of the North. When Dorothy first meets her, the young Kansan naïvely restates the common wisdom on the subject to her face, "I thought all witches were wicked"—only to be assured, "Oh, no, that is a great mistake." Baum; his wife, Maud; and Maud's mother, Matilda Joslyn Gage, were all outspoken feminists. The latter, a colleague of Susan B. Anthony's, put forward the idea that women condemned as witches in the past might in fact have been proto-feminists—women too strong for their own good by the standards of the times in which they lived ("The Man Who Made Oz," by Meghan O'Rourke, *Slate,* posted September 21, 2009; for more detail, see *The Annotated Wizard of Oz,* edited by Michael Patrick Hearn. New York: W. W. Norton, 2000).

10. "I'm Faintly Macabre"

Macabre went into general use during the late nineteenth century as an English-language descriptive meaning "ghastly" or "gruesome." Prior to that, the word was known only from the phrase "danse macabre," associated with a fourteenth-century medieval morality play and used to describe the universal struggle between Death and his doomed victims.

Hans Holbein the Younger illustrated the allegorical theme in a series of engravings created in 1538. Scholars have traced back the word *macabre* as used in this context to "Maccabee," the patronymic of the Jewish warrior brothers whose triumph over Hellenization is chronicled in 2 Maccabees, and is today remembered during the Jewish Hanukkah celebration.

11. Brevity Is the Soul of Wit.

Here Faintly Macabre claims authorship of one of William Shakespeare's most famous aphorisms, a line spoken by Polonius in *Hamlet* (Act 2, Scene 2, line 90).

12. "But power corrupts"

Faintly Macabre here alludes to the famous remark of Lord Acton, the nineteenth-century British historian who, in an 1887 letter to Bishop Mandell Creighton, wrote: "Power tends to corrupt, and absolute power corrupts absolutely. Great men are almost always bad men."

Page 68

13. An Ill-chosen Word Is the Fool's Messenger.

A Juster original. The author recalled: "I wanted four sayings to indicate her [Faintly Macabre's] growing obsession with economic word use. I searched everywhere and could only find three that seemed suitable [and so] I felt obliged to coin one of my own that should seem somewhat venerable and old-fashioned like the others" (N.J. Notes I, p. 26).

14. Speak Fitly or Be Silent Wisely.

A proverb attributed by some scholars to the British metaphysical poet George Herbert.

15. Silence Is Golden.

A proverb sometimes said to be of American origin. But in *Sartor Resartus* (1833–34), the British historian and essayist Thomas Carlyle writes: "As the Swiss inscription says: *Sprechen ist silbern, Schweigen ist gold*—Speech is silvern, Silence is golden"; or, as I might rather express it, speech is of time, silence is of eternity" (book 3, chapter 3).

*An Ill-chosen Word
Is the Fool's Messenger.* [13]

"Soon sales began to fall off in the market. The people were afraid to buy as many words as before, and hard times came to the kingdom. But still I grew more and more miserly. Soon there were so few words chosen that hardly anything could be said, and even casual conversation became difficult. Again I had new signs posted, which said:

Speak Fitly or Be Silent Wisely. [14]

"And finally I had even these replaced by ones which read simply:

Silence Is Golden. [15]

"All talk stopped. No words were sold, the market place closed down, and the people grew poor and disconsolate. When the king saw what had happened, he became furious and had me cast into this dungeon where you see me now, an older and wiser woman.

"That was all many years ago," she continued; "but they never appointed a new Which, and that explains why today people use as many words as they can and think themselves very wise for doing so. For always remember that while it is wrong to use too few, it is often far worse to use too many."

When she had finished, she sighed deeply, patted Milo gently on the shoulder, and began knitting once again.

"And have you been down here ever since then?" asked Milo sympathetically.

"Yes," she said sadly. "Most people have forgotten me entirely, or remember me wrongly as a witch, not a Which. But it matters not, it matters not," she went on unhappily, "for they are equally frightened of both."

"I don't think you're frightening," said Milo, and Tock wagged his tail in agreement.

16. Rhyme and Reason

The well-known idiom that Juster here transforms into the names of two missing persons of note has its origin in a poem by Edmund Spenser, "Lines on his promised pension," as follows: "I was promised on a time / To have reason for my rhyme; / From that time unto this season, / I received nor rhyme nor reason" (see *Bartlett's*). It was Shakespeare, however, who not long afterward popularized the phrase, first in *A Comedy of Errors*, when Dromio of Syracuse remarks: "Was there ever any man thus beaten out of season, / When in the why and the wherefore is neither rhyme nor reason?" (Act 2, Scene 2, lines 47–48); and again in *As You Like It*:

> ROSALIND: But are you so much in love as your rhymes speak?
> ORLANDO: Neither rhyme nor reason can express how much (Act 3, Scene 2, lines 359–60).

"I thank you very much," said Faintly Macabre. "You may call me Aunt Faintly. Here, have a punctuation mark." And she held out a box of sugar-coated question marks, periods, commas, and exclamation points. "That's all I get to eat now."

"Well, when I get out of here, I'm going to help you," Milo declared forcefully.

"That's very nice of you," she replied; "but the only thing that can help me is the return of Rhyme and Reason."

"The return of what?" asked Milo.

16 "Rhyme and Reason," she repeated; "but that's another long story, and you may not want to hear it."

"We would like to very much," barked Tock.

"We really would," agreed Milo, and as the Which rocked slowly back and forth she told them this story.

6. Faintly Macabre's Story

"Once upon a time, this land was a barren and frightening wilderness whose high rocky mountains sheltered the evil winds and whose barren valleys offered hospitality to no man. Few things grew, and those that did were bent and twisted and their fruit was as bitter as wormwood. What wasn't waste was desert, and what wasn't desert was rock, and the demons of darkness made their home in the hills. Evil creatures roamed at will through the countryside and down to the sea. It was known as the land of Null.

"Then one day a small ship appeared on the Sea of Knowledge. It carried a young prince seeking the future. In the name of goodness and truth he laid claim to all the country and set out to explore his new domain. The demons, monsters, and giants were furious at his presumption and banded together to drive him out. The earth shook with their battle, and when they had fin-

1

2

3

4

5

1. Faintly Macabre's Story

Juster recalled: "[In] the manuscript I submitted to Jason Epstein . . . I had not reached Faintly Macabre's Story—or had any idea where my 'episodes' were headed. Milo, I realized, was venturing into a land of much erudition but everything seemed to be askew and didn't often make sense. The banishment of Rhyme and Reason and their ultimate rescue and return gave the story a real framework and purpose" (N.J. Notes I, p. 28).

2. "and their fruit was as bitter as wormwood."

The Book of Proverbs, chapter 5, warns: "For the lips of a strange woman drop as a honeycomb, and her mouth is smoother than oil: But her end is bitter as wormwood, sharp as a two-edged sword" (3 and 4).

3. "and the demons of darkness made their home in the hills."

"The demon," write Carol K. Mack and Dinah Mack in *A Field Guide to Demons, Fairies, Fallen Angels, and Other Subversive Spirits*, "is universally regarded as an incorporeal spirit who can actualize in many ways, yet is usually depicted as a grotesque hybrid: part Homo sapiens, part wild beast, it always walks upright. It has other recognizably human features, but often quite unnatural or uncommon ones, such as way too many fingers or none at all, no bones, no skin, or perhaps several heads. There is something about its mouth and teeth that is always alarming" (New York: Arcade, 1998, p. xxi).

4. "the land of Null"

Null is the German for "zero" or "none," and is derived from the Latin *nullus*.

5. "It carried a young prince"

Juster observed: "You will notice that the prince is a typical imperialist who 'in the name of goodness and

ished, all that remained to the prince was a small piece of land at the edge of the sea.

"'I'll build my city here,' he declared, and that is what he did.

"Before long, more ships came bearing settlers for the new land and the city grew and pushed its boundaries farther and farther out. Each day it was attacked anew, but nothing could destroy the prince's new city. And

grow it did. Soon it was no longer just a city; it was a kingdom, and it was called the kingdom of Wisdom.

"But, outside the walls, all was not safe, and the new king vowed to conquer the land that was rightfully his. So each spring he set forth with his army and each autumn he returned, and year by year the kingdom grew larger and more prosperous. He took to himself a wife

Pages 73–74

6. [The king] took to himself a wife and before long had two fine young sons to whom he taught everything he knew

"Every family," writes Lionel Trilling, "constructs a mythology of its talents and qualities" (*The Portable Matthew Arnold*, edited by Lionel Trilling. New York: Viking, 1949). In laying claim respectively to the superiority of the realms of language and mathematics, the king's two sons embody a centuries-old philosophical debate that assumed renewed urgency in the post–World War II nuclear age. The incredible carnage unleashed during World War I, much of it the by-product of the industrial nations' ever-increasing technological prowess, had already prompted many to question, and some to doubt, the modern West's deep-seated faith in science and the inevitability of industry-driven progress. During the mid-1930s, a small group of British writers and scholars led by C. S. Lewis and his friend J. R. R. Tolkien formed a literary discussion club, called the Inklings, whose members embraced fantasy literature as, in part, a much-needed antidote to their contemporaries' blind worship of scientific reason. A related concern, the fear that a narrowing of human thought might result from the modern tendency toward specialization in all areas of study and research, became a major theme in the writings of Cambridge physicist and novelist C. P. Snow, who, in an influential lecture of 1959 titled "The Two Cultures," lamented the reluctance of modern scientists and humanists to learn from each other. Snow, unlike the earlier writers, had a more affirmative view of science, seeing in its thoughtful application the potential for alleviating world poverty and hunger. While he regretted the lack of interest on the part of scientists in the realms of literature and art, he reserved his strongest criticism for humanists who showed no curiosity for science's potent, and potentially life-enhancing, breakthroughs. Juster, as a young architect with literary aspirations, had read "The Two Cultures" and was still turning it over in his mind as he imagined a world in which word people and number people kept resolutely to themselves in rival cities, thereby dooming themselves to absurdly distorted lives.

Page 74

7. "Each one tried to outdo the other"

Sibling rivalry would seem to be nearly as old as Adam, as witnessed in the story of Cain's slaying of his brother, Abel, in Genesis. Freud understood the phenomenon as an aspect of the Oedipal struggle, waged by each child within his family for the love of the parent of the opposite sex.

8. "'Numbers are more important than wisdom'"

Digitopolis recalls another fantastic realm where an ill-conceived faith in the power of mathematics leads to absurd distortions in the conduct of daily life. Of Laputa, the kingdom visited by Lemuel Gulliver on the third voyage chronicled in *Gulliver's Travels*, Gulliver reports:

"The knowledge I had in mathematics gave me great assistance in acquiring their phraseology, which depended much upon that of science and music. . . . Their ideas are perpetually conversant in lines and figures. [Yet] their houses are very ill built, the walls bevil, without one right angle in any apartment; and this defect ariseth from the contempt they bear to practical geometry, which they despise as vulgar and mechanic" (p. 153).

and before long had two fine young sons to whom he taught everything he knew so that one day they might rule wisely.

"When the boys grew to young-manhood, the king called them to him and said: 'I am becoming an old man and can no longer go forth to battle. You must take my place and found new cities in the wilderness, for the kingdom of Wisdom must grow.'

"And so they did. One went south to the Foothills of Confusion and built Dictionopolis, the city of words; and one went north to the Mountains of Ignorance and built Digitopolis, the city of numbers. Both cities flourished mightily and the demons were driven back still further. Soon other cities and towns were founded in the new lands, and at last only the farthest reaches of the wilderness remained to these terrible creatures—and there they waited, ready to strike down all who ventured near or relaxed their guard.

"The two brothers were glad, however, to go their separate ways, for they were by nature very suspicious and jealous. Each one tried to outdo the other, and they worked so hard and diligently at it that before long their cities rivaled even Wisdom in size and grandeur.

"'Words are more important than wisdom,' said one privately.

"'Numbers are more important than wisdom,' thought the other to himself.

"And they grew to dislike each other more and more.

"The old king, however, who knew nothing of his sons' animosity, was very happy in the twilight of his reign and spent his days quietly walking and contemplating in the royal gardens. His only regret was that he'd never had a daughter, for he loved little girls as much as he loved little boys. One day as he was strolling peacefully about the grounds, he discovered two tiny babies that had been abandoned in a basket under the grape arbor. They were beautiful golden-haired girls.

"The king was overjoyed. 'They have been sent to crown my old age,' he cried, and called the queen, his ministers, the palace staff, and, indeed, the entire population to see them.

"'We'll call this one Rhyme and this one Reason,' he said, and so they became the Princess of Sweet Rhyme and the Princess of Pure Reason and were brought up in the palace.

"When the old king finally died, the kingdom was divided between his two sons, with the provision that they would be equally responsible for the welfare of the young princesses. One son went south and became Azaz the Unabridged, king of Dictionopolis, and the other went north and became the Mathemagician, ruler of Digitopolis; and, true to their words, they both provided well for the little girls, who continued to live in Wisdom.

"Everyone loved the princesses because of their great beauty, their gentle ways, and their ability to settle all controversies fairly and reasonably. People with problems or grievances or arguments came from all over the land to seek advice, and even the two brothers, who by this time were fighting continuously, often called upon

9. "It was said by everyone that 'Rhyme and Reason answer all problems.'"

Here we have Western Enlightenment philosophy in a nutshell, the belief that the orderly, persistent application of reason and scientific thought inevitably leads to greater knowledge and understanding and to the improved well-being of all mankind.

9 them to help decide matters of state. It was said by everyone that 'Rhyme and Reason answer all problems.'

"As the years passed, the two brothers grew farther and farther apart and their separate kingdoms became richer and grander. Their disputes, however, became more and more difficult to reconcile. But always, with patience and love, the princesses set things right.

"Then one day they had the most terrible quarrel of all. King Azaz insisted that words were far more significant than numbers and hence his kingdom was truly the greater, and the Mathemagician claimed that numbers were much more important than words and hence

76

his kingdom was supreme. They discussed and debated and raved and ranted until they were on the verge of blows, when it was decided to submit the question to arbitration by the princesses.

"After days of careful consideration, in which all the evidence was weighed and all the witnesses heard, they made their decision:

"'Words and numbers are of equal value, for, in the cloak of knowledge, one is warp and the other woof. It is no more important to count the sands than it is to name the stars. Therefore, let both kingdoms live in peace.'

"Everyone was pleased with the verdict. Everyone, that is, but the brothers, who were beside themselves with anger.

"'What good are these girls if they cannot settle an argument in someone's favor?' they growled, since both were more interested in their own advantage than in the truth. 'We'll banish them from the kingdom forever.' 10

"And so they were taken from the palace and sent far 11 away to the Castle in the Air, and they have not been seen since. That is why today, in all this land, there is neither Rhyme nor Reason."

"And what happened to the two rulers?" asked Milo.

"Banishing the two princesses was the last thing they ever agreed upon, and they soon fell to warring with each other. Despite this, their own kingdoms have continued to prosper, but the old city of Wisdom has fallen into great disrepair, and there is no one to set things right. So, you see, until the princesses return, I shall have to stay here."

10. "'We'll banish them from the kingdom forever.'"

Juster observed of this passage: "The banishing of Rhyme and Reason . . . renders all learning and knowledge nonsense. The king's ministers—who say the same thing in different ways and who don't care about making sense as long as they can express endless variations on the same thought or word—are prime examples of what happens without Rhyme or Reason" (N.J. Notes I, p. 30).

11. "sent far away to the Castle in the Air"

The expression "castle in the air," conjuring up images of a person's wildest dreams (or ultimate dream house), had currency for centuries before Jonathan Swift vividly described such a place in the surrealistic "Voyage to Laputa" section of *Gulliver's Travels*. "The reader," Lemuel Gulliver records in his journal, "can hardly conceive my astonishment, to behold an island in the air, inhabited by men, who were able (as it should seem) to raise, or sink, or put it into a progressive motion, as they pleased. . . . They conducted me up the stairs, to the top of the island, and from thence to the royal palace . . . and proceeded into the chamber of presence, where I saw the King" (pp. 147, 149).

Gulliver's amazement proves to be short-lived as the troubled nature of life on the island soon reveals itself to him. For Swift, the point was that castles in the air were foolish delusions. But decades later, Scottish lawyer and literary man James Boswell reconsidered the theme with notable sympathy in "Castles in the Air: From Poetical Amusements at a Villa Near Bath," a poem first published in 1781 in the *Scots* magazine (volume 43):

> They who content on earth to stay,
> To earth their views confine;
> With rapture, Miller, will survey
> This paradise of thine!

I, too, my willing voice would raise,
And equal rapture show;
But that the scenes which others praise,
For me are much *too low*.
I grant the hills are crown'd with trees,
I grant the fields are fair;
But, after all, one nothing sees
But what is *really there*.

True taste ideal prospects feigns,
Whilst on poetic wings,
'Bove earth, and all that earth contains,
Unbounded fancy springs.
To dwell on earth, gross element,
Let grov'lling spirits bear;
But I, on nobler plans intent,
Build Castles in the Air.

No less a dreamer than Boswell, Henry David Thoreau declared: "If you build your castles in the air, your work need not be lost. There is where they should be. Now put foundations under them." But Edward Bulwer-Lytton—the English politician and writer who coined the expressions "the pursuit of the almighty dollar" and "The pen is mightier than the sword"—noted less euphorically that while castles in the air are cheap to build, they "cost a vast deal to keep up."

Page 78

12. Milo pressed the button and a door swung open
The first-century AD Greek mathematician Heron of Alexandria conceived plans for the first known automatic door as well as for the first coin-operated vending machine (for the purchase of holy water!), and the first steam engine. Heron is thought to have built prototypes of a number of his inventions, but his speculations seem not to have had a major impact on actual construction practices in his day.

"Maybe we can rescue them," said Milo as he saw how sad the Which looked.

"Ah, that would be difficult," she replied. "The Castle in the Air is far from here, and the one stairway which leads to it is guarded by fierce and black-hearted demons."

Tock growled ominously, for he hated even the thought of demons.

"I'm afraid there's not much a little boy and a dog can do," she said, "but never you mind; it's not so bad. I've grown quite used to it here. But you must be going or else you'll waste the whole day."

"Oh, we're here for six million years," sighed Milo, "and I don't see any way to escape."

"Nonsense," scolded the Which, "you mustn't take Officer Shrift so seriously. He loves to put people in prison, but he doesn't care about keeping them there. Now just press that button in the wall and be on your way."

Milo pressed the button and a door swung open, letting in a shaft of brilliant sunshine.

"Good-by; come again!" shouted the Which as they stepped outside and the door slammed shut.

Milo and Tock stood blinking in the bright light and, as their eyes became accustomed to it, the first things they saw were the king's advisers again rushing toward them.

"Ah, there you are."

"Where have you been?"

"We've been looking all over for you."

78

"The royal banquet is about to begin."

"Come with us."

They seemed very agitated and out of breath as Milo walked along with them.

"But what about my car?" he asked.

"Don't need it," replied the duke.

"No use for it," said the minister.

"Superfluous," advised the count.

"Unnecessary," stated the earl.

"Uncalled for," cried the undersecretary. "We'll take our vehicle."

"Conveyance."

"Rig."

"Charabanc." 13

"Chariot."

"Buggy."

"Coach."

"Brougham." 14

"Shandrydan," they repeated quickly in order, and 15 pointed to a small wooden wagon.

"Oh dear, all those words again," thought Milo as he climbed into the wagon with Tock and the cabinet members. "How are you going to make it move? It doesn't have a——"

"Be very quiet," advised the duke, "for it goes without 16 saying."

And, sure enough, as soon as they were all quite still, it began to move quickly through the streets, and in a very short time they arrived at the royal palace.

Page 79

13. "Charabanc."

An excursion vehicle, the English name for which derives from that for the early-nineteenth-century French *char-á-banc*, or carriage with benches. Popular in early-twentieth-century Britain, a charabanc might either be horse-drawn or motorized.

14. "Brougham."

A four-wheeled one-horse carriage. Pronounced "broom" or "brohm," it was named for Henry Peter Brougham, a titled Scottish Whig politician and jurist who took an interest in educational reform as well as in carriage design. The first brougham was built in 1838. It sat two and was considered quite fashionable. During the late nineteenth century, older broughams that had seen better days were often granted a second life as Victorian hackney cabs, the forerunners of today's London taxis.

15. "Shandrydan."

From the early nineteenth century, a teasing pejorative for any dilapidated, old-fashioned vehicle— the equivalent of the modern-day "junker" or "wreck."

16. "for it goes without saying."

Here the author makes a place for his favorite childhood pun (N.J. Notes I, p. 79).

1. it looked exactly like an enormous book

The author here describes an example of "programmatic" or "mimetic" architecture: a building designed to resemble another kind of object, most commonly for novelty's sake. The oldest known such structure is affectionately called Lucy the Elephant. Located in Margate, New Jersey, it comprises a six-story, pachyderm-shaped building and was constructed in 1881 to serve as a real estate office and roadside promotional extravaganza. It succeeded brilliantly on both counts and has since been entered in the register of National Historic Landmarks. Other more recent notable examples include the Teapot Water Tower (1902) of Lindstrom, Minnesota; the Big Duck (1931) of Flanders, New York, originally built as a poultry farmer's retail outlet; and the Wigwam Motel (1950) of Holbrook, Arizona. Architectural "follies," as such structures are sometimes also called, came to be regarded by some as eyesores but found an ally in architect Robert Venturi and his colleagues Denise Scott Brown and Steven Izenour, who, in their monograph *Learning from Las Vegas: The Forgotten Symbolism of Architectural Form*, made a case for the cultural value of such popular exercises in architectural showmanship and free expression. Mimetic architecture has not been limited entirely to the novelty realm, however. Perhaps the most famous example from the domain of monumental public construction is that of the French National Library, which in 1995 left the center of Paris for a somewhat more remote location in the city's eastern quadrant. Much like those of the palace in Dictionopolis, each of the library's four glass-clad towers, which face each other at the corners of a sunken garden, is designed to suggest an open book standing on its side. Bookshelves were arrayed along corridors just inside the glass walls with the idea that an onlooker would be able to take in the scope and majesty of French print culture in a single glance. Strangely, it

7. The Royal Banquet

"Right this way."

"Follow us."

"Come along."

"Step lively."

"Here we go," they shouted, hopping from the wagon and bounding up the broad marble stairway. Milo and Tock followed close behind. It was a strange-looking palace, and if he didn't know better Milo would have said that it looked exactly like an enormous book, standing on end, with its front door in the lower part of the binding just where they usually place the publisher's name.

Once inside, they hurried down a long hallway, which glittered with crystal chandeliers and echoed with their footsteps. The walls and ceiling were covered with mirrors, whose reflections danced dizzily along with them, and the footmen bowed coldly.

"We must be terribly late," gasped the earl nervously as they reached the tall doors of the banquet hall.

It was a vast room, full of people loudly talking and arguing. The long table was carefully set with gold plates and linen napkins. An attendant stood behind each chair, and at the center, raised slightly above the others, was a throne covered in crimson cloth. Directly behind, on the wall, was the royal coat of arms, flanked by the flags of Dictionopolis.

Milo noticed many of the people he had seen in the market place. The letter man was busy explaining to an interested group the history of the W, and off in a corner

was only as construction neared completion that someone realized that sustained exposure to sunlight would cause irreparable harm to the books, and so an elaborate shutter system was commissioned, at great expense, to solve the problem.

Page 81

2. the history of the W

The *W* was among the last letters to be added to the Latin alphabet (*J* was last), having entered the ranks of the ABCs during the Middle Ages in order to accommodate Germanic-language sounds foreign to Latin. The *W* is an example of a ligature, a new letterform created by combining two preexisting ones, in this case (its English-language name notwithstanding) a pair of Vs. It has been called unreliable, in part for so often standing silent, as in "yellow" and "wriggle," and for having an overlong name (it is the only Latin letterform with a name of more than one syllable) that offers no hint of the sound it represents.

Page 82

3. **"My, how time flies."**

The gist of this familiar expression goes back to the Latin poet Virgil's *Georgics* I, line 284: "Time is flying, never to return."

4. **He was the largest man Milo had ever seen**

Juster recalled: "The castle was my take on all the castles I'd come across in my reading—impossibly large and ornate, and I made the king as all kings should be—ample and full of himself" (N.J. Notes I, p. 32).

5. **and a robe with the letters of the alphabet beautifully embroidered all over it.**

Note that Feiffer chose to ignore this stage direction in creating his illustration on the opposite page.

the Humbug and the Spelling Bee were arguing fiercely about nothing at all. Officer Shrift wandered through the crowd, suspiciously muttering, "Guilty, guilty, they're all guilty," and, on noticing Milo, brightened visibly and commented in passing, "Is it six million years already? My, how time flies."

Everyone seemed quite grumpy about having to wait for lunch, and they were all relieved to see the tardy guests arrive.

"Certainly glad you finally made it, old man," said the Humbug, cordially pumping Milo's hand. "As guest of honor you must choose the menu of course."

"Oh, my," he thought, not knowing what to say.

"Be quick about it," suggested the Spelling Bee. "I'm famished—f-a-m-i-s-h-e-d."

As Milo tried to think, there was an ear-shattering blast of trumpets, entirely off key, and a page announced to the startled guests:

"KING AZAZ THE UNABRIDGED."

The king strode through the door and over to the table and settled his great bulk onto the throne, calling irritably, "Places, everyone. Take your places."

He was the largest man Milo had ever seen, with a great stomach, large piercing eyes, a gray beard that reached to his waist, and a silver signet ring on the little finger of his left hand. He also wore a small crown and a robe with the letters of the alphabet beautifully embroidered all over it.

"What have we here?" he said, staring down at Tock and Milo as everyone else took his place.

6. Illustration

Feiffer drew the characters in this complex scene directly in ink, but he sketched the table and its accoutrements in pencil before inking them in, worried as usual that he lacked the requisite skill to render inanimate objects with conviction.

THE PHANTOM TOLLBOOTH

"If you please," said Milo, "my name is Milo and this is Tock. Thank you very much for inviting us to your banquet, and I think your palace is beautiful."

"Exquisite," corrected the duke.

"Lovely," counseled the minister.

"Handsome," recommended the count.

"Pretty," hinted the earl.

"Charming," submitted the undersecretary.

"SILENCE," suggested the king. "Now, young man, what can you do to entertain us? Sing songs? Tell stories?

Compose sonnets? Juggle plates? Do tumbling tricks? Which is it?"

"I can't do any of those things," admitted Milo.

"What an ordinary little boy," commented the king. "Why, my cabinet members can do all sorts of things. The duke here can make mountains out of molehills. The minister splits hairs. The count makes hay while the sun shines. The earl leaves no stone unturned. And the undersecretary," he finished ominously, "hangs by a thread. Can't you do anything at all?"

Page 85

7. "can make mountains out of molehills"

This expression first appears in the English literary record in John Foxe's *The Book of Martyrs* (1563), as follows: "To much amplifying thinges yt be but small, makyng mountaines of Molehils" [John Foxe, "Acts and Monuments," 1570]. English Puritans made Foxe's book a bestseller and its author a famous man, though not (in the days before royalty arrangements) a rich one. Centuries earlier, the Greek satirical poet Lucian had written of making an elephant out of a mere fly, and it is this latter formulation that carried over into French and German idiomatic language and lore.

8. "splits hairs"

A variant on this familiar idiom, used to express the rhetorical maneuver of making "distinctions without a difference," dates back to the seventeenth century, when William Sancroft wrote of the author of *The Prince:* "Machiavel cut the hair when he advised, not absolutely to disavow conscience, but to manage it with such a prudent neglect, as is scarce discernible from a tenderness" ("Modern Policies, Taken from Machiavel, Borgia, and Other Choise [sic.] Authors," 1652).

9. "makes hay while the sun shines"

This buoyant expression, which recalls a time-honored farming technique for drying grass for fodder, was originally printed in the first English-language book of traditional sayings, John Heywood's *Proverbs* (1546), as follows: "When the sunne shinth make hay." Among the other old chestnuts this little-remembered but extraordinarily influential author helped to popularize are "Haste maketh waste"; "Good to be merry and wise"; "The fat is in the fire"; "All is well that ends well"; "Beggars should be no choosers"; and, of special relevance for a later scene in *The Phantom Tollbooth,* "Look ere ye leap."

10. "leaves no stone unturned"

This idiom goes back to ancient Greece. According to *The History of Origins*: "When Xerxes was conquered by the Greeks, he retreated by the river Salamine, and left Mandonious to finish the war. The general was also unfortunate, and retreated. A report was then circulated that he had buried a large sum of gold and silver in the tent. Polycrates had an earnest desire to possess this enormous wealth, and therefore purchased the whole field in which the camp was placed.

"After digging a long time he was unsuccessful, and therefore repaired to the oracle of Delphos, to ask the advice of Apollo how he was to find the treasure. The oracle answered *"omnem move lapidem,"* move every stone. The advice was followed by Polycrates, who moved every stone, and at length found the treasure" (by a "Literary Antiquary," 1824; Google Books photocopy scanned on Internet).

11. "hangs by a thread"

This expression, used to describe the tenuous nature of a situation, dates back to a story from fourth-century BC Greece. Damocles was a toady in the court of Dionysius II of Syracuse whose flattery so annoyed the ruler that the latter decided to teach him a lesson. Dionysius arranged to trade places with his courtier for a day. At the lavish banquet he prepared for Damocles, a surprise awaited the ruler's unwitting pupil. Damocles was having a high time when he happened to look up— and see that a deadly sword hung directly over his head, suspended by a single horsehair. Fleeing the room in terror, Damocles was said to have learned the intended lesson well, having realized that to hold power was to live in a perpetual state of wariness and fear. Cicero and Horace both retold the story, thereby helping to popularize the "sword of Damocles" as an idiom; centuries later, Shakespeare, taking up the same theme in *Henry IV*, would observe: "Uneasy lies the head that wears a crown."

12 "I can count to a thousand," offered Milo.

"A-A-R-G-H, numbers! Never mention numbers here. Only use them when we absolutely have to," growled Azaz disgustedly. "Now, why don't you and Tock come up here and sit next to me, and we'll have some dinner?"

"Are you ready with the menu?" reminded the Humbug.

"Well," said Milo, remembering that his mother had always told him to eat lightly when he was a guest, "why don't we have a light meal?"

"A light meal it shall be," roared the bug, waving his arms.

The waiters rushed in carrying large serving platters and set them on the table in front of the king. When he lifted the covers, shafts of brilliant-colored light leaped from the plates and bounced around the ceiling, the walls, across the floor, and out the windows.

"Not a very substantial meal," said the Humbug, rubbing his eyes, "but quite an attractive one. Perhaps you can suggest something a little more filling."

The king clapped his hands, the platters were removed, and, without thinking, Milo quickly suggested, 13 "Well, in that case, I think we ought to have a square meal of——"

"A square meal it is," shouted the Humbug again. The king clapped his hands once more and the waiters reappeared carrying plates heaped high with steaming squares of all sizes and colors.

"Ugh," said the Spelling Bee, tasting one, "these are awful."

No one else seemed to like them very much either, and the Humbug got one caught in his throat and almost choked.

"Time for the speeches," announced the king as the plates were again removed and everyone looked glum. "You first," he commanded, pointing to Milo.

"Your Majesty, ladies and gentlemen," started Milo timidly, "I would like to take this opportunity to say that in all the——"

"That's quite enough," snapped the king. "Mustn't talk all day."

"But I'd just begun," objected Milo.

Page 86

12. "I can count to a thousand," offered Milo.

As in *Alice's Adventures in Wonderland*'s "The Pool of Tears" scene, when the frightened girl starts to blather on about her cat to the mouse that has accosted her, Milo here brings up the subject most likely to unnerve the king of Dictionopolis.

13. "I think we ought to have a square meal"

A type of cuisine (or plating style) one might have thought better suited to Digitopolis.

Page 87

14. Illustration

Feiffer's fascination with dance, by then a recurring theme of his *Village Voice* strip, is apparent in this court server's elegant pose.

Page 88

15. **"Roast turkey, mashed potatoes, vanilla ice cream"**

Juster's madcap ode to eating adds memorably to a venerable children's book tradition. Whether or not one accepts the premise that food is the sex of children's fiction, there can be no doubt that eating, and the primal urges, satisfactions, and frustrations associated with it, holds great psychic significance for children. Writers from Lewis Carroll onward have effectively tapped into this mother lode of meaning. How better, for example, to telegraph the genuineness of a storybook character's generosity of spirit than by reporting, as Kenneth Grahame does in the opening pages of *The Wind in the Willows*, the delectable contents of the picnic basket that Water Rat has packed to share with his new friend Mole:

> "There's cold chicken inside it," replied the Rat briefly; "coldtonguecoldhamcoldbeef pickledgherkinssaladfrenchrollscress sandwichespottedmeatgingerbeer lemonadesodawater—"
>
> "O stop, stop," cried the Mole in ecstasies: "This is too much!"
>
> "Do you really think so?" inquired the Rat seriously. "It's only what I always take on these little excursions; and the other animals are always telling me that I'm a mean beast and cut it *very* fine!"
>
> (chapter 1, "The River Bank")

16. **"Hamburgers, corn on the cob, chocolate pudding"**

Juster recalled: "As a child (up till my teens) I was a very poor eater—painfully thin—very picky. A lot of eating propaganda was thrown my way—entreaties, threats, predictions of doom. During my teens, the worm turned and ever since then I have been a devoted eater. The passage in which everyone names their

"NEXT!" bellowed the king.

15   "Roast turkey, mashed potatoes, vanilla ice cream," recited the Humbug, bouncing up and down quickly.

"What a strange speech," thought Milo, for he'd heard many in the past and knew that they were supposed to be long and dull.

16   "Hamburgers, corn on the cob, chocolate pudding— p-u-d-d-i-n-g," said the Spelling Bee in his turn.

"Frankfurters, sour pickles, strawberry jam," shouted Officer Shrift from his chair. Since he was taller sitting than standing, he didn't bother to get up.

And so down the line it went, with each guest rising briefly, making a short speech, and then resuming his place. When everyone had finished, the king rose.

"Pâté de foie gras, soupe à l'oignon, faisan sous cloche, salade endive, fromages et fruits et demi-tasse," he said carefully, and clapped his hands again.

The waiters reappeared immediately, carrying heavy, hot trays, which they set on the table. Each one contained the exact words spoken by the various guests, and they all began eating immediately with great gusto.

"Dig in," said the king, poking Milo with his elbow and looking disapprovingly at his plate. "I can't say that I think much of your choice."

17   "I didn't know that I was going to have to eat my words," objected Milo.

"Of course, of course, everyone here does," the king grunted. "You should have made a tastier speech."

Milo looked around at everyone busily stuffing himself and then back at his own unappetizing plate. It certainly didn't look worth eating, and he was so very hungry.

"Here, try some somersault," suggested the duke. "It improves the flavor."

"Have a rigmarole," offered the count, passing the breadbasket.

"Or a ragamuffin," seconded the minister.

"Perhaps you'd care for a synonym bun," suggested the duke.

"Why not wait for your just desserts?" mumbled the earl indistinctly, his mouth full of food.

"How many times must I tell you not to bite off more than you can chew?" snapped the undersecretary, patting the distressed earl on the back.

"In one ear and out the other," scolded the duke, attempting to stuff one of his words through the earl's head.

"If it isn't one thing, it's another," chided the minister.

"Out of the frying pan into the fire," shouted the count, burning himself badly.

"Well, you don't have to bite my head off," screamed the terrified earl, and flew at the others in a rage.

The five of them scuffled wildly under the table.

"STOP THAT AT ONCE," thundered Azaz, "or I'll banish the lot of you!"

"Sorry."

"Excuse me."

"Forgive us."

favorite foods springs from my constantly pleading with my parents for hot dogs, corn on the cob, and watermelon—which Milo of course never gets to ask for. For me, the whole scene, which was one of the ones I had the most fun doing, was a symphony in linguistic mayhem. The best part was that I was completely in charge" (N.J. Notes I, pp. 32–33).

17. "I didn't know that I was going to have to eat my words," objected Milo.

Concerning the origins of the expression "to eat one's words," word sleuth and literary historian Robert Hendrickson has reported: "'God eateth not his word when he hath once spoken' is the first recorded use of this expression meaning 'to retreat in a humiliating way'—in a 1571 religious work. There are several instances of people literally eating their words, the earliest occurring in 1370 when the pope sent two delegates to Bernabò Visconti bearing a rolled parchment, informing him that he had been excommunicated. Infuriated, Visconti arrested the delegates and made them eat the parchment, words, leaden seal, and all. I doubt that this suggested *to eat one's own words*, but it is a good story" (*The Facts on File Encyclopedia of Word and Phrase Origins*, revised and expanded edition; New York: Facts on File, Inc., 1979, p. 266).

18. Illustration

Jules Feiffer here showed his masterful touch as a choreographer of chaos. The Keystone Kops never looked half this graceful in the thick of a brawl.

18

"Pardon."

"Regrets," they apologized in turn, and sat down glaring at each other.

The rest of the meal was finished in silence until the king, wiping the gravy stains from his vest, called for dessert. Milo, who had not eaten anything, looked up eagerly.

"We're having a special treat today," said the king as the delicious smells of homemade pastry filled the banquet hall. "By royal command the pastry chefs have worked all night in the half bakery to make sure that——"

"The half bakery?" questioned Milo.

"Of course, the half bakery," snapped the king. "Where do you think half-baked ideas come from? Now, please don't interrupt. By royal command the pastry chefs have worked all night to——"

"What's a half-baked idea?" asked Milo again.

"Will you be quiet?" growled Azaz angrily; but, before he could begin again, three large serving carts were wheeled into the hall and everyone jumped up to help himself.

"They're very tasty," explained the Humbug, "but they don't always agree with you. Here's one that's very good." He handed it to Milo and, through the icing and nuts, Milo saw that it said, "THE EARTH IS FLAT."

"People swallowed that one for years," commented the Spelling Bee, "but it's not very popular these days—d-a-y-s." He picked up a long one that stated "THE MOON IS MADE OF GREEN CHEESE" and hungrily bit off the part that said "CHEESE." "Now *there's* a half-baked idea," he said, smiling.

Milo looked at the great assortment of cakes, which were being eaten almost as quickly as anyone could read them. The count was munching contentedly on "IT NEVER RAINS BUT IT POURS" and the king was busy slicing one that stated "NIGHT AIR IS BAD AIR."

"I wouldn't eat too many of those if I were you," advised Tock. "They may look good, but you can get terribly sick of them."

"Don't worry," Milo replied; "I'll just wrap one up for later," and he folded his napkin around "EVERYTHING HAPPENS FOR THE BEST."

19
20
21
22
23
24

Page 91

19. "Where do you think half-baked ideas come from?"

The *Oxford English Dictionary* traces the phrase "half-baked" to a sermon published in England in 1637 in which the Church of England cleric Robert Sanderson railed against "Our profest Popelings, and halfe-baked Protestants." Nearly two and a half centuries later, the term worked equally well in the *Nation* on August 4, 1881, as a put-down of government policy makers' "half-baked measures" aimed at "crippl[ing] the Australian system."

20. "THE EARTH IS FLAT."

Astronomers in ancient Greece—not Christopher Columbus—first realized that the world was spherical. We have the nineteenth-century American writer Washington Irving, in his *Life and Voyages of Christopher Columbus* (1828), to thank for popularizing the mistaken notion that medieval Europeans believed the earth to be as flat as a tabletop.

21. "THE MOON IS MADE OF GREEN CHEESE"

From an English proverb that implied that nobody but a fool would believe such a thing. The earliest printed instance of its use cited in the *Oxford English Dictionary* dates from 1529.

22. "IT NEVER RAINS BUT IT POURS"

This proverb is traceable to the eighteenth-century English physician, mathematician, and satirist John Arbuthnot, who in 1742 published an essay called "It Cannot Rain but It Pours." Arbuthnot had other claims to fame as well. He is credited with having developed the character "John Bull" as the personification of Britain and with having provided his friend Jonathan Swift with the inspiration for part three of *Gulliver's Travels*, the story of Gulliver's visit to the math-crazed kingdom of Laputa. Alexander Pope wrote "Epistle to

Dr. Arbuthnot" in memory of this remarkable polymath.

Swift himself co-authored with Alexander Pope an essay titled "It Cannot Rain but It Pours." A century and a half later, the Morton Salt company adopted the slogan "When It Rains It Pours" to advertise a form of granular salt that maintained its integrity in damp weather.

23. "NIGHT AIR IS BAD AIR."

One of Juster's mother's favorite sayings. As an indication of how popular an expression this was around the time of the author's childhood, consider the following passage from an article published in the May 1924 issue of the *Annals of the American Academy of Political and Social Science*, in which Albert Smith Faught observed: "Nearly every profession is confronted with certain fallacies which seem to be lodged in the mind of the general public. Medical men are familiar with the deep-rooted fallacy that 'Night air is bad air,' while lawyers still find a widespread belief that 'It is necessary to leave an heir one dollar in order to disinherit him'" (p. 311).

24. "EVERYTHING HAPPENS FOR THE BEST."

In Voltaire's *Candide* (1759), Pangloss, wise mentor to the story's eponymous young hero, insists: "In this best of all possible worlds, everything happens for the best." By the end of their shared journey, however, Candide himself is not so sure. Voltaire wrote this satirical work in the aftermath of the Lisbon earthquake of 1755 and in the midst of the Seven Years' War, catastrophic events that rattled the religious faith of many Europeans. The author was among those who, in the face of such massive and seemingly meaningless carnage, could no longer maintain the optimist's view that everything in life occurred for a divinely determined reason.

8. The Humbug Volunteers

"Couldn't eat another thing," puffed the duke, clutching his stomach.

"Oh my, oh dear," agreed the minister, breathing with great difficulty.

"M-m-m-m-f-f-m-m," mumbled the earl, desperately trying to swallow another mouthful.

"Thoroughly stuffed," sighed the count, loosening his belt.

"Full up," grunted the undersecretary, reaching for the last cake.

As everyone finished, the only sounds to be heard were the creaking of chairs, the pushing of plates, the licking of spoons, and, of course, a few words from the Humbug.

"A delightful repast, delicately prepared and elegantly served," he announced to no one in particular. "A feast of rare bouquet. My compliments to the chef, by all means; my compliments to the chef." Then, with a most distressed look on his face, he turned to Milo and gasped, "Would you kindly fetch me a glass of water? I seem to have a touch of indigestion."

"Perhaps you've eaten too much too quickly," Milo remarked sympathetically.

"Too much too quickly, too much too quickly," wheezed the uncomfortable bug, between gulps. "To be sure, too much too quickly. I most certainly should have eaten too little too slowly, or too much too slowly, or too little too quickly, or taken all day to eat nothing, or eaten everything in no time at all, or occasionally eaten something any time, or perhaps I should have——" And he toppled back, exhausted, into his chair and continued to mumble indistinctly.

"Attention! Let me have your attention!" insisted the king, leaping to his feet and pounding the table. The command was entirely unnecessary, for the moment he began to speak everyone but Milo, Tock, and the distraught bug rushed from the hall, down the stairs, and out of the palace.

"Loyal subjects and friends," continued Azaz, his voice echoing in the almost empty room, "once again on this gala occasion we have——"

"Pardon me," coughed Milo as politely as possible, "but everyone has gone."

"I was hoping no one would notice," said the king sadly. "It happens every time."

Study by Jules Feiffer of Azaz the Unabridged. What a difference a crown makes!

"They've all gone to dinner," announced the Humbug weakly, "and just as soon as I catch my breath I shall join them."

"That's ridiculous. How can they eat dinner right after a banquet?" asked Milo.

"SCANDALOUS!" shouted the king. "We'll put a stop to it at once. From now on, by royal command, everyone must eat dinner before the banquet."

94

"But that's just as bad," protested Milo.

"You mean just as good," corrected the Humbug. "Things which are equally bad are also equally good. Try to look at the bright side of things."

"I don't know which side of anything to look at," protested Milo. "Everything is so confusing and all your words only make things worse."

"How true," said the unhappy king, resting his regal chin on his royal fist as he thought fondly of the old days. "There must be something we can do about it."

"Pass a law," the Humbug suggested brightly.

"We have almost as many laws as words," grumbled the king.

"Offer a reward," offered the bug again.

The king shook his head and looked sadder and sadder.

"Send for help."

"Drive a bargain."

"Pull the switch."

"File a brief."

"Lower the boom."

"Toe the line."

"Raise the bridge."

"Bar the door," shouted the bug, jumping up and down and waving his arms. Then he promptly sat down as the king glanced furiously in his direction.

"Perhaps you might allow Rhyme and Reason to return," said Milo softly, for he had been waiting for just such an opportunity to suggest it.

"How nice that would be," said Azaz, straightening

Page 95

2. "Pull the switch."

This idiom most likely originated in connection with the fateful act of initiating an execution by electric chair.

3. "Toe the line."

An idiom associated first with boxing and later with competitive running. Prior to the codification of the Queensberry rules for boxing, British fighters faced one another with feet firmly planted on a pair of lines drawn at the center of the ring. The slugfest continued until one of the combatants literally could stand it no longer. Applied to the realm of track, to "toe the line" meant to place one's forward foot on the starting line in advance of the start of a race.

4. "Bar the door"

Perhaps the most famous appearance of this idiom comes in the raucous old Scots ballad "Get Up and Bar the Door," which tells the outlandish tale of a husband and wife who each insist that the other should be the one to shut their front door against a fearsome wind, and who both pay dearly for their laziness and stubborn pride.

Page 96

5. "Why not indeed?" exclaimed the bug, who seemed equally at home on either side of an argument.

Children of about Milo's age develop the ability to think abstractly and to spot contradictions in the generalizations put forward by others—most especially, of course, those of their teachers and parents, toward whom they can be merciless. Here Milo shows remarkable restraint as he ignores the Humbug's shameless flip-flops in conversation with the king, and prepares to take on the most dangerous challenge of his young life, an attempt to rescue Rhyme and Reason.

Juster commented: "Of all childhood experiences, there is nothing more exhilarating or frightening than suddenly to be put in charge and made ultimately responsible for something" (N.J. Notes I, p. 35).

up and adjusting his crown. "Even if they were a bother at times, things always went so well when they were here." As he spoke he leaned back on the throne, clasped his hands behind his head, and stared thoughtfully at the ceiling. "But I'm afraid it can't be done."

"Certainly not; it can't be done," repeated the Humbug.

"Why not?" asked Milo.

"Why not indeed?" exclaimed the bug, who seemed equally at home on either side of an argument.

"Much too difficult," replied the king.

"Of course," emphasized the bug, "much too difficult."

"You could if you really wanted to," insisted Milo.

"By all means, if you really wanted to, you could," the Humbug agreed.

"How?" asked Azaz, glaring at the bug.

"How?" inquired Milo, looking the same way.

"A simple task," began the Humbug, suddenly wishing he were somewhere else, "for a brave lad with a stout heart, a steadfast dog, and a serviceable small automobile."

"Go on," commanded the king.

"Yes, please," seconded Milo.

"All that he would have to do," continued the worried bug, "is travel through miles of harrowing and hazardous countryside, into unknown valleys and uncharted forests, past yawning chasms and trackless wastes, until he reached Digitopolis (if, of course, he ever reached there). Then he would have to persuade the Mathemagician to agree to release the little princesses—and, of course, he'd never agree to agree to anything that you agreed with. And, anyway, if he did, you certainly wouldn't agree to it.

"From there it's a simple matter of entering the Mountains of Ignorance, full of perilous pitfalls and ominous overtones—a land to which many venture but few return, and whose evil demons slither slowly from peak to peak in search of prey. Then an effortless climb up a two-thousand-step circular stairway without railings in a high wind at night (for in those mountains it is always night) to the Castle in the Air."

He paused momentarily for breath, then began again.

"After a pleasant chat with the princesses, all that remains is a leisurely ride back through those chaotic crags whose frightening fiends have sworn to tear any intruder limb from limb and devour him down to his belt buckle.

"And, finally, after the long ride back, a triumphal parade (if, of course, there is anything left to parade) followed by hot chocolate and cookies for everyone." The Humbug bowed low and sat down once again, very pleased with himself.

"I never realized it would be so simple," said the king, stroking his beard and smiling broadly.

"Quite simple indeed," concurred the bug.

"It sounds dangerous to me," said Milo.

"Most dangerous, most dangerous," mumbled the Humbug, still trying to be in agreement with everybody.

"Who will make the journey?" asked Tock, who had

Page 98

6. "for I have brought you this for your protection."

Gifts with protective or talismanic virtues occur throughout myth, lore, and legend. Typically, such gifts do not solve the hero's problems all by themselves. Rather, the hero must discover their proper use, as Milo does in the course of his quest for Rhyme and Reason.

been listening very carefully to the Humbug's description.

"A very good question," replied the king. "But there is one far more serious problem."

"What is it?" asked Milo, who was rather unhappy at the turn the conversation had taken.

"I'm afraid I can tell you that only when you return," cried the king, clapping his hands three times. As he did so, the waiters rushed back into the room and quickly cleared away the dishes, the silver, the table-cloth, the table, the chairs, the banquet hall, and the palace, leaving them all suddenly standing in the market place.

"Of course you realize that I would like to make the trip myself," continued Azaz, striding across the square as if nothing had happened; "but, since it was your idea, you shall have all the honor and fame."

"But you see——" began Milo.

"Dictionopolis will always be grateful, my boy," interrupted the king, throwing one arm around Milo and patting Tock with the other. "You will face many dangers on your journey, but fear not, for I have brought you this for your protection."

He drew from inside his cape a small heavy box about the size of a schoolbook and handed it ceremoniously to Milo.

"In this box are all the words I know," he said. "Most of them you will never need, some you will use constantly, but with them you may ask all the questions which have never been answered and answer all the questions which have never been asked. All the great books of the past and all the ones yet to come are made with these words. With them there is no obstacle you cannot overcome. All you must learn to do is use them well and in the right places."

Milo accepted the gift with thanks and the little group walked to the car, still parked at the edge of the square.

"You will, of course, need a guide," said the king, "and, since he knows the obstacles so well, the Humbug has cheerfully volunteered to accompany you."

"Now see here," cried the startled bug, for that was the last thing in the world he wanted to do.

Page 99

7. Illustration

Of all the book's drawings, this one most clearly reveals the influence of another of the illustrators Feiffer most admired at the time, that modern English master of cross-hatching, Edward Ardizzone.

"Gevrey Chambertin' 39 — Pommard 45 — and a very old Calvados A splendid finish

The End

© Edward Ardizzone 1991

Black line drawing by Edward Ardizzone from *Sketchbook 12*, 1951.

7

"You will find him dependable, brave, resourceful, and loyal," continued Azaz, and the Humbug was so overcome by the flattery that he quite forgot to object again.

"I'm sure he'll be a great help," cried Milo as they drove across the square.

"I hope so," thought Tock to himself, for he was far less sure.

"Good luck, good luck; do be careful!" shouted the king, and down the road they went.

Milo and Tock wondered what strange adventures lay ahead. The Humbug speculated on how he'd ever become involved in such a hazardous undertaking. And the crowd waved and cheered wildly, for, while they didn't care at all about anyone arriving, they were always very pleased to see someone go.

9. It's All in How You Look at Things

Soon all traces of Dictionopolis had vanished in the distance and all those strange and unknown lands that lay between the kingdom of words and the kingdom of numbers stretched before them. It was late afternoon and the dark-orange sun floated heavily over the distant mountains. A friendly, cool breeze slapped playfully at the car, and the long shadows stretched out lazily from the trees and bushes.

"Ah, the open road!" exclaimed the Humbug, breathing deeply, for he now seemed happily resigned to the trip. "The spirit of adventure, the lure of the unknown, the thrill of a gallant quest. How very grand indeed." Then, pleased with himself, he folded his arms, sat back, and left it at that.

Page 101

1. "Ah, the open road!"

The Humbug's zest for travel and adventure echoes that of *The Wind in the Willows'* Mr. Toad, who, showing off his new horse-drawn caravan, tells his friends, "'There's life for you, embodied in that little cart. The open road, the dusty highway, the heath, the common, the hedgerows, the rolling downs! . . . Here to-day, up and off to somewhere else to-morrow!'" (chapter 2, p. 29).

The Open Road   29

2. "STRAIGHT AHEAD TO POINT OF VIEW"

As improved transportation options allowed tourists and other travelers to venture ever deeper into wilderness terrain, much thought was given to how best they might maximize the experience. According to historian Peter J. Schmitt: "In 1898, geologist Nathaniel Shaler noted that pushing against the winds in open country or peering from a mountain top virtually precluded 'spiritual contact' with nature. Shaler found it difficult to focus on single themes when he was surrounded by beauty. In 'The Landscape As a Means of Culture,' he laid out for readers of *The Atlantic Monthly* a scheme to limit the field of vision by scientific principles, to insure that he could best see into 'the heart of things'" (Peter J. Schmitt, *Back to Nature: The Arcadian Myth in Urban America*, New York: Oxford University Press, 1969, pp. 146–47). By the middle of the twentieth century, roadside viewing points could be found along scenic routes throughout the United States.

3. "Remarkable view"
Norton Juster (right) and a fellow sightseer stopping to enjoy the view at the Grand Canyon, summer of 1949.

In a few more minutes they had left the open country-side and driven into a dense forest.

"THIS IS THE SCENIC ROUTE: STRAIGHT AHEAD TO POINT OF VIEW"

announced a rather large road sign; but, contrary to its statement, all that could be seen were more trees. As the car rushed along, the trees grew thicker and taller and leafier until, just as they'd hidden the sky completely, the forest abruptly ended and the road bent itself around a broad promontory. Stretching below, to the left, the right, and straight ahead, as far as anyone could see, lay the rich green landscape through which they had been traveling.

"Remarkable view," announced the Humbug, bouncing from the car as if he were responsible for the whole thing.

"Isn't it beautiful?" gasped Milo.

"Oh, I don't know," answered a strange voice. "It's all in the way you look at things."

"I beg your pardon?" said Milo, for he didn't see who had spoken.

"I said it's all in how you look at things," repeated the voice.

Milo turned around and found himself staring at two very neatly polished brown shoes, for standing directly in front of him (if you can use the word "standing" for anyone suspended in mid-air) was another boy just about his age, whose feet were easily three feet off the ground.

102

4. for standing directly in front of him . . . was another boy just about his age, whose feet were easily three feet off the ground.

This new alter ego of Milo's—one of Juster's favorite characters—has his own point of view about everything, literally and otherwise, including the most sensible way for a child to grow and mature. While Lewis Carroll before him satirized the simplistic model of child development implied in the unidirectional catchphrase "growing up," Juster here gives the matter his own utterly original, and playful, twist.

Page 104

5. "if Christmas trees were people"

Although both the author's parents were Jewish, the Juster children received Christmas presents. This was in no small part due to the fact that one of Minnie Juster's sisters was married to an Irishman, the young Norton's uncle Bill, a genial man whom Juster appreciated as much for his candor as for his company. Bill would often escort Norton to the dentist's office. When the latter asked, "Will it hurt?" Bill, unlike the other adults he knew, would tell him exactly what to expect.

6. "Well . . . in my family everyone is born in the air"

This passage recalls one from the Laputa section of *Gulliver's Travels*: "There was a most ingenious architect who had contrived a new method for building houses, by beginning at the roof, and working downwards to the foundation, which he justified to me by the like practice of those two prudent insects, the bee and the spider" (part 3, chapter 5, p. 172).

"For instance," continued the boy, "if you happened to like deserts, you might not think this was beautiful at all."

"That's true," said the Humbug, who didn't like to contradict anyone whose feet were that far off the ground.

"For instance," said the boy again, "if Christmas trees were people and people were Christmas trees, we'd all be chopped down, put up in the living room, and covered with tinsel, while the trees opened our presents."

"What does that have to do with it?" asked Milo.

"Nothing at all," he answered, "but it's an interesting possibility, don't you think?"

"How do you manage to stand up there?" asked Milo, for this was the subject which most interested him.

"I was about to ask you a similar question," answered the boy, "for you must be much older than you look to be standing on the ground."

"What do you mean?" Milo asked.

"Well," said the boy, "in my family everyone is born in the air, with his head at exactly the height it's going to be when he's an adult, and then we all grow toward the ground. When we're fully grown up or, as you can see, grown down, our feet finally touch. Of course, there are a few of us whose feet never reach the ground no matter how old we get, but I suppose it's the same in every family."

He hopped a few steps in the air, skipped back to where he started, and then began again.

"You certainly must be very old to have reached the ground already."

"Oh no," said Milo seriously. "In my family we all start on the ground and grow up, and we never know how far until we actually get there." ⁷

"What a silly system." The boy laughed. "Then your head keeps changing its height and you always see things in a different way? Why, when you're fifteen things won't look at all the way they did when you were ten, and at twenty everything will change again." ⁸

"I suppose so," replied Milo, for he had never really thought about the matter.

Page 105

7. "In my family we all start on the ground"

In the "Final Typed Draft" at the Lilly Library, this passage reads: "I'm only ten, but in my family . . ." Juster crossed out "ten" and inserted "nine" in its place. At a later stage, he decided it best simply not to specify Milo's age (Lilly Library, box 5, folder 64).

8. "Why, when you're fifteen things won't look at all the way they did when you were ten"

While Alec's observation is literally true, it also alludes to the concept, evidently foreign to his part of the world, of child and adolescent development—the notion that from infancy through early adulthood all individuals pass through the same sequence of stages in their growth with respect to bodily strength and self-mastery, cognitive functioning, emotional maturity, ego development, and moral awareness. Sigmund Freud, G. Stanley Hall, Jean Piaget, Arnold Gesell, Erik Erikson, and Lawrence Kohlberg are among the twentieth-century theorists who made significant contributions to the study of child and adolescent development.

Page 106

9. visible to the naked eye.

The first known appearance of this expression—"smaller than the smallest hair our naked eyes can discover"—occurs in English physician Henry Power's *Experimental Philosophy* (1664). One of the original Fellows of Britain's Royal Society, Power was writing within decades of the invention of the telescope and at a time when precursors to the modern telescope were being devised.

10. "I'm Alec Bings"

According to the author, this character's curious name has no special significance apart from the fact that it rhymes with the remark spoken immediately following its first mention: "I see through things."

"We always see things from the same angle," the boy continued. "It's much less trouble that way. Besides, it makes more sense to grow down and not up. When you're very young, you can never hurt yourself falling down if you're in mid-air, and you certainly can't get into trouble for scuffing up your shoes or marking the floor if there's nothing to scuff them on and the floor is three feet away."

"That's very true," thought Tock, who wondered how the dogs in the family liked the arrangement.

"But there are many other ways to look at things," remarked the boy. "For instance, you had orange juice, boiled eggs, toast and jam, and milk for breakfast," he said, turning to Milo. "And you are always worried about people wasting time," he said to Tock. "And you are almost never right about anything," he said, pointing at the Humbug, "and, when you are, it's usually an accident."

"A gross exaggeration," protested the furious bug, who didn't realize that so much was visible to the naked eye.

"Amazing," gasped Tock.

"How do you know all that?" asked Milo.

"Simple," he said proudly. "I'm Alec Bings; I see through things. I can see whatever is inside, behind, around, covered by, or subsequent to anything else. In fact, the only thing I can't see is whatever happens to be right in front of my nose."

"Isn't that a little inconvenient?" asked Milo, whose neck was becoming quite stiff from looking up.

106

"It is a little," replied Alec, "but it is quite important to know what lies behind things, and the family helps me take care of the rest. My father sees to things, my mother looks after things, my brother sees beyond things, my uncle sees the other side of every question, and my little sister Alice sees under things."

"How can she see under things if she's all the way up there?" growled the Humbug.

"Well," added Alec, turning a neat cartwheel, "whatever she can't see under, she overlooks." 11

"Would it be possible for me to see something from up there?" asked Milo politely.

"You could," said Alec, "but only if you try very hard to look at things as an adult does."

Milo tried as hard as he could, and, as he did, his feet floated slowly off the ground until he was standing in the air next to Alec Bings. He looked around very quickly and, an instant later, crashed back down to earth again.

"Interesting, wasn't it?" asked Alec.

"Yes, it was," agreed Milo, rubbing his head and dusting himself off, "but I think I'll continue to see things as a child. It's not so far to fall."

"A wise decision, at least for the time being," said Alec. "Everyone should have his own point of view."

"Isn't this everyone's Point of View?" asked Tock, looking around curiously.

"Of course not," replied Alec, sitting himself down on nothing. "It's only mine, and you certainly can't always look at things from someone else's Point of View.

11. "Well," added Alec, turning a neat cartwheel, "whatever she can't see under, she overlooks."

Another play on words worthy of the author's father—or the Marx Brothers. In an earlier version of the text, Juster fleshed out this moment with a bit more detail: "Well," added Alec, "whatever she can't see under, she overlooks," and he leaped up, turned a complete cartwheel and came down flat on his back in the air" (Lilly Library, box 5, folder 5, handwritten p. 11).

For instance, from here that looks like a bucket of water," he said, pointing to a bucket of water; "but from an ant's point of view it's a vast ocean, from an elephant's just a cool drink, and to a fish, of course, it's home. So, you see, the way you see things depends a great deal on where you look at them from. Now, come along and I'll show you the rest of the forest."

He ran quickly through the air, stopping occasionally to beckon Milo, Tock, and the Humbug along, and they followed as well as anyone who had to stay on the ground could.

"Does everyone here grow the way you do?" puffed Milo when he had caught up.

"Almost everyone," replied Alec, and then he stopped a moment and thought. "Now and then, though, someone does begin to grow differently. Instead of down, his feet grow up toward the sky. But we do our best to discourage awkward things like that."

"What happens to *them?*" insisted Milo.

"Oddly enough, they often grow ten times the size of everyone else," said Alec thoughtfully, "and I've heard that they walk among the stars." And with that he skipped off once again toward the waiting woods.

10. A Colorful Symphony

As they ran, tall trees closed in around them and arched gracefully toward the sky. The late-afternoon sunlight leaped lightly from leaf to leaf, slid along branches and down trunks, and dropped finally to the ground in warm, luminous patches. A soft glow filled the air with the kind of light that made everything look sharp and clear and close enough to reach out and touch.

Alec raced ahead, laughing and shouting, but soon encountered serious difficulties; for, while he could always see the tree behind the next one, he could never see the next one itself and was continually crashing into it. After several minutes of wildly dashing about, they all stopped for a breath of air.

"I think we're lost," panted the Humbug, collapsing into a large berrybush.

1. A Colorful Symphony

The image of a symphony composed of colors rather than sounds suggests the special kind of perceptual experience known uniquely by those people—perhaps as many as one in three hundred in the general population—who exhibit one or another form of the phenomenon neuroscientists call synesthesia. What all synesthetes have in common is a hardwired capacity for making some form of automatic, involuntary cross-sensory or -perceptual connection, whether it be by mentally pairing certain words with specific taste sensations or musical tones—or numbers or letters of the alphabet—with particular colors. Researchers have documented a wide range of synesthetic experiences and have found overall that synesthetics tend to be positively impacted, if they are affected at all during the course of their daily lives, by their special "powers." It is quite common for synesthetes to go about their business for years assuming that everyone perceives the world as they do—"seeing" A-flats in music as peach-colored, for instance, or associating the taste of an apple with the texture of linen—until a conversation with a nonsynesthete acquaintance happens to reveal otherwise.

One of modern literature's best-known synesthetes, Vladimir Nabokov, wrote of the phenomenon in the memoir *Speak, Memory:* "On top of this I present a fine case of colored hearing. Perhaps 'hearing' is not quite accurate, since the color sensation seems to be produced by the very act of my orally forming a given letter while I imagine its outline. The long *a* of the English alphabet . . . has for me the tint of weathered wood, but a French *a* evokes polished ebony. This black group also includes hard *g* (vulcanized rubber) and *r* (a sooty rag being ripped). . . .

"To my mother . . . [another synesthete] this all seemed quite normal" (*Speak, Memory: An*

Autobiography Revisited, New York: Knopf/Everyman Library, p. 21).

As a schoolchild, Juster (without apparently realizing there was anything special about it) made good use of a tendency to form one-to-one word/color correspondence—one of the most common forms of synesthesia. Juster had struggled with basic math until he began to assign a different color to each of the numbers, from zero to nine, as he put them on paper. Thereafter, the numbers "made sense" to him and the future architect enjoyed far smoother sailing.

"Nonsense!" shouted Alec from the high branch on which he sat.

"Do you know where we are?" asked Milo.

"Certainly," he replied, "we're right here on this very spot. Besides, being lost is never a matter of not knowing where you are; it's a matter of not knowing where you aren't—and I don't care at all about where I'm not."

This was much too complicated for the bug to figure out, and Milo had just begun repeating it to himself when Alec said, "If you don't believe me, ask the giant," and he pointed to a small house tucked neatly between two of the largest trees.

Milo and Tock walked up to the door, whose brass name plate read simply "THE GIANT," and knocked.

"Good afternoon," said the perfectly ordinary-sized man who answered the door.

Page 111

2. "I'm the smallest giant in the world."

This scene, which toys with the concept of relativity in general and the elasticity of verbal definitions, is also an example of Juster's mischievous campaign to present Feiffer with characters and situations the artist would find impossible to illustrate. Not easily thrown, Feiffer had the last laugh when he realized that he could simply use the same illustration four times, changing only the sign over the doorway (from my interview with J.F., April 24, 2009).

"Are you the giant?" asked Tock doubtfully.

"To be sure," he replied proudly. "I'm the smallest giant in the world. What can I do for you?" 2

"Are we lost?" said Milo.

"That's a difficult question," said the giant. "Why don't you go around back and ask the midget?" And he closed the door.

They walked to the rear of the house, which looked exactly like the front, and knocked at the door, whose name plate read "THE MIDGET."

"How are you?" inquired the man, who looked exactly like the giant.

"Are you the midget?" asked Tock again, with a hint of uncertainty in his voice.

"Unquestionably," he answered. "I'm the tallest midget in the world. May I help you?"

"Do you think we're lost?" repeated Milo.

"That's a very complicated problem," he said. "Why don't you go around to the side and ask the fat man?" And he, too, quickly disappeared.

The side of the house looked very like the front and back, and the door flew open the very instant they knocked.

"How nice of you to come by," exclaimed the man, who could have been the midget's twin brother.

"You must be the fat man," said Tock, learning not to count too much on appearance.

"The thinnest one in the world," he replied brightly; "but if you have any questions, I suggest you try the thin man, on the other side of the house."

Just as they suspected, the other side of the house looked the same as the front, the back, and the side, and

the door was again answered by a man who looked precisely like the other three.

"What a pleasant surprise!" he cried happily. "I haven't had a visitor in as long as I can remember."

"How long is that?" asked Milo.

"I'm sure I don't know," he replied. "Now pardon me; I have to answer the door."

"But you just did," said Tock.

"Oh yes, I'd forgotten."

"Are you the fattest thin man in the world?" asked Tock.

"Do you know one that's fatter?" he asked impatiently.

"I think you're all the same man," said Milo emphatically.

"S-S-S-S-S-H-H-H-H-H-H-H," he cautioned, putting

113

3. "S-S-S-S-S-H-H-H-H-H-H-H," he cautioned . . . "Do you want to ruin everything?"

Norton Juster's copies of the Oz books were among his most prized childhood possessions. Here Juster puts an interesting twist on the speech of the Wizard of Oz, in which that other unremarkable man confesses his true identity:

> "I thought Oz was a great Head," said Dorothy.
> "And I thought Oz was a lovely Lady," said the Scarecrow.
> "And I thought Oz was a terrible Beast," said the Tin Woodman.

"Exactly so! I am a humbug."

> "And I thought Oz was a Ball of Fire," exclaimed the Lion.
> "No; you are all wrong," said the little man, meekly. "I have been making believe."
> "Making believe!" cried Dorothy. "Are you not a great Wizard?"

his finger up to his lips and drawing Milo closer. "Do you want to ruin everything? You see, to tall men I'm a midget, and to short men I'm a giant; to the skinny ones I'm a fat man, and to the fat ones I'm a thin man. That way I can hold four jobs at once. As you can see, though, I'm neither tall nor short nor fat nor thin. In fact, I'm quite ordinary, but there are so many ordinary men that no one asks their opinion about anything. Now what is your question?"

"Are we lost?" asked Milo once again.

"H-m-m-m," said the man, scratching his head. "I haven't had such a difficult question in as long as I can remember. Would you mind repeating it? It's slipped my mind."

Milo asked the question again.

"My, my," the man mumbled. "I know one thing for certain; it's much harder to tell whether you *are* lost than whether you *were* lost, for, on many occasions, where you're going is exactly where you are. On the other hand, you often find that where you've been is not at all where you should have gone, and, since it's much more difficult to find your way back from someplace you've never left, I suggest you go there immediately and then decide. If you have any more questions, please ask the giant." And he slammed his door and pulled down the shade.

"I hope you're satisfied," said Alec when they'd returned from the house, and he bounced to his feet, bent down to awaken the snoring Humbug, and started off, more slowly this time, in the direction of a large clearing.

"Do many people live here in the forest?" asked Milo as they trotted along together.

"Oh yes, they live in a wonderful city called Reality," he announced, smashing into one of the smaller trees and sending a cascade of nuts and leaves to the ground. "It's right this way."

In a few more steps the forest opened before them, and off to the left a magnificent metropolis appeared. The rooftops shone like mirrors, the walls glistened with thousands of precious stones, and the broad avenues were paved in silver.

"Is that it?" shouted Milo, running toward the shining streets.

"Oh no, that's only Illusions," said Alec. "The real city is over there."

"What are Illusions?" Milo asked, for it was the loveliest city he'd ever seen.

"Illusions," explained Alec, "are like mirages," and, realizing that this didn't help much, he continued: "And mirages are things that aren't really there that you can see very clearly."

"How can you see something that isn't there?" yawned the Humbug, who wasn't fully awake yet.

"Sometimes it's much simpler than seeing things that are," he said. "For instance, if something is there, you

4
5

Page 115

4. a magnificent metropolis appeared.

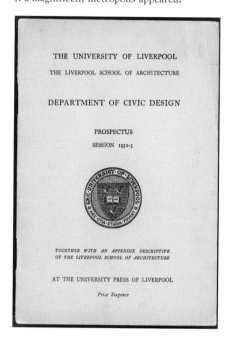

Norton Juster's copy of the University of Liverpool course of study in the city-planning program in which he enrolled in the fall of 1952.

5. The rooftops shone like mirrors, the walls glistened with thousands of precious stones

Apart from its resemblance to that other literary smoke-and-mirrors metropolis, the Emerald City of Oz, "Illusions" suggests a place like mid-twentieth-century midtown Manhattan, where quirky, mixed-use neighborhoods were rapidly giving way to high-rise commercial development, much of it glitzy and otherwise characterless.

6. ". . . Main Street."

The standard American designation for a city or town's principal thoroughfare. High Street, the British equivalent, was introduced in North America during colonial times. But political change often prompts changes in place names as well, and it is likely that following the war of independence, "high" (as in, the king's "high table") fell out of favor with Americans for its unwanted connotation of "superior rank."

can only see it with your eyes open, but if it isn't there, you can see it just as well with your eyes closed. That's why imaginary things are often easier to see than real ones."

"Then where is Reality?" barked Tock.

"Right here," cried Alec, waving his arms. "You're standing in the middle of Main Street."

They looked around very carefully. Tock sniffed suspiciously at the wind and the Humbug gingerly stabbed his cane in the air, but there was nothing at all to see.

"It's really a very pleasant city," said Alec as he strolled down the street, pointing out several of the

sights, which didn't seem to be there, and tipping his cap to the passers-by. There were great crowds of people rushing along with their heads down, and they all appeared to know exactly where they were going as they darted down and around the nonexistent streets and in and out of the missing buildings.

"I don't see any city," said Milo very softly.

"Neither do they," Alec remarked sadly, "but it hardly matters, for they don't miss it at all."

"It must be very difficult to live in a city you can't see," Milo insisted, jumping aside as a line of cars and trucks went by.

"Not at all, once you get used to it," said Alec. "But let me tell you how it happened." And, as they strolled along the bustling and busy avenue, he began.

"Many years ago, on this very spot, there was a beautiful city of fine houses and inviting spaces, and no one who lived here was ever in a hurry. The streets were full of wonderful things to see and the people would often stop to look at them."

"Didn't they have any place to go?" asked Milo.

"To be sure," continued Alec; "but, as you know, the most important reason for going from one place to another is to see what's in between, and they took great pleasure in doing just that. Then one day someone discovered that if you walked as fast as possible and looked at nothing but your shoes you would arrive at your destination much more quickly. Soon everyone was doing

7

---

7. "Many years ago, on this very spot, there was a beautiful city of fine houses and inviting spaces, and no one who lived here was ever in a hurry."

The vibrant city described here has much in common with the ideal of humanly scaled, community-based urbanism praised by Juster's friend Jane Jacobs in her landmark *The Death and Life of Great American Cities*. Jacobs's fiery call to arms issued a stiff rebuke to the leading urban planners and critics of the day, a group that included Juster's own college mentor, Lewis Mumford. While Mumford aligned himself with town and city planners such as Ebenezer Howard and Le Corbusier, who favored the imposition of unified grand designs on population centers, Jacobs argued that the very essence of a city's vitality resided in its crazy quilt of serendipitous, ever-changing confluences of people, resources, and happenings. In her extraordinary book, Jacobs took direct aim at Mumford, who as it happened also published a major work in 1961, *The City in History*, and he responded in kind in the pages of the *New Yorker*. (*The City in History* won the National Book Award for nonfiction in 1962.) Throughout all the fireworks, Juster was able to maintain his friendships with both Jacobs and his old teacher.

Juster commented: "All through my working and teaching [life] I have been interested in the way people see and understand their environment—how they organize and orient themselves to live and work in it, and how much they relegate to 'non-consciousness.'

"I'm sure everyone, at one time or another, has walked down a street they have walked down a thousand times and suddenly noticed something that they seem never to have noticed before. It may be the light, their frame of mind, or any of an endless number of influences that suddenly renders something visible or memorable. We do tend to rush through the 'spaces of our lives' without noticing or taking pleasure (or offense). What a shame" (N.J. Notes I, p. 40).

Embedded within *The Phantom Tollbooth* is a critique of the depersonalization of modern city life that runs parallel to Jacobs's central argument.

it. They all rushed down the avenues and hurried along the boulevards seeing nothing of the wonders and beauties of their city as they went."

Milo remembered the many times he'd done the very same thing; and, as hard as he tried, there were even things on his own street that he couldn't remember.

"No one paid any attention to how things looked, and as they moved faster and faster everything grew uglier and dirtier, and as everything grew uglier and dirtier they moved faster and faster, and at last a very strange thing began to happen. Because nobody cared, the city slowly began to disappear. Day by day the buildings grew fainter and fainter, and the streets faded away, until at last it was entirely invisible. There was nothing to see at all."

"What did they do?" the Humbug inquired, suddenly taking an interest in things.

"Nothing at all," continued Alec. "They went right on living here just as they'd always done, in the houses they could no longer see and on the streets which had vanished, because nobody had noticed a thing. And that's the way they have lived to this very day."

"Hasn't anyone told them?" asked Milo.

"It doesn't do any good," Alec replied, "for they can never see what they're in too much of a hurry to look for."

"Why don't they live in Illusions?" suggested the Humbug. "It's much prettier."

"Many of them do," he answered, walking in the direction of the forest once again, "but it's just as bad to live in a place where what you do see isn't there as it is to live in one where what you don't see is."

"Perhaps someday you can have one city as easy to see as Illusions and as hard to forget as Reality," Milo remarked.

"That will happen only when you bring back Rhyme and Reason," said Alec, smiling, for he had seen right through Milo's plans. "Now let's hurry or we'll miss the evening concert."

They followed him quickly up a flight of steps which couldn't be seen and through a door which didn't exist. In a moment they had left Reality (which is sometimes a hard thing to tell) and stood in a completely different part of the forest.

The sun was dropping slowly from sight, and stripes of purple and orange and crimson and gold piled themselves on top of the distant hills. The last shafts of light waited patiently for a flight of wrens to find their way home, and a group of anxious stars had already taken their places.

"Here we are!" cried Alec, and, with a sweep of his arm, he pointed toward an enormous symphony orchestra. "Isn't it a grand sight?"

There were at least a thousand musicians ranged in a great arc before them. To the left and right were the violins and cellos, whose bows moved in great waves,

Page 119

8. he pointed toward an enormous symphony orchestra.

A modern symphony orchestra averages one hundred musicians, including brass, woodwind, string, and percussion instrumentalists. The evolution of ensembles of this size from smaller-scale groups that we classify today as "chamber orchestras" is attributable to the influence of Beethoven, who brought a new muscularity and grandeur to symphonic composition that called for increased musical firepower. Reinforcing the trend later in the nineteenth century was composer Richard Wagner's ideal of *Gesamtkunstwerk*, or "total artwork." Gustav Mahler's Symphony No. 8 in E-flat major (1906) was dubbed the "Symphony of a Thousand" for the unusually large complement of musicians and singers required to perform it. And Alexander Scriabin conceived his unfinished *Mysterium* (begun in 1903) as a multisensory as well as spiritual extravaganza featuring a large orchestra, a color organ, a massive choir, dancers, incense, and other special effects, to be performed over a period of seven days.

Jason Epstein urged Juster to delete the passage about the mysterious orchestra and its godlike conductor, Chroma, arguing that it contributed little to Milo's story and interrupted the narrative flow. Juster wisely thought otherwise. The Chroma section does stand apart tonally from the rest of the text, with the author for the first and only time venturing headlong into quasi-mystical territory as he spins what amounts to a myth of the origins and wellsprings of color. Still, Juster was right to keep it in. Centrally placed within the tale, this episode, which carries over into the following chapter, is broadly reminiscent of the "Pipers at the Gates of Dawn" chapter in Kenneth Grahame's *The Wind in the Willows*, and it functions similarly as an interlude during which the hero gains a larger perspective that is crucial for navigating the challenges that lie ahead.

Page 120

9. Illustration

Feiffer loosely modeled his portrait of Chroma on Arturo Toscanini (1867–1957), the Italian-born conductor who fled Fascist Italy for New York, where in 1937 he assumed the directorship of the newly created NBC Symphony Orchestra. During his long tenure at NBC, Toscanini reached a vast audience with his fiery yet impeccable brand of musicianship. Much like Albert Einstein, his contemporary from the scientific realm, Toscanini set the popular image of the "musical genius" for an entire generation.

9

and behind them in numberless profusion the piccolos, flutes, clarinets, oboes, bassoons, horns, trumpets, trombones, and tubas were all playing at once. At the very rear, so far away that they could hardly be seen, were the percussion instruments, and lastly, in a long line up one side of a steep slope, were the solemn bass fiddles.

On a high podium in front stood the conductor, a tall, gaunt man with dark deep-set eyes and a thin mouth placed carelessly between his long pointed nose and his long pointed chin. He used no baton, but conducted with large, sweeping movements which seemed to start at his toes and work slowly up through his body and along his slender arms and end finally at the tips of his graceful fingers.

"I don't hear any music," said Milo.

"That's right," said Alec; "you don't listen to this concert—you watch it. Now, pay attention."

As the conductor waved his arms, he molded the air like handfuls of soft clay, and the musicians carefully followed his every direction.

"What are they playing?" asked Tock, looking up inquisitively at Alec.

"The sunset, of course. They play it every evening, about this time."

"They do?" said Milo quizzically.

"Naturally," answered Alec; "and they also play morning, noon, and night, when, of course, it's morning, noon, or night. Why, there wouldn't be any color in the world unless they played it. Each instrument plays a

10

11

Page 121

10. On a high podium in front stood the conductor

Conducting became a discrete musical calling during the nineteenth century as the size of orchestras grew. Prior to then, a senior member of an ensemble, often the principal violinist, might double as the timekeeper during a performance. The musical directors of major orchestras have more than occasionally achieved celebrity status, not least among them the most prominent conductor in New York when *The Phantom Tollbooth* was published, the New York Philharmonic's dashing, young Leonard Bernstein. Known for his wildly gesticulating arms and torso, storm-tossed hair, and perpetually sweaty brow, Bernstein left little doubt, even among skeptics, that conductors did indeed do *something* to earn their salaries.

11. "you don't listen to this concert—you watch it."

The possibility of there being a fundamental correlation between the building blocks of the sound and color spectrums has fascinated philosophers, musicians, artists, and others for a very long time. Speculation along these lines began with the ancient Greek mathematician/philosopher Pythagoras, who hypothesized that the movement of the celestial spheres generated an outpouring of incomparably harmonious musical sounds, a "music of the spheres," that unfortunately lay beyond the ken of human perception.

Intrigued by this notion, Enlightenment thinkers pondered ways to achieve an approximation of the longed-for experience of hearing the celestial music, and hit upon the plan of amplifying the impact of a musical work by pairing it note for note with a display of projected colors. In his *Musurgia Universalis* (1650), the German Jesuit scholar Athanasius Kircher proposed the possibility of establishing precise equivalents between musical tones and the colors of the spectrum. Not long afterward, Sir Isaac Newton, building on the color wheel of his own devising, proceeded to elaborate upon this idea. Then came the earliest instrument, according to artist James Peel, to "attempt a creative synthesis of color and music." In 1725, the French Jesuit scientist Louis-Bernard Castel "conceived of a *clavecin oculaire*, or ocular harpsichord, which he hoped would illuminate the hidden harmonic order thought to exist in the universe. Castel thought of color-music as akin to the lost language of paradise, where all men spoke alike, and he claimed that thanks to his instrument's capacity to paint sounds, even a deaf listener could enjoy music" ("The Scale and the Spectrum," by James Peel, in *Cabinet*, issue 22, Summer 2006).

In late nineteenth-century Europe, color-music organs enjoyed a revival. Inspired by the Impressionists, the British inventors Alexander Rimington and Bainbridge Bishop collaborated on the design and construction of one such instrument. In Germany, Richard Wagner pursued his quest for a *Gesamtkunstwerk*, or sublimely unified, multimedia art, at this time. Wagner in turn inspired Russian composer Alexander Scriabin to write *Prometheus: The Poem of Fire*, a symphony scored for color organ and orchestra. Wassily Kandinsky was among the contemporary painters to associate the colors of his palette with particular musical timbres and emotional resonances.

Closer to our time, the psychedelic music and light shows of the sixties and seventies rock-and-roll era were another attempt at joining color and sound as the two strands of an all-enveloping sensory experience with the power to lift human awareness to a higher plane.

Page 123

12.

Thomas Wilfred at the keyboard of a Clavilux color organ in concerts at the Cleveland Public Auditorium, April 22, 1923 (above), and the Cornish Theater, Seattle, March 5 and 6, 1924 (Manuscripts and Archives, Yale University Library).

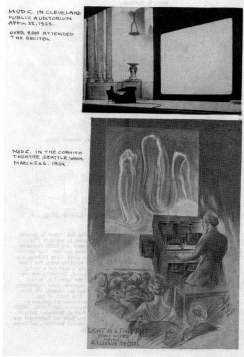

13. "I am Chroma the Great"

Chroma is the Greek word for color. The ancient city-state of Athens, whose citizens prized the arts as much as they did the study of mathematics and philosophy, epitomized the harmonious life of "rhyme and reason" from which the people of Dictionopolis and Digitopolis have both strayed.

different one," he explained, "and depending, of course, on what season it is and how the weather's to be, the conductor chooses his score and directs the day. But watch: the sun has almost set, and in a moment you can ask Chroma himself."

The last colors slowly faded from the western sky, and, as they did, one by one the instruments stopped, until only the bass fiddles, in their somber slow movement, were left to play the night and a single set of silver bells brightened the constellations. The conductor let his arms fall limply at his sides and stood quite still as darkness claimed the forest.

"That was a very beautiful sunset," said Milo, walking to the podium.

"It should be," was the reply; "we've been practicing since the world began." And, reaching down, the speaker picked Milo off the ground and set him on the music stand. "I am Chroma the Great," he continued, gesturing broadly with his hands, "conductor of color, maestro of pigment, and director of the entire spectrum."

"Do you play all day long?" asked Milo when he had introduced himself.

"Ah yes, all day, every day," he sang out, then pirouetted gracefully around the platform. "I rest only at night, and even then *they* play on."

"What would happen if you stopped?" asked Milo, who didn't quite believe that color happened that way.

"See for yourself!" roared Chroma, and he raised both hands high over his head. Immediately the instruments

that were playing stopped, and at once all color vanished. 14
The world looked like an enormous coloring book that 15
had never been used. Everything appeared in simple
black outlines, and it looked as if someone with a set
of paints the size of a house and a brush as wide could
stay happily occupied for years. Then Chroma lowered
his arms. The instruments began again and the color
returned.

"You see what a dull place the world would be without color?" he said, bowing until his chin almost touched the ground. "But what pleasure to lead my violins in a serenade of spring green or hear my trumpets blare out the blue sea and then watch the oboes tint it all in warm yellow sunshine. And rainbows are best of all—and blazing neon signs, and taxicabs with stripes, and the soft, muted tones of a foggy day. We play them all."

As Chroma spoke, Milo sat with his eyes open wide, and Alec, Tock, and the Humbug looked on in wonder.

"Now I really must get some sleep." Chroma yawned. "We've had lightning, fireworks, and parades for the last few nights, and I've had to be up to conduct them. But tonight is sure to be quiet." Then, putting his large hand on Milo's shoulder, he said, "Be a good fellow and watch my orchestra till morning, will you? And be sure to wake me at 5:23 for the sunrise. Good night, good night, good night."

With that he leaped lightly from the podium and, in three long steps, vanished into the forest.

14. and at once all color vanished.
Prior to the late 1960s, most American households that owned a television—by 1955, one out of every two households did—had a black-and-white model. *The Phantom Tollbooth*'s first readers would have had no trouble imagining a world drained of color.

15. The world looked like an enormous coloring book
During the nineteenth century, advances in printing technology made it feasible, for the first time, to print books in color rather than—as had been done for centuries—printing a book's illustrations in black-and-white and then, in some instances, hand-coloring the images page by page, often by means of the *pochoir*, or stencil, method. Books from the earlier period, when sold without the addition of color, were sometimes hand-colored at home, and may thus be considered proto-coloring books of a sort. The first children's book intended expressly to be colored—*The Little Folks' Painting Book*—was issued in 1879 by the enterprising American printer and publisher of juvenile books and games the McLoughlin Brothers. In the company's heyday during the decades that bracketed the turn of the last century, McLoughlin maintained an army of staff illustrators and a vast printing operation that played an important role in the perfection of the color-printing technology of chromolithography.

16. Illustration

This elegant drawing contains a visual pun. To fall silent in musical performance is to "rest."

"That's a good idea," said Tock, making himself comfortable in the grass as the bug grumbled himself quickly to sleep and Alec stretched out in mid-air.

And Milo, full of thoughts and questions, curled up on the pages of tomorrow's music and eagerly awaited the dawn.

16

11. Dischord and Dynne

One by one, the hours passed, and at exactly 5:22 (by Tock's very accurate clock) Milo carefully opened one eye and, in a moment, the other. Everything was still purple, dark blue, and black, yet scarcely a minute remained to the long, quiet night.

He stretched lazily, rubbed his eyelids, scratched his head, and shivered once as a greeting to the early-morning mist.

"I must wake Chroma for the sunrise," he said softly. Then he suddenly wondered what it would be like to lead the orchestra and to color the whole world himself.

The idea whirled through his thoughts until he quickly decided that since it couldn't be very difficult, and since they probably all knew what to do by themselves anyway, and since it did seem a shame to wake anyone so early, and since it might be his only chance

Page 127

1. by Tock's very accurate clock

The degree of accuracy achievable in timekeeping has increased exponentially during the last three centuries. While pre-pendulum mechanical clocks routinely gained or lost half an hour each day, Dutch astronomer Christiaan Huygens's revolutionary mid-seventeenth-century pendulum designs reduced the daily variation to under ten seconds. When King Charles II established the Royal Greenwich Observatory in 1675, he commissioned master London clockmaker Thomas Tompion to build two pendulum clocks of unprecedented precision. Accurate to within seven seconds per day, Tompion's clocks required winding only once a year and provided the timekeeping standard for Britain's maritime trade as well as later for its railroads. In 1721, Tompion's friend George Graham introduced further refinements to the pendulum clock design that yielded accuracy to within one second per day. In 1949, Columbia University physics professor Isidor Rabi built the first working atomic clock— a device that pegged timekeeping to the characteristic vibration of a certain type of molecule. From then onward, advances followed in rapid-fire succession. In 1999, the National Institute of Standards and Technology, in Boulder, Colorado, unveiled its NIST-F1 Cesium Fountain Atomic Clock, a timekeeping apparatus accurate to within one second in every twenty million years.

2. Then he suddenly wondered what it would be like to lead the orchestra

Juster commented: "Milo, impulsively trying to lead the orchestra, is a little like the Sorcerer's Apprentice." When he loses control and then can't stop the changes he has set into motion, the scene briefly becomes a cautionary tale about "the impudent misuse of power." But the happy resolution is equally pointed in its way: "The chaos, and the loss of a week, are the ultimate childhood fantasy of being in charge of the world and escaping disaster" (N.J. Notes I, pp. 42–43).

In the synopsis he prepared for Jason Epstein, Juster writes of this episode (which he refers to as "The Kingdom of Colors"): "where Milo meets Chroma the Great, who composes the world's colors on his magnificent color organ. While there Milo is allowed to try it, with some startling results" (Lilly Library, "Plot Synopsis of Remaining Chapters," box 5, folder 63).

What is striking about this is Juster's decision, for the final version, to recast Milo's experiment in conducting as a matter of his own choosing. Milo is thereby rendered a less passive actor and made wholly responsible for the unintended consequences of his actions.

to try, and since the musicians were already poised and ready, he would—but just for a little while.

And so, as everyone slept peacefully on, Milo stood on tiptoes, raised his arms slowly in front of him, and made the slightest movement possible with the index finger of his right hand. It was now 5:23 A.M.

As if understanding his signal perfectly, a single piccolo played a single note and off in the east a solitary shaft of cool lemon light flicked across the sky. Milo smiled happily and then cautiously crooked his finger again. This time two more piccolos and a flute joined in and three more rays of light danced lightly into view. Then with both hands he made a great circular sweep in the air and watched with delight as all the musicians began to play at once.

The cellos made the hills glow red, and the leaves and grass were tipped with a soft pale green as the violins began their song. Only the bass fiddles rested as the entire orchestra washed the forest in color.

Milo was overjoyed because they were all playing for him, and just the way they should.

"Won't Chroma be surprised?" he thought, signaling the musicians to stop. "I'll wake him now."

But, instead of stopping, they continued to play even louder than before, until each color became more brilliant than he thought possible. Milo shielded his eyes with one hand and waved the other desperately, but the colors continued to grow brighter and brighter and brighter, until an even more curious thing began to happen.

As Milo frantically conducted, the sky changed slowly from blue to tan and then to a rich magenta red. Flurries of light-green snow began to fall, and the leaves on the trees and bushes turned a vivid orange.

All the flowers suddenly appeared black, the gray rocks became a lovely soft chartreuse, and even peacefully sleeping Tock changed from brown to a magnificent ultramarine. Nothing was the color it should have been, and yet, the more he tried to straighten things out, the worse they became.

"I wish I hadn't started," he thought unhappily as a

3

Page 129

3. But, instead of stopping, they continued to play even louder than before

Juster introduces Milo to the "law of unintended consequences," a concept alluded to by economists as far back as John Locke and named by American sociologist Robert K. Merton. In "The Unintended Consequences of Purposive Social Action" (1936), Merton, writing with government policy matters specifically in mind, identified five major sources of unanticipated outcomes to good-faith efforts at rational social planning: ignorance, error, ideological rigidity, willful disregard of the facts, and "self-defeating predictions" (for example, a forecast of famine that spurs changes in agricultural practice that unwittingly increase the chances of famine). Milo here acts out of ignorance, or rather what from a developmental point of view might better be described as the perspective of Jean Piaget's Concrete Operational Stage of cognitive development, when a child is not yet capable of abstract thought and thus unable to foresee the potential consequences of his actions beyond the obvious ones.

4. Illustration

The light beams and otherworldly pose seen in this drawing by Jules Feiffer point to the influence of Rockwell Kent (1882–1971), the American visionary painter, printmaker, illustrator, and author.

In 1927, Kent sketched the logo (pictured below) of the newly renamed, two-year-old publishing firm Random House. The following year, Kent incorporated the same image of a house and walled garden in his colophon-page illustration, depicting the returning hero's home, for the Random House edition of Voltaire's *Candide*.

4

pale-blue blackbird flew by. "There doesn't seem to be any way to stop them."

He tried very hard to do everything just the way Chroma had done, but nothing worked. The musicians played on, faster and faster, and the purple sun raced quickly across the sky. In less than a minute it had set once more in the west and then, without any pause, risen again in the east. The sky was now quite yellow and the grass a charming shade of lavender. Seven times the sun rose and almost as quickly disappeared as the colors kept changing. In just a few minutes a whole week had gone by.

130

At last the exhausted Milo, afraid to call for help and on the verge of tears, dropped his hands to his sides. The orchestra stopped. The colors disappeared, and once again it was night. The time was 5:27 A.M.

"Wake up, everybody! Time for the sunrise!" he shouted with relief, and quickly jumped from the music stand.

"What a marvelous rest," said Chroma, striding to the podium. "I feel as though I'd slept for a week. My, my, I see we're a little late this morning. I'll have to cut my lunch hour short by four minutes."

He tapped for attention, and this time the dawn proceeded perfectly.

"You did a fine job," he said, patting Milo on the head. "Someday I'll let you conduct the orchestra yourself."

Tock wagged his tail proudly, but Milo didn't say a word, and to this day no one knows of the lost week but the few people who happened to be awake at 5:23 on that very strange morning.

"We'd better be getting along," said Tock, whose alarm had begun to ring again, "for there's still a long way to go."

Chroma nodded a fond good-by as they all started back through the forest, and in honor of the visit he made all the wild flowers bloom in a breathtaking display.

"I'm sorry you can't stay longer," said Alec sadly. "There's so much more to see in the Forest of Sight. But I suppose there's a lot to see everywhere, if only you keep your eyes open."

Page 131

5. no one knows of the lost week

In Charles Perrault's classic telling of the story of "Sleeping Beauty" (1697), the eponymous heroine "loses" one hundred years to sleep after a wicked fairy casts a spell of death on her that a good fairy does her best to modify. The latter fairy also exercises her magical powers to put all of Sleeping Beauty's companions at court to sleep for the same long time, so that when the story's heroine is at last awakened by the prince's kiss, she will have missed nothing of the life around her. In contrast, the main point of Washington Irving's humorous short story "Rip Van Winkle" (1819) is to highlight the many world-changing events—the American Revolution, among others—that have transpired during a clueless farmer's epic twenty-year-long nap.

Page 132

6. "It looks like a wagon," cried Milo excitedly.

This moment calls to mind the excitement felt by Mr. Toad, in Kenneth Grahame's *The Wind in the Willows*, when that exuberant traveler first shows off his "gipsy caravan" to Water Rat and Mole.

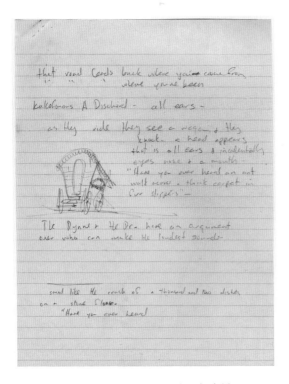

Apart from the endpaper map for which Norton Juster prepared a preliminary sketch, this is the author's only known drawing based on the book (Lilly Library, box 5, folder 34).

They walked for a while, all silent in their thoughts, until they reached the car and Alec drew a fine telescope from his shirt and handed it to Milo.

"Carry this with you on your journey," he said softly, "for there is much worth noticing that often escapes the eye. Through it you can see everything from the tender moss in a sidewalk crack to the glow of the farthest star—and, most important of all, you can see things as they really are, not just as they seem to be. It's my gift to you."

Milo placed the telescope carefully in the glove compartment, and reached up to shake Alec by the hand. Then he stepped on the starter and, with his head full of strange new thoughts, drove out the far end of the forest.

The easy rolling countryside now stretched before them in a series of dips and rises that leaped up one side of each crest and slid gently down the other in a way that made stomachs laugh and faces frown. As they topped the brow of the highest hill, a deep valley appeared ahead. The road, finally making up its mind, plummeted down, as if anxious to renew acquaintance with the sparkling blue stream that flowed below. When they reached the floor of the valley the wind grew stronger as it funneled through the rocks, and directly ahead a bright-colored speck grew larger and larger.

"It looks like a wagon," cried Milo excitedly.

"It *is* a wagon—a carnival wagon," seconded Tock. And that's exactly what it was—parked at the side of the road,

6

painted bright red, and looking quite deserted. On its side in enormous white letters bordered in black was the inscription KAKOFONOUS A. DISCHORD, and below in slightly smaller black letters bordered in white was **DOCTOR OF DISSONANCE**

"Perhaps if someone's at home he might tell us how far we have to go," said Milo, parking next to the wagon.

He tiptoed timidly up the three wooden steps to the door, tapped lightly, and leaped back in fright, for the moment he knocked there was a terrible crash from inside the wagon that sounded as if a whole set of dishes had been dropped from the ceiling onto a hard stone floor. At the same time the door flew open, and from the dark interior a hoarse voice inquired, "Have you ever heard a whole set of dishes dropped from the ceiling onto a hard stone floor?"

Milo, who had tumbled back off the steps, sat up quickly, while Tock and the Humbug rushed from the car to see what had happened.

"Well, have you?" insisted the voice, which was so raspy that it made you want to clear your own throat.

"Not until just now," replied Milo, getting to his feet.

"Ha! I thought not," said the voice happily. "Have you ever heard an ant wearing fur slippers walk across a thick wool carpet?" And, before they could answer, he went on in his strange croaking way: "Well, don't just stand there in the cold; come in, come in. It's lucky you happened by; none of you looks well."

The faint glow of a ceiling lamp dimly illuminated the

7. KAKOFONOUS A. DISCHORD

The author based this shifty character on his childhood doctor, a "loud and gruff [man] with a mustache that made me frightened of men with mustaches for years" (N.J. Notes I, p. 44).

7

wagon as they cautiously stepped inside—Tock first, eager to defend against all dangers; Milo next, frightened but curious; and the Humbug last, ready at any moment to run for his life. 8

"That's right; now let's have a look at you," he said. "T-T-T-T-T-T. Very bad, very bad; a serious case."

The dusty wagon was lined with shelves full of curious boxes and jars of a kind found in old apothecary shops. It 9 looked as though it hadn't been swept out in years. Bits and pieces of equipment lay strewn all over the floor, and at the rear was a heavy wooden table covered with books, bottles, and bric-a-brac. 10

"Have you ever heard a blindfolded octopus unwrap a cellophane-covered bathtub?" he inquired again as the air was filled with a loud, crinkling, snapping sound.

Sitting at the table, busily mixing and measuring, was the man who had invited them in. He was wearing a long white coat with a stethoscope around his neck and a small round mirror attached to his forehead, and the only really noticeable things about him were his tiny mustache and his enormous ears, each of which was fully as large as his head.

"Are you a doctor?" asked Milo, trying to feel as well as possible.

"I am KAKOFONOUS A. DISCHORD, DOCTOR OF DISSONANCE," roared the man, and, as he spoke, several small explosions and a grinding crash were heard.

"What does the 'A' stand for?" stammered the nervous 11 bug, too frightened to move.

8. run for his life.

The origin of this expression is sometimes traced back to 1685, when during the Battle of Sedgemoor a runner in the service of the rebel Duke of Monmouth was captured by the forces of King James II but promised his freedom if he could outrun a horse. The legend records that the runner won his race and that the king's men were as good as their word.

9. of a kind found in old apothecary shops.

The first apothecaries are thought to have set up shop in eighth-century Baghdad.

10. bric-a-brac.

A nineteenth-century term for the grab bag of curios, knickknacks, and other collectibles that tended to clutter Victorian homes. *Bric-a-brac* may derive from the French expression *de bric et de broc*, meaning "by hook or by crook."

11. "What does the 'A' stand for?"

The mad doctor's response is pure Marx Brothers.

Page 136

12. Illustration

Feiffer's Dr. Dischord bears a striking resemblance to Groucho Marx as Dr. Hugo Z. Hackenbush in *A Day at the Races*.

13. "You're suffering from a severe lack of noise."

In the "Final Typed Draft" at the Lilly Library, the following (subsequently deleted) passage comes next:

> "Is it serious?" gasped the Humbug, quickly sitting down and fanning himself.
>
> "SERIOUS," he shouted, leaping from his seat. "Why, if you don't take care of it immediately, in ninety or a hundred years it's sure to be fatal" (Lilly Library, box 3, folder 31).

12

13

"AS LOUD AS POSSIBLE,"

bellowed the doctor, and two screeches and a bump accompanied his response. "Now, step a little closer and stick out your tongues."

"Just as I suspected," he continued, opening a large dusty book and thumbing through the pages. "You're suffering from a severe lack of noise."

He began to jump around the wagon, snatching bottles from the shelves until he had a large assortment in various colors and sizes collected at one end of the table. All were neatly labeled: Loud Cries, Soft Cries, Bangs, Bongs, Smashes, Crashes, Swishes, Swooshes, Snaps and

Crackles, Whistles and Gongs, Squeaks, Squawks, and Miscellaneous Uproar. After pouring a little of each into a large glass beaker, he stirred the mixture thoroughly with a wooden spoon, watching intently as it smoked and steamed and boiled and bubbled.

"Be ready in just a moment," he explained, rubbing his hands.

Milo had never seen such unpleasant-looking medicine and wasn't at all anxious to try any. "Just what kind of a doctor are you?" he asked suspiciously.

"Well, you might say I'm a specialist," said the doctor. "I specialize in noise—all kinds—from the loudest to the softest, and from the slightly annoying to the terribly unpleasant. For instance, have you ever heard a square-wheeled steam roller ride over a street full of hard-boiled eggs?" he asked, and, as he did, all that could be heard were loud crunching sounds.

"But who would want all those terrible noises?" asked Milo, holding his ears. 14

"Everybody does," said the surprised doctor; "they're very popular today. Why, I'm kept so busy I can hardly fill the orders for noise pills, racket lotion, clamor salve, and hubbub tonic. That's all people seem to want these days."

He stirred the beaker of liquid a few more times and then, as the steam cleared, continued:

"Business wasn't always so good. Years ago, everyone wanted pleasant sounds and, except for a few orders during wars and earthquakes, things were very bad. But then the big cities were built and there was a great need for

---

Page 137

14. "But who would want all those terrible noises?" asked Milo, holding his ears.

In his sweeping *The City in History*, architectural historian and critic Lewis Mumford summed up his thoughts on the impact of the myriad sounds to which modern town and city dwellers are routinely exposed: "Today, numerous experiments have established the fact that noise can produce profound physiological changes: music can keep down the bacteria count in milk; and by the same token definite ailments, like stomach ulcers and high blood pressure, seem to be aggravated by the strain of living, say, within sound of a busy motorway or airport" (*The City in History: Its Origins, Its Transformations, and Its Prospects*, New York: Harcourt, Brace, and World, 1961, p. 473).

15. "I'll give it all to the DYNNE for his lunch"

The name DYNNE makes a double play on words as both a homophone of *din* (meaning a confusion of loud, persistent noises) and a rhyming "sight-homophone" of *djinn* (pronounced *gin*), the latter being a variant on the Arabic *jinni* (or *genie*). Like the genies of Arabic folklore, Juster's DYNNE is a shape-shifter capable of concealing himself in a vessel of modest proportions and emerging in full-blown human or other form at his master's command.

In the 2007 musical based on *The Phantom Tollbooth*, by Sheldon Harnick and Arnold Black, Dr. Dischord has three assistants called the Deci-Belles.

honking horns, screeching trains, clanging bells, deafening shouts, piercing shrieks, gurgling drains, and all the rest of those wonderfully unpleasant sounds we use so much of today. Without them people would be very unhappy, so I make sure that they get as much as they want. Why, if you take a little of my medicine every day, you'll never have to hear a beautiful sound again. Here, try some."

"If it's all the same to you, I'd rather not," said the Humbug, backing away to the far corner of the wagon.

"I don't want to be cured of beautiful sounds," insisted Milo.

"Besides," growled Tock, who decided that he didn't much like Dr. Dischord, "there is no such illness as lack of noise."

"Of course not," replied the doctor, pouring himself a small glass of the liquid; "that's what makes it so difficult to cure. I only treat illnesses that don't exist: that way, if I can't cure them, there's no harm done—just one of the precautions of the trade," he concluded, and, seeing that no one was about to take his medicine, he again reached toward the shelf, removed a dark-amber bottle, dusted it carefully, and placed it on the table in front of him.

"Very well, if you want to go all through life suffering from a noise deficiency, I'll give it all to the DYNNE for his lunch," he said, and he uncorked the bottle with a hollow-sounding pop.

For a moment everything was quiet as Milo, Tock, and the Humbug looked intently at the bottle, wondering what Dr. Dischord would do next. Then, very faintly at first, they heard a low rumbling that sounded miles away. It grew louder and louder and louder and closer and closer and closer until it became a deafening, ear-splitting roar that seemed to be coming from inside the tiny bottle. Then, from the bottle, a thick bluish smog spiraled to the ceiling, spread out, and gradually assumed the shape of a thick bluish smog with hands, feet, bright-yellow eyes, and a large frowning mouth. As soon as the smog had gotten completely out of the bottle it grasped the beaker of liquid, tilted back what would have been its head, if it really had one, and drank it all in three gulps.

"A-H-H-H, THAT WAS GOOD, MASTER," he bellowed, shaking the whole wagon. "I thought you'd never let me out. Terribly cramped in there."

"This is my assistant, the awful DYNNE," said Dr. Dischord. "You must forgive his appearance, for he really doesn't have any. You see, he is an orphan whom I raised myself without benefit of governess or any other assistance for——" 16

"No nurse is good nurse," interrupted the DYNNE, doubling up with laughter (if you can imagine a thick bluish smog doubling up with laughter). 17

"For I found him," continued the doctor, ignoring this outburst, "living alone and unwanted in an abandoned soda bottle—without family or relatives——"

"No niece is good niece," roared the DYNNE again, with a laugh that sounded like several sirens going off at once, and he slapped at where his knee should have been.

Page 139

16. **"You must forgive his appearance, for he really doesn't have any."**

First came Illusions, the beguiling (unreal) city of mirrors. Now comes the DYNNE, mystery man of smoke. It speaks well for Milo that he manages not to be distracted for long by smoke or mirrors as he continues on his quest for Rhyme and Reason.

17. **"No nurse is good nurse"**

The first of several clever parodies of the expression "no news is good news," which first appeared in print in British writer and historian James Howell's *Familiar Letters* (June 3, 1640).

18. Illustration

Serendipitously, Feiffer here devised a character from the spirit world who looks quite a lot like a comic-book superhero introduced by Marvel Comics that same fall of 1961, Stan Lee and Jack Kirby's the Thing, member of the Fantastic Four.

19. "No noise is good noise"

Leave it to the Humbug, who, like Carroll's Alice on several occasions, unwittingly makes the most inappropriate—and hostile—remark possible.

18

"And brought him here," continued the exasperated Dischord, "where, despite his lack of shape or features, I trained——"

"No nose is good nose," thundered the DYNNE once again as he collapsed in another fit of hysterics and clutched his sides.

"I trained him as my assistant in the business of concocting and dispensing noise," finished the doctor, mopping his brow with a handkerchief.

19 "No noise is good noise," exclaimed the Humbug happily, trying to catch the spirit of things.

"THAT'S NOT FUNNY AT ALL," sobbed the DYNNE, who went to a corner and sulked.

140

"What is a DYNNE?" asked Milo when he had recovered from the shock of seeing him appear.

"You mean you've never met the awful DYNNE before?" said Dr. Dischord in a surprised tone. "Why, I thought everyone had. When you're playing in your room and making a great amount of noise, what do they tell you to stop?"

"That awful din," admitted Milo.

"When the neighbors are playing their radio too loud, [20] late at night, what do you wish they'd turn down?"

"That awful din," answered Tock.

"When the street on your block is being repaired and the pneumatic drills are working all day, what does everyone complain of?"

"The dreadful row," volunteered the Humbug brightly.

"The dreadful RAUW," cried the anguished DYNNE, "was my grandfather. He perished in the great silence [21] epidemic of 1712."

Milo felt so sorry for the unhappy DYNNE that he gave him his handkerchief, which was immediately covered in bluish smoggy tears.

"Thank you," groaned the DYNNE; "that's very kind. But I certainly can't understand why you don't like noise," he said. "Why, I heard an explosion last week that was so lovely I cried for two days."

The very thought of it upset him so much that he began to sob all over again in a way that sounded almost exactly like a handful of fingernails being scratched across a mile-long blackboard. He buried his head in the doctor's lap.

Page 141

20. "When the neighbors are playing their radio too loud"

In 1931, 12 million of America's 30 million households owned at least one radio. By the end of the decade, an estimated 44 million radios were in use. Television gained in popularity with comparable speed during the 1950s (www.old-time.com/halper).

21. "the great silence epidemic of 1712."

The German people did, as it happens, suffer a major outbreak of influenza in 1712, but as far as anyone knows, silence had nothing to do with it.

Page 142

22. "for noise is the most valuable thing in the world."

While it is unlikely that anyone has ever seriously argued for Dr. Dischord's claim, noise did come to be regarded during the 1970s as a phenomenon to which a market value could and should be assigned under certain circumstances. As excessive urban noise was increasingly recognized as a form of pollution, environmentalists and government regulators invoked the modern economics concept of "externality," making the case that those responsible for creating impactful noise had a legal obligation either to lower the racket or pay a price for not doing so. The city of Portland, Oregon, enacted the first comprehensive noise code in 1975.

"He's very sensitive, isn't he?" asked Milo, trying to comfort the emotional DYNNE.

"It's true," agreed Dr. Dischord. "But he's right, you know, for noise is the most valuable thing in the world."

22

"King Azaz says words are," said Milo.

"NONSENSE," the doctor roared. "Why, when a baby wants food, how does he ask?"

"He screams!" answered the DYNNE, looking up happily.

"And when an automobile wants gas?"

"It chokes!" he shouted again, jumping for joy.

"When a river wants water, what does it do?"

"It creaks!" bellowed the DYNNE as he collapsed into a fit of uncontrolled laughter.

"And what happens when a new day begins?"

"It breaks!" he gasped joyfully from the floor, a look of utter bliss covering his face.

"You see how simple it is," the doctor said to Milo, who didn't see at all. And then, turning to the tear-stained, smiling DYNNE, he remarked, "Isn't it time for you to go?"

"Where to?" asked Milo. "Perhaps we're going the same way."

"I think not," the DYNNE replied, picking up an armful of empty sacks from the table, "for I'm going on my noise collection rounds. You see, once a day I travel throughout the kingdom and collect all the wonderfully horrible and beautifully unpleasant noises that have been made, pack them into my sacks, and bring them back here for the doctor to make his medicines from."

"And a good job he does," said Dr. Dischord, pounding his fist on the table.

"So, wherever the noise is, that's where you'll find me," said the DYNNE with an appreciative smile; "and I must hurry along, for I understand that today there's to be a screech, several loud crashes, and a bit of pandemonium." 23

"And in which direction are you going?" asked the doctor, mixing another brew.

"To Digitopolis," replied Milo.

"How unfortunate," he said as the DYNNE shuffled toward the door; "how very unfortunate, for then you must pass through the Valley of Sound."

"Is that bad?" asked the perpetually worried Humbug.

The DYNNE paused in the doorway with a look of extreme horror on his almost featureless face, and the doctor shuddered in a way that sounded very much like a fast-moving freight train being derailed into a mountain of custard.

"Well you might ask, for you will find out soon enough" was all he would say as he sadly bade them farewell and the DYNNE galloped off on his rounds.

Page 143

23. **"and a bit of pandemonium."**

John Milton coined "Pandemonium" as the name for the capital city of hell in *Paradise Lost*, seat of Satan and the council chamber of evil spirits. Derived from the Greek, *pandemonium* literally means "all demons."

1. not a sound came from his mouth

The Silent Valley, according to Juster, parallels the city of Reality that, because it goes unnoticed by its inhabitants, disappears from view. Likewise in this valley, Juster gives us the "triumph of sound over thought or even the perception of sound itself," another potent image of the world defined by distractions (N.J. Notes I, p. 47).

12. The Silent Valley

"How agreeable and pleasant this valley is," thought Milo as once again they bounced along the highway, with the Humbug humming snatches of old songs, to his own vast amusement, and Tock sniffing contentedly at the wind.

"I really can't see what Dr. Dischord was so concerned about; there certainly couldn't be anything unpleasant along this road." And just as the thought crossed his mind they passed through a heavy stone gateway and everything was very different.

At first it was difficult to tell just what had changed—it all looked the same and it all smelled the same—but, for some reason, nothing sounded the same.

"I wonder what's happened?" said Milo. At least that's what he tried to say, for, although his lips moved, not a sound came from his mouth.

And suddenly he realized what it was, for Tock was no

longer ticking and the Humbug, although happily singing, was doing so in complete silence. The wind no longer rustled the leaves, the car no longer squeaked, and the insects no longer buzzed in the fields. Not the slightest thing could be heard, and it felt as if, in some mysterious way, a switch had been thrown and all the sound in the world had been turned off at the same instant.

The Humbug, suddenly realizing what had happened, leaped to his feet in terror, and Tock worriedly checked to see if he was still keeping time. It was certainly a strange feeling to know that no matter how loudly or softly you chatted or rattled or bumped, it all came out the same way—as nothing.

"How dreadful," thought Milo as he slowed down the car.

The three of them began to talk and shout at once with absolutely no result until, hardly noticing where they were going, they had driven into the midst of a large crowd of people marching along the road. Some of them were singing at the tops of their nonexistent voices and the others were carrying large signs which proclaimed:

"DOWN WITH SILENCE"

"ALL QUIET IS NO DIET"

"IT'S LAUDABLE TO BE AUDIBLE"

"MORE SOUND FOR ALL"

2

Page 145

2. Not the slightest thing could be heard

By 1960, traffic-choked, overcrowded American cities were among the likeliest places on earth to experience this form of sensory overload; the issue that Juster here allegorizes concerned him as an architect and as a student of city planning as well.

Page 146

3. Illustration

Up to this time, Feiffer had drawn only one *Village Voice* strip featuring anything like a protest rally—with comically flat-footed characters like the one depicted here or otherwise. In his strip for January 29, 1958, a lone man in a business suit brandishes a placard whose writing surface has been completely inked out. The accompanying monologue chronicles the sullen man's futile attempts to associate himself with this or that meaningful word or slogan—and the group that would rally around it. Time and again, however, the man's efforts end in failure as another new group comes along to prove the last group's cause to be of no great worth. In the end, the man, his placard broken, finds himself alone as before, and left clinging to the bittersweet pipe dream of one day joining the group whose members are united in their loss of faith in groups.

And one enormous banner stated simply:

"HEAR HERE"

Except for these, and the big brass cannon being pulled along behind, they all looked very much like the residents of any other small valley to which you've never been.

When the car had stopped, one of them held up a placard which said: "WELCOME TO THE VALLEY OF SOUND." And the others cheered as loudly as possible, which was not very loud at all.

"HAVE YOU COME TO HELP US?" asked another, stepping forward with his question.

"PLEASE!" added a third.

Milo tried desperately to say who he was and where he was going, but to no avail. As he did, four more placards announced:

"~~LISTEN~~ LOOK CAREFULLY"

"AND WE"

"WILL TELL YOU"

"OF OUR TERRIBLE MISFORTUNE"

And while two of them held up a large blackboard, a third, writing as fast as he could, explained why there was nothing but quiet in the Valley of Sound.

"At a place in the valley not far from here," he began, "where the echoes used to gather and the winds came to rest, there is a great stone fortress, and in it lives the Soundkeeper, who rules this land. When the old king of Wisdom drove the demons into the distant mountains, he appointed her guardian of all sounds and noises, past, present, and future.

"For years she ruled as a wise and beloved monarch, each morning at sunrise releasing the day's new sounds, to be borne by the winds throughout the kingdom, and each night at moonset gathering in the old sounds, to be catalogued and filed in the vast storage vaults below."

The writer paused for a moment to mop his brow and then, since the blackboard was full, erased it completely and continued anew from the top.

"She was generous to a fault and provided us with all the sound we could possibly use: for singing as we worked, for bubbling pots of stew, for the chop of an ax and the crash of a tree, for the creak of a hinge and the hoot of an owl, for the squish of a shoe in the mud

---

Page 147

4. "sounds, to be catalogued and filed"

The oldest recording of a human voice is thought to be that of a woman singing the French folk song "Au Clair de la Lune." The ten-second clip was recorded on April 9, 1860, using a phonautograph, a device created by French inventor Édouard-Léon Scott de Martinville. The discovery of the recording, which predates that of Thomas Edison singing "Mary Had a Little Lamb" by seventeen years, was announced at a conference of the Association for Recorded Sound Collections, at Stanford University, on March 28, 2008.

Page 148

5. "And, as you know, a sound which is not heard disappears forever and is not to be found again."

This comment alludes to a cluster of concerns that philosophers and scientists have pondered for centuries. The question generally goes something like this: If a tree falls in a forest and no one hears it, did the tree make a sound? The best answer would appear to be yes and no: yes, in the mechanical sense that the event generated sound waves; no, in the subjective, experiential sense that no ear or other receiver, linked to a brain or other perceiving intelligence, was there to capture and interpret the waves. Juster, however, here invokes the old conundrum to highlight the situation of persons who, though physically present, lack presence of mind—the ability to focus their attention sufficiently to savor awareness.

and the friendly tapping of rain on the roof, and for the sweet music of pipes and the sharp snap of winter ice cracking on the ground."

He paused again as a tear of longing rolled from cheek to lip with the sweet-salty taste of an old memory.

"And all these sounds, when once used, would be carefully placed in alphabetical order and neatly kept for future reference. Everyone lived in peace, and the valley flourished as the happy home of sound. But then things began to change.

"Slowly at first, and then in a rush, more people came to settle here and brought with them new ways and new sounds, some very beautiful and some less so. But everyone was so busy with the things that had to be done that they scarcely had time to listen at all. And, as you know, a sound which is not heard disappears forever and is not to be found again.

"People laughed less and grumbled more, sang less and shouted more, and the sounds they made grew louder and uglier. It became difficult to hear even the birds or the breeze, and soon everyone stopped listening for them."

He again cleared the blackboard, as the Humbug choked back a sob, and continued writing.

"The Soundkeeper grew worried and disconsolate. Each day there were fewer sounds to be collected, and most of those were hardly worth keeping. Many people thought it was the weather, and others blamed the moon, but the general consensus of opinion held that the trouble began at the time that Rhyme and Reason were banished. But, no matter what the cause, no one knew what to do.

"Then one day Dr. Dischord appeared in the valley with his wagon of medicines and the bluish smoggy DYNNE. He made a thorough examination and promised to cure everyone of everything; and the Soundkeeper let him try. 6

"He gave several bad-tasting spoonfuls of medicine to every adult and child, and it worked—but not really as expected. For he cured everybody of everything *but* noise. The Soundkeeper became furious. She chased him from the valley forever and then issued the following decree:

"'FROM THIS DAY FORWARD THE VALLEY OF SOUND SHALL BE SILENT. SINCE SOUND IS NO LONGER APPRECIATED, I HEREBY ABOLISH IT. PLEASE RETURN ALL UNUSED AMOUNTS TO THE FORTRESS IMMEDIATELY.'

"And that's the way it has been ever since," he concluded sadly. "There is nothing we can do to change it, and each day new hardships are reported."

A small man, with his arms full of letters and messages, pushed through the crowd and offered them to Milo. Milo took one which read:

Dear Soundkeeper,
    We had a thunderstorm last week and the thunder still hasn't arrived. How long should we wait?

Yours truly,
A friend

---

6. "promised to cure everyone of everything"

The Silent Valley protestor who relates this story to Milo and company here aptly characterizes Dr. Dischord as the kind of charlatan first known in sixteenth-century Britain as a *quacksalver* (hence, our word *quack*), and in the early decades of the American republic as a *medicine man*. The latter term, an unflattering allusion to Native American shamans, came to be associated with the shameless class of itinerant con artists–cum–healers who hawked their nostrums in town after town. To attract a crowd, they typically traveled with a warm-up act of minstrel performers in blackface. Dr. William A. Rockefeller, father of the founder of Standard Oil, was one such humbug in the P. T. Barnum tradition. "I cheat my sons every chance I get," Rockefeller reputedly boasted, to "make 'em sharp" (*QPB Encyclopedia of Word and Phrase Origins*, pp. 595–96).

Page 150

7. "Now do come into the parlor."

Parlor derives from the French *parler*, meaning "to speak." In medieval monasteries, the parlor was the one chamber where monks were free to converse among themselves rather than maintain a studious or prayerful silence. During Victorian times, the word was applied to the showplace of a well-turned-out home—a formal room in which to entertain guests and display the owner's most precious possessions.

8. an enormous radio

An impressive, dark-wood Stromberg-Carlson console radio close both in style and vintage to the one the Justers had in their dining room in Flatbush, Brooklyn (www.antiqueradios.com).

Then he took a telegram which stated:

"BAND CONCERT GREAT SUCCESS STOP WHEN MAY WE EXPECT THE MUSIC STOP"

"Now you see," continued the writer, "why you must help us attack the fortress and free sound."

"What can I do?" wrote Milo.

"You must visit the Soundkeeper and bring from the fortress one sound, no matter how small, with which to load our cannon. For, if we can reach the walls with the slightest noise, they will collapse and free the rest. It won't be easy, for she is hard to deceive, but you must try."

Milo thought for just a moment and then, with a resolute "I shall," volunteered to go.

Within a few minutes he stood bravely at the fortress door. "Knock, knock," he wrote neatly on a piece of paper, which he pushed under the crack. In a moment the great portal swung open, and, as it closed behind him, a gentle voice sang out:

"Right this way; I'm in the parlor."

"Can I talk now?" cried Milo happily, hearing his voice once again.

"Yes, but only in here," she replied softly. "Now do come into the parlor."

Milo walked slowly down the long hallway and into the little room where the Soundkeeper sat listening intently to an enormous radio set, whose switches, dials, knobs, meters, and speaker covered one whole wall, and which at the moment was playing nothing.

"Isn't that lovely?" she sighed. "It's my favorite pro-gram—fifteen minutes of silence—and after that there's a half hour of quiet and then an interlude of lull. Why, did you know that there are almost as many kinds of stillness as there are sounds? But, sadly enough, no one pays any attention to them these days.

"Have you ever heard the wonderful silence just before the dawn?" she inquired. "Or the quiet and calm just as a storm ends? Or perhaps you know the silence when you haven't the answer to a question you've been asked, or the hush of a country road at night, or the expectant pause in a roomful of people when someone is just about

Page 151

9. "It's my favorite program—fifteen minutes of silence"

Fifteen minutes was the standard running time for episodes of the early serialized radio dramas. Silence, however, was the enemy of all radio broadcasters.

Not so composer John Cage, who in 1952 gave the first of many concerts in which he offered his audience an experience of silence, or rather its real-world approximation, as a valid alternative to a more conventional musical performance. Dismissed by some critics as a stunt man and fraud, Cage countered that pure silence did not exist under ordinary circumstances and that the incidental sounds of daily life held untold pleasure for anyone prepared to listen with an open mind. This minimalist—and ultimately mystical—aspect of Cage's concept of music had its art historical counterpart in the all-white and all-black paintings of the composer's contemporaries Robert Rauschenberg, Cy Twombly, and Ad Reinhardt, the impulse for which likewise arose from a desire to free art from artifice and from traditional modes of expression.

10. "But, sadly enough"

In the Lilly Library "Final Typed Draft," this memorable passage reads: "'Why, there are almost as many kinds of stillness as there are sounds, but no one pays any attention to them'"—to which Juster added a concluding "these days" in pencil, thereby further stressing the contrast between the remembered earlier time, when people were far more attuned to sound, and the present day, with its inattentive inhabitants. In a no-longer-extant post-FTD draft, the author continued to refine the passage, splitting it into two sentences and inserting additional text as follows: "'Why, did you know that there are almost as many kinds of stillness as there are sounds? But, sadly enough, no one pays any attention to them these days'" (Lilly Library, box 5, folder 64). The cumulative effect of these changes is to recast the loss at stake as that of a communal heritage rather than merely as one individual's private misfortune.

to speak, or, most beautiful of all, the moment after the door closes and you're all alone in the whole house? Each one is different, you know, and all very beautiful, if you listen carefully."

As she spoke, the thousands of little bells and chimes which covered her from head to toe tinkled softly and, as if in reply, the telephone began to ring, too.

"For someone who loves silence, she certainly talks a great deal," thought Milo.

"At one time I was able to listen to any sound made any place at any time," the Soundkeeper remarked, pointing towards the radio wall, "but now I merely——"

"Pardon me," interrupted Milo as the phone continued to ring, "but aren't you going to answer it?"

"Oh no, not in the middle of the program," she replied, and turned the silence up a little louder.

"But it may be important," insisted Milo.

"Not at all," she assured him; "it's only me. It gets so lonely around here, with no sounds to distribute or collect, that I call myself seven or eight times a day just to see how I am."

"How are you?" he asked politely.

"Not very well, I'm afraid. I seem to have a touch of static," she complained. "But what brings you here? Of course—you've come to tour the vaults. Well, they're usually open to the public only on Mondays from two to four, but since you've traveled so far, we'll have to make an exception. Follow me, please."

She quickly bounced to her feet with a chorus of jingles and chimes and started down the hallway.

"Don't you just love jingles and chimes? I do," she answered quickly. "Besides, they're very convenient, for I'm always getting lost in this big fortress, and all I have to do is listen for them and then I know exactly where I am."

They entered a tiny cagelike elevator and traveled down for fully three quarters of a minute, stopping finally in an immense vault, whose long lines of file drawers and storage bins stretched in all directions from where here began to where there ended, and from floor to ceiling.

"Every sound that's ever been made in history is kept here," said the Soundkeeper, skipping down one of the corridors with Milo in hand. "For instance, look here." She opened one of the drawers and pulled out a small brown envelope. "This is the exact tune George Washington whistled when he crossed the Delaware on that icy night in 1777."

Milo peered into the envelope and, sure enough, that's exactly what was in it. "But why do you collect them all?" he asked as she closed the drawer.

"If we didn't collect them," said the Soundkeeper as they continued to stroll through the vault, "the air would be full of old sounds and noises bouncing around and bumping into things. It would be terribly confusing, because you'd never know whether you were listening to an old one or a new one. Besides, I do like to collect things, and there are more sounds than almost anything else. Why, I have everything here from the buzz of a mosquito a million years ago to what your mother said to

11

12

11. "Every sound that's ever been made in history is kept here"

This phantasmagorical image suggests an affinity between Juster and the Argentine writer Jorge Luis Borges, whose short story "The Library of Babel" first appeared in print in the original Spanish in 1941 and was published in the United States in 1962 in two English-language translations. In this story, Borges imagines the nightmare scenario of a central repository in which every possible combination of printed characters has been collected in book form and stored on shelves in random order. With gibberish and the wisdom of the ages thus residing side by side, the task of finding one's way to the latter is raised to the level of a near impossibility. Juster's Soundkeeper, who takes a more traditional approach to archival organization, has the sense to keep the entire universe of sound in alphabetical order.

12. "Besides, I do like to collect things"

A lifelong pack rat and collector of maps, Juster saved boxloads of draft manuscripts and notes for *The Phantom Tollbooth* and his other books. The author's papers now reside at the Indiana University's Lilly Library, alongside those of Upton Sinclair and Ian Fleming, and the Elizabeth Ball collection of early children's books, among other treasures.

13. "Now where do you think it went?"

Juster commented: "I think almost every child wonders what happens to things after they happen—sounds, events, ideas. Are they gone forever? Lost and irretrievable? Or could they be brought back or are they waiting to be regained? The idea of collecting, organizing, cataloguing, and re-using or re-experiencing sounds seems to intrigue young readers. This is mentioned in many of the letters I receive" (N.J. Notes I, p. 48).

you this morning, and if you come back here in two days, I'll tell you what she said tomorrow. It's really very simple; let me show you. Say a word—any word."

"Hello," said Milo, for that was all he could think of.

"Now where do you think it went?" she asked with a smile.

"I don't know," said Milo, shrugging his shoulders. "I always thought that——"

"Most people do." She hummed, peering down one of the corridors. "Now, let me see: first we find the cabinet with today's sounds. Ah, here it is. Then we look under G for greetings, then under M for Milo, and here it is already in its envelope. So you see, the whole system is quite automatic. It's a shame we hardly use it any more."

"That's wonderful," gasped Milo. "May I have one little sound as a souvenir?"

"Certainly," she said with pride, and then, immediately thinking better of it, added, "not. And don't try to take one, because it's strictly against the rules."

Milo was crestfallen. He had no idea how to steal a sound, even the smallest one, for the Soundkeeper always had at least one eye carefully focused on him.

"Now for a look at the workshops," she cried, whisking him through another door and into a large abandoned laboratory full of old pieces of equipment, all untended and rusting.

"This is where we used to invent the sounds," she said wistfully.

"Do they have to be invented?" asked Milo, who

seemed surprised at almost everything she told him. "I thought they just *were.*"

"No one realizes how much trouble we go through to make them," she complained. "Why, at one time this shop was crowded and busy from morning to night."

"But how do you invent a sound?" Milo inquired.

"Oh, that's very easy," she said. "First you must decide exactly what the sound looks like, for each sound has its own exact shape and size. Then you make some of them here in the shop, and grind each one three times into an invisible powder, and throw a little of each into the air every time you need it." 14

"But I've never seen a sound," Milo insisted.

"You never see them out there," she said, waving her arm in the general direction of everywhere, "except every once in a while on a very cold morning when they freeze. But in here we see them all the time. Here, let me show you."

She picked up a padded stick and struck a nearby bass drum six times. Six large woolly, fluffy cotton balls, each about two feet across, rolled silently out onto the floor.

"You see," she said, putting some of them into a large grinder. "Now listen." And she took a pinch of the invisible powder and threw it into the air with a "BOOM, BOOM, BOOM, BOOM."

"Do you know what a handclap looks like?" 15

Milo shook his head.

"Try it," she commanded.

He clapped his hands once and a single sheet of clean

Page 155

14. "for each sound has its own exact shape and size."

Synesthetes, take note! In the remarkable passage that follows, Juster proposes persuasive visual equivalents for laughter, applause, music, and other familiar sounds, showing that whatever the idiosyncratic wiring of our neurological equipment may or may not have to do with it, a rich sensory life is greatly enhanced by the power to forge metaphorical connections.

15. "Do you know what a handclap looks like?"

The Soundkeeper's puzzling question carries a distant echo of the Zen koan about the sound of one hand clapping. Her matter-of-fact response—and Feiffer's full-page drawing (on the following page)—recalls the festive ticker tape parades that the City of New York has long lavished on heroes from such varied realms as statecraft, space exploration, and sports.

Page 156

16. Illustration

The author's nimble mind at work. Note that item 1e on the list inspired the passage illustrated here (Lilly Library, box 5, folder 34).

SOUND

①

1 - How do sounds look - The soundkeeper explains how the various sounds look & shows them to Milo-
    a - music - Tapestry or lace - some kind of carpets rich & full with the rhythms & weaving melodies woven in.
    b - Drumbeats - wooly & fluffy - cotton balls
    c - laughter - glass bubbles of all sizes and colors
    d - speeches - some light & airy, some sharp, some heavy & shapeless
    e - (hand clap - like sheets of paper (applause - thousands of sheets of paper all fluttering down.

2 - Soundkeeper shows Milo past sounds including what his mother said to him that very morning.

3 - Sound words
pitch	cacophony	polyphony
decibel	noise	
resonance	sonority	
acoustic	audible	
dissonance	tone	

16

white paper fluttered to the floor. He tried it three more times and three more sheets of paper did the very same thing. And then he applauded as fast as he could and a great cascade of papers filled the air.

"Isn't that simple? And it's the same for all sounds. If you think about it, you'll soon know what each one looks like. Take laughter, for instance," she said, laughing brightly, and a thousand tiny brightly colored bubbles flew into the air and popped noiselessly. "Or speech," she continued. "Some of it is light and airy, some sharp and pointed, but most of it, I'm afraid, is just heavy and dull."

"How about music?" asked Milo excitedly.

"Right over here—we weave it on our looms. Symphonies are the large beautiful carpets with all the rhythms and melodies woven in. Concertos are these tapestries, and all the other bolts of cloth are serenades, waltzes, overtures, and rhapsodies. And we also have some of the songs that you often sing," she cried, holding up a handful of brightly colored handkerchiefs.

She stopped for a moment and said sadly, "We even had one section over there that did nothing but put the sound of the ocean into sea shells. This was once such a happy place."

"Then why don't you make sound for everyone now?" he shouted, so eagerly that the Soundkeeper leaped back in surprise.

"Don't shout so, young man! If there's one thing we need more of around here, it's less noise. Now come with me and I'll tell you all about it—and put that down

17. "But——" he started to say

Any word would have served Milo's purpose, but "but"—the contrarian's rhetorical pivot—seems an inspired choice for use in the assault on the Soundkeeper's fortress of stubborn unreason.

immediately!" Her last remark was directed toward Milo's efforts to stuff one of the large drumbeats into his back pocket.

They returned quickly to the parlor, and when the Soundkeeper had settled herself in a chair and carefully tuned the radio to a special hour of hush, Milo asked his question once again, in a somewhat lower voice.

"It doesn't make me happy to hold back the sounds," she began softly, "for if we listen to them carefully they can sometimes tell us things far better than words."

"But if that is so," asked Milo—and he had no doubt that it was—"shouldn't you release them?"

"NEVER!" she cried. "They just use them to make horrible noises which are ugly to see and worse to hear. I leave all that to Dr. Dischord and that awful, awful DYNNE."

"But some noises are good sounds, aren't they?" he insisted.

"That may be true," she replied stubbornly, "but if they won't make the sounds that I like, they won't make any."

"But——" he started to say, and it got no further than that. For while he was about to say that he didn't think that that was quite fair (a thought to which the obstinate Soundkeeper might not have taken kindly) he suddenly discovered the way he would carry his little sound from the fortress. In the instant between saying the word and before it sailed off into the air he had clamped his lips shut—and the "but" was trapped in his mouth, all made but not spoken.

"Well, I mustn't keep you all day," she said impatiently. "Now turn your pockets out so that I can see that you didn't steal anything and you can be on your way."

When he had satisfied the Soundkeeper, he nodded his farewell—for it would have been most impractical to say "Thank you" or "Good afternoon"—and raced out the door.

1. "It's on the tip of my tongue."

The fascinating memory-retrieval phenomenon associated with this expression, which Juster here takes literally to comic effect, has been studied by psychologists for more than forty years but has yet to be satisfactorily explained.

13. Unfortunate Conclusions

With his mouth shut tight, and his feet moving as fast as thoughts could make them, Milo ran all the way back to the car. There was great excitement when he arrived, as Tock raced happily down the road to greet him. The Humbug personally accepted all congratulations from the crowd.

"Where is the sound?" someone hastily scribbled on the blackboard, and they all waited anxiously for the reply.

Milo caught his breath, picked up the chalk, and explained simply, "It's on the tip of my tongue."

Several people excitedly threw their hats into the air, some shouted what would have been a loud hurrah, and the rest pushed the heavy cannon into place. They aimed it directly at the thickest part of the fortress wall and packed it full of gunpowder.

Milo stood on tiptoe, leaned over into the cannon's

mouth, and parted his lips. The small sound dropped silently to the bottom and everything was ready. In another moment the fuse was lit and sputtering.

"I hope no one gets hurt," thought Milo, and, before he had time to think again, an immense cloud of gray and white smoke leaped from the gun and, along with it, so softly that it was hardly heard, came the sound of—

BUT

It flew toward the wall for several seconds in a high, lazy arc and then struck ever so lightly just to the right of the big door. For an instant there was an ominous stillness, quieter and more silent than ever before, as if even the air was holding its breath.

And then, almost immediately, there was a blasting, roaring, thundering smash, followed by a crushing, shattering, bursting crash, as every stone in the fortress came toppling to the ground and the vaults burst open, spilling the sounds of history into the wind.

Every sound that had ever been uttered or made, from way back to when there were none, to way up when there were too many, came hurtling out of the

Page 161

2. Illustration

Study by Jules Feiffer of a "but" shot from a cannon.

In a set of notes headed "Business," Juster recorded his idea for a group of characters to be called "But People. Like butt people. Maybe a goat" (Lilly Library, box 5, folder 34, item 48). This preliminary concept later morphed into the scene played out here.

The author's choice of a word starting with the letter *B* as the one to be fired from the cannon can be said to be linguistically sound. *B*-words are among those that linguists call "plosives"—words starting with a consonant sound that is produced by an interruption of the flow of air in the vocal tract, followed by a sudden burst or release of air.

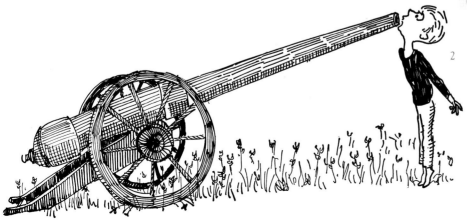

debris in a way that sounded as though everyone in the world was laughing, whistling, shouting, crying, singing, whispering, humming, screaming, coughing, and sneezing, all at the same time. There were bits of old speeches floating about, as well as recited lessons, gunshots from old wars, babies' cries, auto horns, waterfalls, electric fans, galloping horses, and a great deal of everything else.

For a while there was total and deafening confusion and then, almost as quickly as they'd come, all the old sounds disappeared over the hill in search of their new freedom, and things were normal again.

The people quickly went about their busy talkative business and, as the smoke and dust cleared, only Milo, Tock, and the Humbug noticed the Soundkeeper sitting disconsolately on a pile of rubble.

"I'm terribly sorry," said Milo sympathetically as the three of them went to console her.

"But we had to do it," added Tock, sniffing around the ruins.

"What a terrible mess," observed the Humbug, with his knack for saying exactly the wrong thing.

The Soundkeeper looked around with an expression of unrelieved sadness on her unhappy face.

"It will take years to collect all those sounds again," she sobbed, "and even longer to put them back in proper order. But it's all my fault. For you can't improve sound by having only silence. The problem is to use each at the proper time."

As she spoke, the familiar and unmistakable *squinch-squanch, squinch-squanch* of the DYNNE's heavy footsteps could be heard plodding over the hill, and when he finally appeared he was dragging an incredibly large sack behind him.

"Can anyone use these sounds?" he puffed, mopping his forehead. "They all came over the hill at once and none of them are awful enough for me."

The Soundkeeper peered into the sack, and there were all the sounds which had burst from the vaults.

"How nice of you to return them!" she cried happily. "You and the doctor must come by for an evening of beautiful music when my fortress is repaired."

The thought of it so horrified the DYNNE that he excused himself immediately and dashed off down the road in a great panic.

3. "Now remember: they're not for eating, but for listening"

Juster commented: "The nostalgic and nourishing quality of sounds, smells, and other sensory experiences is something we all experience yet we tend to forget or diminish their importance" (N.J. Notes I, p. 48).

"I hope I haven't offended him," she said with some concern.

"He only likes unpleasant sounds," volunteered Tock.

"Ah yes," she sighed; "I keep forgetting that many people do. But I suppose they are necessary, for you'd never really know how pleasant one was unless you knew how unpleasant it wasn't." She paused for a moment, then continued: "If only Rhyme and Reason were here, I'm sure things would improve."

"That's why we're going to rescue them," said Milo proudly.

"What a long, hard journey that will be! You'll need some nourishment," she cried, handing Milo a small brown package, neatly wrapped and tied with string. "Now remember: they're not for eating, but for listening, because you'll often be hungry for sounds as well as food. Here are street noises at night, train whistles a long way off, dry leaves burning, busy department stores, crunching toast, creaking bedsprings, and, of course, all kinds of laughter. There's a little of each, and in far-off lonely places I think you'll be glad to have them."

"I'm sure we will," replied Milo gratefully.

"Just take this road to the sea and turn left," she told them. "You'll soon be in Digitopolis."

And almost before she had finished, they had said good-by and left the valley behind them.

The shore line was peaceful and flat, and the calm sea bumped it playfully along the sandy beach. In the

4. and as soon as he'd said it he leaped from the car, as if stuck by a pin

Here the Humbug becomes the first of the trio literally to "leap to conclusions," with "conclusions" depicted as a barren island. The author recalled: "'Jumping to conclusions' was a phrase that haunted my youth. Teachers, parents seemed to constantly be warning me of the dangers of such a transgression. Doing things, or making up your mind, or giving voice to assumptions without ample thought or evidence was to be avoided at all cost.

"There is a classic story about Calvin Coolidge, who while on a train trip through an open agricultural landscape was looking at a flock of sheep. One of his companions noted that the sheep had been sheared. Coolidge replied thoughtfully, 'Well, at least on this side.'" No jumping to conclusions here! (N.J. Notes I, p. 49).

distance a beautiful island covered with palm trees and flowers beckoned invitingly from the sparkling water.

"Nothing can possibly go wrong now," cried the Humbug happily, and as soon as he'd said it he leaped from the car, as if stuck by a pin, and sailed all the way to the little island. 4

"And we'll have plenty of time," answered Tock, who hadn't noticed that the bug was missing—and he, too, suddenly leaped into the air and disappeared.

"It certainly couldn't be a nicer day," agreed Milo, who was too busy looking at the road to see that the

5. in a split second he was gone also.

In a five-page set of notes for possible characters for the story, Juster considered introducing "the hitch-hiker—who always leads Milo into doing things the easy way. They jump to conclusions together and have a very difficult time getting back. As in all learning he is the hanger-on who wants results without effort" (Lilly Library, box 5, folder 34, item 22).

6. "Can you describe yourself?"

The self-portrait that follows reads like a parody of Walt Whitman's oracular "Song of Myself." While Whitman luxuriates in the opposing tendencies he recognizes within his own compendious nature, this anxious post-Freudian lost soul comes across as a vast bundle of contradictions. His monologue sounds like the captions for a *Feiffer* cartoon. In the accompanying drawing, Feiffer himself dresses the man in a riot of aggressively mismatched patterns and shows him curled up in the fetal position.

5 others had gone. And in a split second he was gone also.

He landed next to Tock and the terrified Humbug on the tiny island, which now looked completely different. Instead of palms and flowers, there were only rocks and the twisted stumps of long-dead trees. It certainly didn't seem like the same place they had seen from the road.

"Pardon me," said Milo to the first man who happened by; "can you tell me where I am?"

"Pardon me," replied the man; "can you tell me *who* I am?"

The man was dressed in a shaggy tweed jacket and knickers with long woolen stockings and a cap that had a peak both front and back, and he seemed as confused as he could be.

"You must know who you are," said Milo impatiently.

"You must know where you are," he replied with equal annoyance.

"Oh dear, this is going to be difficult," Milo whispered to Tock. "I wonder if we can help him."

They conferred for a few minutes and finally the bug 6 looked up and said, "Can you describe yourself?"

"Yes, indeed," the man replied happily. "I'm as tall as can be"—and he grew straight up until all that could be seen of him were his shoes and stockings—"and I'm as short as can be"—and he shrank down to the size of a pebble. "I'm as generous as can be," he said, handing each of them a large red apple, "and I'm as selfish as can be," he snarled, grabbing them back again.

"I'm as strong as can be," he roared, lifting an enormous boulder over his head, "and I'm as weak as can be," he gasped, staggering under the weight of his hat. "I'm as smart as can be," he remarked in twelve different languages, "and I'm as stupid as can be," he admitted, putting both feet in one shoe.

"I'm as graceful as can be," he hummed, balancing on one toe, "and I'm as clumsy as can be," he cried, sticking his thumb in his eye. "I'm as fast as can be," he announced, running around the island twice in no time at all, "and I'm as slow as can be," he complained, waving good-by to a snail. "Is that any help to you?"

Once again they conferred in busy whispers until all three agreed.

"It's really very simple," said the Humbug, twirling his cane.

"If everything you say is true," added Tock.

"Then, without a doubt," Milo concluded brightly, "you must be Canby."

7. "you must be Canby."

Another character from Juster's list that did not make it into the book is Facsimile, the "character who can be just like anything else" (Lilly Library, box 3, folder 1, item 24).

"Of course, yes, of course," the man shouted. "Why didn't I think of that? I'm as happy as can be." Then he quickly sat down, put his head in his hands, and sighed. "But I'm also as sad as can be."

"Now will you tell me where we are?" asked Tock as he looked around the desolate island.

"To be sure," said Canby; "you're on the Island of Conclusions. Make yourself at home. You're apt to be here for some time."

"But how did we get here?" asked Milo, who was still a bit puzzled by being there at all.

"You jumped, of course," explained Canby. "That's the way most everyone gets here. It's really quite simple: every time you decide something without having a good reason, you jump to Conclusions whether you like it or not. It's such an easy trip to make that I've been here hundreds of times."

"But this is such an unpleasant-looking place," Milo remarked.

"Yes, that's true," admitted Canby; "it does look much better from a distance."

As he spoke, at least eight or nine more people sailed onto the island from every direction possible.

"Well, I'm going to jump right back," announced the Humbug, who took two or three practice bends, leaped as far as he could, and landed in a heap two feet away.

"That won't do at all," scolded Canby, helping him to his feet. "You can never jump away from Conclusions. Getting back is not so easy. That's why we're so terribly crowded here."

168

Page 169

8. "But I wouldn't worry too much about it, for you can swim all day"

Juster commented: "Escaping from 'Conclusions' initially gave me great difficulty. But the idea of swimming through the Sea of Knowledge (from which you can emerge totally dry) seemed to be a perfect description of how too many people lead their lives" (N.J. Notes I, pp. 49–50).

That was certainly the truth, for all along the bleak shore and clustered on the rocks for as far as anyone could see were enormous crowds of people, all sadly looking out to sea.

"Isn't there even a boat?" asked Milo, anxious to get on with his trip.

"Oh no," replied Canby, shaking his head. "The only way back is to swim, and that's a very long and a very hard way."

"I don't like to get wet," moaned the unhappy bug, and he shuddered at the thought.

"Neither do they," said Canby sadly. "That's what keeps them here. But I wouldn't worry too much about it, for you can swim all day in the Sea of Knowledge and still

8

9. "But from now on I'm going to have a very good reason"

Milo is developing cognitively, leaving behind Jean Piaget's Concrete Operational Stage, when awareness is largely limited to the impact of one's prior and current experiences, and entering the Formal Operational Stage, when abstract thought and long-term planning add immeasurably to the individual's ability to act purposefully in the real world.

come out completely dry. Most people do. But you must excuse me now. I have to greet the new arrivals. As you know, I'm as friendly as can be."

Over the Humbug's strenuous objections, Milo and Tock decided to swim, and, protesting loudly, the bug was dragged along with them toward the sea.

Canby hurried off to answer more questions, and the last thing he was heard to say was "Pardon me, can you tell me who I am?"

They swam and swam and swam for what seemed like hours, and only Tock's firm encouragement kept Milo struggling through the icy water. At last they reached the shore, thoroughly exhausted and, except for the bug, completely soaked.

"That wasn't bad at all," the Humbug said, straightening his tie and brushing himself off. "I must visit there again."

"I'm sure you will," gasped Milo. "But from now on I'm going to have a very good reason before I make up my mind about anything. You can lose too much time jumping to Conclusions."

The car was just where they'd left it, and in a moment they were on their way again as the road turned away from the sea and began its long climb into the mountains. The warm sun and billowy breezes dried them as they went.

"I hope we reach Digitopolis soon," said Milo, thinking of the breakfast they hadn't eaten. "I wonder how far it is."

14. The Dodecahedron Leads the Way

Up ahead, the road divided into three and, as if in reply to Milo's question, an enormous road sign, pointing in all three directions, stated clearly:

$$D I G I T O P O L I S$$

5	Miles
1,600	Rods
8,800	Yards
26,400	Feet
316,800	Inches
633,600	Half inches

AND THEN SOME

"Let's travel by miles," advised the Humbug; "it's shorter."

"Let's travel by half inches," suggested Milo; "it's quicker."

Page 171

1. The Dodecahedron Leads the Way

In his preliminary notes for the book's characters, Juster envisioned not the Dodecahedron we know but "J. Remington Rhomboid—a two-dimensional character (he has no depth) who is the mathemagician's assistant. As his final reward he becomes three-dimensional." An Oz-like idea! (Lilly Library, box 5, folder 34, item 6).

2. "Let's travel by half inches"

Milo is back to jumping to erroneous conclusions, illustrating the psychological truism that development does not follow an absolutely straight path but more often proceeds by fits and starts.

3. Illustration

As a figurative artist who came of age during the heyday of Abstract Expressionism, Feiffer was bound to feel a bit marginalized. In his depiction of the Dodecahedron, Feiffer here has fun with the very idea of abstraction as he looks back, with tongue in cheek, to the fractured worldview of Cubism.

"But which road should we take?" asked Tock. "It must make a difference."

As they argued, a most peculiar little figure stepped nimbly from behind the sign and approached them, talking all the while. "Yes, indeed; indeed it does; certainly; my, yes; it does make a difference; undoubtedly."

He was constructed (for that's really the only way to describe him) of a large assortment of lines and angles connected together into one solid many-sided shape—somewhat like a cube that's had all its corners cut off and then had all its corners cut off again. Each of the edges was neatly labeled with a small letter, and each of the angles with a large one. He wore a handsome beret on top, and peering intently from one of his several surfaces was a very serious face. Perhaps if you look at the picture you'll know what I mean.

When he reached the car, the figure doffed his cap and recited in a loud clear voice:

3

"My angles are many.
My sides are not few.
I'm the Dodecahedron.
Who are you?"

"What's a Dodecahedron?" inquired Milo, who was barely able to pronounce the strange word.

"See for yourself," he said, turning around slowly. "A Dodecahedron is a mathematical shape with twelve faces."

Just as he said it, eleven other faces appeared, one on each surface, and each one wore a different expression.

"I usually use one at a time," he confided, as all but the smiling one disappeared again. "It saves wear and tear. What are you called?"

"Milo," said Milo.

"That is an odd name," he said, changing his smiling face for a frowning one. "And you only have one face."

"Is that bad?" asked Milo, making sure it was still there.

"You'll soon wear it out using it for everything," replied the Dodecahedron. "Now I have one for smiling, one for laughing, one for crying, one for frowning, one for thinking, one for pouting, and six more besides. Is everyone with one face called a Milo?"

"Oh no," Milo replied; "some are called Henry or George or Robert or John or lots of other things."

"How terribly confusing," he cried. "Everything here is called exactly what it is. The triangles are called triangles, the circles are called circles, and even the same

Page 173

4. "Everything here is called exactly what it is."

The Dodecahedron makes a good case for all things mathematical. Yet as Juster demonstrates in this and subsequent scenes set in Digitopolis, mathematical precision is hardly the same thing as truth or wisdom. Jonathan Swift in *Gulliver's Travels*; William Blake ("Art is the tree of life. Science is the tree of death"); and Friedrich Nietzsche ("Mathematics would certainly have not come into existence if one had known from the beginning that there was in nature no exactly straight line, no actual circle, no absolute magnitude") were outspoken critics of the modern West's worship of quantification and the scientific outlook in general. In 1931, Austrian mathematician and philosopher Kurt Gödel published two "incompleteness theorems" that rocked the scientific world from within by pointing out previously unsuspected limitations in the very foundational structure of mathematics.

Juster had his own perspective on mathematics. "I began," he recalled, "to realize that there must be much humor and whimsy in any discipline that could come up with the idea of negative numbers: how much less than nothing can you get?" (N.J. Notes I, pp. 51–52).

5. "Seventeen!" shouted the Humbug, scribbling furiously on a piece of paper.

In an earlier version of this passage, Juster had Milo, immediately after the Humbug makes this guess, say:

> "Blue," answered Milo to the only part of
> the question he was sure of.
>
> "You'll have to do better than that . . ."

(Lilly Library, box 5, folder 53). The deleted material would seem to be a private reference to Juster's childhood practice of associating numbers with colors.

Harvard researcher Abigail Lipson analyzed this passage for the light it sheds on a range of approaches to problem solving common among mathematics students. According to Lipson, the Humbug's blurted, rapid-fire response typifies that of an inexperienced math student who reacts—whether out of nervousness or a misplaced faith in lightning-strike intuition—as if the most important thing is to answer the teacher's question immediately. She notes that Milo's contrasting hesitation to venture an answer, though expressed in terms of agonizing self-doubt, hints at a more realistic and thus potentially more productive attitude. Were Milo only to realize that a state of confusion was not a sign of personal weakness but rather the necessary starting point of problem solving, he might take courage and focus his powers of reason on the problem at hand. In his attempt to solve the problem, Tock calmly and confidently takes his time—as well a watchdog might—thereby demonstrating his maturity relative to both his traveling companions ("The Road to Digitopolis: Perils of Problem Solving," by Abigail Lipson, in *School Science and Mathematics*, volume 95, October 1995, pp. 282–89).

---

numbers have the same name. Why, can you imagine what would happen if we named all the twos Henry or George or Robert or John or lots of other things? You'd have to say Robert plus John equals four, and if the four's name were Albert, things would be hopeless."

"I never thought of it that way," Milo admitted.

"Then I suggest you begin at once," admonished the Dodecahedron from his admonishing face, "for here in Digitopolis everything is quite precise."

"Then perhaps you can help us decide which road to take," said Milo.

"By all means," he replied happily. "There's nothing to it. If a small car carrying three people at thirty miles an hour for ten minutes along a road five miles long at 11:35 in the morning starts at the same time as three people who have been traveling in a little automobile at twenty miles an hour for fifteen minutes on another road exactly twice as long as one half the distance of the other, while a dog, a bug, and a boy travel an equal distance in the same time or the same distance in an equal time along a third road in mid-October, then which one arrives first and which is the best way to go?"

"Seventeen!" shouted the Humbug, scribbling furiously on a piece of paper.

"Well, I'm not sure, but——" Milo stammered after several minutes of frantic figuring.

"You'll have to do better than that," scolded the Dodecahedron, "or you'll never know how far you've gone or whether or not you've ever gotten there."

"I'm not very good at problems," admitted Milo.

"What a shame," sighed the Dodecahedron. "They're so very useful. Why, did you know that if a beaver two feet long with a tail a foot and a half long can build a dam twelve feet high and six feet wide in two days, all you would need to build Boulder Dam is a beaver sixty-eight feet long with a fifty-one-foot tail?"

"Where would you find a beaver that big?" grumbled the Humbug as his pencil point snapped.

"I'm sure I don't know," he replied, "but if you did, you'd certainly know what to do with him."

"That's absurd," objected Milo, whose head was spinning from all the numbers and questions.

"That may be true," he acknowledged, "but it's completely accurate, and as long as the answer is right, who cares if the question is wrong? If you want sense, you'll have to make it yourself."

"All three roads arrive at the same place at the same time," interrupted Tock, who had patiently been doing the first problem.

"Correct!" shouted the Dodecahedron. "And I'll take you there myself. Now you can see how important problems are. If you hadn't done this one properly, you might have gone the wrong way."

"I can't see where I made my mistake," said the Humbug, frantically rechecking his figures.

"But if all the roads arrive at the same place at the same time, then aren't they all the right way?" asked Milo.

"Certainly not!" he shouted, glaring from his most upset face. "They're all the *wrong* way. Just because

---

6. "as long as the answer is right, who cares if the question is wrong?"

Cooking the books to conceal an unwelcome truth about, say, the financial state of a municipality or corporation, is of course a practice well established among the ranks of number crunchers and their bureaucratic overlords. While numbers don't lie, they can be made to distort reality, whether guilefully or (as in the Dodecahedron's case) through sheer fool-headedness.

Pages 175–176

7. "Just because you have a choice, it doesn't mean that any of them has to be right."

Notwithstanding the ludicrousness of his Boulder Dam example, the Dodecahedron makes an excellent point here that Milo, who during the course of his adventures has grown less self-focused in his approach to problem solving, is now prepared to grasp.

Abigail Lipson observes: "After expending all that problem-solving effort, Milo realizes that all roads lead to Digitopolis. Furthermore, he realizes that 'Which is the right way to go among the three roads?,' 'Which is the right way to go among all possible roads?,' and 'Which roads lead to Digitopolis?' are not necessarily the same question" ("The Road to Digitopolis," *School Science and Mathematics*, volume 95, October 1995, p. 287). As Lipson notes, the Dodecahedron's main point is that effective problem solving requires the ability first to consider a problem in all its varied aspects and then to thread one's way through the maze of hypothetical solutions to the one that achieves one's real-world goal.

you have a choice, it doesn't mean that any of them *has* to be right."

He walked to the sign and quickly spun it around three times. As he did, the three roads vanished and a new one suddenly appeared, heading in the direction that the sign now pointed.

"Is every road five miles from Digitopolis?" asked Milo.

"I'm afraid it has to be," the Dodecahedron replied, leaping onto the back of the car. "It's the only sign we've got."

The new road was quite bumpy and full of stones, and each time they hit one, the Dodecahedron bounced into the air and landed on one of his faces, with a sulk or a smile or a laugh or a frown, depending upon which one it was.

"We'll soon be there," he announced happily, after one of his short flights. "Welcome to the land of numbers."

"It doesn't look very inviting," the bug remarked, for, as they climbed higher and higher, not a tree or a blade of grass could be seen anywhere. Only the rocks remained.

"Is this the place where numbers are made?" asked Milo as the car lurched again, and this time the Dodecahedron sailed off down the mountainside, head over heels and grunt over grimace, until he landed sad side up at what looked like the entrance to a cave.

"They're not made," he replied, as if nothing had

happened. "You have to dig for them. Don't you know anything at all about numbers?"

"Well, I don't think they're very important," snapped Milo, too embarrassed to admit the truth.

"NOT IMPORTANT!" roared the Dodecahedron, turning red with fury. "Could you have tea for two without the two—or three blind mice without the three? Would there be four corners of the earth if there weren't a four? And how would you sail the seven seas without a seven?"

"All I meant was——" began Milo, but the Dodecahedron, overcome with emotion and shouting furiously, carried right on.

"If you had high hopes, how would you know how high they were? And did you know that narrow escapes come in all different widths? Would you travel the whole wide world without ever knowing how wide it was? And how could you do anything at long last," he concluded, waving his arms over his head, "without knowing how long the last was? Why, numbers are the most beautiful and valuable things in the world. Just follow me and I'll show you." He turned on his heel and stalked off into the cave.

"Come along, come along," he shouted from the dark hole. "I can't wait for you all day." And in a moment they'd followed him into the mountain.

It took several minutes for their eyes to become accustomed to the dim light, and during that time strange scratching, scraping, tapping, scuffling noises could be heard all around them.

8. "You have to dig for them. Don't you know anything at all about numbers?"

"If words grew on trees," Juster reasoned as he composed this chapter, "it seemed that numbers must be harder to get at, [that you would have to] dig for them in a mine" (N.J. Notes I, p. 52). The mining metaphor owes something to the author's own unhappy childhood struggles with math. But it also hints at his later appreciation of the power and beauty of mathematics, as brought home to him by an eloquent University of Pennsylvania architecture professor who likened numbers and equations to "jewels" (N.J. Notes I, p. 55).

9. "Could you have tea for two . . . ?"

As raw material for this passage, Juster compiled the following list of number-based idioms:

40 theives [sic]
four flusher
90 like sixty
three blind mice
tea for two
ten pins
four corners of the earth
seven seas (Lilly Library, box 3, folder 44).

Page 178

10. Illustration

At first glance, the miner appears ready to strike. But—as the reader will observe—he is holding his axe with the striking point wrong end to front. Feiffer later attributed this mistake to his chronic nervousness about drawing inanimate objects.

11. Illustration

Jules Feiffer was still in his teens when he produced this accomplished pencil drawing of a man wielding a mallet. Inspired by the superhero comics of the day, the young Feiffer was out to capture action on the page and had not yet developed an interest in the comic possibilities of, say, a man with a paunch (collection of the artist).

10

11

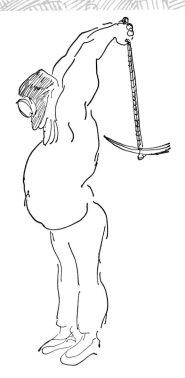

"Put these on," instructed the Dodecahedron, handing each of them a helmet with a flashlight attached to the top.

"Where are we going?" whispered Milo, for it seemed like the kind of place in which you whispered.

"We're here," he replied with a sweeping gesture. "This is the numbers mine."

Milo squinted into the darkness and saw for the first time that they had entered a vast cavern lit only by a soft, eerie glow from the great stalactites which hung ominously from the ceiling. Passages and corridors honeycombed the walls and wound their way from floor to ceiling, up and down the sides of the cave. And, everywhere he looked, Milo saw little men no bigger than himself busy digging and chopping, shoveling and scraping, pulling and tugging carts full of stone from one place to another.

"Right this way," instructed the Dodecahedron, "and watch where you step."

As he spoke, his voice echoed and re-echoed and re-echoed again, mixing its sound with the buzz of activity all around them. Tock trotted along next to Milo, and the Humbug, stepping daintily, followed behind.

"Whose mine is it?" asked Milo, stepping around two of the loaded wagons.

"BY THE FOUR MILLION EIGHT HUNDRED AND TWENTY-SEVEN THOUSAND SIX HUNDRED AND FIFTY-NINE HAIRS ON MY HEAD, IT'S MINE, OF COURSE!" bellowed a voice from across the cavern. And striding toward them came a figure who could only have been the Mathemagician.

He was dressed in a long flowing robe covered entirely with complex mathematical equations and a tall pointed cap that made him look very wise. In his left hand he carried a long staff with a pencil point at one end and a large rubber eraser at the other.

"It's a lovely mine," apologized the Humbug, who was always intimidated by loud noises.

"The biggest number mine in the kingdom," said the Mathemagician proudly.

"Are there any precious stones in it?" asked Milo excitedly.

"PRECIOUS STONES!" he roared, even louder than before. And then he leaned over toward Milo and whispered softly, "By the eight million two hundred and

A full head of hair consists of something closer to 100,000 strands, not counting a beard or a mustache.

13. "But that's a five"

The number five is the third prime number and the fifth Fibonacci number. In most mammals, fingers and toes come in fives. So do the earth's oceans, the books of Moses, the human senses, the rivers of Hades, and the Platonic solids (of which the Dodecahedron is one). The five-pointed star is among the world's most widely used ideograms.

14. an assortment of zeros.

Zero plays two distinctive roles in mathematics, both of them essential to working with numbers. First, zero serves as a placeholder in the accurate expression of numerical values, as in the numbers 206 and 1,004. The introduction into mathematics of a second use of zero, as an integer representing null value, is credited to Indian mathematicians of the ninth century AD. The latter concept—nothingness as a thing in itself—has also proven to be the basis for much philosophical and poetic speculation.

In the pages of notes headed "Business," Juster wrote: "In the land of numbers—use of zeros. Just because a zero equals nothing, don't think you can use them [*sic*] indiscriminately—without serious consequences" (Lilly Library, box 5, folder 34).

15. "We use the broken ones for fractions."

The English word *fraction* derives from the Latin *fractus*, meaning "broken." The concept seems likely to have originated amid the buying and selling in ancient marketplaces.

forty-seven thousand three hundred and twelve threads in my robe, I'll say there are. Look here."

He reached into one of the carts and pulled out a small object, which he polished vigorously on his robe. When he held it up to the light, it sparkled brightly.

13 "But that's a five," objected Milo, for that was certainly what it was.

"Exactly," agreed the Mathemagician; "as valuable a jewel as you'll find anywhere. Look at some of the others."

He scooped up a great handful of stones and poured them into Milo's arms. They included all the numbers 14 from one to nine, and even an assortment of zeros.

"We dig them and polish them right here," volunteered the Dodecahedron, pointing to a group of workers busily employed at the buffing wheels; "and then we send them all over the world. Marvelous, aren't they?"

"They are exceptional," said Tock, who had a special fondness for numbers.

"So that's where they come from," said Milo, looking in awe at the glittering collection of numbers. He returned them to the Dodecahedron as carefully as possible but, as he did, one dropped to the floor with a smash and broke in two. The Humbug winced and Milo looked terribly concerned.

"Oh, don't worry about that," said the Mathemagician 15 as he scooped up the pieces. "We use the broken ones for fractions."

"Haven't you any diamonds or emeralds or rubies?"

asked the bug irritably, for he was quite disappointed in what he'd seen so far.

"Yes, indeed," the Mathemagician replied, leading them to the rear of the cave; "right this way."

There, piled into enormous mounds that reached almost to the ceiling, were not only diamonds and emeralds and rubies but also sapphires, amethysts, topazes, moonstones, and garnets. It was the most amazing mass of wealth that any of them had ever seen.

"They're such a terrible nuisance," sighed the Mathemagician, "and no one can think of what to do with them. So we just keep digging them up and throwing them out. Now," he said, taking a silver whistle from his pocket and blowing it loudly, "let's have some lunch."

And for the first time in his life the astonished bug couldn't think of a thing to say.

1. This Way to Infinity

The English word *infinity* comes from the Latin *infinitas,* meaning "unboundedness." William Blake invoked the concept of the infinite in his critique of what he took to be the excessively materialistic outlook of the Industrial Age. "If the doors of perception were cleansed," the poet admonished, "everything would appear to man as it is, infinite" (from "The Marriage of Heaven and Hell"). Wordsworth, Emerson, and Thoreau wrote eloquently on this same theme, and Juster was influenced by them all.

15. This Way to Infinity

Into the cavern rushed eight of the strongest miners carrying an immense caldron which bubbled and sizzled and sent great clouds of savory steam spiraling slowly to the ceiling. A sweet yet pungent aroma hung in the air and drifted easily from one anxious nose to the other, stopping only long enough to make several mouths water and a few stomachs growl. Milo, Tock, and the Humbug watched eagerly as the rest of the workers put down their tools and gathered around the big pot to help themselves.

"Perhaps you'd care for something to eat?" said the Mathemagician, offering each of them a heaping bowlful.

"Yes, sir," said Milo, who was beside himself with hunger.

"Thank you," added Tock.

The Humbug made no reply, for he was already too

busy eating, and in a moment the three of them had finished absolutely everything they'd been given.

"Please have another portion," said the Mathemagician, filling their bowls once more; and as quickly as they'd finished the first one the second was emptied too.

"Don't stop now," he insisted, serving them again,

and again,

and again,

and again.

"How very strange," thought Milo as he finished his seventh helping. "Each one I eat makes me a little hungrier than the one before."

"Do have some more," suggested the Mathemagician, and they continued to eat just as fast as he filled the plates.

After Milo had eaten nine portions, Tock eleven, and the Humbug, without once stopping to look up, twenty-three, the Mathemagician blew his whistle for a second time and immediately the pot was removed and the miners returned to work.

"U-g-g-g-h-h-h," gasped the bug, suddenly realizing that he was twenty-three times hungrier than when he started, "I think I'm starving."

"Me, too," complained Milo, whose stomach felt as empty as he could ever remember; "and I ate so much."

"Yes, it was delicious, wasn't it?" agreed the pleased Dodecahedron, wiping the gravy from several of his mouths. "It's the specialty of the kingdom—subtraction stew."

2

Page 185

2. "It's the specialty of the kingdom—subtraction stew."

For the 2008 British paperback edition of *The Phantom Tollbooth*, Juster, an enthusiastic home chef, created the recipe for subtraction stew:

Ingredients
4 lbs. (well, maybe 6) of less than nothing
5 lbs. assorted nonexistent ingredients
6 cups (well, maybe 9) of thin air
Less than an iota of something that isn't celery—
    chopped fine
3½ teaspoons of unseasonable seasonings
7 large slices of zilch
½ cup of emptiness
A pinch of zero
A trace of not a darned thing
A large bunch of whatever is not there

How to Make It:
Cut less than nothing into chunks and nonexistent ingredients into small pieces. Put them in a big pot. Add thin air and then all the other ingredients that have been either chopped, mashed, stomped, or forgotten.

Bring to a boil over high heat; cover, turn down, and simmer for just the right time. Taste and if it's not ready, simmer some more for even longer, but be careful not to burn it. Serve in deep bowls so you won't spill any. Garnish with the figment of your imagination.
Yield: 8 Servings

If you have any leftovers, grind them all up and make into a loaf. Bake in a moderate oven.
Yield: 12 Servings

If there is still something left, form into small round croquettes and fry.

Yield: 16 Servings

The dish is particularly good with synonym buns, ragamuffins, and rigmarolls. Careful, if you eat too much you will starve to death.

By the Mathemagician, with sous chef Norton Juster.

"I have more of an appetite than when I began," said Tock, leaning weakly against one of the larger rocks.

"Certainly," replied the Mathemagician; "what did you expect? The more you eat, the hungrier you get. Everyone knows that."

"They do?" said Milo doubtfully. "Then how do you ever get enough?"

"Enough?" he said impatiently. "Here in Digitopolis we have our meals when we're full and eat until we're hungry. That way, when you don't have anything at all, you have more than enough. It's a very economical system. You must have been quite stuffed to have eaten so much."

"It's completely logical," explained the Dodecahedron. "The more you want, the less you get, and the less you get, the more you have. Simple arithmetic, that's all. Suppose you had something and added something to it. What would that make?"

"More," said Milo quickly.

"Quite correct," he nodded. "Now suppose you had something and added nothing to it. What would you have?"

"The same," he answered again, without much conviction.

"Splendid," cried the Dodecahedron. "And suppose you had something and added less than nothing to it. What would you have then?"

"FAMINE!" roared the anguished Humbug, who suddenly realized that that was exactly what he'd eaten twenty-three bowls of.

186

"It's not as bad as all that," said the Dodecahedron from his most sympathetic face. "In a few hours you'll be nice and full again—just in time for dinner."

"Oh dear," said Milo sadly and softly. "I only eat when I'm hungry."

"What a curious idea," said the Mathemagician, raising his staff over his head and scrubbing the rubber end back and forth several times on the ceiling. "The next thing you'll have us believe is that you only sleep when you're tired." And by the time he'd finished the sentence, the cavern, the miners, and the Dodecahedron had vanished, leaving just the four of them standing in the Mathemagician's workshop.

"I often find," he casually explained to his dazed visitors, "that the best way to get from one place to another is to erase everything and begin again. Please make yourself at home."

"Do you always travel that way?" asked Milo as he glanced curiously at the strange circular room, whose sixteen tiny arched windows corresponded exactly to the sixteen points of the compass. Around the entire circumference were numbers from zero to three hundred and sixty, marking the degrees of the circle, and on the floor, walls, tables, chairs, desks, cabinets, and ceiling were labels showing their heights, widths, depths, and distances to and from each other. To one side was a gigantic note pad set on an artist's easel, and from hooks and strings hung a collection of scales, rulers, measures, weights, tapes, and all sorts of other devices for measuring any number of things in every possible way.

Page 187

3. "I often find . . . that the best way to get from one place to another is to erase everything"

The Mathemagician's preferred mode of transportation is not all that different from that of the determined young hero of cartoonist Crockett Johnson's *Harold and the Purple Crayon* (1955).

4. the strange circular room

The Mathemagician occupies a Euclidean geometer—or architect's—dream space, a chamber that doubles as a blueprint or diagram of itself. Juster's description calls to mind the architectural drawings and engravings of such Renaissance masters as Leonardo da Vinci and Jan Vredeman de Vries.

"No indeed," replied the Mathemagician, and this time he raised the sharpened end of his staff, drew a thin straight line in the air, and then walked gracefully across it from one side of the room to the other. "Most of the time I take the shortest distance between any two points. And, of course, when I should be in several places at once," he remarked, writing $7 \times 1 = 7$ carefully on the note pad, "I simply multiply."

Suddenly there were seven Mathemagicians standing side by side, and each one looked exactly like the other.

"How did you do that?" gasped Milo.

"There's nothing to it," they all said in chorus, "if you have a magic staff." Then six of them canceled themselves out and simply disappeared.

"But it's only a big pencil," the Humbug objected, tapping at it with his cane.

"True enough," agreed the Mathemagician; "but once you learn to use it, there's no end to what you can do."

"Can you make things disappear?" asked Milo excitedly.

"Why, certainly," he said, striding over to the easel. "Just step a little closer and watch carefully."

After demonstrating that there was nothing up his sleeves, in his hat, or behind his back, he wrote quickly:

$$4 + 9 - 2 \times 16 + 1 \div 3 \times 6 - 67 + 8 \times 2 - 3 + 26 - 1 \div 34 + 3 \div 7 + 2 - 5 =$$

Then he looked up expectantly.

"Seventeen!" shouted the bug, who always managed to be first with the wrong answer.

"It all comes to zero," corrected Milo.   5

"Precisely," said the Mathemagician, making a very theatrical bow, and the entire line of numbers vanished before their eyes. "Now is there anything else you'd like to see?"

"Yes, please," said Milo. "Can you show me the biggest   6 number there is?"

"I'd be delighted," he replied, opening one of the closet doors. "We keep it right here. It took four miners just to dig it out."

Inside was the biggest **3** Milo had ever seen. It was fully twice as high as the Mathemagician.

"No, that's not what I mean," objected Milo. "Can you show me the longest number there is?"

"Surely," said the Mathemagician, opening another door. "Here it is. It took three carts to carry it here."

Inside this closet was the longest **8** imaginable. It was just about as wide as the three was high.

"No, no, no, that's not what I mean either," said Milo, looking helplessly at Tock.

"I think what you would like to see," said the dog, scratching himself just under half-past four, "is the number of greatest possible magnitude."

Page 189

5. "It all comes to zero," corrected Milo.

This time Milo shows himself to be a confident and patient problem solver, with the degree of concentration needed to follow the mathematical expression through all its twists and turns to the correct answer.

6. "Can you show me the biggest number there is?"

The Phantom Tollbooth had its origins in an impromptu conversation—much like this one—between the author and a child of about Milo's age, about the impossibility of arriving at the "biggest" number. This same realization lies at the core of the concept of infinity. In this scene, Juster also shows that verbal clarity can at times be critical to achieving a desired mathematical result.

7. "Now divide it in half. Now divide it in half again. Now divide it in half again."

Here Juster gives a verbal demonstration of an infinite regress, the phenomenon made visible when, for instance, one positions oneself between two facing mirrors, thereby producing a reflected image that repeats itself, inside itself, endlessly.

"Well, why didn't you say so?" said the Mathemagician, who was busily measuring the edge of a raindrop. "What's the greatest number *you* can think of?"

"Nine trillion, nine hundred ninety-nine billion, nine hundred ninety-nine million, nine hundred ninety-nine thousand, nine hundred ninety-nine," recited Milo breathlessly.

"Very good," said the Mathemagician. "Now add one to it. Now add one again," he repeated when Milo had added the previous one. "Now add one again. Now add one again. Now add one again. Now add one again. Now add one again. Now add one again. Now add——"

"But when can I stop?" pleaded Milo.

"Never," said the Mathemagician with a little smile, "for the number you want is always at least one more than the number you've got, and it's so large that if you started saying it yesterday you wouldn't finish tomorrow."

"Where could you ever find a number so big?" scoffed the Humbug.

"In the same place they have the smallest number there is," he answered helpfully; "and you know what that is."

"Certainly," said the bug, suddenly remembering something to do at the other end of the room.

"One one-millionth?" asked Milo, trying to think of the smallest fraction possible.

"Almost," said the Mathemagician. "Now divide it in half. Now divide it in half again. Now divide it in half again. Now divide it in half again. Now divide it in half again. Now divide it in half again. Now divide——"

"Oh dear," shouted Milo, holding his hands to his ears, "doesn't that ever stop either?"

"How can it," said the Mathemagician, "when you can always take half of whatever you have left until it's so small that if you started to say it right now you'd finish even before you began?"

"Where could you keep anything so tiny?" Milo asked, trying very hard to imagine such a thing.

The Mathemagician stopped what he was doing and explained simply, "Why, in a box that's so small you can't see it—and that's kept in a drawer that's so small you can't see it, in a dresser that's so small you can't see it, in a house that's so small you can't see it, on a street that's so small you can't see it, in a city that's so small you can't see it, which is part of a country that's so small you can't see it, in a world that's so small you can't see it."

Then he sat down, fanned himself with a handkerchief, and continued. "Then, of course, we keep the whole thing in another box that's so small you can't see it—and, if you follow me, I'll show you where to find it."

They walked to one of the small windows and there, tied to the sill, was one end of a line that stretched along the ground and into the distance until completely out of sight.

"Just follow that line forever," said the Mathemagician, "and when you reach the end, turn left. There you'll find the land of Infinity, where the tallest, the shortest, the biggest, the smallest, and the most and the least of everything are kept."

Page 191

8. there, tied to the sill, was one end of a line

In the pages of notes titled "Business," Juster wrote: "an infinitely long line gets loose and panic ensues as they pursue it" (Lilly Library, box 6, folder 34, item 4). In the end, Juster decided it was not necessary to animate the line in order to give readers a vivid sense of the elusive concept of infinity.

9. "Just follow that line forever . . . and when you reach the end, turn left."

In this passage, as in so many others, Juster demonstrates the wisdom of the notion that a game or story that hinges on a playful "reversal of logic" often works better as a teaching device than does a "relentless presentation of sequential facts" (N.J. Notes II, p. 2).

"I really don't have that much time," said Milo anxiously. "Isn't there a quicker way?"

"Well, you might try this flight of stairs," he suggested, opening another door and pointing up. "It goes there, too."

Milo bounded across the room and started up the stairs two at a time. "Wait for me, please," he shouted to Tock and the Humbug. "I'll be gone just a few minutes."

16. A Very Dirty Bird

Up he went—very quickly at first—then more slowly—then in a little while even more slowly than that—and finally, after many minutes of climbing up the endless stairway, one weary foot was barely able to follow the other. Milo suddenly realized that with all his effort he was no closer to the top than when he began, and not a great deal further from the bottom. But he struggled on for a while longer, until at last, completely exhausted, he collapsed onto one of the steps.

"I should have known it," he mumbled, resting his tired legs and filling his lungs with air. "This is just like the line that goes on forever, and I'll never get there."

"You wouldn't like it much anyway," someone replied gently. "Infinity is a dreadfully poor place. They can never manage to make ends meet."

Milo looked up, with his head still resting heavily in his hand; he was becoming quite accustomed to being

---

Page 193

1. "They can never manage to make ends meet."

The expression "to make ends meet" is a compressed version of an older one with the same meaning: "to make both ends of the year meet." According to the *QPB Encyclopedia of Word and Phrase Origins*, Tobias Smollett introduced this saying into literary English in his picaresque novel *The Adventures of Roderick Random* (1748). On entering a public house, Smollett's hero is greeted by the proprietor, who merrily spouts Latin as he offers the gentlemanly new arrival a drink. "In the course of our conversation," reports the narrator, ". . . we understood that this facetious person was a schoolmaster, whose income, being small, was fain to keep a glass of good liquor for the entertainment of passengers, by which he made shift to make the two ends of the year meet" (Google Books, p. 34).

Page 194

2. Illustration

In much of his work—as in this powerful, spare drawing—Feiffer favored a profile view, a tactic that concentrates the viewer's attention on the subject's body language. Here Milo's bent-over posture shows us instantly just how forlorn he feels. Feiffer has also made a virtue of his habitual dislike of background detail. The bareness of the drawing, with its minimalist zigzag line for a staircase, underscores the existential nature of Milo's quest.

3. "It's .58 to be precise"

Postwar social scientists, bureaucrats, and advertising executives reveled in the application of modern statistical analysis to the precise description of demographic groups and societal trends. When government statisticians determined that the average American family had more than two but fewer than three children, satirists jumped on the idea, as Juster does here.

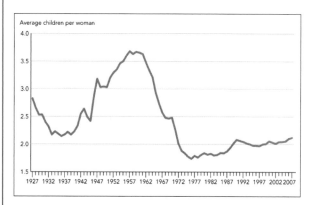

This U.S. government graphic tracks changes in the size of the average American family over several decades.

addressed at the oddest times, in the oddest places, by the oddest people—and this time he was not at all disappointed. Standing next to him on the step was exactly one half of a small child who had been divided neatly from top to bottom.

"Pardon me for staring," said Milo, after he had been staring for some time, "but I've never seen half a child before."

"It's .58 to be precise," replied the child from the left side of his mouth (which happened to be the only side of his mouth).

"I beg your pardon?" said Milo.

"It's .58," he repeated; "it's a little bit *more* than a half."

Page 196

4. "Oh, we're just the average family"

Conformity to the norms of nuclear-family life was one of postwar middle-class American society's most engrossing obsessions.

In *Stuart Little* (1945), E. B. White made light of Americans' quest to produce perfect children. In that story, a typical American couple has a second child who, to all appearances, seems to be a mouse. Published as a chapter book for preteens, White's satirical fantasy was also embraced by a substantial crossover audience of adult readers, presumably including frazzled baby boom–era parents who felt the need for a cathartic laugh.

"Have you always been that way?" asked Milo impatiently, for he felt that that was a needlessly fine distinction.

"My goodness, no," the child assured him. "A few years ago I was just .42 and, believe me, that was terribly inconvenient."

"What is the rest of your family like?" said Milo, this time a bit more sympathetically.

"Oh, we're just the average family," he said thoughtfully; "mother, father, and 2.58 children—and, as I explained, I'm the .58."

"It must be rather odd being only part of a person," Milo remarked.

"Not at all," said the child. "Every average family has 2.58 children, so I always have someone to play with. Besides, each family also has an average of 1.3 automobiles, and since I'm the only one who can drive three tenths of a car, I get to use it all the time."

"But averages aren't real," objected Milo; "they're just imaginary."

"That may be so," he agreed, "but they're also very useful at times. For instance, if you didn't have any money at all, but you happened to be with four other people who had ten dollars apiece, then you'd each have an average of eight dollars. Isn't that right?"

"I guess so," said Milo weakly.

"Well, think how much better off you'd be, just because of averages," he explained convincingly. "And think of the poor farmer when it doesn't rain all year: if there wasn't an average yearly rainfall of 37 inches in this part of the country, all his crops would wither and die."

It all sounded terribly confusing to Milo, for he had always had trouble in school with just this subject.

"There are still other advantages," continued the child. "For instance, if one rat were cornered by nine cats, then, on the average, each cat would be 10 per cent rat and the rat would be 90 per cent cat. If you happened to be a rat, you can see how much nicer it would make things."

"But that can never be," said Milo, jumping to his feet.

"Don't be too sure," said the child patiently, "for one of the nicest things about mathematics, or anything else you might care to learn, is that many of the things which can never be, often are. You see," he went on, "it's very much like your trying to reach Infinity. You know that it's there, but you just don't know where—but just because you can never reach it doesn't mean that it's not worth looking for."

"I hadn't thought of it that way," said Milo, starting down the stairs. "I think I'll go back now."

"A wise decision," the child agreed; "but try again someday—perhaps you'll get much closer." And, as Milo waved good-by, he smiled warmly, which he usually did on the average of 47 times a day.

"Everyone here knows so much more than I do," thought Milo as he leaped from step to step. "I'll have to do a lot better if I'm going to rescue the princesses."

In a few moments he'd reached the bottom again and

5. "Why is it," he said quietly

Here at last Milo is able to articulate the key insights he needs in order to gain mastery over the many confusing aspects of his experiences in the Lands Beyond. Foremost among these is the realization that information and knowledge are not one and the same thing and that conclusions based on false premises cannot possibly yield understanding or wisdom.

burst into the workshop, where Tock and the Humbug were eagerly watching the Mathemagician perform.

"Ah, back already," he cried, greeting him with a friendly wave. "I hope you found what you were looking for."

"I'm afraid not," admitted Milo. And then he added in a very discouraged tone, "Everything in Digitopolis is much too difficult for me."

The Mathemagician nodded knowingly and stroked his chin several times. "You'll find," he remarked gently, "that the only thing you can do easily is be wrong, and that's hardly worth the effort."

Milo tried very hard to understand all the things he'd been told, and all the things he'd seen, and, as he spoke, one curious thing still bothered him. "Why is it," he said quietly, "that quite often even the things which are correct just don't seem to be right?"

A look of deep melancholy crossed the Mathemagician's face and his eyes grew moist with sadness. Everything was silent, and it was several minutes before he was able to reply at all.

"How very true," he sobbed, supporting himself on the staff. "It has been that way since Rhyme and Reason were banished."

"Quite so," began the Humbug. "I personally feel that——"

"AND ALL BECAUSE OF THAT STUBBORN WRETCH AZAZ," roared the Mathemagician, completely overwhelming the bug, for now his sadness had changed to fury and he stalked about the room adding up anger and multiplying wrath. "IT'S ALL HIS FAULT."

"Perhaps if you discussed it with him——" Milo started to say, but never had time to finish.

"He's much too unreasonable," interrupted the Mathemagician again. "Why, just last month I sent him a very friendly letter, which he never had the courtesy to answer. See for yourself."

He handed Milo a copy of the letter, which read:

$$4738 \quad 1919,$$
$$667 \quad 394017 \quad 5841 \quad 62589$$
$$85371 \quad 14 \quad 39588 \quad 7190434 \quad 203$$
$$27689 \quad 57131 \quad 481206.$$
$$5864 \quad 98053,$$
$$62179875073$$

"But maybe he doesn't understand numbers," said Milo, who found it a little difficult to read himself.

"NONSENSE!" bellowed the Mathemagician. "Everyone understands numbers. No matter what language you speak, they always mean the same thing. A seven is a seven anywhere in the world."

"My goodness," thought Milo, "everybody is so terribly sensitive about the things they know best."

"With your permission," said Tock, changing the subject, "we'd like to rescue Rhyme and Reason."

"Has Azaz agreed to it?" the Mathemagician inquired.

"Yes, sir," the dog assured him.

"THEN I DON'T," he thundered again, "for since they've been banished, we've never agreed on anything—

6. "Why, just last month I sent him a very friendly letter"

Juster recalled: "It never occurred to me that the letter (in numbers) that the Mathemagician wrote to Azaz actually had to mean something, since no one in Dictionopolis would be able to read it. I didn't think about it until I began to get mail from puzzled (and sometimes irate) readers who couldn't 'break the code.' Talk about egg on my face" (N.J. Notes II, p. 4).

7. "Then each of you agrees that he will disagree"
Milo outwits the Mathemagician in a flurry of sophistry such as one might ordinarily expect from a dubious character like the Humbug.

and we never will." He emphasized his last remark with a dark and ominous look.

"Never?" asked Milo, with the slightest touch of disbelief in his voice.

"NEVER!" he repeated. "And if you can prove otherwise, you have my permission to go."

"Well," said Milo, who had thought about this problem very carefully ever since leaving Dictionopolis. "Then with whatever Azaz agrees, you disagree."

"Correct," said the Mathemagician with a tolerant smile.

"And with whatever Azaz disagrees, you agree."

"Also correct," yawned the Mathemagician, nonchalantly cleaning his fingernails with the point of his staff.

"Then each of you agrees that he will disagree with whatever each of you agrees with," said Milo triumphantly; "and if you both disagree with the same thing, then aren't you really in agreement?"

"I'VE BEEN TRICKED!" cried the Mathemagician helplessly, for no matter how he figured, it still came out just that way.

"Splendid effort," commented the Humbug jovially; "exactly the way I would have done it myself."

"And now may we go?" added Tock.

The Mathemagician accepted his defeat with grace, nodded weakly, and then drew the three travelers to his side.

"It's a long and dangerous journey," he began softly, and a furrow of concern creased his forehead. "Long before you find them, the demons will know you're there. Watch for them well," he emphasized, "for when they appear, it might be too late."

The Humbug shuddered down to his shoes, and Milo felt the tips of his fingers suddenly grow cold.

"But there is one problem even more serious than that," he whispered ominously.

"What is it?" gasped Milo, who was not sure he really wanted to know.

"I'm afraid I can tell you only when you return. Come along," said the Mathemagician, "and I'll show you the way." And, simply by carrying the three, he transported them all to the very edge of Digitopolis. Behind them lay all the kingdoms of Wisdom, and up ahead a narrow rutted path led toward the mountains and darkness.

"We'll never get the car up that," said Milo unhappily.

"True enough," replied the Mathemagician, "but you can be in Ignorance quick enough without riding all the way; and if you're to be successful, it will have to be step by step."

"But I *would* like to take my gifts," Milo insisted.

"So you shall," announced the Dodecahedron, who appeared from nowhere with his arms full. "Here are your sights, here are your sounds, and here," he said, handing Milo the last of them disdainfully, "are your words."

"And, most important of all," added the Mathemagician, "here is your own magic staff. Use it well and there is nothing it cannot do for you."

He placed in Milo's breast pocket a small gleaming

8. **"I'm afraid I can tell you only when you return."**
    The Mathemagician's words echo almost perfectly those of King Azaz (see page 98), thereby indicating a second matter about which, without realizing it, they are in total agreement.

pencil which, except for the size, was much like his own. Then, with a last word of encouragement, he and the Dodecahedron (who was simultaneously sobbing, frowning, pining, and sighing from four of his saddest faces) made their farewells and watched as the three tiny figures disappeared into the forbidding Mountains of Ignorance.

Almost immediately the light began to fade as the difficult path wandered aimlessly upward, inching forward almost as reluctantly as the trembling Humbug. Tock as usual led the way, sniffing ahead for danger, and Milo, his bag of precious possessions slung over one shoulder, followed silently and resolutely behind.

"Perhaps someone should stay back to guard the way," said the unhappy bug, offering his services; but, since his suggestion was met with silence, he followed glumly along.

The higher they went, the darker it became, though it wasn't the darkness of night, but rather more like a mixture of lurking shadows and evil intentions which oozed from the slimy moss-covered cliffs and blotted out the light. A cruel wind shrieked through the rocks and the air was thick and heavy, as if it had been used several times before.

On they went, higher and higher up the dizzying trail, on one side the sheer stone walls and brutal peaks towering above them, and on the other an endless, limitless, bottomless nothing.

"I can hardly see a thing," said Milo, taking hold of

Page 204

9. a large, unkempt, and exceedingly soiled bird

Juster considered naming this character the "red crested word snatcher." "Takes the words right out of your mouth," he added in a note to himself (Lilly Library, "Demons," box 5, folder 34, item 1).

Elsewhere, Juster commented: "This, of course, is a symphony of taking everything literally, or wrong, or both, and creating total confusion. The Everpresent Wordsnatcher, or dirty bird, is one of those people who don't listen well and take everything you say 'out of context.' Yet how much more fun it is many times to be out of context." The Marx Brothers certainly knew all about shifting contextual gears, as when in *Duck Soup*, Groucho's character, Rufus T. Firefly, shouts: "I've got a good mind to join a club and beat you over the head with it" (p. 116); or in this typically zany exchange between Firefly and Chicolini (Chico):

> FIREFLY: Why should we have a standing army?
>
> CHICOLINI: Because then we save on chairs (*The Marx Brothers: Monkey Business, Duck Soup and A Day at the Races* [filmscripts]. Introduction by Karl French. London and Boston: Faber and Faber, 1993, p. 119).

10. "We're looking for a place to spend the night."

The use of "spend" in this sense predates Chaucer, who wrote: "And thus the longe day in fight they spende" (*OED*, p. 2,956, Geoffrey Chaucer, *The Legend of Good Women*, c. 1385).

Tock's tail as a sticky mist engulfed the moon. "Perhaps we should wait until morning."

"They'll be mourning for you soon enough," came a reply from directly above, and this was followed by a hideous cackling laugh very much like someone choking on a fishbone.

9

Clinging to one of the greasy rocks and blending almost perfectly with it was a large, unkempt, and exceedingly soiled bird who looked more like a dirty floor mop than anything else. He had a sharp, dangerous beak, and the one eye he chose to open stared down maliciously.

10

"I don't think you understand," said Milo timidly as the watchdog growled a warning. "We're looking for a place to spend the night."

"It's not yours to spend," the bird shrieked again, and [11] followed it with the same horrible laugh.

"That doesn't make any sense, you see——" he started to explain.

"Dollars or cents, it's still not yours to spend," the bird replied haughtily.

"But I didn't mean——" insisted Milo.

"Of course you're mean," interrupted the bird, closing the eye that had been open and opening the one that had been closed. "Anyone who'd spend a night that doesn't belong to him is very mean."

"Well, I thought that by——" he tried again desperately.

"That's a different story," interjected the bird a bit more amiably. "If you want to buy, I'm sure I can arrange to sell, but with what you're doing you'll probably end up in a cell anyway."

"That doesn't seem right," said Milo helplessly, for, with the bird taking everything the wrong way, he hardly knew what he was saying.

"Agreed," said the bird, with a sharp click of his beak, "but neither is it left, although if I were you I would have left a long time ago."

"Let me try once more," Milo said in an effort to explain. "In other words——"

"You mean you have other words?" cried the bird happily. "Well, by all means, use them. You're certainly not doing very well with the ones you have now."

"Must you always interrupt like that?" said Tock irritably, for even he was becoming impatient.

11. **"It's not yours to spend"**

The author here shows that being "out of context" can be a learning experience, however unnerving it may seem at first. For Milo, the repeated jolt of being compelled by the Dirty Bird to question his choice of words and their potential for miscommunication proves to be a liberating experience, a chance to "steer," as Juster commented, his "perceptions and reactions— even [his] sense of the possible [beyond] a narrow range of responses: What is 'expected'; What is 'logical'; What is 'true'" (N.J. Notes II, pp. 5–6).

"Naturally," the bird cackled; "it's my job. I take the words right out of your mouth. Haven't we met before? I'm the Everpresent Wordsnatcher, and I'm sure I know your friend the bug." And then he leaned all the way forward and gave a terrible knowing smile.

The Humbug, who was too big to hide and too frightened to move, denied everything.

"Is everyone who lives in Ignorance like you?" asked Milo.

"Much worse," he said longingly. "But I don't live here. I'm from a place very far away called Context." 12

"Don't you think you should be getting back?" suggested the bug, holding one arm up in front of him.

"What a horrible thought." The bird shuddered. "It's such an unpleasant place that I spend almost all my time out of it. Besides, what could be nicer than these grimy mountains?"

"Almost anything," thought Milo as he pulled his collar up. And then he asked the bird, "Are you a demon?"

"I'm afraid not," he replied sadly, as several filthy tears rolled down his beak. "I've tried, but the best I can manage to be is a nuisance," and, before Milo could reply, he flapped his dingy wings and flew off in a cascade of dust and dirt and fuzz.

"Wait!" shouted Milo, who'd thought of many more questions he wanted to ask.

"Thirty-four pounds," shrieked the bird as he disappeared into the fog.

"He was certainly no help," said Milo after they had been walking again for some time.

Page 207

12. "I'm from a place very far away called Context."

Juster commented: "One of the important jobs a writer has (especially a children's book writer) is to help his readers understand that there is more than one way to look at things—some of them improbable and often *out of context*.

"As an example:

> Grown-ups love figures. When you tell them that you have made a new friend, they never ask you any questions about essential matters. They never say to you, 'What does his voice sound like? What games does he love best? Does he collect butterflies?' Instead, they demand: 'How old is he?' 'How many brothers has he?' 'How much does he weigh?' 'How much money does his father make?' Only from these figures do they think they have learned anything about him. If you were to say to the grown-ups: 'I saw a beautiful house made of rosy brick, with geraniums in the windows and doves on the roof,' they would not be able to get any idea of that house at all. You would have to say to them: 'I saw a house that cost $20,000.' Then they would exclaim: 'Oh, what a pretty house that is!'

"That of course is from *The Little Prince* and illustrates how differently adults and children think. Facts and/or information often mean entirely different things to them; and, equally important, kids have less real experience from which to judge the 'importance' of facts. So, $3 \times 4 = 12$ can be no more meaningful and a lot less interesting than 'There's a giant asleep under my bed' or 'The moon is made of green cheese.'"

Page 208

13. Illustration

This drawing looks back to Feiffer's apprenticeship during the late 1940s in Will Eisner's studio, where he assisted in the creation of *The Spirit*. Feiffer's rendering of the Terrible Trivium recalls the creepy Max Scarr (below left), a German banker turned butler (and assassin in disguise), who appears in the April 14, 1946, issue of *The Spirit*, with shades also of two of the saga's creepy cephalopodic villains, the Octopus (various issues between July 14, 1946, and March 18, 1951) and the Squid (below right; January 18, February 15, and April 5, 1942).

© Will Eisner Studios, Inc.

14. a very elegant-looking gentleman.

This stranger proves to be the Terrible Trivium, a demon described by Juster in autobiographical terms as representing "my way of keeping myself from doing what I was supposed to do or what was demanding or difficult" (N.J. Notes II, p. 7). Considering the origins of *The Phantom Tollbooth* as a procrastinatory diversion, it's fitting that this demon should occupy pride of place as the first of the rogues' gallery of demons to be encountered by Milo and his companions.

13

14

"That's why I drove him off," cried the Humbug, fiercely brandishing his cane. "Now let's find the demons."

"That might be sooner than you think," remarked Tock, looking back at the suddenly trembling bug; and the trail turned again and continued to climb.

In a few minutes they'd reached the crest, only to find that beyond it lay another one even higher, and beyond that several more, whose tops were lost in the swirling darkness. For a short stretch the path became broad and flat, and just ahead, leaning comfortably against a dead tree, stood a very elegant-looking gentleman.

He was beautifully dressed in a dark suit with a well-pressed shirt and tie. His shoes were polished, his nails were clean, his hat was well brushed, and a white handkerchief adorned his breast pocket. But his expression was somewhat blank. In fact, it was completely blank, for he had neither eyes, nose, nor mouth.

"Hello, little boy," he said, amiably shaking Milo by the hand. "And how's the faithful dog?" he inquired, giving Tock three or four strong and friendly pats. "And who is this handsome creature?" he asked, tipping his hat to the very pleased Humbug. "I'm so happy to see you all."

"What a pleasant surprise to meet someone so nice," they all thought, "and especially here."

"I wonder if you could spare me a little of your time," he inquired politely, "and help with a few small jobs?"

"Why, of course," said the Humbug cheerfully.

"Gladly," added Tock.

"Yes, indeed," said Milo, who wondered for just a moment how it was possible for someone so agreeable to have a face with no features at all.

"Splendid," he said happily, "for there are just three ¹⁵ tasks. Firstly, I would like to move this pile from here to there," he explained, pointing to an enormous mound of fine sand; "but I'm afraid that all I have are these tiny tweezers." And he gave them to Milo, who immediately began transporting one grain at a time.

"Secondly, I would like to empty this well and fill the other; but I have no bucket, so you'll have to use this

Page 209

15. **"there are just three tasks."**

Here Juster takes up two traditional fairy-tale motifs: the assignment to the hero of a series of seemingly impossible tasks and the structuring of events around the number three. In "Rumpelstiltskin," "Three Billy Goats Gruff," "Cinderella," and many other old stories, an action repeated three times results, finally, in a wished-for outcome. Here, however, repetition leads only to a sense of deepening frustration, the meaning of which is made clear by events in the following chapter.

eye dropper." And he handed it to Tock, who undertook at once to carry one drop at a time from well to well.

"And, lastly, I must have a hole through this cliff, and here is a needle to dig it." The eager Humbug quickly set to work picking at the solid granite wall.

When they had all been safely started, the very pleasant man returned to the tree and, leaning against it once more, continued to stare vacantly down the trail, while Milo, Tock, and the Humbug worked hour after hour——

210

17. Unwelcoming Committee

Page 211

1. The Humbug whistled gaily at his work

The Humbug's surprisingly sensible strategy for passing the time in a trying situation echoes that of Snow White in the eponymous Disney animated film (1937), when the heroine cheerfully urges her animal helpers to "Whistle While You Work" as they tidy up the Seven Dwarfs' cottage. Closer to the time of *The Phantom Tollbooth*'s publication, Broadway theatergoers (and later film audiences as well) were captivated by the Rodgers and Hammerstein show tune "I Whistle a Happy Tune," which highlighted a key moment in the musical *The King and I* (1951), when the new English tutor to the King of Siam's children arrives in court and must assure her own child that their life there will not be as frightening as seems likely at first.

The Humbug whistled gaily at his work, for he was never as happy as when he had a job which required no thinking at all. After what seemed like days, he had dug a hole scarcely large enough for his thumb. Tock shuffled steadily back and forth with the dropper in his teeth, but the full well was still almost as full as when he began, and Milo's new pile of sand was hardly a pile at all.

"How very strange," said Milo, without stopping for a moment. "I've been working steadily all this time, and I don't feel the slightest bit tired or hungry. I could go right on the same way forever."

"Perhaps you will," the man agreed with a yawn (at least it sounded like a yawn).

"Well, I wish I knew how long it was going to take," Milo whispered as the dog went by again.

"Why not use your magic staff and find out?" replied

2. Milo . . . quickly calculated

Even before rescuing Rhyme and Reason, Milo himself applies reason, in the form of basic math, to the solution of a real-world problem.

Tock as clearly as anyone could with an eye dropper in his mouth.

Milo took the shiny pencil from his pocket and quickly calculated that, at the rate they were working, it would take each of them eight hundred and thirty-seven years to finish.

"Pardon me," he said, tugging at the man's sleeve and holding the sheet of figures up for him to see, "but it's going to take eight hundred and thirty-seven years to do these jobs."

"Is that so?" replied the man, without even turning around. "Well, you'd better get on with it then."

"But it hardly seems worthwhile," said Milo softly.

"WORTHWHILE!" the man roared indignantly.

"All I meant was that perhaps it isn't too important," Milo repeated, trying not to be impolite.

"Of course it's not important," he snarled angrily. "I wouldn't have asked you to do it if I thought it was important." And now, as he turned to face them, he didn't seem quite so pleasant.

"Then why bother?" asked Tock, whose alarm suddenly began to ring.

"Because, my young friends," he muttered sourly, "what could be more important than doing unimportant things? If you stop to do enough of them, you'll never get to where you're going." He punctuated his last remark with a villainous laugh.

"Then you must——" gasped Milo.

"Quite correct!" he shrieked triumphantly. "I am the

Terrible Trivium, demon of petty tasks and worthless jobs, ogre of wasted effort, and monster of habit."

The Humbug dropped his needle and stared in disbelief while Milo and Tock began to back away slowly.

"Don't try to leave," he ordered, with a menacing sweep of his arm, "for there's so very much to do, and you still have over eight hundred years to go on the first job."

"But why do only unimportant things?" asked Milo, who suddenly remembered how much time he spent each day doing them.

"Think of all the trouble it saves," the man explained, and his face looked as if he'd be grinning an evil grin—if he could grin at all. "If you only do the easy and useless jobs, you'll never have to worry about the important ones which are so difficult. You just won't have the time. For there's always something to do to keep you from what you really should be doing, and if it weren't for that dreadful magic staff, you'd never know how much time you were wasting."

As he spoke, he tiptoed slowly toward them with his arms outstretched and continued to whisper in a soft, deceitful voice, "Now do come and stay with me. We'll have so much fun together. There are things to fill and things to empty, things to take away and things to bring back, things to pick up and things to put down, and besides all that we have pencils to sharpen, holes to dig, nails to straighten, stamps to lick, and ever so much more. Why, if you stay here, you'll never have to think again—

3

Page 213

3. he tiptoed slowly toward them with his arms outstretched and continued to whisper

The Terrible Trivium goes about his business in much the same way that a hypnotist might, lulling his subjects by limiting the sensory stimulation to which they are exposed while planting suggestions intended for internalization by them as the basis for new habitual behaviors.

The author clearly enjoyed this opportunity to lampoon—and exorcise himself of—a whole world of demons.

Juster's scribbled ideas for the characters who would do their frightful, ludicrous best to trip up Milo and his friends. Some of these demons made it into the story as described or in modified form while others landed on the cutting-room floor (Lilly Library, box 5, folder 34).

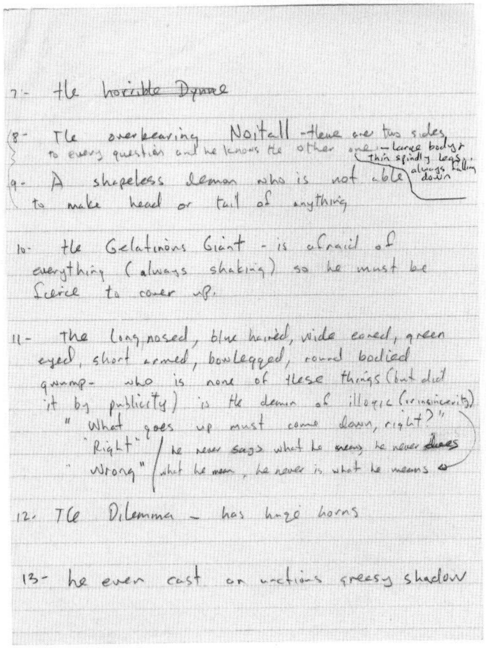

7- the ~~horrible Dynne~~

8- The overbearing Noitall - there are two sides to every question and he knows the other one - large body & thin spindly legs, always falling down

9- A shapeless demon who is not able to make head or tail of anything

10- the Gelatinous Giant - is afraid of everything (always shaking) so he must be fierce to cover up.

11- The long nosed, blue haired, wide eared, green eyed, short armed, bowlegged, round bodied grump - who is none of these things (but did it by publicity) is the demon of illogic (or insincerity)
" What goes up must come down, right?"
"Right" / he never says what he means he never ~~does~~
" Wrong" / what he mean, he never is what he means

12. The Dilemma - has huge horns

13- he even cast an unctious greasy shadow

Page 214

4. what felt very much like a waist-deep pool of peanut butter.

In 1950s and 1960s films and television adventure shows, a hero struggling to survive in a hostile locale was far more apt to land in quicksand than in peanut butter; here Juster is winking at the reader.

and with a little practice you can become a monster of habit, too."

They were all transfixed by the Trivium's soothing voice, but just as he was about to clutch them in his well-manicured fingers a voice cried out, "RUN! RUN!"

Milo, who thought it was Tock, turned suddenly and dashed up the trail.

"RUN! RUN!" it shouted again, and this time Tock thought it was Milo and quickly followed him.

"RUN! RUN!" it urged once more, and now the Humbug, not caring who said it, ran desperately after his two friends, with the Terrible Trivium close behind.

"This way! This way!" the voice called again. They turned in its direction and scrambled up the difficult slippery rocks, sliding back at each step almost as far as they'd gone forward. With a great effort and many helping paws from Tock, they reached the top of the ridge at last, but only two steps ahead of the furious Trivium.

"Over here! Over here!" advised the voice, and without a moment's hesitation they started through a puddle of sticky ooze, which quickly became ankle-deep, then knee-deep, then hip-deep, until finally they were strug-
4 gling along through what felt very much like a waist-deep pool of peanut butter.

The Trivium, who had discovered a mound of pebbles which needed counting, followed no more, but stood at the edge shaking his fist, shouting horrible threats, and promising to rouse every demon in the mountains.

"What a nasty fellow," gasped Milo, who was having great difficulty just getting his legs to move. "I hope I never meet him again."

"I believe he's stopped chasing us," said the bug, looking back over his shoulder.

"It's not what's behind that worries me," remarked Tock as they stepped from the sticky mess, "but what's ahead."

"Keep going straight! Keep going straight!" counseled the voice as they continued to pick their way carefully along the new path.

"Now step up! Now step up!" it recommended, and almost before they knew what had happened, they had all taken a step up and then plunged to the bottom of a deep murky pit.

"But he said *up!*" Milo complained bitterly from where he lay sprawling.

"Well, I hope you didn't expect to get anywhere by listening to me," said the voice gleefully.

"We'll never get out of here," the Humbug moaned, looking at the steep, smooth sides of the pit.

"That is quite an accurate evaluation of the situation," said the voice coldly.

"Then why did you help us at all?" shouted Milo angrily.

"Oh, I'd do as much for anybody," he replied; "bad advice is my specialty. For, as you can plainly see, I'm the long-nosed, green-eyed, curly-haired, wide-mouthed, thick-necked, broad-shouldered, round-bodied, short-armed, bowlegged, big-footed monster—and, if I do say

Page 215

5. "For, as you can plainly see"

In his notes about demons, Juster sketched this talkative, self-satisfied character as follows: "the long nosed, blue haired, wide eared, green eyed, short armed, bow legged, round bodied Gwump, who is none of these things (but [does] it all by publicity). . . . The demon of illogic (or insincerity). He never says what he means, he never does what he means, he never is what he means" (Lilly Library, box 5, folder 34, item 11).

Page 216

6. but Milo . . . reached for his telescope

Juster once again presents concrete evidence of Milo's having attained Jean Piaget's Formal Operations Stage of cognitive development. In this stage, young people become capable of thinking like real scientists as they methodically put their prior expectations to the test of experience while holding their mind open to the possibility of reaching conclusions at variance with those proposed by others.

so myself, one of the most frightening fiends in this whole wild wilderness. With me here, you wouldn't dare try to escape." And, with that, he shuffled to the edge of the pit and leered down at his helpless prisoners.

Tock and the Humbug turned away in fright, but Milo, who had learned by now that people are not always what they say they are, reached for his telescope and took a long look for himself. And there at the rim of the hole, instead of what he'd expected, stood a small furry creature with very worried eyes and a rather sheepish grin.

"Why, you're not long-nosed, green-eyed, curly-haired, wide-mouthed, thick-necked, broad-shouldered,

round-bodied, short-armed, bowlegged, or big-footed—and you're not at all frightening," said Milo indignantly. "What kind of a demon are you?"

The little creature, who seemed stunned at being found out, leaped back out of sight and began to whimper softly.

"I'm the demon of insincerity," he sobbed. "I don't mean what I say, I don't mean what I do, and I don't mean what I am. Most people who believe what I tell them go the wrong way, and stay there, but you and your awful telescope have spoiled everything. I'm going home." And, crying hysterically, he stamped off in a huff.

"It certainly pays to have a good look at things," observed Milo as he wrapped up the telescope with great care.

"Now all we have to do is climb out," said Tock, placing his front paws as high on the wall as he could. "Here, hop up on my back."

Milo climbed onto the dog's shoulders. Then the bug crawled up both of them and, by standing on Milo's head, just managed to hook his cane on the root of an old gnarled tree. With loud complaints he hung on doggedly until the other two had climbed out over him and pulled him up, somewhat dazed and discouraged.

"I'll lead the way for a while," he said, brushing himself off. "Follow me and we'll stay out of trouble."

He guided them along one of five narrow ledges, all of which led to a grooved and rutted plateau. They stopped for a moment to rest and make plans, but before

7. **And, crying hysterically**
   The demon's crybaby behavior further highlights Milo's newfound maturity.

Page 218

8. Illustration

Feiffer enjoyed capturing the Rube Goldberg–like precariousness and well-timed precision of the companions' balancing act.

they had done either the whole mountain trembled violently and, with a sudden lurch, rose high into the air, carrying them along with it. For, quite accidentally, they had stepped into the callused hand of the Gelatinous Giant.

"AND WHAT HAVE WE HERE!" he roared, looking curiously at the tiny figures huddled in his palm—and licking his lips.

He was an incredible size even sitting down, with long unkempt hair, bulging eyes, and a shape hardly worth speaking of. He looked, in fact, very much like a colossal bowl of jelly, without the bowl.

"HOW DARE YOU DISTURB MY NAP!" he bellowed furiously, and the force of his hot breath tumbled them over in his hand.

"We're terribly sorry," said Milo meekly, when he'd untangled himself, "but you looked just like part of the mountain."

"Naturally," the giant replied in a more normal voice (but even this was like an explosion). "I have no shape of my own, so I try to be just like whatever I'm near. In the mountains I'm a lofty peak, on the beach a broad sand bar, in the forest a towering oak, and sometimes in the city I'm a very handsome twelve-story apartment house. I just hate to be conspicuous; it's really not safe, you know." Then he looked at them again with hungry eyes and wondered how well they'd taste.

"You look much too big to be afraid of anything," said Milo quickly, for the giant had already begun to open his mouth wide.

Page 220

9. Illustration

Feiffer's Giant does indeed look "just like part of the mountain." With his big feet, saucer eyes, and unkempt hair, he might be taken as well for a slightly older relative of the Wild Things that Maurice Sendak created for his most famous picture book two years later.

10. Illustration

Study by Jules Feiffer of the Gelatinous Giant.

9
10

"I'm not," he said, with a slight shiver that ran all over his gelatinous body. "I'm afraid of everything. 11 That's why I'm so ferocious. If the others found out, I'd just die. Now do be quiet while I eat my breakfast." He raised his hand toward his gaping mouth and the Humbug shut his eyes tightly and clasped both hands over his head.

"Then aren't you really a fearful demon?" Milo asked desperately, on the assumption that the giant had been brought up well enough not to talk with a mouthful.

"Well, approximately yes," he replied, lowering his 12 arm to the vast relief of the bug: "that is, comparatively no. What I mean is, relatively maybe—in other words, roughly perhaps. What does everyone else think? There, you see," he said peevishly; "I'm even afraid to make a positive statement. So please stop asking questions before I lose my appetite altogether." Then he raised his arm again and prepared to swallow the three of them in one gulp.

"Why don't you help us rescue Rhyme and Reason? Then maybe things will get better," shouted Milo again, this time almost too late, for in another instant they would have all been gone.

"Oh, I wouldn't do that," said the giant thoughtfully, lowering his arm once more. "I mean, why not leave well enough alone? That is, it'll never work. I wouldn't take a chance. In other words, let's keep things as they are—changes are so frightening." As he spoke he began to look a bit ill. "Maybe I'll just eat one of you," he

Page 221

11. "I'm afraid of everything."

Of this demon, Juster commented: "I guess [he is] my Cowardly Lion without any redeeming traits. I think it was my desire to be invisible in school—and often [later] in life [as well]" (N.J. Notes II, p. 8).

12. "Well, approximately yes,"

The author made good use of this list, using four of the seven words in a single paragraph (Lilly Library, box 5, folder 34).

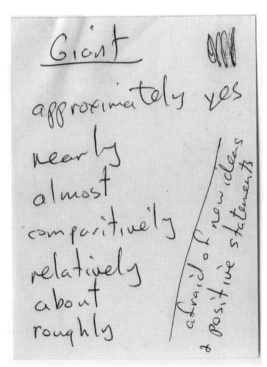

Page 222

13. "I have a box full of all the ideas in the world"

Not quite: King Azaz gave Milo a box filled with words. But in light of the developmental changes evidenced in Milo's recent actions, the boy clearly is far better equipped than before to use those words "well and in the right places," as the King had admonished him to do (p. 99).

14. who began to shake like an enormous pudding.

Some characters about whom Juster made notes did not end up in the book. One who didn't make the final cut was the Chocolate Moose, a creature "always afraid that he is not light enough or that he will be eaten before dessert" (Lilly Library, box 5, folder 34, "King Azaz" [and other characters listed], page 4, item 14). Juster appears to have put the essence of his idea for that character into the simile in this passage.

remarked unhappily, "and save the rest for later. I don't feel very well."

"I have a better idea," said Milo.

"You do?" interrupted the giant, losing any desire to eat at all. "If it's one thing I can't swallow, it's ideas: they're so hard to digest."

13 "I have a box full of all the ideas in the world," said Milo, proudly holding up the gift King Azaz had given him.

14 The thought of it terrified the giant, who began to shake like an enormous pudding.

"PUT ME DOWN AND JUST GO AWAY," he pleaded, forgetting for a moment who had hold of whom; "AND PLEASE DON'T OPEN THAT BOX!"

In another moment he'd set them down on the next jagged peak and, with panic in his eyes, lumbered off to warn the others of this terrible new threat.

But news travels quickly. The Wordsnatcher, the Trivium, and the long-nosed, green-eyed, curly-haired, wide-mouthed, thick-necked, broad-shouldered, round-bodied, short-armed, bowlegged, big-footed monster had already spread the alarm throughout the evil, unenlightened mountains.

And out the demons came—from every cave and crevice, through every fissure and crack, from under the rocks and up from the mud, stomping and shuffling, slithering and sliding, through the murky shadows. And all had only one thought in mind: destroy the intruders and protect Ignorance.

From where they stood, Milo, Tock, and the Humbug

could see them moving steadily forward, still far away but coming quickly. On all sides the cliffs were alive with this evil collection of crawling, looming, creeping, lurching shapes. Some could be seen plainly, others were but dim silhouettes, and yet still more, only now beginning to stir from their foul places, would be along much sooner than they were wanted.

"We'd better hurry," barked Tock, "or they're sure to catch us." And he started up the trail again.

Milo took one deep breath and did the same; and the bug, now that he knew what lay behind, ran ahead with renewed enthusiasm.

18. Castle in the Air

Higher and higher they climbed, in search of the castle and the two banished princesses—from one crest to the next, from jagged rock to jagged rock, up frightful crumbling cliffs and along desperately narrow ledges where a single misstep meant only good-by. An ominous silence dropped like a curtain around them and, except for the scuffling of their frantic footsteps, there wasn't a sound. The world that Milo knew was a million thoughts away, and the demons—the demons were *there* in the distance.

"They're gaining!" shouted the Humbug, wishing he'd never looked back.

"But there it is!" cried Milo at the same instant, for straight ahead, climbing up from atop the highest peak, was a spidery spiral stair, and at the other end stood the Castle in the Air.

Page 225

1. Illustration

This illustration is unique within the book as a technical experiment in the controlled application of splattered ink. Feiffer anticipated by several years the use of this technique by two English illustrators who later became closely associated with it, Gerald Scarfe and Ralph Steadman.

1

"I see it, I see it," said the happy bug as they struggled up the twisting mountain trail. But what he didn't see was that, curled up right in front of the first step, was a little round man in a frock coat, sleeping peacefully on a very large and well-worn ledger.

A long quill pen sat precariously behind his ear, there were ink stains all over his hands and face as well as his clothing, and he wore a pair of the thickest eyeglasses that Milo had ever seen.

"Be very careful," whispered Tock when they'd finally reached the top, and the Humbug stepped gingerly around and started up the stairs.

"NAMES?" the little man called out briskly, just as the startled bug reached the first step. He sat up quickly,

Page 226

2. "I'm the official Senses Taker"

The enumeration of this Kafkaesque taskmaster's list of absurd demands points up the stifling consequences of bureaucratic procedure run amok. The Senses Taker, Juster commented, is "the demon of welcome distractions and endless tasks and chores" (N.J. Notes II, p. 7).

3.

Norton Juster compiled this list of idioms—ninety in all—with seemingly nothing in common except that each somehow caught his fancy as promising story material. The author may have given the fastidious Senses Taker a hint of his own compulsive personality, but without the ability to see the humor in it (Lilly Library, box 5, folder 34).

```
1.  Drop in
2.  hit the jackpot.
3.  all sewed up.
4.  over a barrel
5.  in a pigs ear.
6.  all there
7.  upset the applecart
8.  tied to apron strings
9.  the long arm of the law
10. acid test
11. all at sea
12. put all one's eggs in one basket
13. an axe to grind
14. bad egg
15. his bark is worse then his bite.
16. beat a dead horse
17. a bee in ones bonnet
18. ants in your pants
19. bite someone's head off
20. the bitter end
21. black sheep
22. once in a blue moon
23. bone to pick
```

pulled the book out from under him, put on a green eye-shade, and waited with his pen poised in the air.

"Well, I——" stammered the bug.

"NAMES?" he cried again, and as he did he opened the book to page 512 and began to write furiously. The quill made horrible scratching noises, and the point, which was continually catching in the paper, flicked tiny inkblots all over him. As they called out their names, he noted them carefully in alphabetical order.

"Splendid, splendid, splendid," he muttered to himself. "I haven't had an M in ages."

"What do you want our names for?" asked Milo, looking anxiously over his shoulder. "We're in a bit of a hurry."

"Oh, this won't take a minute," the man assured them. "I'm the official Senses Taker, and I must have some information before I can take your senses. Now, if you'll just tell me when you were born, where you were born, why you were born, how old you are now, how old you were then, how old you'll be in a little while, your mother's name, your father's name, your aunt's name, your uncle's name, your cousin's name, where you live, how long you've lived there, the schools you've attended, the schools you haven't attended, your hobbies, your telephone number, your shoe size, shirt size, collar size, hat size, and the names and addresses of six people who can verify all this information, we'll get started. One at a time, please; stand in line; and no pushing, no talking, no peeking."

The Humbug, who had difficulty remembering anything, went first. The little man leisurely recorded each answer in five different places, pausing often to polish his glasses, clear his throat, straighten his tie, and blow his nose. He managed also to cover the distressed bug from head to foot in ink.

"NEXT!" he announced very officially.

"I do wish he'd hurry," said Milo, stepping forward, for in the distance he could see the first of the demons already beginning to scale the mountain toward them, no more than a few minutes away.

The little man wrote with painful deliberation, finally finished with both Milo and Tock, and looked up happily.

"May we go now?" asked the dog, whose sensitive nose had picked up a loathsome, evil smell that grew stronger every second.

"By all means," said the man agreeably, "just as soon as you finish telling me your height; your weight; the number of books you read each year; the number of books you don't read each year; the amount of time you spend eating, playing, working, and sleeping every day; where you go on vacations; how many ice-cream cones you eat in a week; how far it is from your house to the barbershop; and which is your favorite color. Then, after that, please fill out these forms and applications—three copies of each—and be careful, for if you make one mistake, you'll have to do them all over again."

"Oh dear," said Milo, looking at the pile of papers, "we'll never finish these." And even as he spoke the demons swarmed stealthily up the mountain.

Page 228

4. the gay and exciting circus

The devious Senses Taker makes a suitably tempting choice for Milo's distraction. Here Juster has aligned himself with children's book authors before him who were intrigued by the dark undercurrents of circus life and festivity. In *Toby Tyler; or, Ten Weeks with a Circus* (1880), James Otis tells a tale of the cruel exploitation of a ten-year-old orphan who has run away to the circus in search of a better life. And in *The Adventures of Pinocchio* (1883), Carlo Collodi sets his wayward hero on the road to ruin when, after being transformed into a donkey in the Land of Play, Pinocchio is promptly sold to a circus, where, like Toby Tyler, he is treated inhumanely.

5. "And wouldn't you enjoy a more pleasant aroma?"

A dog's sense of smell is approximately one thousand times more sensitive than that of a human. While dogs have an estimated 220 million olfactory receptors in their noses, man, their best friend, has a mere 5 million.

"Come, come," said the Senses Taker, chuckling gaily to himself, "don't take all day. I'm expecting several more visitors any minute now."

They set to work feverishly on the difficult forms, and when they'd finished, Milo placed them all in the little man's lap. He thanked them politely, took off his eyeshade, put the pen behind his ear, closed the book, and went back to sleep. The Humbug took one horrified look back over his shoulder and quickly started up the stairs.

"DESTINATION?" shouted the Senses Taker, sitting up again, putting on his eyeshade, taking the pen from behind his ear, and opening his book.

"But I thought——" protested the astonished bug.

"DESTINATION?" he repeated, making several notations in the ledger.

"The Castle in the Air," said Milo impatiently.

"Why bother?" said the Senses Taker, pointing into the distance. "I'm sure you'd rather see what I have to show you."

As he spoke, they all looked up, but only Milo could see the gay and exciting circus there on the horizon. There were tents and side shows and rides and even wild animals—everything a little boy could spend hours watching.

"And wouldn't you enjoy a more pleasant aroma?" he said, turning to Tock.

Almost immediately the dog smelled a wonderful smell that no one but he could smell. It was made up of all the marvelous things that had ever delighted his curious nose.

"And here's something I know you'll enjoy hearing," he assured the Humbug.

The bug listened with rapt attention to something he alone could hear—the shouts and applause of an enormous crowd, all cheering for him.

They each stood as if in a trance, looking, smelling, and listening to the very special things that the Senses Taker had provided for them, forgetting completely about where they were going and who, with evil intent, was coming up behind them.

The Senses Taker sat back with a satisfied smile on his puffy little face as the demons came closer and closer, until less than a minute separated them from their helpless victims.

But Milo was too engrossed in the circus to notice, and Tock had closed his eyes, the better to smell, and the bug, bowing and waving, stood with a look of sheer bliss on his face, interested only in the wild ovation.

The little man had done his work well and, except for some ominous crawling noises just below the crest of the mountain, everything was again silent. Milo, who stood staring blankly into the distance, let his bag of gifts slip from his shoulder to the ground. And, as he did, the package of sounds broke open, filling the air with peals of happy laughter which seemed so gay that first he, then Tock, and finally the Humbug joined in. And suddenly the spell was broken.

Page 229

6. The bug listened . . . to something he alone could hear

The hypnotic effect on the Humbug of the Senses Taker's wildly cheering virtual crowd—and indeed all three of his demonic ploys—suggests the Chinese mind-control, or "brainwashing," techniques, including partial sensory deprivation, that first became known to Americans during the time of the Korean War. Richard Condon's bestselling novel *The Manchurian Candidate* (1959) made *brainwashing* a household word in Cold War America.

7. "what they're *not* looking for"

Ideas set down in this sheet of notes by the author found their way into the text on this page, as well as that of pages 231 and 234 (Lilly Library, box 5, folder 34).

CASTLE IN THE SKY

1. use term cold light of reason
   stands to reason

2. Read between the lions – (pun to be used for social lions)

3. Its not what you say, its the way that you say it, for people can use the same words and mean entirely different things.

4. People only hear what they want to hear
   see what they want to see
   say what they want to say and
   make figures do whatever they want for
   without rhyme, reason, honesty – anything goes

5. Rhyme – with a laugh or writing as the mailmans ring when you know there's a letter for you.

6. Just off the map bit – Milo. I'll bet you can see everything----. Oh no, see R.R.-Here are many things j ust—l the map.

8. "As long as you have the sound of laughter, . . . you've nothing to fear from me."

Underlying the Senses Taker's admission is one of Juster's core beliefs. As he once told an interviewer: "Having a sense of humor can be an essential thing in your life. I have a kind of 'gallows humor' for times when things are really too terrible. My wife will say

"There is no circus," cried Milo, realizing he'd been tricked.

"There were no smells," barked Tock, his alarm now ringing furiously.

"The applause is gone," complained the disappointed Humbug.

"I warned you; I warned you I was the Senses Taker," sneered the Senses Taker. "I help people find what they're *not* looking for, hear what they're *not* listening for, run after what they're *not* chasing, and smell what isn't even there. And, furthermore," he cackled, hopping around gleefully on his stubby legs, "I'll steal your sense of purpose, take your sense of duty, destroy your sense of proportion—and, but for one thing, you'd be helpless yet."

"What's that?" asked Milo fearfully.

"As long as you have the sound of laughter," he groaned unhappily, "I cannot take your sense of humor—and, with it, you've nothing to fear from me."

"But what about THEM?" cried the terrified bug, for at that very instant the other demons had reached the top at last and were leaping forward to seize them.

They ran for the stairs, bowling over the disconsolate Senses Taker, ledger, ink bottle, eyeshade, and all, as they went. The Humbug dashed up first, then Tock, and lastly Milo, almost too late, as a scaly arm brushed his shoe.

The dangerous stairs danced dizzily in the wind, and the clumsy demons refused to follow; but they howled with rage and fury, swore bloody vengeance, and watched with many pairs of burning eyes as the three small shapes vanished slowly into the clouds.

"Don't look down," advised Milo as the bug tottered upward on unsteady legs.

Like a giant corkscrew, the stairway twisted through the darkness, steep and narrow and with no rail to guide them. The wind howled cruelly in an effort to tear them loose, and the fog dragged clammy fingers down their backs; but up the giddy flight they went, each one helping the others, until at last the clouds parted, the darkness fell away, and a glow of golden sunrays warmed their arrival. The castle gate swung open smoothly. They entered the great hall on a rug as soft as a snowdrift and they stood shyly waiting.

"Come right in, please; we've been expecting you," sang out two sweet voices in unison.

At the far end of the hall a silver curtain parted and two young women stepped forward. They were dressed all in white and were beautiful beyond compare. One was grave and quiet, with a look of warm understanding in her eyes, and the other seemed gay and joyful.

"You must be the Princess of Pure Reason," said Milo, bowing to the first.

She answered simply, "Yes," and that was just enough.

"Then you are Sweet Rhyme," he said, with a smile to the other.

Her eyes sparkled brightly and she answered with a laugh as friendly as the mailman's ring when you know there's a letter for you.

9

9. a silver curtain parted and two young women stepped forward.

Neither Feiffer nor Juster came away particularly satisfied with their portrayals of Rhyme and Reason—Feiffer, because the women looked too conventional, like a pair of thinking-man's beauty pageant contestants; Juster, because, despite their being so necessary to the story, the characters of Rhyme and Reason acted "too much like the girls in my classes in elementary school—well behaved, responsible, orderly, a force for good, but a damper on the chaos I thrived on as a child. They are, of course, so important, and the problem for all of us is to incorporate them into our lives and not lose the spirit, fun, and adventure of life" (N.J. Notes II, p. 8).

10. Illustration

Seated between Rhyme and Reason, Milo does not so much look tired as bewildered—like a typical Feiffer character caught up in an existential dilemma and unable (here literally) to choose which way to turn.

10

"We've come to rescue you both," Milo explained very seriously.

"And the demons are close behind," said the worried Humbug, still shaky from his ordeal.

"And we should leave right away," advised Tock.

"Oh, they won't dare come up here," said Reason gently; "and we'll be down there soon enough."

"Why not sit for a moment and rest?" suggested Rhyme. "I'm sure you must be tired. Have you been traveling long?"

"Days," sighed the exhausted dog, curling up on a large downy cushion.

"Weeks," corrected the bug, flopping into a deep comfortable armchair, for it did seem that way to him.

"It *has* been a long trip," said Milo, climbing onto the couch where the princesses sat; "but we would have been here much sooner if I hadn't made so many mistakes. I'm afraid it's all my fault."

"You must never feel badly about making mistakes," explained Reason quietly, "as long as you take the trouble to learn from them. For you often learn more by being wrong for the right reasons than you do by being right for the wrong reasons."

"But there's so *much* to learn," he said, with a thoughtful frown.

"Yes, that's true," admitted Rhyme; "but it's not just learning things that's important. It's learning what to do with what you learn and learning why you learn things at all that matters."

"That's just what I mean," explained Milo as Tock and the exhausted bug drifted quietly off to sleep. "Many of the things I'm supposed to know seem so useless that I can't see the purpose in learning them at all."

"You may not see it now," said the Princess of Pure Reason, looking knowingly at Milo's puzzled face, "but whatever we learn has a purpose and whatever we do affects everything and everyone else, if even in the tiniest way. Why, when a housefly flaps his wings, a breeze goes round the world; when a speck of dust falls to the ground, the entire planet weighs a little more; and when you stamp your foot, the earth moves slightly off its course. Whenever you laugh, gladness spreads like the

Page 233

11. "if I hadn't made so many mistakes."

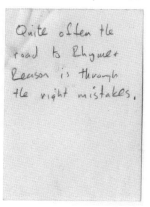

Quite often the road to Rhyme & Reason is through the right mistakes.

Juster may have first set down the gist of Reason's memorable response to Milo's apology on this index card (Lilly Library, box 5, folder 34).

12. "but it's not just learning things that's important. It's learning what to do with what you learn"

Rhyme here sounds like an advocate for American progressive education, whose proponents favored what Bank Street College of Education founder Lucy Sprague Mitchell called "relationship thinking" over traditional forms of rote learning.

13. "Why, when a housefly flaps his wings, a breeze goes round the world"

Here the author offers examples of the unanticipated consequences in a dynamic system that sometimes result from a seemingly minor event—a theme of post-Newtonian science and especially of what later came to be known as Chaos Theory. The idea was already in the air in 1952 when Ray Bradbury published "A Sound of Thunder," a short story about time travel in which the accidental crushing of a single butterfly during the time travelers' excursion into the past sets off a chain of events that lead to alterations in the language, architecture, and politics of their present-day world. Serendipitously, in 1961, the year of *The Phantom Tollbooth*'s publication, Edward Lorenz made his first computer-based studies of weather systems, the surprising findings from which he later encapsulated in the phrase "the butterfly effect."

ripples in a pond; and whenever you're sad, no one anywhere can be really happy. And it's much the same thing with knowledge, for whenever you learn something new, the whole world becomes that much richer."

"And remember, also," added the Princess of Sweet Rhyme, "that many places you would like to see are just off the map and many things you want to know are just out of sight or a little beyond your reach. But someday you'll reach them all, for what you learn today, for no reason at all, will help you discover all the wonderful secrets of tomorrow."

"I think I understand," Milo said, still full of questions and thoughts; "but which is the most important——"

At that moment the conversation was interrupted by a far-off chopping noise. With each loud blow, the entire room and everything in it shook and rattled. Down below, on the murky peak, the demons were busily cutting the stairway loose with axes and hammers and saws. Before long the whole thing collapsed with a tremendous crash and the startled Humbug leaped to his feet just in time to see the castle drifting slowly off into space.

"We're moving!" he shouted, which was a fact that had already become obvious to everyone.

"I think we had better leave now," said Rhyme softly, and Reason agreed with a nod.

"But how will we get down?" groaned the Humbug, looking at the wreckage below. "There's no stairway and we're sailing higher every minute."

14. **"I'll take everyone down."**

In *The Poetics of Space,* the French philosopher Gaston Bachelard remarks: "Common sense lives on the ground floor." Reason has long been associated metaphorically with groundedness, as in the expression "down to earth." The mythic Icarus defies reason when, held aloft only by wings made of wax, he flies too close to the sun and plummets to earth. By contrast, Milo and his companions, with Rhyme and Reason at their side, make it safely back to terra firma.

"Well, time flies, doesn't it?" asked Milo.

"On many occasions," barked Tock, jumping eagerly to his feet. "I'll take everyone down."

"Can you carry us all?" inquired the bug.

"For a short distance," said the dog thoughtfully. "The princesses can ride on my back, Milo can catch hold of my tail, and you can hang on to his ankles."

"But what of the Castle in the Air?" the bug objected, not very pleased with the arrangement.

"Let it drift away," said Rhyme.

"And good riddance," added Reason, "for no matter how beautiful it seems, it's still nothing but a prison."

Tock then backed up three steps and, with a running start, bounded through the window with all his passengers and began the long glide down. The princesses sat tall and unafraid, Milo held on as tight as he could, and the bug swung crazily, like the tail on a kite. Down through the darkness they plunged, to the mountains and the monsters below.

14

19. The Return of Rhyme
and Reason

Sailing past three of the tallest peaks, and just over the outstretched arms of the grasping demons, they reached the ground and landed with a sudden jolt.

"Quick!" urged Tock. "Follow me! We'll have to run for it."

With the princesses still on his back, he galloped down the rocky trail—and not a moment too soon. For, pounding down the mountainside, in a cloud of clinging dust and a chorus of chilling shrieks, came all the loathsome creatures who choose to live in Ignorance and who had waited so very impatiently.

Thick black clouds hung heavily overhead as they fled through the darkness, and Milo, looking back for just a moment, could see the awful shapes coming closer and closer. Just to the left, and not very far away, were

Page 238

1. the Triple Demons of Compromise

Juster's notes on demons include the following: "Twin demons. As tall as one was that's how short the other was. As round as one was that's how square the other was, as rough as one was, that's how [smooth] the other was. They are not at all alike, but [yet] exactly the same. THE TWIN DEMONS OF COMPROMISE" (Lilly Library, box 5, folder 34, item 4).

The author recalled: "I must admit I concocted [them] only to plague Jules" (N.J. Notes II, p. 8). Not to be so easily undone, Feiffer chose to leave the Triple Demons to the reader's imagination.

2. the Gorgons of Hate and Malice

In Greek mythology, a Gorgon is a fearsome female creature with snakes for hair and a gaze capable of turning anyone in her line of vision to stone. Homer writes of only one Gorgon in the *Iliad* and the *Odyssey*, but later Greek writers attest to the existence of three Gorgon sisters, two of whom are immortal, while the third, Medusa, is not.

1 the Triple Demons of Compromise—one tall and thin, one short and fat, and the third exactly like the other two. As always, they moved in ominous circles, for if one said "here," the other said "there," and the third agreed perfectly with both of them. And, since they always settled their differences by doing what none of them really wanted, they rarely got anywhere at all—and neither did anyone they met.

Jumping clumsily from boulder to boulder and catching hold with his cruel, curving claws was the Horrible Hopping Hindsight, a most unpleasant fellow whose eyes were in the rear and whose rear was out in front. He invariably leaped before he looked and never cared where he was going as long as he knew why he shouldn't have gone to where he'd been.

2 And, most terrifying of all, directly behind, inching along like giant soft-shelled snails, with blazing eyes and wet anxious mouths, came the Gorgons of Hate and Malice, leaving a trail of slime behind them and moving much more quickly than you'd think.

"FASTER!" shouted Tock. "They're closing in."

Down from the heights they raced, the Humbug with one hand on his hat and the other flailing desperately in the air, Milo running as he had never run before, and the demons just a little bit faster than that.

From off on the right, his heavy bulbous body lurching dangerously on the spindly legs which barely supported him, came the Overbearing Know-it-all, talking continuously. A dismal demon who was mostly mouth, he was ready at a moment's notice to offer misinformation on any subject. And, while he often tumbled heavily, it was never he who was hurt, but, rather, the unfortunate person on whom he fell.

Next to him, but just a little behind, came the Gross Exaggeration, whose grotesque features and thoroughly unpleasant manners were hideous to see, and whose rows of wicked teeth were made only to mangle the truth. They hunted together, and were bad luck to anyone they caught.

Riding along on the back of anyone who'd carry him was the Threadbare Excuse, a small, pathetic figure whose clothes were worn and tattered and who mumbled the same things again and again, in a low but piercing voice: "Well, I've been sick—but the page was torn out—I missed the bus—but no one *else* did it—well, I've been sick—but the page was torn out—I missed the bus—but no one *else* did it." He looked quite harmless and friendly but, once he grabbed on, he almost never let go.

Closer and closer they came, bumping and jolting each other, clawing and snorting in their eager fury. Tock staggered along bravely with Rhyme and Reason, Milo's lungs now felt ready to burst as he stumbled down the trail, and the Humbug was slowly falling behind. Gradually the path grew broader and more flat as it reached the bottom of the mountain and turned toward Wisdom. Ahead lay light and safety—but perhaps just a bit too far away.

And down came the demons from everywhere, frenzied creatures of darkness, lurching wildly toward their

Page 239

3. Riding along on the back of anyone who'd carry him was the Threadbare Excuse

Writing in 1996, Maurice Sendak observed: "The dumbing down of America is proceeding apace. Juster's allegorical monsters have become all too real. The Demons of Ignorance, the Gross Exaggeration . . . and the shabby Threadbare Excuse are inside the walls of the Kingdom of Wisdom, while the Gorgons of Hate and Malice, the Overbearing Know-it-all, and most especially the Triple Demons of Compromise are already established in high office all over the world" ("An Appreciation," by M.S. for the 35th-anniversary U.S. edition, 1996).

Page 240

4. Illustration

Feiffer considered this drawing one of his favorite illustrations for the book, in part because it was such a complete departure from his signature cartoon style, in which white space typically defines the figures. For this complex composition, Feiffer found inspiration in the epic, fever-pitch graphics of the prolific nineteenth-century French engraver, sculptor, and illustrator Gustave Doré.

4

Illustration by Gustave Doré from Milton's *Paradise Lost*, 1866.

Page 242

5. the ugly Dilemma

Dilemma derives from a Greek compound word meaning "two premises or things taken for granted," and was first used as a technical term in the realm of debating. A dilemma in this sense is a rhetorical trap calculated to leave the opposing debater with only two possible responses, neither one of them desirable. Medieval philosophers referred to a predicament of this kind as an *argumentum cornutum*, or "horned argument." Eventually, the two idioms merged in the familiar expression "on the horns of a dilemma" (*Arcade Dictionary of Word Origins*; *QPB Encyclopedia of Word and Phrase Origins*).

prey. From off in the rear, the Terrible Trivium and the wobbly Gelatinous Giant urged them on with glee. And pounding forward with a rush came the ugly Dilemma, snorting steam and looking intently for someone to catch on the ends of his long pointed horns, while his hoofs bit eagerly at the ground.

The exhausted Humbug swayed and tottered on his rubbery legs, a look of longing on his anguished face. "I don't think I can——" he gasped as a jagged slash of lightning ripped open the sky and the thunder stole his words.

Closer and closer the demons loomed as the desperate chase neared its end. Then, gathering themselves for one final leap, they prepared to engulf first the bug, then the boy, and lastly the dog and his two passengers. They rose as one and——

And suddenly stopped, as if frozen in mid-air, unable to move, staring ahead in terror.

Milo slowly raised his weary head, and there in the horizon, for as far as the eye could see, stood the massed armies of Wisdom, the sun glistening from their swords and shields, and their bright banners slapping proudly at the breeze.

For a moment everything was silent. Then a thousand trumpets sounded—then a thousand more—and, like an ocean wave, the long line of horsemen advanced, slowly at first, then faster and faster, until with a gallop and a shout, which was music to Milo's ears, they swept forward toward the horrified demons.

Page 243

6. Illustration

When Feiffer came to the passage on the previous page specifying a "long line of horsemen," he informed Juster that he did not like to draw horses, and made a sketch for the scene in which the warriors were shown mounted on the backs of cats. Juster was not amused. To placate him, Feiffer reluctantly drew a side view of a single horse, extended it in the simplest possible way to suggest the presence of two more horses in line beside it, and left it at that. Note the absence of the soldiers' swords and of their "bright banners slapping proudly at the breeze." Equally curious, there appears to be one more rider than horse in this scene.

7. Everyone Milo had met during his journey had come to help

Here Juster gathers everyone onstage for the grand finale. Of all the characters he considered incorporating into the story but ultimately chose to do without, he made the most extensive notes for one called "The Exact Moment," whose obsession was to have been with such matters as: "1. The exact moment you pass from wakefulness into sleep; 2. The exact moment water becomes ice; 3. The exact moment forward motion becomes backward motion; 4. The exact moment good becomes bad. Looks like the dot of light when you turn off the television set" (Lilly Library, box 5, folder 34).

There in the lead was King Azaz, his dazzling armor embossed with every letter in the alphabet, and, with him, the Mathemagician, brandishing a freshly sharpened staff. From his tiny wagon, Dr. Dischord hurled explosion after explosion, to the delight of the Soundkeeper, while the busy DYNNE collected them almost at once. And, in honor of the occasion, Chroma the Great led his orchestra in a stirring display of patriotic colors. Everyone Milo had met during his journey had come to help—the men of the market place, the miners of Digitopolis, and all the good people from the valley and the forest.

The Spelling Bee buzzed excitedly overhead shouting, "Charge—c-h-a-r-g-e—charge—c-h-a-r-g-e." Canby, who, as everyone knew, was as cowardly as can be, came all the way from Conclusions to show that he was also as brave. And even Officer Shrift, mounted proudly on a long, low dachshund, galloped grimly along.

Cringing with fear, the monsters of Ignorance turned in flight and, with anguished cries too horrible ever to forget, returned to the damp, dark places from which they came. The Humbug sighed with relief, and Milo and the princesses prepared to greet the victorious army.

"Well done," stated the Duke of Definition, dismounting and grasping Milo's hand warmly.

"Fine job," seconded the Minister of Meaning.

"Good work," added the Count of Connotation.

"Congratulations," proposed the Earl of Essence.

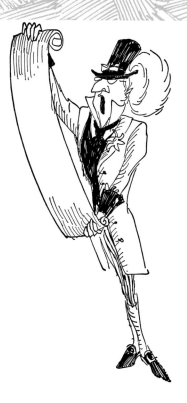

Page 245

8. "CHEERS"

Although as far as can be told, the Undersecretary is not raising a glass to Milo and friends, his choice of a word associated with toasting and drinking is historically apt. The clinking of glasses prior to the consumption of an alcoholic beverage has been a popular custom as far back as medieval times—in part with the purpose in mind of dislodging the devil or demons who might be lurking in the "spirits" contained in the drinkers' cups.

"CHEERS," recommended the Undersecretary of Understanding. 8

And, since that's exactly what everyone felt like doing, that's exactly what everyone did.

"It's we who should thank——" began Milo, when the shouting had subsided, but, before he could finish, they had unrolled an enormous scroll.

And, with a fanfare of trumpets and drums, they stated in order that:

"Henceforth,"

"And forthwith,"

"Let it be known by all men"

"That Rhyme and Reason"

"Reign once more in Wisdom."

The word *folly* here means a "theatrical court entertainment."

The two princesses bowed gratefully and warmly kissed their brothers, and they all agreed that a very fine thing had happened.

"And furthermore," continued the proclamation,

"The boy named Milo,"

"The dog known as Tock,"

"And the insect hereinafter referred to as the Humbug"

"Are hereby declared to be"

"Heroes of the realm."

Cheer after cheer filled the air, and even the bug seemed a bit embarrassed at having so much attention paid to him.

"Therefore," concluded the duke, "in honor of their glorious deed, a royal holiday is declared. Let there be parades through every city in the land and a gala carnival of three days' duration, consisting of jousts, games, feasts, and follies."

The five cabinet members then rolled up the large parchment and, with many bows and flourishes, retired.

Swift horsemen carried the news to every corner of the kingdom, and, as the parade slowly wound its way through the countryside, crowds of people gathered to cheer it along. Garlands of flowers hung from every house and shop and carpeted the streets. Even the air shimmered with excitement, and shutters closed for many years were thrown open to let the brilliant sunlight shine where it hadn't shone in so long.

Milo, Tock, and the very subdued Humbug sat proudly in the royal carriage with Azaz, the Mathemagician, and the two princesses; and the parade stretched for miles in both directions.

As the cheering continued, Rhyme leaned forward and touched Milo gently on the arm.

"They're shouting for you," she said with a smile.

"But I could never have done it," he objected, "without everyone else's help."

"That may be true," said Reason gravely, "but you had the courage to try; and what you *can* do is often simply a matter of what you *will* do."

"That's why," said Azaz, "there was one very important thing about your quest that we couldn't discuss until you returned."

"I remember," said Milo eagerly. "Tell me now."

"It was impossible," said the king, looking at the Mathemagician.

"Completely impossible," said the Mathemagician, looking at the king.

"Do you mean——" stammered the bug, who suddenly felt a bit faint.

"Yes, indeed," they repeated together; "but if we'd told you then, you might not have gone—and, as you've discovered, so many things are possible just as long as you don't know they're impossible." 10

And for the remainder of the ride Milo didn't utter a sound.

Finally, when they'd reached a broad, flat plain midway between Dictionopolis and Digitopolis, somewhat to the right of the Valley of Sound and a little to the left of the

Page 247

10. "so many things are possible just as long as you don't know they're impossible."

The author's version of "I think I can, I think I can," and one of the passages most often cited by readers as inspirational.

Page 248

11. Ferris wheels

The handiwork of bridge builder George Washington Gale Ferris, Jr.—the world's first Ferris Wheel was a star attraction of the 1893 World's Columbian Exposition—and Chicago's answer to the Eiffel Tower. When an amusement park entrepreneur from Juster's native Brooklyn, New York, tried unsuccessfully to purchase the Chicago landmark for reinstallation at Coney Island, the wily showman built a somewhat smaller Wonder Wheel of his own and posted a sign that proclaimed it the "world's largest."

12. and bedlam

A contraction of *Bethlehem*, which in Hebrew means "house of bread," *bedlam* was first associated with the Hospital of St. Mary of Bethlehem. Originally founded as a priory in 1247 in Bishopsgate, London, St. Mary's had become a hospital by 1330, and by about 1400 it was admitting patients with maladies that today would be classified as forms of mental illness. It was officially designated as an asylum for the insane three centuries later. By the late seventeenth century, *bedlam* could also mean any scene of considerable chaos or confusion.

13. recounting in great detail his brave exploits

In the "Final Typed Draft," Juster crossed out *adventures* and inserted the more highly colored *exploits* in its stead (Lilly Library, box 3, folder 31, p. 179).

Forest of Sight, the long line of carriages and horsemen stopped, and the great carnival began.

Gaily striped tents and pavilions sprang up everywhere as the workmen scurried about like ants. Within minutes there were racecourses and grandstands, side shows and refreshment booths, gaming fields, Ferris wheels, banners, bunting, and bedlam, almost without pause.

The Mathemagician provided a continuous display of brilliant fireworks made up of exploding numbers which multiplied and divided with breathtaking results—the colors, of course, being supplied by Chroma and the noise by a deliriously happy Dr. Dischord. Thanks to the Soundkeeper, there was music and laughter and, for very brief moments, even a little silence.

Alec Bings set up an enormous telescope and invited everyone to see the other side of the moon, and the Humbug wandered through the crowd accepting congratulations and recounting in great detail his brave exploits, most of which gained immeasurably in the telling.

And each evening, just at sunset, a royal banquet was held. There was everything imaginable to eat. King Azaz had ordered a special supply of delicious words in all flavors and, for those who liked exotic foods, in all languages, too. The Mathemagician had provided innumerable platters of division dumplings, which Milo was very careful to avoid, for, no matter how many you ate, when you finished there was more on your plate than when you began.

And, of course, following the meal came songs, epic

Page 249

14. Illustration

Months after the publication of *The Phantom Tollbooth*, Jules Feiffer created a *Feiffer* strip featuring another troubadour, this one singing a ballad that pokes cynical fun at the concept of Santa Claus (*Explainers*, strip dated December 21, 1961, p. 273).

© Jules Feiffer

poems, and speeches in praise of the princesses and the three gallant adventurers who had rescued them. King Azaz and the Mathemagician pledged that every year at this same time they would lead their armies to the Mountains of Ignorance until not one demon remained, and everyone agreed that no finer carnival for no finer reason had ever been held in Wisdom.

But even things as fine as all that must end sometime, and late on the afternoon of the third day the tents were struck, the pavilions were folded, and everything was packed ready to leave.

"It's time to go now," said Reason, "for there is much to

Page 250

15. He wanted very much to go back

Unlike Dorothy in the Land of Oz, Milo needs no one to tell him how to get back home.

16. yet somehow he could not bear the thought of leaving.

Juster commented: "Milo's departure, for me, was like leaving summer camp when summer ends. Leaving a magical world of special friends and going back to reality and all its problems (but somewhat more able to handle them)" (N.J. Notes II, p. 11).

17. and he looked very hard

Here Milo seems to be acting on the lessons learned from his visit to the cities of Reality and Illusions.

do." And, as she spoke, Milo suddenly remembered his home. He wanted very much to go back, yet somehow he could not bear the thought of leaving.

"And so you must say good-by," said Rhyme, patting him gently on the cheek.

"To everyone?" said Milo unhappily. He looked around slowly at all the friends he'd made, and he looked very hard so as not to forget any of them for even an instant. But mostly he looked at Tock and the Humbug, with whom he had shared so much—the perils, the dangers, the fears, and, best of all, the victory. Never had anyone had two more steadfast companions.

"Can't you both come with me?" he asked, knowing the answer as he said it.

"I'm afraid not, old man," replied the bug. "I'd like to, but I've arranged a lecture tour which will keep me occupied for years."

"And they do need a watchdog here," barked Tock sadly.

Milo embraced the bug who, in his most typical fashion, was heard to mumble gruffly, "BAH," but whose damp eyes told quite a different story. Then the boy threw his arms around Tock's neck and, for just a moment, held on very tightly.

"Thank you for everything you've taught me," said Milo to everybody as a tear rolled down his cheek.

"And thank you for what you've taught us," said the king—and, as he clapped his hands, the little car was brought forward, polished like new.

18. "Surely you don't think numbers are as important as words?"

Juster commented: "Once the victory was won there was little else to do but get Milo home. It was a great victory but I didn't want to imply that it was a total victory, for all time. This fight would have to be won again and again" (N.J. Notes II, pp. 10–11).

Milo got in and, with one last look, started down the road, with everyone waving him on.

"Good-by," he shouted. "Good-by. I'll be back."

"Good-by," shouted Azaz. "Always remember the importance of words."

"And numbers," added the Mathemagician forcefully.

18 "Surely you don't think numbers are as important as words?" he heard Azaz shout from the distance.

"Is that so?" replied the Mathemagician a little more faintly. "Why, if——"

"Oh dear," thought Milo; "I do hope they don't start it all again." And in a moment they had faded from sight as the road dipped, turned, and headed for home.

20. Good-by and Hello

As the pleasant countryside flashed by and the wind whistled a tune on the windshield, it suddenly occurred to Milo that he must have been gone for several weeks.

"I do hope that no one's been worried," he thought, urging the car on faster. "I've never been away this long before."

The late-afternoon sun had turned now from a vivid yellow to a warm lazy orange, and it seemed almost as tired as he was. The road raced ahead in a series of gentle curves that began to look familiar, and off in the distance the solitary tollbooth appeared, a welcome sight indeed. In a few minutes he reached the end of his journey, deposited his coin, and drove through. And, almost before realizing it, he was sitting in the middle of his own room again.

"It's only six o'clock," he observed with a yawn, and

Page 253

1. Good-by and Hello

Forty-four years after the publication of *The Phantom Tollbooth*, Juster wrote *The Hello, Goodbye Window*, a picture book about a young girl's visit to her grandparents. In that story, a certain ground-floor window of the grandparents' cozy home plays a key role in several of the affectionate threesome's favorite games and activities.

Chris Raschka won the 2006 Caldecott Medal for his illustrations for *The Hello, Goodbye Window*.

Norton Juster at home reading *The Hello, Goodbye Window* with his granddaughter, Tori, who was the inspiration for the book, 2005.

then, in a moment, he made an even more interesting discovery.

"And it's still today! I've been gone for only an hour!" he cried in amazement, for he'd certainly never realized how much he could do in so short a time.

Milo was much too tired to talk and almost too tired for dinner, so, without a murmur, he went off to bed as soon as he could. He pulled the covers around him, took a last look at his room—which somehow seemed very different than he'd remembered—and then drifted into a deep and welcome sleep.

School went very quickly the next day, but not quickly enough, for Milo's head was full of plans and his eyes could see nothing but the tollbooth and what lay beyond. He waited impatiently for the end of class, and when the time finally came, his feet raced his thoughts all the way back to the house.

"Another trip! Another trip! I'll leave right away. They'll all be so glad to see me, and I'll——"

He stopped abruptly at the door of his room, for, where the tollbooth had been just the night before, there was now nothing at all. He searched frantically throughout the apartment, but it had vanished just as mysteriously as it had come—and in its place was another bright-blue envelope, which was addressed simply: "FOR MILO, WHO NOW KNOWS THE WAY."

He opened it quickly and read:

Dear Milo,
You have now completed your trip, courtesy of the

Phantom Tollbooth. We trust that everything has been satisfactory, and hope you understand why we had to come and collect it. You see, there are so many other boys and girls waiting to use it, too.

It's true that there are many lands you've still to visit (some of which are not even on the map) and wonderful things to see (that no one has yet imagined), but we're quite sure that if you really want to, you'll find a way to reach them all by yourself.

Yours truly,

The signature was blurred and couldn't be read.

Milo walked sadly to the window and squeezed himself into one corner of the large armchair. He felt very lonely and desolate as his thoughts turned far away—to the foolish, lovable bug; to the comforting assurance of Tock, standing next to him; to the erratic, excitable DYNNE; to little Alec, who, he hoped, would someday reach the ground; to Rhyme and Reason, without whom Wisdom withered; and to the many, many others he would remember always.

And yet, even as he thought of all these things, he noticed somehow that the sky was a lovely shade of blue and that one cloud had the shape of a sailing ship. The tips of the trees held pale, young buds and the leaves were a rich deep green. Outside the window, there was so much to see, and hear, and touch—walks to take, hills to climb, caterpillars to watch as they strolled through the garden. There were voices to hear and conversations to listen to in wonder, and the special smell of each day.

255

Page 255

2. And yet, even as he thought of all these things

This tender valedictory message, like the equally memorable one with which *Alice's Adventures in Wonderland* concludes, highlights the qualities of sensitivity and awareness that young Milo, having journeyed to the Lands Beyond and back, now has a far better chance of sustaining throughout the rest of his life.

Page 256

3. "There's just so much to do right here."

Or, as Voltaire's Candide expressed much the same sentiment: "We must cultivate our garden."

4. Illustration

Feiffer made the interesting choice to depict Milo's room not in terms of the specific objects to be found in it but rather as a kind of Blakean force field, as a whirlwind of energy both potential and real.

And, in the very room in which he sat, there were books that could take you anywhere, and things to invent, and make, and build, and break, and all the puzzle and excitement of everything he didn't know—music to play, songs to sing, and worlds to imagine and then someday make real. His thoughts darted eagerly about as everything looked new—and worth trying.

"Well, I *would* like to make another trip," he said, jumping to his feet; "but I really don't know when I'll have the time. There's just so much to do right here."

APPENDIX

14. the chocolate moose who is always afraid he is not light enough or that he will be eaten before desert.

15. Chroma the great- the color symphonist, the great musician who plays the color organ & floods the world with beauty or not as he sees fit.

16. The star gazer - who wonders about everything & takes care of the stars like a shepherd.

17. The seal of approval - who passes judgment on everything with stern impartiality.

18 The social lion - the arbiter of good manners and social taste - always does the correct thing even when its wrong.

19- Nosy ——

Norton Juster, avid list maker and note taker, produced this undated roster of characters while in the thick of completing the manuscript (Lilly Library, box 5, folder 34).

20 - the animals no one has heard of - who appear throughout the story -

21. the inventor - who never leaves well enough alone and is always trying to improve things or invent new ones that haven't any use yet - he invents straight bananas & square oranges for easy packing - a spherical car, etc -

22. the hitch-hiker - who always leads Milo into doing things the easy way - they jump to conclusions together and have a very difficult time getting back - ~~As~~ As in all learning he is the hanger on who wants results without effort.

23. the optomitrist - who fits the rose colored glasses.

24 Facsimile - the character who can be just like anything else.

Words for use

1. ambiguous - ambiguity
2. alliteration
3. quagmire
4. grotesque
5. flabbergast
6. claptrap
7. ballyhoo
8. shenanigan
9. upholstery
10. fanfare
11. gargoyle
12. bamboozle
13. tantamount (name of mountain?)
14. humbug — (insect)
15. slipshod
16. ✱ Serendipity - the art of finding what your not looking
           for -
17. thingamabob, thingamajig
18. Syllabus & omnibus
19. Somersault
20. use of words which when not negitive change meaning
      unkempt — kempt
      uncouth - couth
21. bedlam.

This list hints at the author's fascination with the sounds and rhythms of language, as well as with the power of idiosyncratic words to stimulate a young reader's imagination. In the end, Juster found a use for several of these enticing verbal morsels (Lilly Library, box 5, folder 35).

22 curmudgeon (miser, churl or avaricious)
23 expunge
24 filibuster
25 gauntlet
26 gymnasium
27 melancholy
28 intransigent
29 meander
30 sarcophagus
31.   hearse & rehearse
        treat & retreat
        main & remain
32. Panjandrum - petty pompous official.

not just once in a while, but all the time

Milo never knew what to do with himself. "It seems strange for an eight year old boy to be so uninterested in things," thought his parents, but as hard as they tried there simply wasn't anything he really liked to do.

"It seems to me that almost everything is a waste of time," Milo would say as he sat staring out of the window at nothing— "There is nothing to do and nothing to say" and he said nothing and did nothing.

NOW, of all the things Milo didn't like to do, going to school was what he didn't like to do most do least, and each day he sat dreamily in the classroom learning as little as possible. "I just can't see the point in learning sums or subtracting apples or where Madagascar is or how to spell February", and since no one bothered to tell him otherwise (a somewhat unhappy lack in the educational system) he continued to regard the process of amassing knowledge as an ~~serious~~ inconvenient interruption to the important business of day dreaming.

but as unpleasant as the class room was

An early handwritten draft of page one, chapter one (Lilly Library, box 5, folder 37).

I

Milo didn't know what to do with himself —

Not just sometimes, but always. When he was in school he longed to be out and when he was out he longed to be in. On the way he thought about coming home and coming home he thought about going. Wherever he was he longed to be somewhere else and when he got there he wondered why he'd bothered. Nothing interested him — especially the things that should.

"It seems to me that almost everything is a waste of time", he said one day as he walked dejectedly home from school.

"I just can't see the point of learning large sums or subtracting apples or where Australia is or how to spell February." And, since no one bothered to explain otherwise he regarded the process of seeking knowledge as the greatest waste of time of all.

As he and his unhappy thoughts hurried through the streets (for while he was never very anxious to be where he was going, he liked to get there as quickly

Page one, chapter one of the handwritten first complete draft, which Norton Juster gave to his mother to be typed. Note that Milo complains about having to study "Australia," rather than "Ethiopia," as in the published book. At every stage of the writing, the author fiddled with certain words, listening for the most pleasing cadence (Lilly Library, box 5, folder 47).

CHAPTER I.

There was once a little boy, named

A Milo ^who didn't know what to do with himself——Not just sometimes, but always.

When he was in school he longed to be out and when he was out he longed to be in. On the way he thought about coming home and coming home he thought about going. Whereever he was, he longed to be somewhere else, and when he got there he wondered why he'd bothered.

Nothing interested him—especially the things that should.

"It seems to me that almost everything is a waste of time," he said one day as he walked dejectedly home from school.

"I ~~just~~ can't see the point of learning large sums or subtracting apples *fromapples* or where ~~Australia~~ *Madagascar* is, or how to spell February." And, since no one bothered to explain otherwise he regarded the the process of seeking knowledge as the greatest waste of time of all.

As he and his unhappy thoughts hurried through the streets (for while he was never very anxious to be where he was going, he liked to get there as quickly as possible) it seemed a great wonder that the world which was so large could sometimes feel so small and empty.

"There is nothing for me to do, no place for me to go and hardly anything worth seeing," and he punctuated this ^*Last* thought with such a sad, deep sigh that a crested poppenjay singing nearby, stopped, and rushed home to be with his family.

- 1 -

Page one, chapter one of a draft originally thought to be the one submitted to Jason Epstein but that, based on internal evidence, seems clearly to represent a later stage in the writing (Lilly Library, box 5, folder 56).

PLOT SYNOPSIS OF REMAINING CHAPTERS

Chapters one through seven represent about one third of the book. The remaining chapters concern Milo's adventures as he and Tock and the Humbug who accompanies them as guide, leave Diction-opolis and set out for Digitopolis to make peace between words and numbers.

Since Digitopolis lies at the opposite end of the country, they must first visit the places that lie in between:

1. "The Land of Sound" where they meet the Soundkeeper, visit the great storage vaults of past sounds and speeches and rescue present and future sound which has been imprisoned in the old fortress, thereby saving the people from a life of silence.

2. "Conclusions," an island in the sea of knowledge which can only be reached by jumping. It is easy to get to but very difficult to return from, and so is densely populated. While there they meet Alec Bings, who seems through things, a little boy with X-ray vision who literally and figuratively can see through everything, but can't see what's in front of his nose.

3. "The Kingdom of Colors," where Milo meets Chrome the Great who composes the world's colors on his magnificent color organ. While there Milo is allowed to try it, with some startling results.

4. "The Land of Tomorrow," where Milo meets the men who invented progress and sees how new things come to be and what happens to the things that are not needed like square oranges, straight bananas and answers for which there are no questions.

After Juster finished his handwritten draft, Minnie Juster typed her son's synopsis for submission to Jason Epstein at Random House (Lilly Library, box 5, folder 63).

They finally reach Digitopolis where Milo meets the Mathemagician, his assistants J. Remington Rhomboid, Peter Paradox and the Adding Machine, a friendly robot. They pay a long visit to Infinity and a shorter one to the town of Averages where they meet the average man and the average woman and learn a lesson in logic.

The Mathemagician is pleased to see them but is as stubborn as AZAZ and so they finally decide to make the dangerous trip to the Castle in the Sky and rescue Rhyme and Reason themselves.

They go forth into the mountains of Ignorance, trick the slow witted but terrible Gelatinous Giant and climb the long stair to the Castle. There they meet the two princesses and their pets, the Seal of Approval and the Social Lion, rescue them and return in triumph to WISDOM.

Milo then says goodbye to his friends, heads for home and after one more detour in the land if Illusions he reaches the tollbooth and his room. The next day when he eagerly rushes home from school to take another trip he finds that the booth has disappeared as mysteriously as it came. In its place is a letter which tells him that there are many other little boys and girls who have to use it also and that now he must find the lands beyond by himself. At first he is very unhappy but then he realizes that he doesn't have time to be because there is so much to do.

Select Reviews of *The Phantom Tollbooth*

Bernkopf, Elizabeth. *The Boston Globe*, December 24, 1961.

Bishop, C. H. *Commonweal*, November 10, 1961, p. 186.

The Bulletin of the Center for Children's Books, Vol. XV, No. 7, p. 112.

Crosby, John. "Child's Book." *New York Herald Tribune*, September 22, 1961, p. 23.

Goodwin, Polly. *Chicago Tribune*, December 17, 1961, p. 7.

Holmstrom, John. *New Statesman*, December 21, 1962, p. 332.

Jackson, Charlotte. *The Atlantic Monthly*, December 1961, p. 120.

Jacobs, Jane. "Books." *The Village Voice*, December 7, 1961, p 9.

Leslie, Andrew. "Words and More." *The Guardian*, November 16, 1962, p. 6.

Mathes, Miriam. *Library Journal*, January 15, 1962, p. 332.

Maxwell, Emily. "The Smallest Giant in the World, and the Tallest Midget." *The New Yorker*, November 18, 1961, p. 222.

McGovern, Ann. "Journey to Wisdom." *The New York Times Book Review*, November 12, 1961, p. 35.

New York Herald Tribune, November 12, 1961, p. 14.

Richler, Mordecai. *The Spectator*, November 9, 1962, p. 732.

San Francisco Chronicle, December 10, 1961, p. 48.

Saturday Review of Literature, January 20, 1962, p. 27.

Time, December 15, 1961, p. 89.

Times Literary Supplement, November 23, 1962, p. 892.

Winthrope, Isabel. "Contemporary Carroll?" *Schoolmaster*, November 30, 1962.

Wood, Jean. New York *Newsday*, February 17, 1962, p. 25.

Select Anthologies that Excerpt *The Phantom Tollbooth*

"Giant, Midget, Fatman, Thinman," in Pamela Pollack (ed), *The Random House Book of Humor for Children*. New York: Random House, 1988.

Junior Great Books, Series 5. Chicago: The Great Books Foundation, 1992.

"Milo and the Mathemagician," in Clifton Fadiman (ed), *The Mathematical Magpie*. New York: Simon & Schuster, 1962.

"Milo Conducts the Dawn," in Diana Wynne Jones (ed), *Fantasy Stories*. New York: Kingfisher, 1994.

"The Royal Banquet," in Eric S. Rabkin (ed), *Fantastic Worlds*. New York: Oxford University Press, 1979.

"The Royal Banquet," in *New Basic Readers*, Curriculum Foundation Series. Chicago: Scott Foresman, 1965.

What the Dormouse Said, Amy Gash (ed). Chapel Hill, NC: Algonquin Books, 1999.

"The Word Market," in Bennett Cerf (ed), *Bennett Cerf's Houseful of Laughter*. New York: Random House, 1963.

The Phantom Tollbooth First Editions Around the World

United States (English): Epstein & Carroll, 1961
United Kingdom (English): Collins, 1962
Sweden (Swedish): Bonnier, 1967
Italy (Italian): Mondadori, 1971
Switzerland (German): Benziger, 1976
Israel (Hebrew): Zmora Bitan Modan, 1977
Germany (German): Rowohlt, 1978
Netherlands (Dutch): Querido Uitgeverij, 1983
Spain (Catalan): Editorial Barcanova, 1998
Japan (Japanese): PHP Institute, 1998
Spain (Spanish): Grupo Anaya, 1998
Brazil (Portuguese): Companhia das Letras, 1999
Mexico (Spanish): Edivisión Compañía Editorial, 2000
United States (Spanish): SeaStar, 2001
Poland (Polish): Grupa Wydawnicza Bertelsmann Media, 2001
Croatia (Croatian): Mozaik Knjiga, 2002
France (French): Hachette Jeunesse, 2002
Thailand (Thai): Matichon, 2002
Russia (Russian): Inostranka, 2005
Greece (Greek): Kedros, 2006
People's Republic of China (Simplified Chinese): Jilin wen shi chu ban she, 2007
Turkey (Turkish): Yapi Kredi, 2008
South Korea (Korean): Okdang Books, 2009
Lithuania (Lithuanian): Baltos Lankos, 2010
Taiwan (Complex Chinese): Eurasian, 2011

PICTURE CREDITS

ACKNOWLEDGMENTS

A great many individuals came to my aid during the course of my own journey to the Lands Beyond and back. For timely assistance in sharing needed information and for granting access to needed materials, I wish to express my appreciation to: Kathleen Ahrens, Jean Albano, Igor Aleksic, Kristin Angel, Ron Barbagallo, Hosea Baskin, Jennifer Belt, Ruth Black, Sarah Bodine, Allison Bruce, John Canemaker, Clelia Carroll, Catherine Casley, Laura Cecil, Nick Clark, Christinna Clemence, Erzsi Deàk, Sara Duke, Jason Epstein, Judy Feiffer, Meredith Gillies, David R. Godine, Kari Haijima, Elizabeth Hammill, Sheldon Harnick, Laura Harris, Gail B. Hochman, Barbara Hogenson, Schuyler Hooke, Karen Nelson Hoyle, Naomi Kojima, Mary Krienke, Lily Lawes, Miri Leshem-Pelly, the late David Levine, Nicolette A. Lodico, Meredith Lue, Mary Ellen Mark, Marianne Merola, Richard Michelson, Yumi Mitobe, Diane Muldrow, Yumi Myung, Idelle Nissela-Stone, Sharyn November, Cynthia Ostroff, Ingemar Perup, Alice Playten, Kimberly Tishler Rosen, Dominique Sandis, Karlan Sick, Joe Strube, Lori Styler, Nan A. Talese, Holly Thompson, Rosemary A. Thurber, Francis Turner, Jason Turner, Alan Voorhees, and Joshua White.

My thanks also to the archivists and other staff members at the following institutions for their help and guidance during the research phase of this project: Andersen Library (University of Minnesota), Edward Ardizzone Estate, Art Resource, Ashmolean Museum of Art and Archaeology (University of Oxford), Bobst Library (New York University), Brandt & Hochman Literary Agents, Brooklyn Historical Society, Brooklyn Public Library, Eric Carle Museum of Picture Book Art, Laura Cecil Literary Agency, Cumberland Rare Books, George Eastman House, Will Eisner Estate, Ford Foundation Archives, Barbara Hogenson Agency, *The Horn Book Magazine*, Library of Congress, Mary Ellen Mark Library/Studio, R. Michelson Galleries, Museum of Modern Art, Music Library (University of Buffalo), New York Public Library, Official Marx Toy Museum, Society of Children's Book Writers and Illustrators, Sterling Lord Literistic, Nan A. Talese Books, Visual Artists and Galleries Association, and Yale University Library.

My gratitude goes to Cherry Williams, curator of manuscripts, and to her colleagues at the Lilly Library, Indiana University, for the ready access they provided to research materials and for their hospitality during my visit to Bloomington to study Norton Juster's papers. In addition, I thank them for their prompt and meticulous handling of requests for images for reproduction.

Jules Feiffer graciously answered my questions about his role as *The Phantom Tollbooth*'s illustrator and about his early working life as a member of a circle of Brooklyn artist and writer friends. I also thank him for the many examples of his published and unpublished art that he made available for reproduction. I'm grateful too for the warm welcome that he and his wife, Jennifer Allen, his archivist, Katie P. Korman, and his assistant, Mike James, all extended to me during my visits to the archaeological site that is the amazing, art-filled Feiffer home, where long-forgotten outtake drawings for *The Phantom Tollbooth* were among the treasures that emerged.

Norton Juster gave most generously of his time and prodigious energy. I thank him for sitting for hours of interviews; for jotting down pages of backstory recollections for my use; for lending family photographs, unpublished drawings, and other research materials from his files; and not least of all, for making me laugh. My warm thanks too to Norton's wife, Jeanne Juster, for her help in gathering bibliographical information, fielding telephone messages, and making my visits to Massachusetts all the more memorable.

I want to express my heartfelt gratitude to everyone at Random House for their commitment to this book and for all their many and varied efforts on its behalf. To my editor, Michelle Frey, and her capable editorial team, Michele Burke and Kelly Delaney, a special thanks for their Tock-like steadfastness and good sense as, together, we navigated the landscape of a project of labyrinthine complexity. And to art director Isabel Warren-Lynch and designer Cathy Bobak, an appreciative tip of my hat for the Chroma-esque elegance and flair with which they harmonized the old and new elements of this book-within-a-book. Thanks also to executive copy editor Artie Bennett for an eagle eye with words that would be the envy of Dictionopolis.

As always, I thank my agent, George M. Nicholson of Sterling Lord Literistic, and his assistant, Erica Rand Silverman, for their clear judgment, wise counsel, and unwavering support.

I thank my wife, Amy Schwartz, for her friendship and encouragement; and my son, Jacob, for being himself and for already knowing *there's just so much to do right here*.

—L.S.M.

BIBLIOGRAPHY

Books

Amidi, Amid. *Cartoon Modern: Style and Design in Fifties Animation*. San Francisco: Chronicle Books, 2006.

Ammer, Christine. *The American Heritage Dictionary of Idioms*. Boston and New York: Houghton Mifflin, 1997.

Ayto, John. *Dictionary of Word Origins*. New York: Arcade Publishing, 1990.

Bachelard, Gaston. *The Poetics of Space*. Translated from the French by Maria Jolas. Boston: Beacon Press, 1994.

Baum, L. Frank. *The Annotated Wizard of Oz: Centennial Edition*. Illustrated by W. W. Denslow. Edited, with an introduction and notes, by Michael Patrick Hearn. New York: W. W. Norton & Co., 2000.

Canemaker, John. *Winsor McCay: His Life and Art*. Foreword by Maurice Sendak. New York: Abbeville Press, 1987.

Capote, Truman. *A House on the Heights*. Introduction by George Plimpton. New York: Little Bookroom, 2002.

Carroll, Lewis. *The Annotated Alice: The Definitive Edition*. Illustrated by John Tenniel. Introduction and notes by Martin Gardner. New York: W. W. Norton & Co., 2000.

Cerf, Bennett. *At Random: Reminiscences of Bennett Cerf*. New York: Random House, 1977.

The Compact Edition of the Oxford English Dictionary (2 Vols.). New York: Oxford University Press, 1971.

Couch, N. C. Christopher, and Stephen Weiner. *The Will Eisner Companion*. Introduction by Dennis O'Neil. New York: DC Comics, 2006.

Devine, C. Maury, et. al., eds. *The Harvard Guide to Influential Books*. New York: Harper & Row, 1986.

Epstein, Jason. *Book Business: Publishing Past, Present, and Future*. New York: W. W. Norton & Co., 2001.

Feiffer, Jules. *Backing into Forward: A Memoir*. New York: Nan A. Talese Books/Doubleday, 2010.

—————. *Clifford*. The Collected Works, Vol. 1. Foreword by Pete Hamill. Seattle: Fantagraphics Books, 1988.

—————. *Explainers: The Complete* Village Voice *Strips (1956–1966)*. Introduction by Gary Groth. Seattle: Fantagraphics Books, 2008.

—————. *Feiffer's Children*. Kansas City and New York: Andrews, McMeel & Parker, 1986.

—————. *The Great Comic Book Heroes*. New York: Dial Press, 1965.

—————. *Passionella and Other Stories*. The Collected Works, Vol. 4. Seattle: Fantagraphics Books, 2006.

French, Karl, ed. *The Marx Brothers:* Monkey Business, Duck Soup, *and* A Day at the Races. London: Faber and Faber, 1993.

Furniss, Maureen, ed. *Chuck Jones: Conversations*. Jackson, MS: University Press of Mississippi, 2005.

Gibson, Walker, ed. *The Limits of Language*. New York: Hill and Wang, 1962.

Hendrickson, Robert. *QPB Encyclopedia of Word and Phrase Origins*. New York: Facts on File, 1997. (First published in 1984 under the title *The Facts on File Encyclopedia of Word and Phrase Origins*.)

Hill, Draper. *The Satirical Etchings of James Gillray*. New York: Dover Publications, 1976.

Jacobs, Jane. *The Death and Life of Great American Cities*. New York: Random House, 1961.

Juster, Norton. *Alberic the Wise and Other Journeys*. Illustrated by Domenico Gnoli. New York: Pantheon, 1965.

—————. *The Dot and the Line: A Romance in Lower Mathematics*. New York: Random House, 1963.

—————. *The Hello, Goodbye Window*. Illustrated by Chris Raschka. New York: Michael di Capua Books/Hyperion, 2005.

—————. *The Odious Ogre*. Illustrated by Jules Feiffer. New York: Michael di Capua Books/Scholastic, 2010.

——————. *So Sweet to Labor: Rural Women in America, 1865–1895*. New York: Viking Press, 1979. (Reissued as *A Woman's Place: Yesterday's Women in Rural America*. Golden, CO: Fulcrum Publishing, 1996.)

Lindberg, Gary H. *The Confidence Man in American Literature*. New York: Oxford University Press, 1982.

Mack, Carol K., and Dinah Mack. *A Field Guide to Demons, Fairies, Fallen Angels, and Other Subversive Spirits*. New York: Arcade Publishing, 1998.

Marcus, Leonard S., ed. *Funny Business: Conversations with Writers of Comedy*. Somerville, MA: Candlewick Press, 2009.

——————. *Minders of Make-Believe: Idealists, Entrepreneurs, and the Shaping of American Children's Literature*. Boston: Houghton Mifflin Harcourt, 2008.

Martin, Robert M. *There Are Two Errors in the the Title of This Book: A Sourcebook of Philosophical Puzzles, Problems, and Paradoxes*. Toronto: Broadview Press, 2002.

Marx, Harpo, and Rowland Barber. *Harpo Speaks . . . About New York*. Introduction by E. L. Doctorow. New York: Little Bookroom, 2000.

Mumford, Lewis. *The City in History: Its Origins, Its Transformations, and Its Prospects*. New York: Harcourt, Brace, & World, 1961.

Nabokov, Vladimir. *Speak, Memory: An Autobiography Revisited*. New York: Knopf, Everyman's Library, 1999.

O'Sullivan, Judith. *The Great American Comic Strip: One Hundred Years of Cartoon Art*. Boston: Bulfinch Press, 1990.

Phillips, Robert, ed. *Aspects of Alice: Lewis Carroll's Dreamchild as Seen Through the Critics' Looking-Glasses*. New York: Vintage, 1977.

Pink, Steven. *The Stuff of Thought: Language as a Window into Human Nature*. New York: Viking Penguin, 2007.

Rosten, Norman. *Neighborhood Tales*. New York: George Braziller, 1986.

Saxon, Arthur H. *P. T. Barnum: The Legend and the Man*. New York: Columbia University Press, 1983.

Schmitt, Peter J. *Back to Nature: The Arcadian Myth in Urban America*. New York: Oxford University Press, 1969.

Seuss, Dr. *The Annotated Cat: Under the Hat of Seuss and His Cats*. Introduction and annotations by Philip Nel. New York: Random House Children's Books, 2007.

Silverman, Kenneth. *Begin Again: A Biography of John Cage*. New York: Knopf, 2010.

Singer, Jerome L. *Daydreaming: An Introduction to the Experimental Study of Inner Experience*. New York: Random House, 1966.

Snow, C. P. *The Two Cultures and the Scientific Revolution: The Rede Lecture*. New York: Cambridge University Press, 1959.

Spufford, Francis. *The Child That Books Built: A Life in Reading*. New York: Metropolitan Books, 2002.

Swift, Jonathan. *Gulliver's Travels*. Edited, with an introduction, by John F. Ross. New York: Holt, Rinehart and Winston, 1948.

Tatar, Maria. *Enchanted Hunters: The Power of Stories in Childhood*. New York: W. W. Norton & Co., 2009.

Tebbel, John. *Between Covers: The Rise and Transformation of Book Publishing in America*. New York: Oxford University Press, 1987.

Tippins, Sherill. *February House*. Boston and New York: Houghton Mifflin Harcourt, 2005.

Tolkien, J. R. R. *The Tolkien Reader*. New York: Ballantine Books, 1966.

Venturi, Robert, Denise Scott Brown, and Steven Izenour. *Learning from Las Vegas: The Forgotten Symbolism of Architectural Form* (revised edition). Cambridge, MA: MIT Press, 1977.

Voltaire, François-Marie Arouet de. *Candide*. Illustrated by Rockwell Kent. New York: Random House, 1928.

White, Gabriel. *Edward Ardizzone: Artist and Illustrator*. New York: Schocken Books, 1979.

Articles and Essays

Bellafante, Ginia. "Suburban Rapture." *The New York Times Book Review*, December 24, 2008, p. 23.

Carey, Joanna. "Liquid Inspiration." *The Guardian*, October 26, 1999, p. 2.

Cohen, Amy L. "How I Finally Found *The Phantom Tollbooth*." *The Horn Book Newsletter for Parents*, Vol. 8, No. 4, Fall 1987, p. 3.

Dirda, Michael. "Comedy Tonight." *Washington Post Book World*, August 16, 1998, p. 15.

Dizikes, Peter. "Our Two Cultures." *The New York Times Book Review*, March 22, 2009, p. 23.

Giltz, Michael. "Lot of Good Tomes: In the Library with . . . Michael Chabon." *New York Post*, August 26, 2001, p. 48.

Goldscheider, Eric. "At Home with Norton Juster." *The Boston Globe*, July 5, 2001, p. 2.

Greenfield, Karen. "Musicians on Reading." *Washington Post Book World*, December 12, 1999, p. 16.

Heller, Steven. "Insight by a Thousand Strokes." *The New York Times*, January 3, 2010, p. WK3.

——————. "Jules Feiffer: Interview by Steven Heller." *The Master Series: Jules Feiffer* (School of Visual Arts exhibition catalog), Fall 2006, pp. 3–19.

"Is Greenwich Village Moving to the Heights?" *Brooklyn Heights Press*, January 31, 1957, p. 1.

Klinger, Eric. "The Power of Daydreaming." *Psychology Today*, October 1987, pp. 36–44.

Krisher, Bernard. "A View of the Heights: Newcomers Like Link with Past, Feel Area Is Symbol of Frontier." *New York World Telegram and Sun*, January 25, 1957, pp. 1–2.

Lask, Thomas. "Repeat Performances (Juvenile Division)." *The New York Times Book Review*, November 1, 1959, p. 59.

——————. "Repeat Performances (Juvenile Division)." *The New York Times Book Review*, November 13, 1960, p. 54.

——————. "Some New Looks at Old Favorites." *The New York Times Book Review*, May 8, 1960, p. 34.

——————. "Repeat Performances (Juvenile Division)." *The New York Times Book Review*, November 12, 1961, p. 62.

Lipson, Abigail. "The Road to Digitopolis: Perils of Problem Solving." *School Science and Mathematics*, Vol. 95, No. 6, October 1995, pp. 282–89.

Looking Glass Library (display advertisement). *The New York Times Book Review*, November 8, 1959, p. 17.

Margolick, David. "Levine in Winter." *Vanity Fair*, November 2008, pp. 168–78.

Miller, Laura. "'A Good Book Should Make You Cry.'" *The New York Times Book Review*, August 22, 2004, p. 12.

Nichols, Lewis. "In and Out of Books." *The New York Times Book Review*, May 7, 1961, p. 8.

——————. "In and Out of Books." *The New York Times Book Review*, December 17, 1961, p. 8.

"Oliver Smith Likes the Heights for Its 'Gracious Living,'" *Brooklyn Heights Press*, February 21, 1957, p. 1.

Peel, James. "The Scale and the Spectrum." *Cabinet*, Issue 22, Summer 2006, pp. 24–28.

Powers, Alan. "Milo the Mindbender." *Building Design*, June 7, 2002.

Quindlen, Anna. "Enough Bookshelves." *The New York Times*, August 7, 1991, p. A21.

"Random House to Distribute New Children's Series." *Publishers Weekly*, April 6, 1959, p. 29.

RoseEtta Stone. "An Interview with Norton Juster, Author of *The Phantom Tollbooth*," underdown.org/juster.htm, September 11, 2004.

Schine, Cathleen. "On Books." *Barnard*, Winter 1994, p. 26.

Weber, Bruce. "David Levine, Political Caricaturist with Wit and Bite, Is Dead at 83." *The New York Times*, December 30, 2009, p. B9.

Weich, Dave. "Norton Juster, Beyond Expectations." Powells.com, April 2002. (powells.com/authors/juster.html)

Whittemore, Katharine. "Phantom Tollbooths." *The Boston Globe Magazine*, December 4, 1994.

INDEX

Note: *Italic* page numbers refer to illustrations.